MW01025519

POLYBIUS

POLYBIUS

COLLIN ARMSTRONG

G

GALLERY BOOKS

NEW YORK AMSTERDAM/ANTWERP LONDON
TORONTO SYDNEY/MELBOURNE NEW DELHI

G

Gallery Books
An Imprint of Simon & Schuster, LLC
1230 Avenue of the Americas
New York, NY 10020

First Gallery Books hardcover edition April 2025

GALLERY BOOKS and colophon are registered trademarks
of Simon & Schuster, LLC

Interior design by Hope Herr-Cardillo

Manufactured in the United States of America

10 9 8 7 6 5 4 3 2 1

Library of Congress Cataloging-in-Publication Data is available.

ISBN 978-1-6680-4497-1
ISBN 978-1-6680-4499-5 (ebook)

For Natalie, Ellison, and Cooper

POLYBIUS

SINNESLÖCHEN. AN ODD NAME. THOM COULDN'T TRACE ITS ORIGIN—GERMAN, Scandinavian? In the end, it didn't matter where the company had come from. What mattered was it had folded and Thom was parked outside its former office, ready to pick over its remains after its owners had permanently closed up shop.

While the brochures he had printed and the ads he ran in the *Mercury News* in San Jose, California, read "Mazzy Asset Management," Thom saw his business for what it really was—trash collecting. Everything he'd pull from the offices of bankrupt businesses around the area—furniture, fixtures, wiring, whatever was left behind—went to an auction house. Which was essentially a dump, albeit for nicer garbage. It wasn't that Thom didn't take his work seriously; he just disliked having to dress up what he did for a living. But people wouldn't want to do business with someone calling himself a garbageman, so Thomas Mazzy long ago rebranded himself as an "asset manager," complete with an ad in the yellow pages that proclaimed, "Yes, MAM!"

All around Silicon Valley, as it was increasingly known to the outside world, every conversation seemed to involve some bullshit pretense about the other person's job—who they knew, why they were in town, what *amazing whatever* they were working on. Companies offering vague services, with inscrutable names like Symantec, Activision, and Electronic Arts were springing up left and right. Everyone claimed they were someone, or something, they most likely were not.

Thom joked he was in the business of failure. After all, if other companies weren't going under, his would. He made a living out of picking up the pieces when things went belly-up. Silicon Valley was the new Wild West. Being the guy who hauled bodies out of the street after a shoot-out wasn't glamorous, but there was no shortage of work.

But this kind of blithe cynicism helped mask an inadequacy he'd long felt, having to work with his hands in a city where your head was what mattered. If he was flippant about what he did, Thom figured, no one could accuse him of taking too seriously a job that was more likely to give him a hernia than it was a comfortable retirement.

Thom's first "asset management" job for the month of September 1982 was at its outset no different from the rest. An auction house he worked with regularly, Gordon-Smith Antiquities, had acquired ownership of everything that wasn't considered structural inside a warehouse that had served as a research and development center for Sinneslöchen. Thom and his crew were being paid to go in and pull anything Gordon-Smith could potentially sell. "Anything" meant *anything*, in some cases down to in-wall wiring and light bulbs. The irony that the same items would just shift to another space he might end up gutting a year later wasn't lost on Thom; sometimes he wondered how often he'd pulled and coiled the same runs of phone cable without realizing it.

He watched as Bernie Coen pulled into the parking lot in front of Sinneslöchen's now-vacant office, a pair of seventeen-year-old meatheads jostling about the bed of his rusting F-150. Besides himself and Bernie, he'd hire college and high school students off the books. They'd get a little beer money; he'd get extra muscle so he could give his own a break.

Bernie introduced the boys as Kevin and Chris. As soon as they were out of the truck, they were horsing around the parking lot. Thom shot Bernie a wary look as they started for the entrance. "You know them?"

"Through Kevin's mom," Bernie replied, drawing a half-cocked eyebrow from Thom. "Not like *that*."

Thom wasn't so sure. For a middle-aged guy with zero prospects and about a quarter of his hair left, Bernie got around.

You never knew what to expect on a job. Gordon-Smith paid Thom for every pallet he could load down, but there was always the risk of a lean exchange. You might walk into a warehouse on the first day of a job to find it was all but empty. Sinneslöchen, at first glance, seemed promising—short of a coffeepot, the reception area looked intact. A front desk with pens and a stapler neatly arranged on top, leather chair, large potted palm in need of a long drink; Thom half expected a receptionist to wander out and say they had the wrong address.

They moved from the offices to the maw of a research and development wing, which sat behind heavy steel doors fixed with twin dead bolts. Thom cycled through the keys Gordon-Smith had provided until he found one that fit the locks, each opening with a heavy clank. Passing through the doors, they were staggered by how much had been left behind. Thom kept tabs on big items like furniture and fixtures so Bernie could track the rest—tools, electronics, raw materials for fabricating who knows what.

It didn't take long for them to realize this job was a serious windfall—and for Thom to develop a vague, uneasy sense about the space. It was *too* complete, as if whoever had been working there simply . . . vanished. In the corner of one cluttered workspace, he noted a desk calendar open to March 5, 1982.

Bernie caught him staring. "What is it?"

Thom nodded toward the date. "You suppose that's the last time someone was here? That was . . . almost seven months ago."

Uninterested, Bernie was already moving on. "My sister gave me one for Hanukkah. I forgot about it and stopped tearing off pages. Lousy gift."

But something about it bothered Thom. *Everything's just been sitting here, all this time*? Running his finger along a workspace, it cut a line through a thick layer of dust.

It called to mind a story he remembered reading as a child, in a book about ghost ships. A boat had been found adrift at sea—dinner on tables in the mess hall untouched, nothing amiss but no crew to be seen. It was as if they'd all decided to jump ship at the same spontaneous moment, for no clear reason.

In four hours, they'd loaded ten pallets with everything from the front offices—seemingly new, mod-ish furniture, rows of gunmetal-gray filing cabinets, box after box of desk supplies. When Thom tried to lift the palm, the fronds shuddered off and onto the floor—it wound up in a dumpster outside, but the rest of what they'd collected filled the company's rusted box truck.

After all that, the R&D area was still untouched.

Thom drove to Gordon-Smith Antiquities and unloaded the pallets solo, so Bernie and the boys could continue working. He poked his head past the door of account manager Mila Novik—very pretty and, per several past interactions, very uninterested in anything beyond a professional relationship with Thom.

"Hey, Mila."

"Oh. Hi." Something in her voice, a register of apprehension, hollowed out Thom's stomach—like she was girding herself to turn him down again.

He was quick to try to deflect. "I was just— What do you, uh— Do you know anything about this job? This place? Sinne-something."

Mila shrugged. "They were making video games, I think."

That was it. Thom thought about pressing for more information but feared he'd come off sounding like an idiot.

As the day progressed and the crew worked its way across the R&D space, stacking and tagging pallet after pallet of workbenches, tools, and industrial-sized spools of jacketed copper wire, Thom's unease was replaced by confusion. Granted, he knew next to nothing about what went on inside the places he was hired to pick over—"research," "fabrication," "testing" were all words he understood, just not in the context of Silicon Valley. But he'd seen enough spaces over the years to recognize the usual tools of the trade.

Everything here looked off—not wrong or amateur. *Unorthodox.* Rows of rectangular glass screens had a kind of artisan appearance on their concave insides, covered in what had to be thousands of pinprick dimples made from a kind of silvery resin. They weighed far more, by themselves, than a full TV set of equal size. The circuit boards and power plants all looked too complex, too densely constructed. The fact that there wasn't a finished product or prototype in sight, or even a clear endgame in the form of blueprints or schematics, only served to deepen this enigmatic quality.

But Thom kept these musings to himself, and work continued at a steady clip through lunch, which the group took inside the cavernous space on account of a steady rain that had blown in. By late afternoon they'd made two additional trips back to Gordon-Smith, and the R&D floor was starting to look empty.

In clearing parts, boxed and otherwise, off several rows of wire racks toward the back of the space, Thom came upon something unexpected: a door, set flush with the wall and without a handle. Another pair of heavy-duty twin dead-bolt locks kept it sealed shut. It wasn't hidden per se, but the nature of its construction and the way the racks had been arranged made it hard to spot. If they hadn't been picking the space over, they would've missed it.

Freeing a key ring from his battered denim pocket, Thom began trying keys to see which might fit. Bernie soon joined him, with curiosity getting the better of Chris and Kevin, too.

Chris tossed a nod at the door. "Take it off the hinges."

Tagging his shoulder, Kevin pointed toward the seam. "They're on the inside, dumbass."

Stepping closer, Bernie examined the strange construction. "You sure you don't have the key?"

Thom tossed him the ring. "Maybe I missed it." But he hadn't, and he knew it. Fishing a pry bar out of a weathered tool bag, he walked back up to the door. Still trying keys, Bernie saw what his boss was about to do and quickly took a step back.

Wedging the bar in between the door and the jamb, Thom put his weight against it. The frame began to creak, slowly starting to give. As Thom leaned into the door, a small sheet of paper slipped up and out of his flannel pocket. Pulled through the air, it flattened itself against the seam. For a moment they all stared, uncertain what had just happened.

Breaking their daze, Thom reached out and peeled the paper away from the seam, then ran his hand along it, feeling a mild vacuum. Taking a step back, he let go of the paper again. They all watched as it was grabbed midflight and plastered against the seam once more. Cautioning the others to step back, Thom resumed leaning on the pry bar—the drywall began to splinter—until finally, the door was flung open with a loud crack.

The interior of the hidden room looked like something out of *2001: A Space Odyssey*—floor to ceiling white, smooth surfaces with few visible lines, antiseptic in appearance. There seemed to be a separate ventilation system running inside, louder than the one in the main space and powerful enough you could feel its chilled push-pull when you passed through the right spots.

"It's a clean room," Bernie said, receiving three blank stares in response. "When you don't want anything contaminating what you're building. Or whatever you're building contaminating you."

Chris froze. "You serious? Is it dangerous?"

Bernie smirked a little as he explained. "This room's not going to kill you. There's no masks or suits or glove boxes. It's just, the kind of work that's done in these places is sensitive. Speck of dust or a stray hair and you're shit out of luck."

As usual, Thom thought, when someone wasn't familiar with whatever esoteric concept Bernie found a way to drum up, the man went out of his way to make it seem as though this was something *everyone else* knew about. Thom had known Bernie for years and valued his work ethic and friendship, but sometimes he wanted to bust his jaw for being such a smarmy son of a bitch.

True to its name, a few tools had been left on a workbench, but other than those—and of course, the lone arcade cabinet standing in its center—the clean room was, well, exceptionally clean.

Of course, the cabinet.

It was a coin-operated video game, but there was no marquee above the screen, no printed graphics on the sides, just a white particleboard box with a coin door and the usual joystick-plunger configuration. Like a generic, store-brand equivalent. Still on its way to being finished, it had been abandoned just like everything else inside.

Chris spotted a cord around the cabinet's back and plugged it in. As a cascade of boot files crisscrossed the flickering screen, it was obvious they were looking at something different. The display was unbelievably vibrant, with the visuals—just text to this point—so crisp and clear that anyone who'd even wandered past an arcade before would know that this was unusual.

Finally, a title appeared on-screen—*Polybius.*

Press Start, the display beckoned.

"Neat. Back to work," Bernie chuffed, herding Chris and Kevin from the room and leaving Thom to complete an inventory.

"What's it doing in here?" It took Thom a moment to realize there was no one around to speculate on an answer—they'd all left. He hadn't noticed.

Thom started to walk the space, taking stock. It was difficult not to glance back at the display as he moved and eventually he couldn't take his eyes off it. He crossed the floor and stood in front of it, transfixed. He didn't care about video games—the Atari 2600 he'd bought a few years ago was boxed up in his garage—but here, he couldn't refuse the vibrant lure.

He fished a quarter from his pocket, dropped it in, and pressed the small lighted button labeled START. Hands hovering over the analog stick and two plungers that made up the control scheme, Thom watched as a series of lines appeared around the title on-screen, gradually overtaking its shape and forming a maze that grew more and more complex, faster and faster, until its structure overwhelmed the screen and the in-game camera swooped down toward its entrance.

Thom was awestruck—he'd never seen anything like this. The level of detail and fluidity of motion felt cinematic. A path extended before him, into a dark space bounded on either side by stone walls. Almost like a cavern.

He nudged the joystick forward, stepping inside. Looked left, right. Tried the plungers: one caused him to jump; the other raised a torch. Tipping the joystick back rotated his point of view—there was something in the distance behind him. Vaguely humanoid but cloaked by the dark, not clear or defined enough at this range to rightly call it a figure. More like a *figment*, looming there in the dark. As it shifted, mass gently swaying, glints of what looked like silvery eyeshine could be seen, flowing tiny arcs of mercury that dissolved into then re-emerged from the dark.

Maybe I'm supposed to go that way, Thom thought. But as he walked in the direction of the figment, it started moving toward him. Instinctively, Thom let go of the joystick, and his character froze. For a moment, so did the figment, as if mirroring his actions. But then it took another step toward him. Then another. Again, deliberate, ground crunching beneath heavy feet as it advanced.

It felt *wrong.*

Jamming the joystick forward, Thom ran into the cavern, finding himself inside the maze that had formed moments earlier.

As he moved, he could hear the figment behind him, gaining ground. It was almost as if Thom could feel its breath on his neck. He knew he couldn't stop—if he did, it would be on him, and it'd be over.

It was Bernie's hand on his shoulder that snapped Thom back to reality.

"You all right, boss?"

It felt to Thom as if he was coming out of a deep sleep. He had absolutely no idea how much time had passed since he'd stepped in front of the cabinet. As Bernie considered him, amused by his confusion, Thom felt a sudden, burning swell of resentment at the smirk curling over his old friend's face.

Glancing at the spartan inventory Thom had taken of the room's contents, Bernie asked, a little disbelievingly, "This everything?"

Thom snapped, "I'm too stupid to write a fucking list?" The truth was that Thom *had* missed more than a few items, including most obviously the cabinet itself. But his mind was elsewhere, replaying what he saw as *another* jab at his intellect from Bernie.

Thrown by the venom in Thom's voice, Bernie raised a hand as if to say *no harm intended*, but the gesture had the opposite effect—Thom's eyes narrowed at being told how to feel.

In a flash Thom found himself springing forward, hands seizing Bernie's neck. Bernie struggled, but Thom was driven by a dark energy so primal there was nothing Bernie could do to escape his grasp. The same anger he buried every time he absorbed one of life's little slights—cut off in traffic, interrupted in a conversation, rebuffed by a woman—bubbled back all at once. It turned out that everything he'd taught himself to shake off was still there, waiting for its moment to scream out from the dark.

Thom could feel bone twisting beneath the weathered skin of Bernie's neck, see the veins in his eyes bursting as his friend gasped for air and struggled to break free. The wet, stuttering cracks Bernie's spine made as it snapped were a rhapsody to Thom. He cast the lifeless body to the floor and left the clean room, searching for Chris and Kevin. *Little fuckers.* He'd never felt such pure, focused purpose in all his life.

But in reality, Thom hadn't moved an inch—and there was Bernie, hand still raised.

The realizations came in waves, each hitting harder than the last. It had been inside his head, a horrible thing to let himself imagine—worse because he'd taken a kind of elemental pleasure in snapping the life out of another person. One he knew and trusted.

Thom felt sick, couldn't stop sweating, stop thinking about how real it had all seemed . . . how distressingly *right* it had all felt. He silently reassured himself he'd lost a moment of time to a perverse kind of daydream. That was it. Strange, but not representative of his true self. *It must be this place.* All day it had been giving him bad vibes, and he'd let it get into his head.

Recognizing something was wrong, Bernie set the inventory aside and approached his friend. Struggling to parse dream from reality, Thom was suddenly seized with terror—Bernie had been dead on the floor seconds earlier, now he was moving toward him? He backpedaled, fear in his eyes, bumping into a workbench. Bernie froze in response. He didn't understand what or why something might set Thom off and simply asked again, "You all right, boss?"

For a long moment Thom just stared, finally shaking off the feeling as much as he could and nodding in response. Checking his watch, he couldn't make sense out of what he saw. "What time do you have?"

Bernie checked his Casio. "Five thirty. Are you sure you're—"

"Five thirty?"

It had been two hours since they'd found the room. Probably ninety minutes since Thom jimmied open the door, and at least an hour since he'd been left alone inside. When had he started playing? He couldn't remember anything since Bernie, Chris, and Kevin had left him to take inventory.

"Did you get enough sleep last night?" Bernie, too, was trying to figure out what the hell had just happened but didn't know the right questions to ask.

"I just zoned out." Thom's eyes drifted from Bernie for a moment, floating over the stark white of the clean room. "This place is a little weird, huh?" Thom asked. He added a laugh, hoping to cut the tension, but his unease was clear. Bernie went to say something, but before he could, Thom nodded toward the door. "We have an hour. Just keep those two on track, okay?" Thrown by the strange interaction, Bernie nodded and went. He was glad to get out of there. Away from Thom.

Left alone again, Thom tried to reconsider the sequence of events. But whatever he did, however he came at it, there was a hole in his memory, a gap where he couldn't say what he'd done, said, thought, or felt. It simply wasn't there. Which was on top of the fact that he'd imagined killing someone so vividly, he felt compelled to peer out of the clean room to make sure Bernie still drew breath.

The clean room.

Like that, Bernie's peculiar turn of phrase suddenly dug its way back under Thom's skin. *For fuck's sake. Why'd he have to say it? Why even bring it up? Who cares? He probably made those kids feel like idiots too. They're just kids. But* everyone knows, *right, Bernie?*

I swear to God, if he does that one more time, I'll fucking kill him.

Thom's mind slammed into reverse. *I wouldn't do that,* he thought. *Couldn't.* The push-and-pull of perspectives made him paranoid he'd say or do something he shouldn't. He was frozen, mind racing between deep regret over what he'd imagined doing and furious indignance toward Bernie that made him hot, as if a fire had caught inside and was spreading, boiling his blood and bones.

On his periphery he could see the display flashing, shimmering so brightly it seemed to burn in around the corners of his eyes. Wherever he looked, he saw trails of light, a ghostly form lingering a step out of sight. He squeezed his eyes shut in an attempt to will the light away, but instead it clarified, from faint wisps into an enveloping, fluid rush of dark lines that wrapped around the room, pulsing in time with his heartbeat. Boom, pulse, boom, pulse.

But then something intruded—a sharp crunch. The sound of the figment stepping toward him out of the dark.

Thom's eyes sprang open, and he found himself standing in front of the cabinet, hands hovering over the controls. But he hadn't felt himself move, hadn't taken a step.

Or had I?

Suddenly the screen went blank, the audio silent. Thom saw Chris crouched nearby, coiling the power cord then taping it to the cabinet's back. By the door, Kevin waited with a dolly. "We're done in the other room. Mr. Coen asked us to start emptying this one," he said. Thom stepped aside as the boys shuffled the cabinet onto the dolly, not thinking to offer any help. He just watched, once again lost and struggling to recall what had happened, where his time had gone.

He saw Bernie eyeing him from the R&D floor, a peculiar smile curling over his lips as Chris wheeled the cabinet away. It seemed genuine—like he'd caught Thom slacking but still understood the need to take a moment for yourself now and then, even on the job.

Or was Bernie happy in tacitly embarrassing him, by sending some dumb kid to do *his* job? Silently chiding, reminding him he'd wasted an hour staring at that screen like an idiot—that he'd caught him shirking his responsibilities—that things would be better off with *him* in charge and Thom taking orders?

Fuck him, Thom thought as he crossed the now-empty R&D floor, footsteps echoing in the cavernous space. *I'll kill him.*

MONEY FROM SILICON VALLEY HAD FLOWED SO GRADUALLY INTO THE SMALL northern California town of Tasker Bay, the question of when the area had really started changing was one of the most debated topics among its "original" locals. Many still regarded their home as a fishing town, a farming town. In truth it was now more or less *just* a town, a place where people spent their evenings and weekends, not where they made a living or contributed anything meaningful to the world.

A combination of lower-priced real estate relative to San Jose coupled with proximity to Silicon Valley had, over the last five years, transformed the area from a hardscrabble, working-class coastal town into a high-end suburb. Locals who didn't sell out and move elsewhere found it harder and harder to make ends meet in an area where the price of everything was rising faster than their own wages. The things their town had for years provided—hauls of mushrooms, peppers, and greens; nets teeming with striped bass that filled the town's namesake bay; services needed to keep the like operational—were not of interest to this new breed of resident. Their only concern was acquiring property, and they'd pay far enough above market to the point that, for most locals, it seemed foolish to say no.

There was a sense among those who hadn't sold that the ground was shifting uncontrollably beneath their feet. That someday soon, most if not all of them would be priced out of their town. Their *home*. This made people uneasy, and that unease echoed. Nerves perpetuated more nerves. Resentment simmered. And even though no one would acknowledge it, it felt like it was only a matter of time before those ill feelings would manifest in real-world consequences.

Andi Winston and her mother, Rachel, were part of Tasker Bay's new wave, though they hadn't come looking for cheap real estate. They were looking for refuge. Rachel's marriage to Andi's father, Devon, had gone from unstable to unsustainable over the past few years. His open disdain for her had begun to infect Andi, and the mood swings he suffered had increased not only in frequency, but volatility. Devon had long refused treatment for his condition, and while Rachel was a practicing MD, she was also his wife, whom he saw fit to blame for whatever went wrong. Doctor or not, he didn't care—she was the last person he'd take advice from. Especially after she'd suggested that he might be bipolar.

The damage this was doing to her own relationship with Andi finally grew too great to bear, so Rachel closed her family practice in the San Jose suburb of Dobern, uprooting herself and a then-sixteen-year-old Andi to Tasker Bay, where the burgeoning population of transplants readily embraced a doctor who'd come from the same "modern" world they'd all recently left.

Andi wasn't oblivious, understanding that things weren't well between her parents. She didn't know why, though she had her theories—many centered around things her father had said about her mother's lack of faith in the software company he'd been trying to start and, indirectly, in him. She knew her father wasn't perfect but never knew the full story, because Rachel worked to hide it from her—spare her, she'd argue.

There had always been technology around the house, thanks to Devon. He was an early adopter who would bring home whatever had just hit store shelves, cameras or video games or personal computers, immediately disassembling them to see how they worked.

As a child, Andi had had a habit of turning her toys upside down to see how they fit together, so it made sense that, at a young age, she'd been drawn to her father's kitchen-table engineering. The two would spend hours in their own quiet world, painstakingly breaking devices down piece by piece, speculating on how they worked and what they might do to modify or improve them. These moments left Rachel on the outside looking in and cemented Andi's vision for her future.

Moving's never easy, but it's especially hard on a teenager halfway through high school. Andi had no desire to start over in Tasker Bay, and, before the Mayflower trucks had departed Dobern, she knew she wouldn't be staying long. Her home, her future, was in Silicon Valley. Devon often talked about Andi apprenticing with him straight out of high school. Her ability to learn by doing was so accelerated, he said, that she'd get far more out of working than she would going to college and studying theory; practice was what she needed.

Rachel knew that the kind of hands-on experience Devon was dangling wasn't common in Silicon Valley, especially for young women. But she also knew something would go wrong and Andi would be left holding the bag, because there was always that moment with Devon when he would throw up his hands and walk away. Just as he'd done with her, he'd lure Andi into making a major life decision, then fail to uphold his end of the bargain. Where would that leave her?

But he'd also been there for Andi in ways that Rachel hadn't. It had been Devon who saw how Andi struggled to distinguish certain colors, and who found a way to use their engineering sessions to help her cope. She learned to recognize minute differences in shading and to identify components by shape and feel, all with his guidance.

That was always the duality with Devon. Here was an act of pure love, of deeply patient compassion, that he couldn't extend to Rachel. In private, he'd lambaste her—*a doctor*—for failing to recognize Andi's issue. Rachel was grateful he'd helped their daughter. But in her darker moments, she resented the fact that Andi's deadbeat father—not her, the one who kept a roof over their heads, food on the table, and who for years endured Devon's psychological and sometimes physical abuse—was the one who'd molded their daughter's self-image.

Andi knew Rachel saw her father as a quitter. She'd heard this said behind closed doors more than once. Rachel would trot out a list of half-finished—what she'd call half-assed—ideas and business proposals, the failures of which she insisted could be blamed on no one else but Devon. Eventually, Andi was left to wonder whether

her mother believed *she* could do the kind of work she dreamed of. After all, she doubted her husband—why wouldn't she doubt her own daughter, too? In the end, she told herself, it didn't matter. The day she graduated high school, she'd be on a bus back to San Jose—to her father, her future. Her real home.

Kids from five surrounding small towns were sent to West Bay High School, but in total there were still only a little over four hundred students across four grades. Such small class sizes made it difficult *not* to get to know other people, but Andi made a point to defy those odds. She didn't want any connections to her temporary home, no matter how immaterial. She'd taken a stand upon her and Rachel's arrival to keep herself separate from Tasker Bay, and up to this point—early in her senior year—there had been no reason to back down. She'd gone nearly two years without making new friends. Why start now?

In a sense, it wasn't all that difficult. She kept to herself, avoided anything extracurricular, and when classmates made overtures, she made her rebuttal loud and clear.

I don't have time.

That doesn't really sound fun.

Why would I want to do that?

It didn't take long for the rest of West Bay High to recognize she wanted nothing to do with them. And with a steady influx of new students thanks to the never-ending stream of transplants moving to Tasker Bay from San Jose, she was old news before long anyway.

But by far the biggest reason why Andi had successfully dodged real interaction with her classmates, and been able to deflect attempts by her mother at getting her to socialize, was by finding a job. Home Video World was a rental shop—VHS, Beta, CED—as well as an arcade. And Andi spent most of her time keeping its forty-some cabinets operational.

Situated on a downtown block that housed dour-looking businesses including a small accounting firm, a used book seller, and Tasker Bay's only liquor store, the Bottle Shoppe, Home Video World stood out via a collection of neon signs burning in its windows and the glow of arcade cabinets humming and buzzing within. It was colorful and noisy in an agreeable way, able to draw customers in with the promise of casual, harmless fun. Wire racks lined with boxes from videotapes—a tag underneath each to indicate whether it was in stock or rented out—took up half the floor space. The other half was filled with rows of arcade games, a few pinball machines, and the random small table and chairs.

Malcolm Petty, the shop's owner, had been relying on expensive house calls from an area electrician to triage his library of games before hiring Andi. The naturally suspicious type, Mal—he'd always thought his full name sounded weak—had come to believe poor work was being done on purpose so he'd have to keep forking over cash for repairs. Andi, though, could see it was simply a case of someone doing work outside their depth; an electrician wasn't a technician, and vice versa.

Mal gave her considerable leeway around the shop because she saved him money and showed no interest in slacking off with her classmates or spending time playing rather than fixing games. In fact, more than once, Andi made it clear she had no love for the act of gaming. Dumping change into a box for sixty seconds' worth of dopamine made no sense to her.

It also didn't hurt that, as Mal lecherously put it—sometimes within earshot—she was "easy on the eyes." On the taller side, hair thinning and middle growing thick as he reached the end of his thirties, Mal tried hard to project an air of male superiority that Andi easily saw through. She wasn't naive—she knew regardless of whatever value she brought to the table, Mal had hired her in part because he wanted to sleep with her. From the bevy of part-time jobs she'd had over the years, she'd long ago arrived at an ugly truth: in almost any given situation, there was *always* a Mal. Just one, if you were lucky. She also knew herself well enough to be certain that, if Mal ever *did* try to pull some shit, she could hit hard enough to make him regret it.

Finding her way to the arcade every day after school, Andi routinely worked through closing, sometimes doing full days—up to twelve hours per—on the weekends. She made decent money, socking everything away to pad her eventual flight back to San Jose. She wasn't going out, wasn't buying beer, didn't have hobbies outside of programming and cobbling together computers. And part of her arrangement with Mal—that she kept anything she couldn't bring back to full working order—meant she didn't have to pay for raw materials when it came to the latter.

Things being what they were, they weren't *terrible*. Andi had found both a refuge from society and a way to avoid her mom through work. She was making a little money doing something she didn't hate, even if she *did* hate Mal. And most importantly, unlike a lot of people, she knew exactly where she was going in life: southeast, back home, the first chance she got.

While Home Video World's doors opened every day at ten a.m., business didn't pick up until the afternoon. This was fine with Mal—he could sell a little weed, some pills out of the back of the shop and take it easy in the morning, then share the load with Andi in the afternoon. For the son of a Tasker Bay fisherman with no interest in continuing his father's back-breaking business after he'd passed away, Mal had done well finding a niche for himself, one that catered to the influx of Silicon Valley migrants and their considerable bank accounts.

The video rental business into which Mal had dipped a toe over the last few years had proven surprisingly lucrative, particularly the adult titles, but the arcade was his cash cow—and with Andi there to keep it on its feet, he intended to milk it for everything it was worth. This had come to include rotating in new cabinets.

It was Andi who turned him on to the idea of prowling auction houses in and around San Jose and San Francisco for deals. Not only did he consistently find the parts needed to keep his older cabs running, he lucked into new ones too. *Joust*, *Dig Dug*, and *Tempest* had all recently turned up, steeply discounted to boot. Andi was full of these kinds of creative, cost-cutting ideas. In his very occasional reflective moments, Mal could admit that if she decided to change the locks after he left, and take over the shop, she wouldn't miss a beat.

The latest of these auction house finds was due in Tasker Bay later that afternoon, bought for next to nothing. Something called *Polybius*. Mal didn't know the title—it hadn't turned up in any of his trade magazines—but the price made it a no-brainer. Annoyingly, he'd have to paint the cabinet—its sides were stark white. There wasn't even a marquee. But that wouldn't cost him much, so all that was left was to take delivery, plug it in, and collect Tasker Bay's loose change.

The problem was that the delivery came late, in the middle of what Mal referred to as the shop's "rush hour," a combination of out-of-school kids crowding the arcade floor and parents on their way home from work picking up a video for the night. He was forced to put Andi behind the counter—the most public-facing and therefore her least favorite spot in the shop—so he could oversee the delivery.

This left Andi doing what she tried hardest to avoid: talking to her classmates. The assignment was made worse by the fact that, under the counter and in plain view, was a loaded .38 Mal kept on hand for "emergencies." Andi felt no safer knowing it was there. Mal was more likely to end up shot with it than saved by it, she'd decided.

Daydreaming about Mal meeting an untimely end couldn't last forever, though—Andi was snapped back to reality by a boy her age loosely waving a hand, trying to get her attention so he could change a five-dollar bill. She recognized him from school. Every now and then she'd swear he was eyeing her from across the room during Algebra II, but she hadn't bothered tuning in when someone had spoken his name.

"Hey, Andi," the boy offered from behind a shy smile. She pushed the quarters to him then snatched the five, looking to busy herself with something below the counter so he'd get the message, take his change, and shuffle off. As she hovered there, Andi felt a little like kicking herself. Why not say hi, or at least smile? Why didn't she know his name? It wouldn't hurt *not* to be an asshole.

Another customer stepped up to the counter, but Andi stayed down, having resolved she wasn't coming back up until she at least remembered his name. She'd heard it in the background before at school, and it was interesting. Or at least not boring.

"Yo," came an annoyed call from the other side of the counter, followed by the rap of a fist against the laminate top. She raised a hand in response, motioning for another moment of respite while she tried recalling his name. *Ronald—no. Ray—Raymond? Richard . . . Roland?*

CHAPTER 2

ROMAN KEMP HAD LONG BEEN AN OUTWARDLY SOCIAL KID. HIS PERSONA HAD BEEN forged in reaction to tragedy, the death of his mother, Cheryl, who passed from cancer when he was only ten. It was evidence of things Ro hadn't been ready to confront: mortality, unpredictability, chaos. He'd sought an escape in others—friends, teammates, a large social circle. A life too busy to dwell.

But what Ro wanted now was to do nothing, or at least nothing he *had* been doing. He needed something different but couldn't figure out what that "something" was. The feeling crept up early in his junior year and lingered, leading him to drop out of every student organization and sport he'd been a part of as he entered his final year of high school. He alienated teammates and lost friends, but the life he was leading—despite all outward appearances—had begun to feel empty and devoid of meaning.

To the naked eye, Ro seemed troubled. He wasn't oblivious to the signals he was sending out. Maybe he was troubled. But all those years spent hiding from his feelings through others had left him deeply uncertain of everything. He wanted to learn who he really was, what he was capable of, and decided it was something he needed to do largely on his own.

He wasn't so much burning bridges as he was finding new routes. He was still affable around other West Bay students, ready to lend a hand when someone needed help. He didn't mind being called a friend and remained a familiar face around town. These were parts of himself he still liked and wouldn't let go of, which made the withdrawal from his old hypersocial ways all the more baffling for those around him.

Teachers, coaches, friends, their parents, his own father had all tried decoding what was going on. There was no satisfactory answer he could give. He wanted time, and space, and the chance to figure out who he was apart from others. To find what *he* wanted, and whether it—whatever *it* was—wanted him.

He'd found himself drawn to video games late in his junior year and had begun amassing books and magazines on the industry. Specifically, the subject of writing game code. He'd always enjoyed writing in school, essays and short pieces of fiction, but with games the end results were visual. In a lot of cases they were designed by just one or two people. The ability to tell a story and bring it to life, all in relative isolation, felt worth exploring.

Ro also thought that because she worked at the arcade where he'd been spending most of his time, the very quiet, very pretty girl from his Algebra II class shared his passion for gaming. He knew there was only one way to find out but had also grown skilled at talking himself out of bolder moves, like attempting to initiate a conversation with a girl on whom he'd had a crush since she'd moved to town.

Still, he *felt* something for her, even after he'd stopped feeling much about anything. The emptiness he felt flew out of his mind when he thought about Andi. He knew he should do something about it.

He was, of course, wrong. Andi didn't work at the arcade because she scored free plays on *Tempest*. But there *was* something they had in common, an aspect to their personalities neither could, at their age, fully understand or properly grasp—both were desperately ready for something different from life.

That particular day, Ro had resolved to say something to her—and he had—but she'd stopped him short at "Hi, Andi" by ducking down, then staying out of sight. It was . . . odd. And more than a little deflating. But as he walked back toward the arcade floor, quarters jangling in his pocket, he glanced over his shoulder just as Andi popped up from behind the counter. She looked toward him, and for a moment their eyes locked.

Ro assumed it was happenstance and was the first to look away. Still, his stomach twisted into knots as he settled in front of *Robotron: 2084*. He glanced back once more, stealing a look, but by then she was busy with another customer. He turned back to the cabinet, dropped in a quarter, and grabbed the twin joysticks as gameplay began.

What he couldn't have known was, after the customer had stepped away, Andi's eyes roamed the floor in search of him. Why did he know her name, she wondered—say it . . . say hi? It wasn't *that* unusual. People did that sort of thing all the time. Just not to her.

Behind the shop, a deliveryman rolled an arcade cabinet mummified in moving blankets and shrink-wrap down the metal ramp of a nondescript box truck. Light rain fell as Mal scribbled his signature on the corner of a carbon receipt, thin paper wilting from the mist.

He noted as he scanned the form that the delivery was costing him half of what he'd paid for the cabinet itself. But it was still a deal, and the last time he'd tried moving a game on his own, it had ended in a cracked screen Andi's magic couldn't mend and a sore back that for a week forced him to sleep in the ratty old recliner that had once been his father's domain. Mal swore it still smelled like the Tasker Bay docks, even though his father had been gone for nearly ten years. It was worth paying for delivery, he'd decided, if it kept him out of that goddamned chair. In truth, he had no attachment to it and probably should've replaced it years ago. But he *did* have an attachment to his money. When the chair fell apart, he'd replace it. Maybe see if Andi could fix it, first. He stuffed the receipt into a tattered accordion folder that had long substituted for a proper filing cabinet, then headed back inside and out of the rain.

The cabinet was wheeled to a space behind the shop floor that served as a combination office, workshop, and storage area. It was crowded with a handful of in-process repair jobs spread over a workbench, a desk covered in trades and junk food wrappers, and racks that held the adult titles that Mal rented out. Initially, he'd been surprised how willing people were to walk up to a relative stranger and ask for pornography. But vice was vice, whether it was pumping quarters into a game or peering into humanity's exotic corners.

If people were willing to pay, he'd find a way.

And *that* was his real service, he told himself. To provide whatever, whenever asked. If Tasker Bay had a kingpin, Mal liked to think he was it. It made him feel alive, that willingness to say yes when timid types would not.

He cleared a path to an outlet and plugged the new cabinet in. The internal cooling fans began to spin as a wave of static crackled through the speakers and across the display. Using a key he found taped to the cabinet's back, Mal opened the coin door and toggled a few credits. Everything seemed in working order. The controls were tight. It felt as if the game was brand-new. As his hand glanced the start button, the door leading to the shop's floor opened. Andi leaned through, spotting the new cabinet.

"What's that?" she asked, barely interested in the answer.

"Don't know," Mal shrugged. "Never heard of it. But it was cheap."

"Yeah, well, it's crazy out there. So come help," Andi ordered as she walked over and unplugged the cabinet, then headed back toward the shop floor.

"Rude," Mal called after as he followed her out. "And I'm *your* boss." It pissed Mal off that Andi always seemed to have the upper hand in these moments. In truth, he just failed to see that hers was consistently the more practical point of view. He simmered but still returned to the floor without protest. His self-image might have been Tasker Bay's resident crime lord, but this moment hewed closer to the truth—being pushed around by a much sharper subordinate.

Left alone in back, the cabinet's display still glowed faintly with the ghostly outline of the game's attract screen. As the picture tubes cooled, the image faded, and the screen went dark.

Andi knew Mal would lean on her to stay and set up the new cabinet, but she'd been anxious to leave work all night. Something about Ro—whose name she'd finally managed to remember—left her unsettled. She wasn't used to feeling this kind of intense focus toward another person. So she slipped away right after close, hopping on her bike and pedaling toward home before Mal had a chance to suggest otherwise.

It was in this short window of time Andi could muster a little appreciation for what Tasker Bay was, and wasn't. The road was quiet, the woods that lined it tall and lush, with treetops swept by cool winds blown in from the bay. That two-mile stretch between work and home offered a sense of peace she'd never experienced within the relative bustle of San Jose. In the year and a half she'd worked at the arcade, this nightly ride home had become one of the few things she looked forward to.

As she pulled up to the front of the side-split home her mom had purchased before their move, *without* consulting her, Andi told herself that whatever she was feeling about Ro would pass with time. She'd already managed to go a good four hours without thinking about him. *Just get through the rest of the night without doing it again, and things will be fine.*

The house was nothing like their home in Dobern. It reminded Andi of a lodge, big rooms with high ceilings, ancient-looking redwood beams crisscrossing throughout. The walls were painted in shades of the same color, creating a rich scheme that stood in stark contrast to the white finishes of their newly constructed two-story home back in San Jose. That house was nicely appointed but boxy and full of right angles that, Andi had to admit, felt bland in comparison. While she wouldn't miss Tasker Bay, she might miss this place.

She found her mom at the dining room table, sifting through a sea of patient charts she'd brought home from her office. Rachel had dialed back the hours she spent at her practice upon the move to Tasker Bay but not the amount of work she did; she'd just started doing it from home. This was, Andi decided, worse than her mom being gone all the time. There were papers everywhere that she wasn't supposed to touch, meaning she had almost nowhere to go that wasn't her room. When she'd pointed out that moving someone's records was better than spilling cereal all over them, Rachel wasn't amused. They were *private*. And she was *trying*. Her mom did a lot of *trying* these days, though what she was trying to do wasn't clear. Trying to make a mess? Job well done. Trying to be more present? Being chained to a desk at home was still being chained to a desk.

"How was work?" Rachel asked as Andi dumped her things in the only empty spot she could find and rooted in the refrigerator for something to eat. "There are cold cuts in the drawer."

"Work was fine, school was fine," Andi replied, pulling what she needed for a sandwich—turkey, Swiss, lettuce and tomato, honey mustard. No pickled jalapeños, though—still. They'd been out for a week. She started to complain, but the sight of her mother boxed in by literal stacks of paperwork gave her pause. She could run to the store tomorrow herself.

"I stitched a fingertip back on today," Rachel said matter-of-factly.

"Mom, I'm making dinner."

It was like she hadn't heard Andi. "I hadn't done that before. I've stitched other things, never a fingertip."

Andi continued constructing her sandwich, but morbid curiosity—of which she had an abundance—finally got the better of her. "So, what happened? With the finger?"

"He was cutting a turkey breast—"

Andi stopped and stared at the slices of turkey piled up before her, before shooting her mom a withering look. "Are you trying to make me *not* eat?"

"Yours is already sliced. You're fine. He was cutting a turkey breast with an electric carving knife, and the phone rang. He set the knife down without switching it off, turned around to answer"—by this point, Rachel was pantomiming—"and passed a finger *right* over top of the blade."

Andi winced a little. "So he's too lazy to use a regular knife," she said, flashing the chef's knife she was using to slice her sandwich in half for effect. "Then he's too stupid to shut it off?"

"These are the people who pay our mortgage," Rachel replied with a sly smile, before returning to her work.

It was, severed fingertip and all, a nicer-than-average conversation between the two of them. Andi had perhaps been more willing to engage because she suspected that time alone with her thoughts would lead back to Ro. But she also worried that lingering too long, instead of retreating to her room per usual, would seem suspicious and prompt questions from her mom that she didn't want to answer. Questions that would *also* likely lead back to Ro.

"Homework," Andi blurted out as she disappeared down the hall, forgetting her backpack—and homework—in her haste.

She settled in at a desk strewn with electronic components,

setting to work on a computer she'd been building from scratch. Her room wasn't exactly spartan; she liked to think of it as curated. But aside from posters for the Dead Kennedys and the Dils, part of the San Francisco punk scene she'd identified with growing up, there wasn't much personality to it. It was the myriad of home-brewed engineering projects, the computers, shortwave radios, and satellite TV descramblers that defined the space.

She understood more about her parents than she used to. Than Rachel realized. She knew her dad wasn't well. But she also still believed in him, and she still found great comfort in opening something up and taking it apart, piece by piece, like they used to do.

Mal piloted *Polybius*, ratchet-strapped to a two-wheeled dolly, through the maze of cabinets on the shop floor to a spot he kept reserved for new titles. He'd relocated his previous new addition, *Moon Patrol*, earlier that evening and now worked *Polybius* off the dolly and into place.

After plugging the cabinet in and powering it on, Mal then walked to the front door. He unlocked and propped it open with a rubber doorstop, then pulled and sparked a joint he'd tucked into a pack of Marlboro Reds. After a couple of deep drags, he turned to see the game's attract screen once again staring back, flashing an invitation to him just as it had in the back room.

Kicking the stop away, he walked back over and stooped in front of the coin door, keying it open and toggling a handful of credits. Rising back up and pressing the start button, he gripped the controls and watched the field of play take shape.

He glanced left, right at the other displays still glowing around him—next to this thing their graphics were shit. The images were an order of magnitude sharper, with far more depth and color. They seemed . . . alive. Even the audio was different, abstract layered tones that sounded like something out of a movie. He'd have said it was orchestral, if he'd known that word *and* believed an instrument could've produced such oddly compelling sounds. If this is what they were working on in Silicon Valley, Mal thought, then they were doing *something* right.

Not only was the game a visual knockout, but, as play commenced, it proved more tightly controlled and engaging than anything else he'd encountered. He raced forward through the cavern-like maze, whatever the hell was chasing him pounding after. Symbols carved on the walls—like the runes he'd seen in some Viking movie with Cameron Mitchell on KNTV the other night—whipped by as he ran. His heartrate was rising, thumping as the tension increased—with each turn he gained ground on his pursuer, only to cede it back in the next straightaway.

How long has it been?

Mal felt like he was waking from a coma, except he was upright, on his feet, and holding the game's controls. The screen flickered back at him—*Press Start.* Somewhere along the line he must have lost and then . . . played through the rest of his credits? He wasn't sure. He couldn't remember *anything* past walking over to play the game.

Cool air rushed through the room, blowing a tumbleweed of

crinkling plastic candy wrappers past his feet. Mal glanced over, watching the front door swing open. *Did I leave it unlocked?* He checked his watch—nearly midnight. Shaking off his malaise, he went to finish locking up when he heard them: *footsteps*, heavy, moving through the dark across the floor. He spun, expecting to see someone behind him, but the space was empty. Just rows of glowing screens.

"Hey!" There was no response to Mal's call, just more unseen shuffling. He moved for the counter, fishing out the .38 and checking the cylinder—loaded with six shots.

"I've got a gun and I'm calling the cops, so you can get shot, get arrested, or get the fuck out now. Your choice."

Thinking he'd caught sight of something—a vaguely human shape, calling to mind the figment that had been chasing him in the game—he froze.

This is ridiculous, he told himself. *You're high, and paranoid.*

But still, he stood and stared, waiting it out, making sure whatever he *thought* he saw wasn't going anywhere. As he finally lowered the gun, the figment seemed to come alive and shift in response, disappearing into the dark.

The gun flew back up. "Goddamn it, I'm warning you!" Reaching over the counter, Mal grabbed the phone. He could hear movement as he went to dial. Suddenly the dial tone began to fluctuate in time with the footsteps, undulating like an electronic pulse—buzz-step, buzz-step. He spun the rotary dial—as it clicked back into place, it synced with the encroaching movements too, click-buzz-step, click-buzz-step. Every sound was swirling into a thumping rhythm—first the footsteps and the dial tone, then Mal's heartbeat, finally a throbbing in his head that swelled from nowhere. What felt like a surge of electricity passed through him, blurring his vision and drowning everything but the cycle of noise from his ears.

As a deep, primal fear gripped him, Mal began to wilt. Gun still in hand, he dropped the phone and gripped his head, squeezing his eyes shut as he crumpled to the floor. The sound grew louder and more urgent, reverberating to the point Mal could feel himself shaking with each beat—until it abruptly stopped.

His body and mind were so tensed, it took Mal a long moment to realize the psychic assault had come to an end. As his wits returned, he shot to his feet and jammed the gun against the dark, firing a single shot that slammed into a VHS copy of *The Watcher in the Woods*. But he was alone, a fact he confirmed after every single light had come on, every corner of the shop and back room had been checked and rechecked, all at the barrel of the .38.

Snatching the ruined tape from its shelf, Mal started to leave the shop floor. As he went, he glanced back at *Polybius*, finding himself slowing, staring. But the feeling passed as quickly as it had cropped up. He disappeared through the back room then out into the chilly Wednesday night air.

CHAPTER 3

DAVID KEMP HAD HOPED ARRIVING HOME EARLY FROM WORK THAT THURSDAY afternoon would be a pleasant surprise for his son. Ro usually had to fend for himself until David was able to pull away from Tasker Bay's small police station, where he served as a Sonoma County resident deputy sheriff. Tasker Bay was a small town, but when you wore that hat, there was always something requiring your attention, something to demand energy you might otherwise have been able to direct elsewhere. In David's case, he would have preferred having more time to try to understand what had happened to his son over the past several months. He didn't seem to be the same person.

Ro had been a leader on and off the field, cocaptain of the football team and an active member of West Bay High's student council. People responded to him, looked to him for an example of how to be, what to do. Ro could be *something*, but he didn't seem to want it—or anything else—anymore. To see him give all that up troubled David.

Ro was *also* a teenager. Teenagers went through phases. David had turned forty-three earlier that year but wasn't so old he'd forgotten what it was like to be eighteen. And besides, his son was nothing if not resilient. He'd come around.

David had first noticed that ability to internalize and overcome stress after the passing of his wife and Ro's mother, Cheryl. This was when Ro started finding ways to engage after school, all on his own. David was there for him more back then but, upon reflection, often found himself wondering whether Ro actually needed him. He seemed preternaturally self-sufficient. And so, as Ro had grown older, David just assumed that independent streak meant his son was all right being on his own most of the time.

But maybe he'd been wrong?

Even when Cheryl was alive, there'd been adversity—David was white; she was Black. They'd always lived in what could be considered more progressively minded parts of the country, gradually making their way from the edge of Los Angeles up the coast while David searched for work following an emotionally draining stint in the LAPD. But it didn't change the fact that, wherever they went, their family unit was not viewed as the norm.

David knew as a result of his withdrawing from his friends, from sports, Ro was losing a crutch—not just one that had helped him connect with others but had helped him deal with a loss they both still felt. It never went away, the sense that Cheryl should've been—but wasn't—there. If Ro didn't have something to focus on, didn't have a sense he was part of something bigger, David worried his son might start to spiral. He knew from experience. When it seemed like Ro hadn't needed *him* anymore, he took it hard and threw himself deeper into work to compensate. If there was something Ro was missing that could help with the questions, fears, doubts that came from feeling alone, feeling different, David worried about him trying and perhaps failing to find it on his own.

David tried turning his attention to the day's copy of the local paper, the *Tasker Bay Trader*, but it wasn't much use. He'd heard the gist of every story over the radio or in conversation around town, which caused his thoughts to drift in other, distressing directions.

People in Tasker Bay gossiped a lot, and for a while now he'd heard rumblings that a recently formed "town council"—made up almost exclusively of wealthy newcomers and overseen by real estate developer Bob Colson—was engineering his exit. Among other plans the council was pursuing, in the name of making Tasker Bay their own, was the installation of someone from the Santa Clara Sheriff's Department in David's position.

Despite years spent with the LAPD, he'd apparently been in Tasker Bay too long. Read too much as a "townie" for the area's new blood. It surely hadn't helped that he'd served as a character witness for a local, Carl Delano, who'd become involved in a protracted legal dispute over a parcel of land with Colson's development company, Bayview Holdings. Or that he and his deputies had ticketed Colson—fond of flaunting the posted speeds on Tasker Bay's winding roads in his DeLorean—on nearly a dozen occasions that year alone.

David had only ever been a soldier and then a cop. He wasn't sure what else he would or could do. His job gave him focus, kept his mind occupied, away from dark places. Without it, the same worries he felt for Ro echoed for him. Could he face what he was running from, find what was missing when he stripped away life's distractions?

As Ro entered through their home's back door, David snapped happily to, but concern flashed in Ro's eyes at seeing his dad. "Is everything all right?" were the first words out of his mouth, not *Hi, Dad*, or *Great, you're home early*. Instead, Ro assumed some random, local tragedy was the only reason to see his father during daylight hours. Right away David began second-guessing his decision.

"Everything's fine. I just thought I'd take off a little early. Jeff's at the station, Charlie's on later tonight," David said, referring to the two deputies his office was afforded. "Thursdays are always quiet anyway. I was thinking we could go to Ford's, get a bite."

"I'm supposed to see Laurel"—Ro checked his watch—"in, like, forty-five minutes. I'm her ride."

Recognizing that he hadn't planned this well enough, David saw no sense in letting the disappointment he felt infect his son. "See your friends," he replied with a smile. "We'll do it next week."

"You sure?" Ro asked, a hint of relief somewhere in his voice that wounded David, even if he understood it.

He nodded. "Yeah. Go on. Next week."

"Thanks, Dad. You good?"

"Good," David replied. "You?" Ro nodded. It was a simple question he'd taken to asking Ro after his mother passed, a quick way to check in and remind his son it was okay to talk, share. A shorthand way of saying *I see you. I'm here. I love you.* It became part of their dynamic, although for a while now David suspected Ro wasn't being honest in his answers. Then again, at the moment, neither was he.

As Ro disappeared into the house, David stared off for a moment, silently kicking himself for not thinking things through. He rose and grabbed his jacket from its hook near the back door, then headed for his sheriff's cruiser parked outside as daylight waned. With a new baby at home, his deputy Jeff wouldn't mind a night off.

Laurel Greene and Ro had dated most of their junior year. After they'd split, and Ro had started withdrawing from his old social circles, he realized that he still wanted her in his life and was grateful she felt the same way. They knew each other well—when to call bullshit, when to listen. The life of a teenager being what it was, Ro understood it took an extraordinary amount of self-confidence to stand by someone who projected "otherness" and appreciated Laurel all the more for it.

Short, tan, with sandy blond hair and a surfer's lithe body, Laurel possessed a kind of effortless poise in everything she did. She was her own person in a way Ro envied and deeply admired, moving effortlessly between West Bay High's social classes without compromise. She could be found most afternoons with her nose buried in a dog-eared sci-fi paperback and happily spent weekend nights with her parents, but she was also somehow always the first to know about—and usually the first invited to—anything going on around West Bay.

Going back three generations, her family had owned Tasker Bay's sole grocery store, Greene's. Unimaginative name aside, it was an institution. But as much as the area's new residents appreciated its small-town charm, that wasn't enough. Earlier that year a competitor,

Paulson's, had opened up on the edge of town, easily accessible for those commuting to and from San Jose. Nearly the size of West Bay High, it stocked more, could do more, all for less than Greene's ever could. As their customers shifted away, Laurel's family felt the walls closing in.

Uncertainty bred tension. Tension bred acrimony. And for Laurel, the doom-and-gloom vibe that had overtaken the household was fast becoming something she couldn't handle. Neither parent had bothered telling her what she'd learned by accident, when she'd found a letter left on the kitchen counter. The family was filing for bankruptcy.

For the first time in her life, she found herself wanting to be somewhere else, anywhere other than home, and was grateful Ro was on his way that night to pick her up. Sequestered in her room since getting back from school, she'd picked up a copy of a Harlan Ellison anthology and started reading "I Have No Mouth, and I Must Scream" but couldn't maintain focus over all the very loud *discussing* going on between her parents downstairs. They weren't even arguing about the shop—its problems had started infecting every interaction between them.

Finally hearing a car horn honking outside, Laurel snatched a sketchbook from underneath a stack of loose papers—all of them covered in intricate pencil drawings of futuristic landscapes—and ducked out the front door fast enough to avoid running into her mom or dad.

Ro reached over and opened up the passenger door as she approached. When they were dating, he'd park, walk up to the front door. Now it was a foot on the brake pedal, a hand on the horn, and up to Laurel to shovel whatever random crap was left in the passenger seat out of her way. Neither seemed to mind these or the other small shifts that had occurred in their dynamic, post breakup. Things were just easier this way.

Ro noted the sketch pad sticking out of the bag Laurel stashed in the back seat. "What's that for?"

"I'm not *playing*," she said. "It's a waste of money. I'm just coming with."

Ro pulled away, cutting down a side street toward Tasker Bay's small downtown. "You'd have fun if you actually tried. And you'd like the sprites—like the level designs and the characters, that kind of stuff."

"I can see that without giving my money away." Laurel shrugged.

Stopped at a red light, Ro plucked the sketchbook from her bag and flipped through a series of drawings inspired by a book about overpopulation, *Stand on Zanzibar*. Bodies were crammed together in dingy trams and seedy streets. "These are great," he said. "When are you going to sketch something for one of my ideas?" Ro asked, part of a long-running game of cat and mouse they played.

"What's on the box and what's in the game are not remotely the same," Laurel shot back. "I'm not spending a bunch of time drawing spaceships that end up looking like triangles. And people don't take anything away from playing games. They don't change the way they think."

The arcade floor was packed. But most of the cabinets weren't in use—everyone was crowded around the shop's newest title, *Polybius*. People stepped up and tucked quarters along the marquee, forming an unofficial queue for the next play. Laurel said hi here and there as she retreated to a corner where a few graffiti-covered card tables sat, finding an incomplete sketch then setting to work.

Surveying the space, Ro finally spotted Andi as she emerged from in back, taking up a position behind the counter. She looked annoyed at being there. But as he started toward her, he found himself with a better angle on the new game and stopped for a moment to watch.

Mark Casey, a hulking ex-teammate of Ro's, ducked and dodged his way through a seemingly endless cavern, a dark shape occasionally appearing on the periphery as it gave chase. Everything about the game—the mechanics, the visuals, the intense speed at which it was played—set it apart. Ro even noted a handful of unfamiliar faces in the regular crowd. Mal had the next big thing, it seemed.

Accidentally bumped by another customer, Ro snapped to. He felt a flash of anger at his eyes being pulled from the screen. He watched as the boy who'd pushed past him, another ex-teammate named Cliff Young, jostled to the front of the line.

Even when Ro had been on the team, neither Mark nor Cliff had ever warmed up to him. He'd heard enough muffled comments to know it was his race that they disliked. That, and the fact his dad often broke up the raucous parties they and a handful of others liked to throw along Tasker Bay's windy coast. Linebackers both, they tended to act as aggressively off the field as they did on. Ro had no business messing with either of them but in that moment wanted to part the crowd and get in Cliff's face for bumping him—until, just as quickly, he didn't.

He wasn't an aggressive person. Not like that, anyway. The feeling left him uneasy.

Spotting Andi, still behind the counter, helped him refocus.

As Ro approached, Andi felt her cheeks flush. She was pissed at seeing him in person, given she'd failed at keeping him off her mind the night before and throughout the day that followed. Ro offered a small smile as he set a five on the counter. Andi stared at the crinkled bill for a moment, debating whether to speak.

After watching her stare for what felt like an eternity, Ro finally asked, "Are you . . . okay?" Without a response, Andi snatched up the bill and opened the register.

"You could just use the change machine," she finally managed, still not meeting his eyes.

"It's busted. Takes your money but won't give you quarters. Mal probably set it up that way on purpose." Ro laughed a little at his own joke, trying unsuccessfully to sell it. He glanced away, hoping he wasn't visibly wincing. He felt like he was wincing. "I don't think I've seen this many people in here before."

"It's that new game," Andi said, still pulling change.

She'd spoken. It was a window. Ro leapt through, still incorrectly assuming they had a common area of interest. "I haven't seen anything like it. *Speed Race*, I guess."

"*Speed Race* was electromechanical. That game's real 3D," Andi said as she slid his change over the counter and fixed her eyes on *Polybius*. "I guess it kind of plays the same."

Ro was impressed. And intimidated. "You . . . know about this stuff?" He immediately realized it was a dumb question. Obviously Andi did. He went to correct himself. "I meant—"

"I don't like playing games. I like the programming, the hardware," she cut in.

"Oh. That's cool. I want to write games. The code, I mean.

The stories, too. I'm trying to learn how, but there isn't a lot out there."

"Andi," Mal barked from in back. Without a word she turned and slipped through the door leading to the back room. Ro was once again left to gather his change and shuffle off. At least she'd said something this time.

"*Ro.*" He turned to find Laurel nearby, still with her sketchbook, an exaggerated look of disbelief on her face. "Were you *talking* to her?"

"Not really," he replied, trying to deflect the flack he assumed was incoming. "Almost literally. It was a . . . thirty-second conversation."

"She can actually speak? English? To other people?" Laurel smirked. "I guess that's cool. But you should've tried talking to her, like, a year ago." She'd known Ro had an eye for Andi, even when they were together. Never understood why. Andi was cute in a way that stood out—tall, pale, with sharp eyes and short black hair—but so what? She clearly didn't want *anything* to do with *anyone*. If there was a colder shoulder to be given at West Bay, Laurel hadn't felt it.

"I'm not *talking* to her," Ro corrected. "That was the only conversation we've ever had."

"Gotta start somewhere," Laurel said, returning to her sketchbook. "And that girl never talks to anybody, so if she talked to you, it means something. Be happy, dummy." Looking back up, she nodded at the counter. "She's watching you."

Ro peered over his shoulder, trying to remain inconspicuous. Sure enough, Andi was back, and he'd caught the tail end of a look in his direction. It felt remarkably good, but the sensation was short-lived. Scuffling came from somewhere within the rows of cabinets, more frantic moment to moment. Ro and Laurel glanced at each other, then moved toward the noise.

"Mal!" Andi called over her shoulder as she hurried toward the commotion. She pushed through a sea of bodies ringing a brawl between Mark, Cliff, and a scrawny twentysomething man Andi didn't recognize. Mark was holding the man back, Cliff was landing body blows.

Ro and Laurel arrived in time to watch Andi force her way into the scrum, grabbing Cliff's arm just as he drew back. "Out—*now*," she shouted.

Cliff yanked himself free. Andi had expected resistance but not a full-on swing at her head. The crowd gasped as she managed to duck, springing back up and cracking Cliff across the face with a right cross. As impressive as the punch was, it didn't faze her hulking opponent, who proceeded to grab her by the shoulders and toss her, hard, to the floor.

Head smacking scuffed linoleum, Andi could see Cliff standing over her, glaring down as he raised a foot. She knew she needed to move, but with her head still hazy, the signal wasn't loud or clear enough for her body to receive. All she could think was *This is going to fucking hurt.*

Suddenly Ro barged in front of Cliff, ramming him back with a shoulder, then pushing him through the crowd and up against a wall. Springing forward, Cliff was met by a forearm shoved first into his chest then pinned under his throat. "Calm down!" Ro shouted, putting everything he had into keeping the much bigger man in place. It seemed like Cliff couldn't hear him, so wound-up that everything around him had turned to white noise.

Still holding on to the stranger, Mark tossed him aside then started toward Ro, eyes on fire.

"Hey, it's over," Laurel snapped, stepping in front of Mark and waiting for him to back down. "Gonna hit me next?" she asked, standing her ground until he finally wavered. Mark had been chasing after her for years—including while she and Ro were dating—and Laurel had no problem exploiting the power she held over him, given the moment. "*Go,*" she snapped, pointing toward the door.

A look of vague recognition flashed in Mark's eyes. He glanced at Ro and Cliff, then the stranger he'd been pummeling.

"Get out," boomed Mal as he threw on every light in the shop and stormed onto the floor, .38 tucked conspicuously into his waistband. "Cops are on their way, so go out now if you don't want to spend the night in lockup." For a moment the crowd milled, assuming he was only talking to the troublemakers. "We're closed. *Out!*"

Andi felt someone reach under her arms from behind, pulling her onto her feet—Laurel. "Are you okay?" she asked. Still foggy, overwhelmed by everything, Andi didn't respond.

"What the fuck? Come on, Ro. Let go of me, man." Whatever had come over Cliff seemed to pass. He'd even given up pushing back. Ro let him loose, stepping aside.

No sooner was Cliff free than Mal was clamping a hand on his arm, pulling him toward the door. "You come in here again and I call the cops, you got it? I don't want to see you, or your friend."

As they reached the exit, Cliff tore free from Mal's grip, then huffed off. Out of nowhere, Mark blindsided Mal, shoving and sending him backpedaling across the shop floor. "There's *a lot* of shit going down here the cops could find out about. I don't think you're calling anybody, asshole," he said, staring Mal down for a long moment before turning and following Cliff into the crowd milling outside.

"You too," Mal said to Ro as he climbed back to his feet. "Out!"

For a moment Ro stared, incredulous—he'd *stopped* the fight—but let it go. Starting for the exit, he glanced back toward Laurel, still with Andi. "Hey, Laurel," Ro called. "We're going. Come on." She said something to Andi that he couldn't hear, then followed him out.

With the arcade finally clear, Mal approached Andi, cautious. "You need a doctor?"

"I'll see one when I get home," Andi said, before starting after Ro. "And the guy you just threw out was the one who broke up the fight."

"Like I give a shit!" Mal shouted after, angry at being questioned. He surveyed the empty room, all the lost business already eating at him.

Outside, Ro and Laurel were walking toward Ro's car when they heard Andi calling after. "Hey, Roman."

"*Roman*," Laurel quietly chided. As she continued on, Ro waited for Andi to catch up.

"You didn't have to do that," Andi snapped at him as she approached. It was a normal expression of gratitude, but the way she said it gave Ro pause—was she angry he'd stepped in?

"I was only trying to help." Ro's voice wavered a little as he spoke. He was unsure whether or not this was supposed to be an apology.

"I didn't need it."

"You were flat on your back, and he was going to put a boot in your ribs," Ro said. "I'm not just going to stand around and let that happen because it's . . . better for your pride."

Ro was right, which for Andi made things even more awkward. She had no immediate response, knowing she ought to apologize and thank him, neither of which she felt able to do.

"We gotta go," Ro said, a tinge of bitterness in his voice as he started toward the car.

For a moment Andi stewed, then surprised herself by speaking up. "Roman."

He stopped, turning toward her, waiting for something else—but she just stared, not sure what to say next. "It's just Ro," he finally offered.

"Roman's better."

Ro had to laugh a little—one minute she was mad because he stood up for her, the next she was telling him to ditch his childhood nickname. "I'll take it under advisement," he said, waiting for a response that didn't come. Andi looked like she'd rather vanish off the face of the earth before saying anything further. Ro felt just as helpless, no idea what to say that would put her at ease.

Then suddenly Laurel was by his side. "I stashed some beer at my parents' shop," she said. "Come with."

"Oh. I just—have to get home."

"Suit yourself," Laurel said, going. With a half-hearted wave, Ro followed.

Andi watched as they hopped into Ro's car, then pulled away. *What the hell is wrong with you?* she thought.

After heading back into the arcade and locking the door behind her, she was surprised to find Mal standing at the *Polybius* cabinet, playing. She watched him for a moment, expecting him to turn around, say something, offer *some* acknowledgment. He didn't, staying fixed on the screen instead. "After I zero the register, I'm done," Andi said, huffing past him. Still no response.

As she tallied the day's receipts, Andi glanced at Mal, who remained transfixed by the game. Finally starting for the door, she was curious whether he'd notice. But it was like she wasn't even there.

She pedaled away from the shop, took a short detour, and wound past Greene's Market. The lights were out inside, and Ro's car was nowhere to be seen. Circling the block to make sure she hadn't missed them, she finally headed on her way.

If Andi hadn't diverged from her normal route, she would've passed Bar Harbor, the gathering spot for fishing crews from Tasker Bay's docks. There'd been fishing in town since the first settlers arrived some hundred and fifty-odd years ago, and among the sprawling patchwork of slips and shacks, a few of those original structures still stood.

Summer was the busiest season for the bay's many crews, and the striped bass the area was known for were plentiful. But as the season changed, an annual rite of adjustment began. Bass dwindled, but sturgeon, crabs, and leopard sharks could be found if you were willing to travel a little, while crews that stayed local shifted their focus onto rockfish.

There was always a flow of people in and out as the seasons changed. That meant that while there were regulars at Bar Harbor, there was also always a stream of new faces—tonight, that included the man who'd had his ass handed to him in Home Video World by Mark and Cliff. He ducked into the shotgun-styled building, bypassing booths wrapped in deep red vinyl for a backless stool at the long bar top, crafted from slabs of Douglas fir coated with yellowed layers of marine epoxy.

No one knew he wasn't a fisherman, wouldn't have cared if they did, but they did watch with curiosity as he downed shots to try to dull the pain from what was clearly a fresh beating. The owner and regular bartender, Larry Danna, had tried making small talk, but the man hadn't engaged. He just wanted to drink and be left alone, so he was.

This meant that no one paid any mind when after an hour, two beers, and four shots of Jim Beam, he rose unsteadily and staggered out the front door. It also meant that no one saw the two figures lurking in the shadows outside who proceeded to follow him down the street, into the night.

CHAPTER 4

THE LETTER HAD BEEN WAITING ON DAVID'S DESK WHEN HE'D RETURNED TO THE office earlier that night. For all the chatter he'd heard, it was harsher than he'd expected. The town council had amassed the signatures necessary and filed the paperwork to have him recalled. With Bob Colson using his plentiful resources to exert influence, he'd be out of a job in a month. The whole thing was rotten, arranged in secret and predicated on his actions as a private citizen, not some failure in his role as a public servant. The text made it clear the intention was not just to oust him from office; it was to smear him with suggestions of incompetence and corruption. It was vindictive, and its outcome inevitable.

The steady drizzle that had started when he'd left home earlier was now a full-on downpour as he cruised through town on patrol. It was no surprise this time of year, but it served to further sour his already glum mood. He didn't miss much about LA, but under the circumstances, he'd gladly take a dry heat over this.

Catching movement in the shadows as he rolled past an alley, David slowed down to observe. The rain made it hard to tell if he'd seen three drunks staggering off together . . . or two people dragging a third.

Tasker Bay had more than its share of heavy drinkers. It seemed to come part and parcel with a life on the water, and they were probably just stumbling home. Better on foot than behind the wheel, especially in the rain. But a gut instinct forced David to stop and, with a closer look, see the situation differently: two figures much bigger in stature *did* seem like they were carrying the smaller third down the alley. And it looked like the third was weakly resisting.

Opting to approach on foot instead of hitting the lights and siren, David rolled to a stop and grabbed a flashlight from inside the glove box. Pulling the hood up on his poncho, he made his way across the rain-slicked pavement toward the alley. Arriving, he found it empty.

He'd seen bodies in motion, that much he knew. There had to have been someone in the alley not twenty seconds prior, and unless they knew he was coming, or felt otherwise compelled to run, they couldn't have cleared his line of sight in that amount of time—especially not if two were dragging a third who was pulling in the opposite direction. As he moved his flashlight up and down, its beam glanced over a handful of garbage cans and a dumpster—all big enough for someone to hide behind.

Shit.

David's hand dipped to the service revolver strapped to his belt and unfastened the clasp holding the gun in place. He'd drawn his weapon three times in the decade he'd served as a member of Tasker Bay's police force, all of them to ward off bears that had wandered up to the edge of town. LA had been a different story, David reminded himself, and being out of practice wasn't the same as being out of your depth. If it came to that, he knew what he was capable of.

An itch, like the one that moments before had told him he needed to step out of the car, was now telling David *be ready*. Not much for superstition or anything that went beyond what he could see with his own two eyes, David still made a point of listening to his gut. It had saved his life in the war and on the streets more than once, and right now it was on full alert.

Cautiously, he swept forward. On either side, rain splattered brick walls, bubbled out of clogged gutters, rushed down storm drains. Every bit of sound seemed amplified the deeper he moved into the alley. He'd have a hard time hearing if someone was moving in his direction. It was one big, tall echo chamber.

Up first was a row of garbage cans, rain pinging off dented metal lids. Angling wide and fast around them, David found nothing. A short distance ahead sat the dumpster. He moved toward it, tensing with each step. It was big enough to effectively block his view of whoever might be on its other side, lying in wait. David slipped the revolver halfway out of its holster as he approached, but there was nothing behind—or inside—the massive, rusted bin, either.

As he reached the alley's end, the sense of danger dissipated. He panned his light, starting to wonder if his eyes had been playing tricks. After a moment spent watching, listening—as best he could over the storm, anyway—he decided to call it. But as he turned to head back toward the car, something odd shimmered in the periphery of his flashlight's beam. It looked like blood. A lot of it, splashed along the facade of a building and splattered across the sidewalk nearby. He knelt down for a closer look before the storm could wash it away.

Scanning his surroundings, he saw no tracks leading to or from the area, no sign of a struggle. But it hadn't leaked from the building or bubbled up out of the ground unless something biblical was going on. It had to have come from someone, somewhere close by. Recently, too—otherwise the storm would've taken care of it by now.

A piercing scream from somewhere in the dark shocked him to his feet and cranked his nerves to their zenith. Drawing his weapon, he moved in search of a source.

Emerging from the alley and onto a cross street, David caught sight of a large, dark figure. For a brief moment, the two stared at each other before the figure took off.

Training his weapon, David barked at the figure, "Stop! Show me your hands!" But the figure was already dashing around a corner. Driven by years of training, suppressing the feeling that this wouldn't end well, David holstered his gun and raced after.

Boots pounding wet pavement, David tracked the figure as it skidded around another corner, once again vanishing from sight. As he raced past another alley, he caught sight of what had to be the *second* figure he'd seen, dragging the now unconscious third toward a distant, nondescript sedan. In this split second of distraction, David lost track of his periphery and was too slow to react as the figure he'd been chasing charged at him from the dark, slamming into him with such force he was lifted off his feet and thrown backward. His body thudded onto the sidewalk, head cracking against the pavement.

He could see someone approaching but in the dark and momentarily dazed couldn't make out a face. What he *could* see, as he feebly pawed at his gun, was the figure raising a boot over his head.

Before the figure could cave in his face, a distant voice echoed, jolting it to a halt. Again, the voice called—words failing to register in David's still-ringing ears—and after a moment, the looming figure hustled away.

Staggering to his feet, David could hear a car firing to life and tires peeling out. By the time he made it to the alley where he'd seen the vehicle, whoever it was that he'd been chasing was long gone.

Slumping against the side of a building, David tried to collect himself and figure out what the hell had just happened. He hadn't seen a face, hadn't been able to make out specifics on the car. Realizing he needed to move while whatever detail he might be able to recall was still fresh in his mind, he reached for his flashlight and went to stand.

As he rose off the ground, something glinted when his light passed over top. Stooping back down, he reached forward and plucked a small object off the ground. For a moment, he couldn't figure out what he was looking at—after all, it wasn't every day that you saw a human tooth, ripped out at its root and left in an alley.

CHAPTER 5

WHEN DAVID WASN'T HOME FRIDAY MORNING, RO FELT THAT MUCH WORSE ABOUT rebuffing him the night before. As the son of a cop, you never knew. Before heading to school, he phoned the station and managed to catch his father for a quick chat. David promised he'd see Ro later that evening.

While he felt better knowing his father was all right, Ro was still sweating the idea of seeing Mark and Cliff at West Bay following the scuffle at Home Video World the night before. Both were a hell of a lot bigger than him and prone to set things off without provocation. But it turned out his fears were unfounded. Neither showed up until halfway through the day and didn't even react when they saw him in passing.

After getting kicked out of Home Video World and picking up the beer Laurel had stashed at her parents' shop, the two drove to a spot along the coast they'd come to frequent the previous summer. The weather had turned fast as October arrived, and they weren't ready for the cold sting the night air delivered near the water. A few other West Bay kids Laurel had invited showed up, and the group built a fire that kept them warm until the rain really cut loose. They sheltered in a large outcropping of rock hollowed out over time by the surf, waiting out the weather. Ro took the opportunity to sober up, although he wound up wishing he hadn't, as Laurel peppered him with questions about Andi.

What did she say to you?

Are you going to try and talk to her again?

Do you think she could be some kind of robotics project that escaped from a lab in San Jose and that the two of you are going to end up creating the first human-robot hybrid baby?

"I mean she does act like a robot trying to pass itself off as human," Laurel mockingly offered.

As the others gradually filtered off, Ro and Laurel ended up alone. There was no escaping the conversation. "No to the escaped robot, and I don't know to the rest," Ro finally said.

"She likes you."

Ro shook the suggestion off, genuinely unsure. It seemed to him that Andi took every opportunity she could to avoid him.

"I'm going to talk to her," Laurel said.

"No, you're not." Ro tried to come off sounding definitive but knew that was a losing battle. Laurel had spoken.

"Be serious. What do you want? Do you want to talk to her?" She eyed him incisively, already aware of the answer but recognizing that he needed to say it out loud to really hear it for himself.

"I don't know. I mean, I do. But—"

"But you're not going to."

Ro threw up a hand as he stepped out into the rain, kicking sand over the embers still glowing in the makeshift firepit. "She's not . . . I don't know. I really don't think she likes me."

Laurel followed him into the rain, the two of them walking together toward Ro's Land Cruiser. "You're making me say cliché shit. I hate saying cliché shit. You won't know whether she likes you until you ask. Ugh. *Such a cliché.*" No one was better at feigning disgust than Laurel.

"You're drunk," Ro needled, as he fired on the engine. But he hadn't said, *You're wrong.*

So, in a decent mood owing to Cliff and Mark having already forgotten about their scuffle the night before, Ro found himself scanning the crowd at lunch for Andi. He'd been weighing whether he should try to talk to her, but as it turned out, he was too late—Laurel had beaten him to it. She was at that very moment taking a seat across from Andi and, when she spotted Ro gawking, covertly waved him away so she could put her plan into motion.

"What do you want?" Andi asked without looking up, curt and clearly uninterested in seeing Laurel again.

"First, hi. Second, to talk about Ro. Sorry, *Roman.*"

At Laurel's labored pronunciation of Ro's full name, Andi finally glanced up with a withering look. "Why would I want to talk about him?"

"Seriously? Because I sat there and watched you checking him out yesterday. More than once. *Before* he decided to play hero and keep Cliff from breaking your ribs."

For a moment, Andi considered getting up and walking away or just telling Laurel to fuck off—she *had been* sitting there first—but instead she stayed put, stayed quiet. *Did* she want to talk about him? She tried forcing her mind onto something else—she didn't want to think about the answer.

"He's really sweet, and funny," Laurel continued rapid-fire, trying not to give Andi room to turn her away before she could make her case. "And smart. *And* smart enough to know he's not *that* smart."

Andi's brain raced back and forth, trying to figure out what to say. In that moment she realized socialization is like a muscle—if it isn't being worked, it atrophies. She had cloistered herself for so long now that it was hard to find the words—simple words, *any words*—about a boy who deep down she'd come to realize she liked.

"You don't have to say anything if you don't like him. And I won't ask again. But if you do, what's the problem?"

Andi eyed Laurel as she spoke. "I always see you with him. You're saying you're *not* dating?"

"We were. But we're friends. It's better that way."

"Why?"

Laurel shrugged. She didn't know, but she did see an opening Andi had, intentionally or not, provided. "So, you knew we were together?"

"Why do you care what I know?" Andi jabbed, retreating as Laurel pressed.

"Because Ro's my friend. If someone likes *him*—and he likes *them*—then I'm going to find out if it makes sense."

"He—" *Likes me?* At least that's what Andi meant to ask. But something had caught in her throat, stopping her. Instead of finishing the thought out loud like a normal person, she proceeded to silently chew it over in her head.

Laurel waited a moment to see if there was more coming but, growing tired of the conversational vacuums Andi tended to leave, decided to fill this one herself. "We're coming to the arcade later. If you can get"—she gestured in Andi's general direction, unsure exactly what her problem was—"*this* under control, you should talk to him. And don't guilt-trip him because I talked to you about it—it wasn't his idea. I want him to be happy, I don't want him getting hurt, so just . . . talk to him and see whether you're right about how you feel." With that Laurel grabbed her tray and stood to leave, having guessed correctly that Andi would rather be left alone.

"I'm not interested in dating anybody," Andi managed, just as Laurel had started away.

"Talking's not dating," Laurel replied without stopping, disappearing into the crowd.

David made it home shortly before Ro was set to head back out. Happy to see his son after being away for close to twenty-four hours straight, David was also exhausted and found himself falling asleep on the couch while Ro cleaned up from dinner.

He'd decided against saying anything about what had happened the night before. He didn't want to worry Ro and, even though he trusted him, knew that kids lacked the filters necessary to keep gossipy secrets to themselves. The last thing anyone needed was a rumor that a tooth-pulling psychopath was prowling Tasker Bay's back alleys and beating up cops.

By the time Ro left for the night, David had roused himself a little and was half watching a rerun of a TV movie he remembered first seeing with Cheryl, about a resort that turned out to be a kind of purgatory for its amoral guests. As the increasingly rattled characters searched for a way out—fighting through an endless maze of tropical vegetation while the canopy grew to block out more and more light, robbing them of any sense of direction—David found his eyes drifting shut.

He was shocked awake as he started to slump over; the deep purple bruise covering his chest where he'd been hit suddenly pinched. For a panicky moment the pain made him think his assailant had come back to finish the job.

There were moments like this from his past that still rattled him. While serving in Vietnam, he'd often been assigned to long-range patrols at night. He saw more than one friend snared by lethal booby traps or caught off guard by enemy combatants who knew how to lurk undetected mere feet away. Somehow he'd come home from the war with nothing to show but a few scratches, an improbable streak of cosmic luck that continued during his time with the LAPD. He'd dodged certain death three times by his count—twice by a knife attack, once by a bullet that caught a bounce and whizzed past inches from his head.

But in ten years, nothing that had happened in Tasker Bay had ever left that same kind of dark, indelible mark on his psyche. Until now.

As it turned out, Andi's problem that night wasn't being forced to confront Ro. It was that he didn't show up. She decided her initial instinct was right, that she shouldn't get involved with anyone in Tasker Bay . . . *and he probably doesn't like me, anyway.*

At least she knew where she stood. This was easier, even if it stung. It wouldn't have worked. Couldn't have. *Because I'm* not *getting attached.*

Mal lurked here and there all evening, agitated by something. He had a hit on his hands with the new game and should've been happy, Andi thought. Maybe it was the brawl? She knew about his various illegal side grinds, at least some of them, and he didn't want or need the cops showing up. Not looking to suggest any deeper interest in him or his problems by asking, she was perfectly fine living with her hunch. The less she knew about whatever Mal was up to when things inevitably came back to bite him in the ass, the better.

His moodiness was such that, when he said he was thinking of going home early, Andi felt relieved. She'd rather close by herself than walk on eggshells, let alone risk Mal feeling the need to unload his problems on her. Forced out of the back and behind the counter on account of his early exit, she was surprised to see him heading for the front door—he was parked out back—and watched with mild curiosity as he lingered on the edge of the crowd queuing to play *Polybius*. For a moment it looked like he'd forgotten what he was doing.

Called away to change bills for a customer, by the time Andi glanced back, Mal was gone and Ro had taken his place. Approaching the counter, he smiled.

She didn't. "We're closing in ten minutes."

Ro waited, but that was it. He was being brushed off. "Right. Thanks," he said as he started to go. But halfway into turning back toward the shop floor he thought twice. *What's the worst that could happen—go back to not talking instead of barely talking?*

"We were supposed to be here earlier. Laurel's parents were—" Ro caught himself before saying they were arguing, with Laurel stuck in the middle this time. It was too personal a detail to offer.

Andi waved him off in a way that suggested she understood, both where he was going *and* what it was like. Ro was reminded of how little he knew about her. Maybe she was dealing with the same problem. Either way, he thought, he shouldn't have bothered. With a little nod goodbye, he committed to walking away.

But then Andi called after him, voice growing a little stronger word to word. "I have to close, but if you want to . . . hang out, you could wait out front until I kick everybody else out."

As she dipped a master light switch to warn the crowd it was time to finish up, Andi tried to push everything out of her mind—doubt, fear, excitement—and chose to focus on battening the shop down for the night.

The group ringing *Polybius* had expanded. Of the forty or so customers in the shop, at least thirty lingered around it. Andi had watched as a few jostled each other for a clearer look at the screen, but no one took it as far as Mark and Cliff had the night before. The energy seemed different, too, the electricity of seeing "the next big thing" replaced by fixed eyes and focused thoughts. It was intense. And very odd.

After a few stubborn players failed to register that she wanted them gone, Andi walked over and pulled the plug, powering *Polybius* down. Rising back up, she found every pair of eyes that had been staring at the game staring at her, instead. She froze, hairs on the back of her neck at sudden attention. It only lasted a moment, as people broke off and headed for the door, but it was more than enough to rattle her nerves.

For a moment after the doors were locked, she contemplated ducking out the back and leaving Ro and Laurel waiting out front. After a few minutes she figured they'd just leave, and she'd be off the hook. But instead, once the crowd had moved on, she found herself unlocking the door and waving them in. It felt like an out-of-body experience, like she was standing there watching herself move but couldn't control her actions.

She'd turned away plenty of other guys and a few girls since coming to town. They'd all thrown up their hands and moved on when she'd brushed them off. She was skilled at making her disinterest land. But not with Ro. Was the reason she just opened the door that simple—that he'd kept trying? Was she taking pity? Or was there really something about him that she liked?

Guess I'll find out, she thought as Ro and Laurel stepped inside out of the rain.

"Mal's gonna think this is busted if I don't plug it back in," Andi said as she reached around *Polybius* and powered it back on. While the game booted up, she watched Ro fail to interest Laurel in it. *At least she doesn't like wasting her time on this crap either*, Andi thought. But it wasn't fifteen seconds later that Laurel's eyes were glued to the display.

While Andi set about organizing the counter, Ro leaned against the other side. His gaze drifted, landing on Laurel as she dropped a quarter into *Polybius*. "Huh. Laurel *hates* video games."

"Yeah. I don't get it," Andi said as she disappeared in back. Ro wasn't sure if he was meant to follow, and as he glanced back at

Laurel, he found himself drawn to watching the game. Gradually, it was as if the lights in the room started to dim. The shop's vibrant, random color scheme—a combination of glowing, flashing displays and colorful box art—grew dull and muted until only *Polybius*'s screen shone out from an almost pitch-black void.

"You don't have to wait out there." Andi's voice snapped Ro awake. He shook off the momentary trance he'd found himself in and followed her into the back of the shop.

As Andi started returning tools from the workbench to a frayed canvas bag, Ro lingered nearby. When she lifted a cardboard box filled with tangled nests of wire and parts salvaged from dead cabinets, the bottom started to give way. Both rushed to try to stop the contents from falling—failed—and cracked their heads together instead.

"Shit!" Andi winced, dumping the rest of the box's contents onto the floor.

Ro felt like an idiot. "Sorry. I wasn't—I was trying to help."

Andi stooped down and refolded the bottom of the box, then started tossing the salvage that had spilled out back inside. Ro joined her, and for a moment they worked in silence. He chewed his lip, trying to figure out what he was supposed to say before settling on another apology. "I really didn't—"

Andi shook her head at him. "Don't worry about it. Unless you were trying to headbutt me. In which case, *what the hell*?"

Ro scoffed a little. She was funny. Or at least sarcastic. He liked that.

With the mess off the floor, Andi leaned back against the workbench. "Is that one popular?" She nodded at *Polybius*, just visible through the doorway leading back to the shop floor.

"I don't know." Ro shrugged. "I'd never heard of it until I saw it here. Compared to everything else on the floor, it's way more advanced. If you're used to playing the same thing over and over again, seeing something *that* different gets people excited, I guess."

As Andi continued to straighten up, Ro quietly examined the space. What he assumed to be Mal's desk was in one corner, all trash and unopened mail. A dirty bathroom sat nearby, cleaning supplies ironically stacked inside. Boxes of the snacks Mal loved marking up sat against an otherwise empty wall.

But most of the space appeared to be Andi's. A row of game cabinets had been opened up, guts spilled across a plywood workbench that stretched nearly the length of one wall. Fastened along the bench's edges were a series of heavy-duty magnifying lamps, with pieces of what looked like canvas taped between them. On each piece of canvas was a swatch of paint—all of them different shades of gray, with the words "yellow," "blue," or variants of either color written out next to a given swatch.

Ro leaned in to examine one of the canvas slips. "What is this?"

"Nothing," Andi snapped, swinging the magnifiers away and stuffing a motherboard back into a cabinet for safekeeping.

"Sorry," Ro said, uncertain what he'd done.

Andi knew right away she'd overreacted. "It's fine," she said, voice a little smaller. "Just . . . I'm color-blind. Kind of. Certain colors, shades are hard to tell apart. Yellows and blues, mostly. It's called tritanopia."

"Oh. Sorry. I didn't know."

"Yeah, why would you?" she asked. "It's just . . . something you live with, I guess."

"You can still do all this stuff?" Andi shrugged in response, as if none of it was *that* hard. "That's . . . kind of incredible," Ro said, a touch of genuine marvel in his voice.

Andi eyed him as she continued tidying up, his earnestness curling her lips into a small smile. "Yeah, I mean, I don't want it defining me or whatever, but it's a part of who I am. It's why I wear so much black. It's just easier."

She waved a hand over the workbench. "This whole system was my dad's idea. I wanted—*want*—to be a computer engineer. He and I would do these projects together and he saw I couldn't tell things apart based on color. So he helped me figure out a way to do it, and I've . . . just kept refining it, I guess."

Ro considered a printed circuit pulled from a *Zaxxon* cabinet. "I don't understand any of this stuff."

"You said you want to learn how to write code?" Andi asked. "You should learn about the hardware, too. Here."

Clearing space, she pulled a hand-hewn device the size of a paperback book from a milk crate under the bench and set it in front of Ro. One end was designed to connect with a computer's parallel port, and the other was an unfinished-looking knot of wires. Ro picked it up, examining it, no idea what he was holding.

"It's kind of a reverse universal programmer. Instead of writing data to the P-ROM chips on the motherboards, it reads them—shows me the code from each chip," Andi explained.

Ro looked lost. Remembering what Laurel had said—that he was smart enough to know what he didn't know—Andi took pity. "P-ROM is programmable ROM. Read-only memory—it's what drives the cabinet. Holds the code. It *is* the game."

Ro was listening—but he was also paying mind to the fact that, in order for them both to get a good look at the device, they were standing right next to each other, close enough that Andi's hand had brushed his arm. Twice. If it bothered her, he figured, she'd pull away. If he leaned into it, he might spoil the moment. Better to just stay put.

Andi stayed too.

"So, this shows you how the games are written?" he asked.

"Not 'how,' exactly—it just exports a finished script. So you still have to know *why* it was written that way. What the code's saying. But more or less, yeah. I copied a few boards when I was swapping them out. I could . . . show you the code sometime. If you wanted."

"Seriously? That'd be awesome."

Andi coiled the loose cables around the rest of the device and slipped it into the crate underneath the workbench before heading toward the back of the shop. "I need to lock up. I'll see you out front."

Ro nodded as she went, lingering for a moment to take in the strange world where Andi spent her time. As he made his way back to the shop floor, he found Laurel still in front of the *Polybius* controls, her game over.

"What'd you think?" Ro asked, stepping up next to her. She didn't respond to his words or presence. It seemed like she didn't know he was there at all. "Laurel? Hey—"

As Ro put a hand on her shoulder, Laurel titled her head toward him. "What?" She sounded confused, like she'd just woken up and couldn't remember where she was.

"Are you okay?" he asked, craning his neck to get a better look at her. "You seem . . . kind of spaced out."

Shaking her head, Laurel retreated to a stool nearby. "That's why games are dumb. Put you in a trance."

Ro scoffed. It wasn't the first time Laurel had taken shots at his hobby, but he didn't snipe back as his attention had drifted to *Polybius*'s attract screen. The in-game camera raced through the cavernous maze, whipping backward to catch sight of the looming, shadowy figment in pursuit. The walls of the cavern seemed to extend forever into the dark, runic symbols barely visible in the shadows, the whole image so expertly rendered it seemed to Ro like he could reach past the screen and feel the wet, cold stone for himself.

"How do you suppose they made it look like that?" Laurel asked, the fog that had settled over her mind finally starting to lift. "Ro? Ro. *Roman*."

"Hm?" Ro turned toward her, sluggish, a moment too slow to understand what he'd just been asked.

Seeing that she had his attention, Laurel tried again. "What makes that game . . . like that?"

"Like what?" Andi asked as she appeared from in back, a ring of keys spinning around one of her fingers.

"So different from everything else," Laurel replied. "I look at the rest of these and I don't care. I don't want play." She gestured around the shop floor as she spoke, before landing back on *Polybius*. "I want to play *that*."

"Once I get the time, I want to open it up. It's the game, but I think it's the display, too—the screen," Andi said as she started flipping off the overhead lights. "I don't play either, by the way. And I don't want to play it. But I guess I get why people do. I just want to know how it's possible to make something that looks like that."

"You think it's sixteen-bit?" Ro asked. "*Pole Position* was sixteen-bit."

Andi nodded toward a *Pole Position* cabinet nearby. There was no comparison. It was apples and something that wasn't even fruit. "It's gotta be more than that," she said.

Laurel was lost. "What's a bit?"

"The number of instructions a system can handle. The more bits, the more instructions, the more complex the result you can . . ." Andi would've kept on, but she realized Laurel's eyes had drifted back to the screen. For a moment it was funny—Laurel talked tough but was clearly as much of an addict as every other gamer who came through the front door. Then Andi noticed Ro was staring too. Their collective glazed-over look started to annoy, then finally unnerve her.

"Hey. I want to close up. I need to get home. *Hey*." Andi laid a hand on Ro's shoulder—he flinched, head whipping toward her. Andi took an instinctive step back when she saw an agitated look in his eyes, but it passed from them so quickly she told herself that she'd simply startled him. "I need to get going."

All three headed outside, where Andi locked and double-checked the front doors. "I'll see you around," she said, before starting unceremoniously away.

Ro looked to Laurel for advice, but she just shrugged. Andi was a mystery to her, too.

After a moment of deliberation, he hustled after and found Andi unlocking her bike from a drainpipe she'd chained it to behind the shop. "I'm sorry if we kept you too late."

"I was on my own all day. Mal took off at six. I'm just tired," she said as she wheeled her bike onto the sidewalk.

"Are you . . . working this weekend?"

"Every weekend."

It felt like she might have been brushing him off, but Ro wasn't sure. "Oh. Well, there's a party tomorrow. I actually don't know the kid's name. Just moved here. I didn't know if you'd heard about it."

Andi's blank face answered for her.

"Anyway. Laurel's always on me to go out, and I thought, maybe, if you wanted to come, it'd be more fun."

"For who?"

Ro had to laugh a little, although he suspected that kind of bluntness was normal and not a joke with Andi. "Me, I guess. Hopefully you. If you wanted to go."

Andi searched for a response. "Your friend seems nice—you're nice—but I'm not . . . I just don't think it's a good idea."

Ro realized that might be it, things between them already fizzling out. It felt like someone had pulled a plug and whatever was holding him upright had started whooshing out. But something pushed him not to let go just yet. "Can I ask why?"

Andi didn't have an answer. Well, she *did*, but it was increasingly apparent to her how strange and unnecessarily cold an answer it was. She didn't want friends, or whatever it was she could perhaps have with Ro, here in Tasker Bay.

He pushed through the uneasy silence. "*I* don't want to go to that party. I don't even know the guy. I don't like . . . most people. But it seems like we at least have things we can talk about. So maybe we could do something else. Together. Instead. If you wanted."

For a long moment, Andi looked everywhere but at Ro, fighting to understand why she was having such a hard time just telling him she wasn't interested so she could end the awkwardness and go home to sulk. Of course she knew why—she *was* interested and therefore found it difficult lying to him. It was, she decided shortly before finally answering, kind of an awful feeling being compelled to be completely honest with another person. *Who wants that all the time?*

"We close late on the weekend. You could come by at, like, nine thirty. Or earlier if you want to . . . be here."

"Yeah." Clocking the eagerness in his tone, Ro quickly backed off. "If that's okay."

Nodding, Andi started to go, but there was a separate thought that had been rattling in her head all night that she decided to let out. "That was weird, right? Inside, with the game?"

"With Laurel?" Ro asked. "I think she was just impressed. That game does look really good."

"Okay, but it wasn't just her. I was talking to you, and it was like you didn't hear me. I thought you were ignoring me." While her tone implied a joke, Andi's eyes said something different.

Ro realized he might have fucked up and was quick to respond. "I wouldn't do that. I just . . . didn't hear you, I guess."

"Okay. So, if you didn't hear me, but you weren't ignoring me, then what happened?" Neither had any idea.

CHAPTER 6

BLOODSTAINED ROOTS TWISTING SKYWARD, THE TOOTH SAT IN A VIAL ON DAVID'S desk where he'd left it, greeting him when he arrived at Tasker Bay's sheriff's office early Saturday morning. Steaming mug of coffee in hand, he sat and stared at the mysterious object in silence.

Despite calls to a few contacts in the LAPD, he had no leads or clear path forward to figure out where the tooth had come from or what its appearance, in conjunction with his assault, might portend. There were forensic specialists who could try to trace its identity, but David's was a low-profile, low-priority case.

His other deputy Charlie had suggested checking it against area dental records, which wasn't a bad idea in a vacuum, but it was needle-in-a-haystack odds of finding a match. They were left to question people they thought could've had ties to some hypothetical incident, who lived nearby or ran businesses in the area.

The most obvious spot where a scuffle might have broken out and made its way onto the street was Bar Harbor. Its owner, Larry, told David he did remember seeing someone come through who looked like he'd been in a fight, but that was *before* he sat down at the bar and started knocking back shots. It was the most substantive account David and his deputies had gathered, and it hadn't changed a thing.

So David was moving on to another tack. As he scanned his contact sheet for the town's doctor, he noted the sheer volume of names and numbers that had been crossed out over the last few years. The turnover in Tasker Bay's public offices and private businesses was staggering. Soon enough, they'd strike his name from that list too.

He finally found it: Rachel Winston, MD. It was a long shot, but if anyone had come to see her in the past day or so who'd been roughed up—ideally, with a missing tooth—she might be able to help.

Before he could pick up the phone to dial, however, it rang. When he answered, the panic, anger, palpable horror in Carl Delano's trembling voice was so great it set his own nerves on edge, to the point David realized his hand was shaking when he went to replace the receiver.

By the time David arrived at Delano Stables, the town's veterinarian, Johann Almr, was already there. Known to most as John, he was a perpetually tired-looking man in the middle of his sixties who had for many years looked after not only Tasker Bay's pets, but its livestock, too. He'd put down David and Ro's spaniel, Titus, after the dog had been crippled in a hit-and-run. A fire still crept up the back of David's neck whenever his mind flashed back to the image of an anonymous driver speeding off, eight-year-old Ro chasing after and screaming at them to stop while Titus lay twitching by the side of the road.

Johann walked to meet David as he pulled up. Carl was nowhere to be seen, nor his wife Julie. "What the hell's going on?" David asked, stepping from his cruiser.

"You need to see for yourself," Johann replied, a whiff of his Icelandic accent still present despite forty years of life in the States.

David thought the man looked shaken and, recalling the terror in Carl's voice over the phone, wasn't sure he *wanted* to see. Still, he followed as Johann walked toward the barn. As they approached, it was quiet. There was *nothing*, no sound other than the breeze and a thin hiss from the rain that continued pelting down.

As Johann placed a hand on the stable doors, he glanced at David as if to ask, *Are you ready?* David nodded but within moments understood Johann's apprehension. The smell of blood, of death hit him in a series of waves that nearly forced him to turn away so he could wretch.

Inside was unlike anything David had seen, including during his time in Vietnam. His mind raced, trying to process it all.

Is this what the inside of a slaughterhouse looks like?

The horses the Delanos kept—four of their own, plus eight others belonging to area families—had been sliced apart, hulking bodies reduced to ribbons of flesh and sinew. Blood caked the shiplap walls, pooled on the dirt floor; in some spots it nearly reached the ceiling in arcing, crimson fans. Amid the carnage, David could see bones broken and crudely stripped of flesh, entrails heaped and seeping bile, partial limbs . . . flanks splayed open . . . skulls fractured, faces split. There was no apparent pattern to it, no method beyond wild brute force.

He was careful to remain on the perimeter, not wanting to spoil any potential evidence . . . or stand any closer to the carnage than he absolutely had to. In truth, he just wanted to leave. "Any way another animal could've done all this, John?" he finally asked. "Mountain lion? Or a bear?"

Picking up a broom and using the handle, Johann exposed a section of raggedly sliced flesh. "These aren't bite marks, or cuts from claws. Looks to me like they were hacked apart."

David forced himself to imagine the scene—the agitation that the first blow must have struck among the animals, the determination of an attacker willing to wade into the middle of a room full of thousand-pound creatures throwing their weight around in a blind panic.

The whole scene reminded him of images he'd seen in one of the art history books his wife had been fond of. Francis Bacon, or Goya. Basically, hell on earth. The question of *why* kept knocking around his head, over and over. What would someone stand to gain by doing something like this?

There had to be a motive. To consider the alternative, that this was done for no reason, was too dark for him to contemplate.

Why would have to remain elusive for now, but *how* might have just presented itself. Spotting the edge of a weathered-looking wood handle sticking out from under the shattered rib cage of one of the fallen animals, David waved Johann over. "Bring that broom," he called, as he angled for a better look while pulling a handkerchief from his pocket.

Following David's direction, Johann levered the flank off the ground just enough for him to grab ahold of the handle—but whatever it was attached to was still lodged in the animal's side. "Hang on," David grunted as he worked the handle back and forth, finally pulling it loose with a sickening *scritch* as metal raked bone.

Standing, he considered the strange-looking blade he now held. It had to be ten, maybe twelve inches in length, with a wicked-looking concave hook topping its face. "Fuck is this?" David asked, mystified.

"A billhook," Johann offered, tilting his head for a better look. Thin ribbons of red-and-black flesh dotted its broad surface. "It's for clearing brush."

Nodding, David turned the blade in his hand. Whatever it was meant for, someone had found a far, far darker use for it here.

Outside, a still-unsteady David leaned against his cruiser for support. He radioed Jeff and Charlie, directing them into the field to start questioning everyone living or working nearby.

Johann stopped on the way to his truck, waiting for David to finish his call. "I'll handle the bodies when you're ready. It's better to be quick about it—you're going to have scavengers before long." With a nod, he kept walking, just as ready to get away from the horrific scene as David.

Looking toward the Delano home, David saw Carl had emerged. He stood motionless on the front porch, eyes trained on the stable. The two men were friends—had history. A little over a year ago, Carl had been accused of assaulting a surveyor sent by Bob Colson and Bayview Holdings who'd let himself into the stables without permission. David had believed the accusation was more about impugning Carl than it was anyone truly feeling threatened.

Bob was convinced half of Carl's land constituted unclaimed wilderness he should be able to purchase and develop—Carl contested it was his, dating back to the initial sale of the land to his family over a hundred years ago.

David knew Carl was a gentle soul—he'd seen how he worked with animals, how he doted on children after he and his wife had given up on having their own years prior. But he'd also seen a change in him as both the assault charge and legal proceedings dragged on. He was weary, more cynical. Approaching the two-story farm home's front porch, David feared what this latest rotten turn might do to him.

"David." Carl sounded tired, voice on the edge of breaking. "You need me to do anything?"

"No. John's going to take care of the stable. And we're going to do everything we can to figure out what happened here. I know it's probably not something you want to do right now, but I need to ask you a few questions before we lose any more time," David said. "Did you see anyone around here you didn't recognize yesterday? Not just last night, any time on Friday?"

Carl glanced at David. "Some folks from Bayview were out here."

"You're sure about that?" Anything to do with Bayview Holdings was a prickly topic with Carl, and David needed to keep him focused. "You know who it was? What they were doing?"

Carl shook his head. "Taking pictures. Measurements. I don't know how all that crap works."

"On your property?" David tried to clarify. Carl nodded. "Anyone, anything else that seemed out of place?"

"We were in bed by ten, asleep probably . . . twenty minutes later? Anything after that, I don't know." Carl's face tightened as his voice lowered, barely able to speak the words out loud. "Who the hell would do something like this? I mean, who—those animals, they were—" He had to cut himself off, too overwhelmed to finish the thought.

"Did you keep a knife in the barn? A billhook? " Carl nodded. "Okay," David said. "That's all I need right now. We're going to get into it. I'll check in later, all right?"

As David walked back toward the stable, Carl called out after him. "You ask Bob Colson about it," he said, sounding very certain that would lead to an answer.

"Carl. There's no way that Bob was—" David just stopped. The suggestion was insane, but he didn't want Carl to feel any more attacked than he already did. So he left the notion alone, nodding toward the house. "Be with Julie. I know she's torn up. And so are you. We're going to handle it."

Barely an hour after he'd started canvassing Carl's neighbors, David heard a name. Four houses down, septuagenarians Donald and Sally Larado were certain they'd seen Malcolm Petty walking along Glenora Lane in the direction of the road they shared with the Delanos, Route Nine.

"I just saw someone walking. He was tall like Mal, but I didn't see a face," Don said. "Sal saw his face in the mirror. So she says."

"Plain as day." Sally nodded, dismissing her husband's skeptical tone.

It wasn't ironclad proof of anything, but it warranted a talk. If

Mal *had* been there, maybe he'd seen something and not realized it. Instructing Jeff and Charlie to continue their sweep, David headed toward Tasker Bay's sleepy downtown and Home Video World. There was a small crowd—teens and twentysomethings, mostly—loitering outside when he arrived, waiting for the shop to open. Mal wasn't there, so David drove toward his bungalow on the edge of town. Situated in a cluster of modest houses that had traditionally belonged to fishermen and their families, Mal's place hadn't seen any improvements or even much upkeep in years. As David pulled up outside, its damp, weathered exterior against a cold October sky made it look all the more depressing.

David and Mal had had a few run-ins in the past—a drunk-and-disorderly, a brawl at Bar Harbor. And he'd long suspected Mal was selling drugs out of his shop but didn't have resources to commit to a long-term surveillance project.

At the door, he knocked. No answer. Knocked again. Nothing, still.

Reaching out, he gripped the handle and gave it a half twist—unlocked. As he opened the door, he called out, "Mal, it's Sheriff Kemp. I'd like to talk with you."

The scent of cigarette butts and stale beer was overpowering as David passed through the doorway. Everywhere he looked, he found disarray—laundry strewn about, trash overflowing from cans and spilling onto the floor. Scraps of meals, emptied liquor and beer bottles cluttered tables.

The home was small and naturally dark, with fewer windows than needed to give it proper illumination. As David glanced around, it was obvious Mal hadn't bothered updating anything since his father had willed him the home after he passed. Apparently, he hadn't cleaned much since then either—the floral wallpaper, shag carpet, Formica counters were all covered in a thick, sticky yellow sheen from years of cigarette smoke.

A radio hissed static in the kitchen; the TV buzzed in the living room. David scanned the space, eyes settling on something he recognized from his training on controlled substances at the academy—a few tabs of acid, sitting on the coffee table.

The sight of an old recliner ripped open, fabric torn apart into twisted, fraying ribbons, gave him pause, a flashback to what he had seen earlier that morning at the stable. As he moved deeper into the house without sign of Mal, his gut began to tighten. Something was off, and he'd stepped right into the middle of it.

A trio of doors lined the only hallway that branched off from the living room. "Mal? It's Sheriff Kemp. We need to talk. Come on out." Silence in response. David stepped forward, cautiously opening the first door—a spare room, as cluttered as the rest, with no sign of Mal. It looked like storage for anything Mal didn't know what to do with. Old newspapers, broken radios, random car parts. The next was a bedroom, Mal's he assumed, disheveled but devoid of life, and plain as day. Not a picture on the walls or knickknack on the beat-up dresser and nightstand. Finally, he came to a small bathroom.

David took a step inside, opening a mildew-encrusted shower curtain to check the tub for any sign of blood or hair having been washed off. Kneeling, he examined the fixtures, basin, but found nothing besides months' if not years' worth of caked-on, waxy grime. Nothing here was going to shed light on what had happened to Carl's horses. But as David started to stand, he felt a cool rush across the nape of his neck. The kind of short, thin breeze you feel when something nearby moves, briefly pushing air in your direction.

Trying not to telegraph his intention, tilting his eyes as he carefully angled for his weapon, he caught sight of a pair of shoes barely a foot away from where he was crouched. *Someone was standing right behind him.*

"Mal?" David finally asked, trying hard to stay composed. "That you?"

No response. The feet stayed put.

"I'm going to stand up now. I'd like to talk to you." Pushing himself off and up from the lip of the enamel-coated cast-iron tub, David carefully turned, finding himself face-to-face with a dead-eyed, trancelike Mal. He felt his breath catch, a cold sweat creeping over him. "Mal," he started, "I'm just going to take a step around you, and then we can—"

That's when Mal started screaming.

Jumping back in shock, David stumbled into the tub, landing flat on his ass inside it. But as he went for his gun, something stopped him—Mal *still* wasn't looking at him. The sound of his scream bounced around the tiled walls and tore at David's ears, a kind of guttural cry from someplace deep and dark within.

CHAPTER 7

ANDI SAW THE LINE OUTSIDE AS SHE APPROACHED HOME VIDEO WORLD THAT Saturday afternoon. *Where the hell's Mal? He should've opened up hours ago.* After pedaling her bike around back and locking it up, she keyed inside. There was commotion out front—loud voices, bodies jostling—and it kept her on edge as she moved from station to station, rushing to get the doors open. It was bad enough Mal was a no-show with no notice, and now there was a crowd. That had literally never happened. If people saw the shop was closed, they'd just come back later.

She knew they were waiting for *Polybius*. But who stands in line, in the rain, to play a video game? Glancing at the cabinet, she was hit with a wave of unease, a sense that something about the shop and the people who frequented it had changed after its arrival. It sounded ridiculous. And she had no proof. But none of that changed how she was feeling as she unlocked the door. Bodies pushed past her and made a line for, then formed a ring around, the game.

Given that she was on her own, Andi lost track of the hours, and the day went by fast. She'd tried calling Mal's place but got no answer, and the waitress she managed to get on the phone over at Bar Harbor hadn't seen him come in. Andi wasn't worried that she couldn't track him down; she was annoyed at him for going completely dark on her without warning.

All afternoon, she watched player after player circle *Polybius*. If there had been thirty the night before, there were at least that many now. More. Recalling that Mal had said he'd found no mention of the game in any of the trade magazines he kept behind the counter, Andi weaved through the crowd and slipped into a small runway between cabinets. She scanned the back, sides of *Polybius*. Mal had made her spray-paint the plain cabinet black, and now she was kicking herself for not bothering to check for a manufacturer's mark or model number before she had. There was only an access door, sealed by security screws with intricate-looking drives that Andi didn't recognize.

Ducking in back she grabbed a handful of metal rasps and some loose pieces of thin rebar. Settling in behind the counter, she started crafting a screwdriver capable of opening the cabinet.

Rachel Winston found a spot in front of Tasker Bay's police station, glancing up at the storm clouds roiling overhead as she walked toward an entrance set into the building's stucco facade, painted an appealing mix of nickel with light brown and green accents. For being less than ninety miles north of San Jose, Rachel still wasn't used to the amount of rainfall Tasker Bay received, or how intensely gray the fall and winter seasons were. She'd read about doctors at the National Institute of Mental Health working on a study to do with the effects of weather patterns on a person's mood. Based on the way her own annual blues coincided with the onset of Tasker Bay's dreary season, she was pretty sure they were onto something.

As she entered the station and approached the receptionist's desk, Rachel recognized the bubbly red-haired young woman seated behind it as a patient of hers. "Hi, Evie. Sheriff Kemp asked to see me."

"Dr. Winston? Oh!" Evie's face lit up at seeing her. "I'll get him. It's been so busy here this morning."

Wondering if Evie—who had a knack for oversharing during her checkups—could offer context for whatever it was she was being pulled into, Rachel trailed after her instead of waiting in the lobby. "Busy how?"

"The Delano farm," Evie said as she weaved through a small bullpen housing half a dozen desks toward David's office. "And now Mal's in lockup for something and is just completely out of his mind."

"What about a farm?" Rachel asked.

"Oh my God, it's so awful. It—" Before Evie could dish, David stepped out from the hall leading to the station's two-cell lockup, right into their path. "Oh! Sheriff. Dr. Winston's here."

David smiled as he stepped aside, motioning Rachel into his office, where both took a seat. "I'm David—Sheriff Kemp. But David's fine. Thanks for coming. Sorry it had to be on a Saturday."

"That's all right. Rachel," she said reaching out her hand, their eyes locking for a moment. David was handsome, with dark brown eyes and a mop of salt-and-pepper hair he kept pushing back and off his forehead, almost like a tic. Catching herself staring, Rachel quickly broke off. "So. What, uh, am I doing here?"

David exhaled, loath to dredge up details of what had happened. "We had an incident last night. Someone killed a dozen horses in a stable on the edge of town."

Rachel recoiled. "That's awful. But you know I'm a doctor. I'm not a veterinarian."

David had called to ask her about the tooth he'd found, but for now, that had to wait. "No, I know. We have someone in custody who might have seen something. The problem is he's—not catatonic; I don't know the right word. Not well. Not talking. I'd like you to take a look. We need to be able to ask him some questions."

Mal sat hunched on an aluminum-and-canvas cot inside one of the station's small, spartan holding cells. His hands remained cuffed, a distant look in his eyes suggesting his mind was still somewhere else.

David entered the cell first, trailed by Rachel. He stepped aside, allowing her access to Mal while staying close enough to lay hands on him if the need arose. Scribbling notes, Rachel worked her way through a series of cursory exams with tools from a worn, brown leather satchel she carried—pulse, temperature, reflexes, recognition. He showed no awareness she was there, had no response to her touch.

Watching Rachel more than he was keeping an eye on Mal, David had to check himself. She was pretty, a good foot shorter than him with wavy, auburn hair tucked behind her ears and tied up with a torn sliver of navy bandana. The University of California San Francisco sweatshirt she wore must have been a favorite, left thin from wash and wear. While it seemed impossible he or Ro hadn't needed a doctor since theirs retired and Rachel became the town's sole practitioner, he was certain he'd remember if he'd seen her before.

She glanced back at David. "Has he been like this the whole time?"

"He'll come around and say a few words. Just nonsense. Then it's this again," David said as he gestured toward Mal, who kept on staring dead ahead at nothing from the edge of his cot. "We found a couple of tabs of acid at his place. A lot of booze. Some speed. But we don't know what he took. If he took *anything*." David watched as she smoothed her hands over Mal's, examining his skin, nail beds. "What do you see?"

She shook her head. "Nothing. I mean, if he did what you described, there ought to be some sign of trauma. To kill an animal, multiple animals of that size, I think you'd see stress in the hands. Lesions, blistering, bruising."

"If he was wearing gloves? Work gloves, something heavy duty?"

"Maybe." Rachel rose to her feet. "But I'm not trained in forensics."

David nodded at Mal. "What about him? Otherwise? Is he in any danger or . . . ?"

"Without his medical history and blood work, I'm honestly just taking shots in the dark. There's no sign of blood loss or trauma, which pretty much rules out shock. From the way you found him, it sounds like he might have gone on a bender and took it too far." Rachel took a penlight from her satchel and passed it back and forth over Mal's eyes. "Here. His pupils are dilated and unresponsive. Has he been sleeping?" David shook his head. "But then his heart rate's normal, skin tone seems even, and he's not . . . uncoordinated. He's just not moving. A drug like LSD affects different people differently, and if he took a high dose, the effects would be even less uniform. If you want my advice, get him transferred to the county hospital. They're going to be better equipped to make this kind of evaluation than I am."

"I put the request in this morning, but they wouldn't even give me a timeline. They're already having to triage because of the rain. A lot of accidents."

"I know a couple of people up there," Rachel said. "I'll put in a call. See if it helps."

"I appreciate it."

For a long moment, Rachel considered Mal. He still hadn't budged. He just stared ahead at the cell's dull cinder-block walls. "At the farm," Rachel finally asked, "could a person actually do that?"

"I grew up on a farm in the Antelope Valley. Cattle, pigs. It takes energy to butcher an animal by hand. *One animal.*" David leaned back against the bars as he spoke, bits of weathered-looking gray paint flaking off at his touch. "I've seen people on angel dust look pretty superhuman, but cutting up a dozen horses, live horses . . . I don't know."

"And mentally?" Rachel asked, eyes returning to Mal and his unflinching, thousand-yard stare.

"Cops learn to never say never. You think you know the worst thing another person can do, and then . . ." David shook his head. "Thing is, if I can figure out a *why*, I can usually find a *who*. The part that worries me here is, I can't see any reason why anyone would do anything like this. Ever."

While David took a call from his junior deputy Jeff, Rachel waited in his office with a cup of coffee. There wasn't much personality to the space, mostly boxes of departmental files and papers. A copy of Woodward and Bernstein's *The Final Days* peeked out from under a stack of case files. The only real window into David that any of it provided was a framed photo of who she assumed were his wife and son. As she picked it up for a closer look, David returned.

"That's your family?" Rachel asked, replacing the photo. "What does your wife do?"

"She was a professor at Berkeley. English lit. She passed away." It was always a little awkward when people found out about Cheryl. He knew they felt bad for asking, which could make him feel bad for telling them. So David tried to offer whoever had asked a nod, as if to say he understood and didn't take offense.

Still, Rachel blanched. "Oh God, I'm sorry. What, uh—"

"Cancer. That's my son there. Ro. Roman. He's a senior at West Bay. How about you? Kids?"

"A daughter, Andi. She goes to West Bay too. Same year."

"Really? Maybe they know each other."

"Maybe." Rachel decided it wasn't worth going into why Andi's antisocial tendencies made this highly unlikely. "She works for him. Mal. At the arcade." Rachel couldn't mask the concern this made her feel. "What are you going to do with him?"

"We can't hold him forever. Obviously can't let him go like this, either. He'll come around and we'll question him, or that transfer comes through, and we'll talk to him over at County."

The conversation hit a lull and Rachel took the cue to start buttoning up her satchel. "Well, if there's anything else I can do—"

Raising a hand—*one second*—David rooted in a desk drawer until he found the vial containing the tooth and set it between the two of them. "*This* is actually why I called you. I was hoping you could tell me if anyone had come by your office in the last forty-eight hours who looked like they'd been in a fight. Pretty beat-up. Maybe missing a tooth. Maybe not."

"No," Rachel said, picking up the vial for a closer look. "Where'd you find it?"

"In the street," David said. *In the middle of a pool of blood*, he almost added but then thought twice. Rachel didn't need another reason to worry.

It was fifteen minutes past closing when Andi resorted to tripping the breakers in back, cutting power to force the crowd out. It had been the single biggest day the shop had seen since she started working there, and she'd managed it entirely by herself.

She knew better than to steal from Mal. The one thing he cared enough about to keep track of was his money. But today was an exception. Once Ro arrived, she had pizza delivered with cash from the drawer, then raided the makeshift bar Mal maintained in a rusty filing cabinet in back, fixing them both a bottom-shelf whiskey and Coke.

Andi's thoughts seemed to be elsewhere, even as Ro tried making small talk out of her day. "So, Mal just leaves you here like this? Laurel's parents don't even let her run the registers."

"Yeah, well, apparently she's stealing beer. So that's probably for the best. You want to help me with something?" Andi asked, not waiting for Ro to answer before hopping up and starting toward

Polybius. "I want to dump the code to see what it's doing. We'll have to open it up."

Ro followed her onto the shop floor. "I still don't know what any of that means." He eyed the cabinet as Andi ducked behind to pull the plug. "Have you played it yet?"

"No. Why?" she called out from in back of the machine.

"I don't know. What if it gets busted?" Ro shrugged. "Maybe you ought to try it first."

Andi mulled it over. She was doing this because she felt like the game might be having an effect on people. Playing felt counter-intuitive. But she also hadn't felt anything herself, and she'd been staring at it off and on all week. Maybe she *was* overreacting, seeing something that didn't actually correlate with the game. She finally nodded, easing out from the dusty alley running behind the cabinets. "All right. Let's try it."

Andi opened the coin door and toggled a few credits, then took up the controls and managed to outrun the figment to the point it seemed like she was getting the hang of things and maybe even enjoying herself. Then she abruptly stepped back from the cabinet. "Yeah. I don't get it." She expected a response from Ro, but one never came. Glancing over her shoulder, she found his eyes fixed on the screen. "Ro? *Roman*."

"Hm?"

Andi studied him for a moment, waiting for him to come out of his fog. It would've been annoying to her if it wasn't starting to feel so concerning. Ro, Laurel, Mal, seemingly everyone who played would go blank afterward, snapping back to normal at random. *Why?* And what was going through their heads when they were . . . elsewhere?

"Sorry," Ro finally said. He stepped up to the controls and in no time had navigated much deeper into the maze than Andi had managed. The cavern walls, illuminated by quick, erratic flashes of torchlight, twisted and turned faster and faster to the point that the runes lining them seemed to strobe. The threat of the figment forced Ro to keep his character running full tilt, amplifying the effect.

Andi appreciated the mild hypnotic rhythm the visuals possessed, but it was nothing she *had* to watch. Eventually it grew overwhelming. She didn't see how anyone could stand it, but not only had Ro been playing for at least five minutes, it seemed to her he hadn't so much as blinked. He hadn't spoken, either.

"Hey. Check this out," Andi said, presenting the makeshift screwdriver she'd fashioned to crack open the cabinet. "Ro?" Nothing. Waving it in front of his face, she watched him, leaning in to look for some sign of recognition, but his eyes stayed fixed on the screen. So she did the only thing that had worked thus far and pulled the power cord. As life drained from the screen, Ro's gaze drifted toward her, a hollow, inscrutable look that lasted several moments too long for comfort.

"Are you okay?" she asked, using the cabinet's edge to hoist herself off the floor. As Ro's glassy eyes tracked her, she found her hand instinctively tightening around the screwdriver in case she suddenly needed to defend herself. Ro's nostrils flared, muscles tensed, and she clutched the would-be shank tighter.

But finally, and without clear provocation, the spell broke. "What?" came Ro's voice, distant and lost.

"Let's sit down," Andi said, guiding him to a chair and kneeling beside him to look him over. He angled for his half-empty drink, which she managed to slide just out of reach. "Maybe not a great idea."

The gears turning in Ro's brain were practically visible as he worked his way up to asking a question. "I—where were—what happened?"

"What do you remember?" Andi asked, trying to avoid coloring his recollection.

Ro was quiet for a long moment. His gaze drifted, finally landing on the cabinet. "How long was I playing?"

A sense of relief washed over Andi, but she wasn't ready to let the screwdriver slip from her hand just yet. "Maybe ten minutes."

"Felt like . . . I don't know. I don't really remember anything past . . ." Trailing off, Ro stood and started pacing the room at random. "What the hell *happened*?"

"You got black-out drunk off a couple of glasses of cheap whiskey but stayed on your feet and kicked that game's ass, or . . ." Andi nodded toward the cabinet with a shrug.

"You played it too, right? What happened to you?"

Andi had forgotten, but Ro was right. And she was fine. "Nothing. I got bored so I quit. I was watching you."

Ro found himself wondering if that was true. If he couldn't remember, how could she? Something about the answer felt wrong, but so did doubting her. Why lie? His suspicion passed as quickly as it had taken hold, but questions lingered.

Andi's attention had drifted back to the cabinet, the only place left she could think of to look for answers. "Let's open it up," she said, flashing the screwdriver at Ro.

CHAPTER 8

THE RAIN THAT HAD PLAGUED TASKER BAY FOR THE PAST SEVERAL DAYS HAD slowed for the moment, but reports of flooding in surrounding areas were coming across David's radio every few hours. Local roads washed out every fall, and in storms past a poorly maintained access road once used to haul equipment for a logging operation had been the only way in or out of town.

David knew the weather might amplify nerves, which were already buzzing over what had happened at the stable. In a town as small as Tasker Bay, people saw anything out of the ordinary as cause for concern. Once worries started, they spread, anxiety passing between family and friends over something that *typically* amounted to nothing.

Only this time wasn't typical. And it wasn't nothing.

As David wound his cruiser through downtown, Mal rode silently in back. It was late, after midnight. Mal had come around a couple of hours ago, answering all of David's questions without protest. It hadn't helped.

"I went to Bar Harbor after I left the shop. Had . . . I don't know, two beers. Went home after, kept on drinking, and fell asleep on the couch," Mal had said. With a little pressure and an assurance there was no jeopardy for him in telling truth, Mal had admitted he had taken two tabs of acid, too. It wasn't a great look, but it wasn't evidence of anything either. In fact, other than the Larados' specious claim they'd seen Mal walking near the farm, there was *nothing* linking him to the crime.

He'd seemed genuinely shocked to hear about the scene at the stables and expressed sympathy for Carl and Julie. "True locals," he'd called them, who hadn't deserved what had happened.

David pulled up to Mal's home, made his way around, and opened Mal's door. "We need to talk about a few things."

Mal nodded and David stepped aside, following him to the front door.

Mal kicked a path through the living room to the couch, where he flopped down, then threw an upturned hand toward David, who wasn't sure if he was being invited to sit or told to hurry up.

"I'm going to need you to stick around town," David said, cutting to the chase.

"Am I being charged with something?" Mal asked, sizing up how worried he should be.

David shook his head as he spoke. "No, but it'll be easier on everyone, you included, if you stay local." He could see Mal was about to start grousing and pressed on. "I had someone telling me you were out walking near the Delano farm after hours, before their animals were attacked. Now I heard your side of it too, but that's still reason enough. Just stay local, and once this thing's been wrapped up, we can all move on."

Mal watched as David glanced at the recliner. Mal had no idea why he'd destroyed it. He hated it, which was reason enough, but that might not land for David. And he'd picked a stupid time to finally take out his pent-up frustrations on it. Anything getting carved to pieces after what had happened to those horses was a bad look. "Had a mouse in there," Mal finally offered. It was bullshit, but believable—he *did* have mice, on account of living like a slob.

Long after he'd heard the cruiser fire on and pull away, Mal ruminated on the couch. His head swam with thoughts, everything seeming to come at him at once. *Did they take anything? What else did they find?* Most unnerving of all: *Why the hell would they think I'd do something like that to poor old Carl?* Aware he retained few memories from the past twenty-four hours, Mal had been drunk and stoned but refused to believe he could've blacked out and gone on some kind of murder spree.

He finally rose to his feet, walked to a window, and peered out through yellowed slats. David was gone, and there didn't seem to be anyone else from the sheriff's office lurking on a surveillance detail.

Comfortable that he was alone, Mal made his way down the hall and into the bathroom. Grasping the sides of a medicine cabinet set into the wall, he jimmied it loose, pulling it out and setting it down on the floor.

After confirming that the stash he kept hidden inside the hollowed-out space—a few sheets of acid, packets of pills, a few ounces of skunk triple-walled in plastic cling wrap—was still there, he went to replace the medicine cabinet. But something caught his eye: a streak of blood along the edge of the hole cut into the drywall. Mal leaned in, staring, uncertain where it could have come from. He checked his hands, arms—nothing. If David or one of his deputies had been in here messing around and found all of this, he'd be on his way to the county lockup. The blood couldn't be theirs. So it had to be his. Only it wasn't.

Andi's rig was busy pulling code from *Polybius*'s motherboard, which left her and Ro free to gut the cabinet itself. They'd removed everything inside the plywood box, careful to lay it out in such a way it was clear how it would all fit back together. The only piece left was the monitor.

"Why's it so heavy?" Ro asked, straining to pull the screen out while Andi, wedged inside the service door, pushed it toward him from below.

"It's a *screen*," she replied, as if everyone should know how much one ought to weigh. Together, they managed to get the monitor pushed out of the cabinet, at which point Andi sprang up, helping Ro lower it down onto a pile of discolored shop towels. With it finally safe on the floor, the two slumped beside it.

"I've taken every cab on the floor apart, and none of the screens weighed that much. Half that much," Andi huffed, catching her breath. "That's gotta be ninety pounds."

Realizing Ro had fallen silent, she glanced back to find him staring at something on the floor. She angled for a look herself. The phosphor screen—the portion that lights up and shows a picture when bombarded by particles from the electron gun—blacked out most of the display's face, save for a razor-thin bevel around its edge. It was through that transparent sixty-fourth or so of an inch that a shaft of light, shining down from a fixture overhead, was being caught and split into dozens of vibrant shades.

Ro reached forward and jostled the screen. The colors danced in response, blending into brilliant new hues before separating back out as the gentle motion subsided. "Can you—" he started to ask Andi.

"Some of it," she cut in. "So, like, not really here. Or here. Those are mostly gray. But here, I can see. This."

"It's like a prism," Ro marveled.

"Prisms break visible light into basic colors. Red, orange. Roy G. Biv, remember? That's grade-school physics. This isn't that."

"You see how the game looks. It has to be some kind of new technology. Maybe this is part of it." Ro gestured toward the psychedelic sprawl of color, kneeling down to pass his hand through the stream of light. His skin began heating up the moment it glanced the beam, and he jerked back to find a red welt puffing up just below his knuckles.

"Shit!" Andi saw smoke rising from the floor. Thinking fast, she killed the lights, then fished a rag out from under the counter and tossed it over the display. She flipped the lights back on and checked the linoleum. Sure enough, there were burn marks where the screen's focused light had nearly set the floor on fire, in a matter of seconds.

As she moved through the shop, Andi dipped every light switch save for a few that controlled fixtures on the fringes. After bandaging his burn, Ro wheeled a dolly carrying the display into the back room, where the two of them hefted it into an open spot Andi had cleared on her workbench. One by one, she started clicking the lights back on while Ro adjusted the display's position, trying to give themselves as much light as possible to work with while not burning the place down.

They pried the glass front away from the display's body, revealing its internals. To Andi's semi-trained eye, they were far more densely constructed than usual, but the components seemed normal. The glass front itself was anything but.

It was extremely heavy, easily accounting for half the display's weight despite measuring just nineteen inches across. In profile it looked as if multiple layers of razor-thin glass, far too many to count, had been laminated together. Its inner surface was covered in thousands of small shiny peaks, each no bigger than the tip of a needle.

Eventually moving on to the cluster of components housed behind the screen, which translated data from the motherboards to drive the display, Andi cautiously removed them one by one and laid them out across the workbench in similar fashion to the pieces she and Ro had removed from the cabinet. While she tried walking Ro through how each functioned in service of producing an image on-screen, she soon found herself at a loss. Despite a decade's worth of picking over the insides of everything—toasters, TVs, radios, computers—she'd never seen anything like this before.

"It doesn't make sense," she finally admitted, uncurling a crick in her neck and standing to stretch. Not knowing was far and away her biggest pet peeve. She hated feeling lost, somehow behind someone else. Noticing the clock, she felt a little overwhelmed. It was pushing one a.m., and the entire cabinet had to be reassembled before they could leave. It had been a bust. "We better start putting things back together."

When Ro arrived home, David wasn't there. It was late, past two. *Where is he?*

Ro tried calling the sheriff's office but didn't get an answer. He sat down and watched the door for a while, hoping that his dad would step through before starting to wonder whether he should drive over to make sure he was all right. It wasn't the first time that this had happened, but the palpable depth of his worry felt different, as if he could sense something was wrong.

He didn't have aunts or uncles, cousins. Not that he spoke to, anyway. There'd been bad blood on both sides when David and Cheryl were married, and when his mom passed, Ro and David fell out of whatever minor touch they'd been in with the rest of the family. David *was* his family. All that was left. There was always a risk in his line of work, but Tasker Bay had felt like a relatively safe space all these years. Suddenly, though, doubts were surging through Ro.

Noise from somewhere deeper in the house snapped him out of his funk. Rough and shuffling, like footsteps. Ro sat up. "Dad? Are you here?"

Nothing. The silence lasted long enough that Ro assumed he'd heard something else, or nothing at all. But just as the momentary, anxious surge he'd felt was starting to wane, he heard the same sound right behind him.

He sprang up from his seat, spinning to find nothing. He was alone. Suddenly a voice inside him spoke, its words draining the sound from his ears, sight from his eyes—*he's dead.*

Ro found himself in darkness, deaf and mute, other senses dulled by a cold sensation he couldn't shake, like floes of ice roiling under his skin. He could feel himself in motion but couldn't get his bearings. He dug deep and tried to scream, but every time he went to force the sound out, it felt as if his lungs were flat. He stumbled back onto what he thought was the couch, feeling his face, looking for some tether to reality. Patting up from his jawline, he found his eyes and began rubbing, then started clawing, desperate to somehow jump-start his senses. Terror overtaking him, he doubled over and began convulsing, pitching himself off the couch.

Cracking his head against the side of a coffee table as he fell, Ro could sense the faintest shift inside as he hit the floor. The pitch black in which he'd been swimming was slowly fading up into a mass of grays, finally providing him with a hazy view of the living room as he lay on his side. His ears adjusted, fingers and toes wriggled, hands and feet moved.

He stayed on the ground, trying to convince himself that his body didn't just do that, that whatever that was, it wasn't real. But as he felt the skin around his eyes, it stung at the lightest touch.

CHAPTER 9

RACHEL HAD STARTED KEEPING LIMITED SUNDAY HOURS UPON HER AND ANDI'S arrival in Tasker Bay. There wasn't another doctor around for ten square miles, no hospitals for twenty, so she figured the need was there. Somewhere inside, she felt a little swell of pride in going that extra step to uphold the oath she'd taken. If someone needed her, she'd be there. When she'd decided to practice those extra hours, she opted not to have her receptionist come in, figuring she could handle a small amount of weekend traffic herself. That *had* been true, until today.

A line of patients snaked around her practice's small, sterile waiting room, all the way out the front door. They weren't coughing or sneezing, not for the most part. Some looked spent, like they might lie down and stay there. Others were agitated, knees bouncing, heads swiveling. Many of the patients were younger and had parents with them, although an older few waited on their own. There was a tension, a nervousness hanging in the air as they waited their turn to speak with Rachel.

"I can't sleep."

"She's not eating."

"He just keeps crying."

"I watched her slump over at the dinner table. Like she passed out."

"He . . . he punched the wall. I think his hand might be broken."

"She said she's hearing things."

"I—I feel like someone's watching me."

Every consultation led somewhere different, none of them adding up to offer any logical conclusion about why so many people were suddenly suffering.

As the day wore on and reports of strange symptoms mounted, Rachel scribbled a note to herself in the margins of an evaluation form: *Collective psychosis?* It was vague, too broad, but then again so were the claims patient after patient had made. Whatever this was, very suddenly it had Tasker Bay in its grip.

Just down the block from Rachel's practice, Laurel sliced through box after box on the loading dock behind her parents' grocery, prepping produce for the floor. As a young girl, she'd once found a spider inside a box of bananas—huge, dead, gnarled up like an arthritic fist—and since then always went slow when it came to unpacking fruit and vegetables. As such, it usually took her a full morning to prep a produce delivery, but today she was done in a little under two hours. She hadn't worked faster, there was just less in the order compared to usual.

It wasn't just the produce. Stock had been dipping around the store for a while, shelves looking sparser. And she'd been working more shifts as other employees were let go. Clearly, her parents were trying to cut down on expenses.

Other kids her age were ambivalent or downright hostile toward their families, but Laurel *loved* her parents. They had been her best friends for as long as she could remember. And it was killing her to watch them spiral into debt and acrimony trying to keep the store afloat. It had become a millstone hung from their necks, dragging them deeper and deeper underwater. Laurel wanted to help, which is why she always came in without complaint when asked. But when it came to anything truly meaningful, the kind of act that could affect change at a higher level, she felt powerless. They were going to lose everything, and she didn't know what that meant for their or her future.

She loaded a cart and headed out to stock the shelves. She recognized faces as she went, regulars and parents of friends. She smiled and waved. But her thoughts never strayed far from her family's troubles. Which is what made seeing Mrs. Abernathy—it was Christine, Laurel was pretty sure—so upsetting. Her family owned the Paulson's grocery chain, and she and her husband ran Tasker Bay's location, on the outskirts of town. The one that had steadily been siphoning away business from Greene's. Christine had made a point of coming into their store every now and again as an olive branch, but it pissed Laurel off, and she took no solace in her father's explanation that the Abernathys were "just trying to coexist."

Fuck that, Laurel had told herself. *And fuck you for coming in here, bitch,* she thought as Christine strolled past with a mostly empty basket. Her rich family had given her and her asshole husband a golden ticket. They didn't work for it, didn't have to build anything for themselves. Maybe *Christine's* parents earned it, but *she* hadn't. And that was more than Laurel was able to stomach.

Abandoning her cart, she banged through the service doors in the back of the store then stepped off the loading dock and out into the rain. She wasn't just pissed off; it was something more. Deeper. She began to feel her heart race, temples pound. If she knew it wasn't a euphemism, she could've sworn her blood was running hotter, rising to a boil inside her veins.

Heading back inside, she snatched up the box cutter she'd been using just a few minutes prior, then marched back onto the shop floor with a singular purpose, to slice Christine Abernathy open like a midsummer eggplant.

Stalking, closing in on her target with each step, Laurel froze at the sound of her mother Sarah's voice. "Laurel, are you going to finish the produce? The cart's just sitting in the middle of the aisle."

The box cutter fell from her hand, clattering to the floor, and all at once Laurel was aware of where she was, what she was supposed to be doing. Just not what she'd *almost* done. The fire she'd felt toward Christine moments earlier was gone, as if wiped from her memory.

"Are you all right?" her mother asked, approaching. But Laurel waved her off, nodding as she stooped down to pick up the blade before shuffling off. In truth, she wasn't. Where had her thoughts gone? And why, when she passed Christine a few moments later, was she gripped by a cold sweat?

David was en route to break up a brawl at Bar Harbor. Like many of Tasker Bay's old-school locals, its owner, Larry, preferred to handle problems on his own. People tended to picture California as full of free-love hippies composting their own shit, but the truth was more complicated. People liked their autonomy. So, for someone like Larry—who believed they ought to dissolve the town's entire governmental structure so people could handle their own business—to call for help, something out of the ordinary was going on.

As he pulled up, David kept the rack lights spinning atop his cruiser and chirped the siren, hoping an early warning might encourage whoever was going at it inside to stand down. But as he stepped up to the front door, something big crashed against the textured window that highlighted the shotgun-styled building's facade. A moment later the glass splintered, bowing out around leaded accents as a heavy-duty fillet knife pierced the window inches from David's face. Staggering back, he drew the revolver clipped to his belt and stepped with caution through the door.

Besides Larry, sheltering behind the counter, there were half a dozen others cowering on the bar's periphery as three men engaged in an all-out brawl. Two, whose faces David didn't immediately recognize, were trying to dodge the third as he swung the knife. That was Robby Sapp Jr., third-generation fisherman who'd graduated West Bay High a few years prior and gone right to work alongside his father, Rob Sr. Battered in the fight, the jukebox was stuck blurting out the same five-second snippet of Creedence's "Fortunate Son" over and over.

"I need you to separate, then stay where you are," David boomed, but his edict fell on deaf ears. Robby charged at one of the men, but they ducked clear and Robby slammed uncontrolled against the bar. Seeing a window, David holstered his gun and bodychecked Robby. It felt like he was built out of concrete, but the impact still sent him to the floor. Pinning him down, David grabbed the knife, then quickly clamped handcuffs around his wrists.

Pulling Robby to his feet, David started shuffling him toward the door. Larry stepped out from behind the bar and propped the entrance open, then hustled out and opened the rear door on the cruiser, as David continued inching Robby forward.

"Make sure they all stay put," David said, jerking his head back toward the bar. Larry nodded, hurrying back inside.

Anticipating a struggle at the cruiser door, David was thrown as the fight vanished from Robby. He went slack—David couldn't keep him off the pavement, doing his best to soften his fall. Figuring it could be a ploy and that Robby was going to rear up, David took a step back and once again gripped his gun. But instead Robby just sat up, eyes blank, with an expression that landed somewhere between confusion and exhaustion. After helping him into the cruiser, David headed back inside.

He found Larry sweeping glass off the floor, jukebox mercifully now unplugged. The patrons unlucky enough to have been caught in the middle, along with the two men Robby had fought, sat stone-faced at the bar. David glanced around the room as he spoke. "I'm going to need to take statements from everyone. I have to ask you not to leave until I do."

He turned to Larry. "Can I talk to you?" The two men made their way into a dim storage area in back that reeked of stale beer, stocked with bottles and kegs. "What the hell happened?" David asked.

"Robby came in . . . I don't know, a couple of hours ago. About noon," Larry said, clearly still shaken.

"How much did he drink?"

"Nothing. Coffee."

"You're saying—" David stopped himself. Larry's answer was clear, even if it made no sense. "Did you see what set him off?"

Larry shook his head. "I didn't see what started it, but he'd said something to those two boys in there that they didn't like hearing. They got in his face, and Robby just lost his damn mind."

"Who are they? The two he was fighting with?" David asked as he nodded back toward the bar.

"Elliot and John . . . Kerr, I think? Brothers. They've been talking up some fishing tour they want to start. Rubs a lot of the folks down at the docks the wrong way. You get a bunch of tourists zooming around the bay, you can forget about fishing for a living."

"Has Robby ever flipped a switch like that in front of you before? You ever hear about him doing anything like that?"

"No. Robby's about as easygoing as they come." Taking a dusty bottle of vodka down from a shelf, Larry offered David a swig, but he waved him off. Larry still took a long swallow. "But people talk. Locals point fingers at folks like those two boys out there. It's not *them*, these new people they hate. It's *change*. It's seeing what they know turned into something they don't. A lot of them just . . . can't deal with it."

Robby sat in the back seat of David's cruiser. As his thoughts returned, he grew aware of what he'd done. He'd felt frustrated all morning. An offer he'd put in on a slip, which he hoped would help him expand his family's fishing business, had been trumped by the two men he'd attacked. The Kerrs. So, yes, he was pissed off. But he doesn't . . . didn't . . . attack people. With a fucking knife.

He *had* followed them into the bar, though. And stuck to coffee instead of something that could've taken the edge off, listening to the brothers talk about setting up a business that would destroy his way of life. If Tasker Bay didn't fish, it didn't do anything. That was the last thing he could remember, feeling upset. Now here he was, in the back of a police car, more scared than he'd been in his entire life.

This *wasn't* him.

Except now it was.

As David climbed into the cruiser and pulled away from the curb, Robby turned toward his window, staring out. Nothing much registered as the scenery blew by, save for the line that snaked out the door at Home Video World. *They're probably there to play that game*, he thought. The same one he'd mindlessly pumped twenty quarters into the night before.

Ro finally saw his dad when David returned home early that morning, and chalked up the sudden, debilitating episode he'd suffered the night before to a combination of alcohol and exhaustion. He'd retreated to his room after, where he'd been out cold since. He was still asleep when Laurel called, but the palpable worry in her voice snapped him to.

The two met at the docks, the punchline to a long-running joke

Laurel liked to tell—how anything could be made to sound dirty if you added "down by the docks" at the end in a low voice. In Ro's estimation it worked about half the time.

Laurel wasn't herself. She brooded, unloading about her parents fighting, the letter from the bank she'd seen, the lapses in memory she'd been having. "When I feel like I do remember things, they're awful," she said. "And they feel real, like they happened. Like I . . . I did them."

"I had something happen," Ro offered. "This nightmare. I knew my dad had been killed. *I knew it.* I felt like I couldn't stand, couldn't do anything. I couldn't help him. But I saw him this morning. He was fine. So, we both had bad dreams, but—"

"No!" Laurel snapped, so fast it left them both startled. "These *aren't* dreams. I have them . . . at work. In the morning. And yours are about wanting to help someone. In mine I'm trying to *kill* someone."

David moved Robby into one of his office's two holding cells after a transfer to the county lockup he'd requested couldn't reach them. Flooding, mudslides, washed-out roads had all slowed municipal response time to a crawl. For now, Robby wasn't going anywhere.

A string of violent incidents in a remarkably short window of time felt like it should mean something. David believed in following patterns. But the only common thread here appeared to be chaos. The Delanos' horses, the tooth, the brawl. There were no threads to follow.

Carl had been calling the station every few hours in search of an update, but David's answers weren't changing. They hadn't made progress on the stable. They had no eyewitnesses, no evidence from the crime scene save for the bloodied billhook—which had been dusted for fingerprints without success; only Carl's were present.

He could feel the man's temperature rising with each call. He continued insisting that someone from Bayview Holdings had slaughtered his animals to try to drive him off his land. "I'll just have to do something about it myself," Carl finally said.

"Carl. You won't. You so much as go near Bob Colson with any kind of intent, and you know what happens," David cautioned. "You're going to lose your land. You're going to go to jail."

"Are you going to talk to Bob? Or am I?"

"Carl. I'm telling you, you *can't* do that," David practically yelled into the phone, patience waning.

"Then do your goddamned job," Carl spat before hanging up.

For a moment David just sat there, receiver slack in his hand, blurting out a sharp off-hook tone. He decided he'd better go and see Bob before Carl did.

The home Bob Colson had settled into was the nicest in town, a sprawling Monterey Colonial that the Colsons had opulently updated. A middle-aged couple who were both high-powered real estate brokers in San Jose, Bob and his wife, Carol, had started the run on Tasker Bay real estate by moving there first, then letting a select group of clients know about their "new find," getting them in cheap on easily improvable land. Representing nearly every home in town that went up for sale, the Colsons froze out buyers they didn't approve of, quietly reengineering Tasker Bay in their own image.

As a result, Bob had become a bogeyman for locals like Carl, who he'd tried to steamroll for one reason or another—a caricatured, scheming swindler out to steal their town from under them.

For his part, David wasn't so paranoid. He just didn't like the man. Shortly after relocating to Tasker Bay, Bob had purchased the two apartment complexes the town accommodated. A few at a time, he'd evicted the tenants, leaving their units empty. Within two years he'd cleared out both buildings, demolished them, and built a run of generic-looking suburban mansions in their place. He could've made more by managing the buildings, but it wasn't about money. It was about finding a legal path to pricing certain buyers out of town. Even a townie could see that. Especially a townie. David and his deputies were forced to serve *every single* eviction notice. And now Bob was running him out of a job too.

Bob immediately soured at finding David outside his front door. "What can I do for you, Resident Deputy Sheriff?" he asked, drawing out his full title when everybody else was fine with sheriff. Or David.

"You heard about the Delanos?"

"Yeah, it's terrible. You know, if you need help with it, I have a contact in the San Jose PD that I can—"

"Carl Delano's property," David cut in.

"What?" Bob's voice shot up an octave as he realized what David meant. "For fuck's sake. Does he— He thinks *I* did something?"

"He thinks you paid somebody to do it, because he doesn't think you'd have the balls to do it yourself. His words." But David *might* have enjoyed delivering them.

"He's an asshole."

"I know the two of you are still tied up in court, so you can understand—"

"He convinced *one* judge he owns that acreage," Bob spat. "But he's going to have to do it again, and it won't be getting any cheaper. You can tell him that."

"I'm giving you a chance to get out in front," David said, raising a hand in peace. "If you'll tell me Carl's wrong—"

"He's way the fuck wrong."

"Then we're done. If I find out otherwise, I'll be back. That's it," David said, and started to go.

"David," Bob called after a moment, forcing him to turn and walk back to the door. In the rain. "If I think . . . someone's missing, what do I do about that?"

"Missing? Who?"

"Mike—Michael Newton. He works in our office. Sort of a trainee. He's the son of a friend in Sacramento," Bob said.

David sized him up for a moment. He looked concerned, a side of Bob he wasn't used to seeing. "When's the last time you saw him?"

"Three days ago. He was supposed to be in for work this weekend. I tried his phone. His address this morning."

"Has he done this before? Missed work? Gone away unannounced?"

"No. He's, uh . . . a little boring. It was a favor, hiring him. His father works for the state."

That tracked. There was always an angle with Bob. "Did you call his parents?" David asked.

"They're out of the country. I'm still trying to reach them. But I talked to his brother, and he didn't come home."

"All right. Get me his info," David said, "whatever you have. Photos, too. And call Evie about it. She can get things started."

Late Sunday afternoon, Andi and Ro met at Ford's Diner, a hole-in-the-wall that survived on account of quality cooking. It had been barely twelve hours since they'd last seen each other, but both already had news to share. Settling into a booth in a quieter corner, Andi ordered coffee, black—Ro played along, then struggled to covertly choke his down for the rest of their talk.

"I started going through the code last night," she said. "There can be thousands of lines in a game. But that thing . . . it's ten times that. More. I don't know where to start. And there's this."

Andi pulled a book on Greek history from her bag and opened it to a bookmarked page, then spun it around to face Ro. The name Polybius was highlighted.

"He was a politician, historian, a bunch of stuff. Including a mathematician. And this"—Andi indicated an illustration of a graph, five columns by five rows, twenty-four Greek letters spread across it—"is a cryptograph he designed. Like a system to generate secret codes. People would use them to send signals by firelight, back and forth."

Andi watched Ro study the entry, impatient for him to reach the same conclusion she had. "He came up with a way to use light to send messages. And whoever made that game put his name on it," she finally said, trying to cut through the haze. "You see what it does to people. What if it's . . . *sending messages*?"

Andi felt silly saying it, but as Ro's odd conversation with

Laurel flashed silently in his mind, she clocked discomfort on his face. *He understood.*

Ro still shook his head. *It's crazy.* "Why would—"

"I don't know," Andi cut in. "But you see it?" she asked, voice wavering a little as she put her ill-formed theory out there. "The game . . . what it's doing?"

"I don't know what I see." Ro had come there intending to tell Andi about his episode the night before, but in the moment thought twice. She was grasping at something wild, and he felt wrong enabling her. At least for now. "I found this."

Setting a copy of *RePlay* magazine in front of Andi, he flipped to a dog-eared page. On it was an advertisement from a company called Sinneslöchen, featuring their new game, *Cortex*. Andi snatched it up, checking the publication date—December 1981—before flipping back to the ad.

"It's not the same," she said, failing to see whatever connection Ro had drawn.

"Look at the screenshots," Ro said, indicating a row of images along the page's outer edge.

Andi leaned in. The graphics were as vibrant and rich as *Polybius*'s. "I mean, sure. It looks the same, the image quality or whatever, but it's not the same game." She was right. The screenshots looked closer to *Asteroids* or *Tempest*. "Why make a game, advertise it, change *everything* about it? And then take your name off it?"

"Read the bottom," Ro suggested, tapping a block of copy.

New worlds are waiting to be explored, and only Sinneslöchen can take you there. With our state-of-the-art, patent-pending Infinite Matrix technology, gameplay explodes off the screen.

On the road. In space. In fantastical realms of wizards and witchcraft. No company brings you closer to the action with cutting-edge graphics light-years ahead of the competition. Prepare yourself for the future of gaming.

"Maybe Sinneslöchen didn't make the game, but if they made that screen, they could probably tell us something about it," Ro said. He noticed Andi zeroing in on an address and phone number in tiny print. "The number was disconnected. I tried information, but they couldn't find another listing. Does Mal keep trades around the shop?"

When she and Ro arrived at Home Video World a little before five p.m., Andi was surprised to find the counter empty. She ducked in back, but there was no sign of Mal there, either. Somewhere between alarm and anger, she made her way back onto the floor, where she finally found a familiar face. Patrick, an old friend of Mal's—based on how little she saw Mal socialize, maybe his *only* friend—lingered on the fringes of the crowd surrounding *Polybius*. Short in stature, quiet, he was so low-key he was easy to miss. He'd pick up shifts from time to time in exchange for a dime bag or a few tabs of acid, but never worked solo.

Andi approached and tapped his shoulder. "Hey. Where's Mal?"

Surprised, Patrick jerked away. He seemed on edge. "Oh, hey. Yeah, I, uh, I don't know."

Andi eyed him. Patrick was one of those people who always seemed a little bit nervous. But it was getting harder to tell who might've been influenced by the game, and who was just reacting to how strange those who'd played were behaving. "How long have you been here?"

Patrick checked his watch. "Half hour? I was on my way home. Thought I'd stop in."

Andi's confusion grew. "Wait. You aren't working?"

"No. But, I mean, you guys weren't here." Patrick shrugged. "I figured I should stay until somebody showed up."

With Ro's help, Andi made her rounds, and everything in the shop looked okay—no one had messed with the register; the cabinets and change machine were all fine. She tried calling Mal but got no response. Accepting that this was her new abnormal, she gathered then stacked two feet of trade publications in front of her and Ro. They began paging through them, looking for any mention of Sinneslöchen.

Leaving Ro at the counter so she could pull a couple of adult titles for a customer from in back of the shop, Andi heard the unmistakable crunch of glass underfoot as she passed through the darkened space. Pausing, she swept her shoe back and forth, kicking a pile of shards aside.

She switched on a light clipped to her workbench and panned it across the floor then around the room, landing on an open window—one of the panes had been broken inward. She hurried to Mal's desk and, sweeping trash out of the way, found a phone and tried Mal again. This time he picked up.

Before his voice had even crackled over the line, Andi cut in. "Did you come in today?"

"What?" It sounded like Mal had just woken up.

"Mal, it's Andi. Did you come into the shop today?"

"No. Are *you* there?"

"No one's been here? You didn't have Patrick open?"

"No."

A chill came over Andi as she glanced through the door leading from the back room onto the shop floor. *Someone broke in here then what, unlocked the front door? What the actual fuck?*

"Andi? Hey, are you—" She dipped the cradle and ended the call before Mal could finish, walking back out to find Ro behind the counter with his nose still buried in an old trade. Without a word, she picked up the phone and dialed the sheriff's office.

"I need to report a break-in," Andi said, voice hushed.

Ro's ears perked up, and he set the magazine down.

"Home Video World, on Main. I don't know. They broke a window in back. I don't know if they're still here." As she listened, Andi found herself looking for Mal's .38. "There's a—a gun that's missing too."

David and Jeff arrived in under five minutes. David was thrown to find his son behind the counter with the girl who'd reported the break-in, but it wasn't the time to ask. He directed Jeff into the crowd to start talking with customers. It struck David how no one seemed to care that they'd walked in. If whoever had broken in was still there, they were either very oblivious, or very good at suppressing their nerves.

"Andi, I'm Sheriff Kemp. And Ro's father."

Ro's eyes rolled. "She knows, Dad."

David half raised a hand. "I put a call into Mal, and the gun's with him. So there's that. If nothing's missing, and nothing was vandalized, you're saying someone broke in to—do what? Open up the shop?" David took care to make sure he didn't come off as dismissive. He was genuinely confused.

"I don't know," Andi said, aware of how ridiculous it sounded. From the corner of her eye, she could see the crowd jostling around *Polybius*.

David followed her gaze, failing to connect the cabinet, crowd, and crime the same way she appeared to. "My deputy will talk to everyone on the floor. If anyone knows anything, we'll find out. Ro?" David looked to his son. "See if you can find something to patch that window in back."

"There's some scrap wood over by the—the porn," Andi said, immediately regretting her choice of waypoints.

David made sure Ro was in back and out of earshot before he continued. "We're *familiar* with Mal. I won't ask why you might think it, but is there *anything* else here worth stealing?"

"If he's hiding something here, it's his business. Not mine. As far as I know, no."

A moment of study lead David to believe her. Curiosity finally getting the better of him, he nodded in Ro's direction and started to ask, "How do you two know—" but was cut short as Jeff approached.

"Found 'em," Jeff said. Taking stock of his expression, David wondered why he didn't look more resolved. Why he seemed so puzzled.

David was surprised to see a mild-looking young woman, early twenties, handcuffed and in the back seat of Jeff's cruiser.

"Her knuckles were all torn up. Cuts looked fresh. I don't think I made it through the first question before she confessed to the whole thing," Jeff said. His tone made it clear it still made no sense to him.

Opening the door, David crouched down to speak with the young woman face-to-face. She was nervously wringing her hands, and blood had started seeping through the bandages Jeff had applied. "You okay, miss?" David asked. She nodded slowly, clearly aware of him but seemingly unaware of her circumstances. "You broke the window in back? Then unlocked the front doors?" Another dreamy nod in response. "What was it you didn't feel like waiting on?"

The young woman gradually tilted her head to face David. Something about the way she moved, mechanical and deliberate, unnerved him. When she locked her eyes with his, it was as if she was looking past him, at something in the distance.

"I know you," she finally said.

David wanted to turn away, so put off by her strange manner that he struggled to hide his unease. "I'm sorry?"

"You came to our apartment. Kicked us out." There was no trace of animosity in her words, just indifferent truth.

As David studied the young woman, a sense of recognition came over him. He could still recall every face he'd evicted on behalf of Bob Colson. "You're Kelly. Kelly Braun."

"I just wanted in," she said. David followed her gaze to a window in front of the shop, where *Polybius* could be seen. Kelly was staring at it.

"You just . . ." Seeing that the already faraway look on Kelly's face had moved further still, David knew he wasn't getting anything else out of her for the time being. Rising to his feet, he turned to Jeff. "Did you give her a sobriety test?" Jeff shook his head. "Do it down at the station. No reason for her to go through anything else out here."

Jeff climbed into the driver's seat. He rolled down the window before pulling away. "Sheriff? The way she's acting, does she remind you of anyone?"

David didn't have to think long. "Yeah. Mal. Let's just help her get her head right, okay?"

As Jeff nodded then pulled away, David headed back inside, passing the game that had caught Kelly's eye. Even without a frame of reference, he recognized that it looked different from the other games around it. He slowed a step, suddenly finding himself drawn in.

"*So?*" Andi's voice snapped him to.

Shaking off the momentary lapse of focus, David headed over to speak with her. "It was a young woman. Said she just wanted inside. Strange as that sounds, I'm inclined to believe her." Before David could speak further, his radio chirped, Charlie's voice crackling over the speaker. "Got a 10-54d reported along Peck Creek near the intersection of White Hall and DeQuincy. Alpha Two is en route, requesting backup." Ro's eyes widened a little at the call.

David pulled the handset from his belt. "Copy, this is Alpha One, coming to you now." Tucking the radio away, he fished his keys from his pocket as he spoke. "You're okay here? If you want to close, I can help clear the place out."

"We're fine," Andi said.

She looked certain enough that David didn't push any further.

He glanced at Ro. "You're staying?" Ro nodded. "Good. Just . . . be careful." With that he went, pace brisk.

Andi turned to Ro, confused. "What the hell just happened?"

"I used to memorize police codes so I could follow on a scanner when my dad was on patrol. 10-54d is a body, deceased. They found a body."

CHAPTER 10

RAIN SPLATTERED THE WINDSHIELD OF DAVID'S CRUISER AS HE WOUND ALONG White Hall Road. Rooster tails kicked up as the car passed over water that was rapidly pooling on saturated ground. With heavy winds picking up, he had to slalom around downed branches and debris.

He'd been in communication with Charlie on and off as he drove, thankful he was the one who'd taken the initial call instead of Jeff. Time that Charlie had spent with Oakland PD had given him experience dealing with bodies, something Jeff didn't have. Charlie had transferred from Oakland to Tasker Bay a few years ago, to live closer to his mother after she'd begun showing signs of early-onset Alzheimer's. Circumstances aside, David was glad to have him around, as he knew firsthand how time spent in a major metropolitan area hardened you to the rigors of the job.

After pulling his cruiser behind Charlie's along the side of the road, David started walking. He could see a flashlight and the hazy glow of flares burning in the distance.

In the middle of the woods, in the middle of a storm, the

acrid smell of dead flesh still found its way inside David's mouth and nose as he approached. On more occasions than he cared to remember, first in Vietnam then with the LAPD, he'd come across bodies decomposing in hundred-plus-degree heat. *This* wasn't akin to *that*, thankfully, but nothing ever seemed to fully neutralize the ghastly odor.

Charlie had pulled what was left of what looked like a twenty-something man's body from the rushing, swollen creek and onto some plastic sheeting beneath a tarp he'd strung overhead. He looked relieved to see David, stepping clear and angling his flashlight to provide a better view of the deceased.

From the look of it, the man had been in the water two or three days at most. The skin hadn't developed the greenish, blackish hues a body takes on after being submerged over weeks. Dozens of small wounds were visible, though none appeared to be the cause of death. More likely, they'd resulted from the current dragging the body over rocks, branches, other debris. He'd been badly beaten, face disfigured beyond any hope of recognition. There were already signs of putrefaction around the wounds, potentially compromising forensic evidence. That process would only continue as the body's temperature—no longer cooled by the creek's frigid waters—continued to rise. They needed to work quickly.

"Clarence is on his way," Charlie said as David examined a series of dark bruises around what was left of the body's neck.

Clarence Meeks had been a medical examiner in Portland before relocating to Tasker Bay, where he'd been elected and re-elected to the position of coroner more times than most locals could recall. He also ran the town's sole funeral home, which meant anybody who passed away, passed by him. He was well into his seventies but still sharp as a tack, and David valued Clarence's expertise when it came to cause of death. In this case, though, David needed no help. Ligature marks encircling the throat and the pulpy remains of a collapsed windpipe suggested this poor soul had been strangled to death.

As David inched closer for a better look, the mottled skin around the throat began to vibrate, as if something was moving from the top of the breastbone and into the lower jaw.

Something was.

Slick with bile, a crawfish pulled itself out of the body's mouth, slipping down what was left of the face before disappearing into the murky water rushing nearby.

David and Charlie both recoiled back at the sight, with Charlie jerking his head away, squeezing his eyes shut. "Fuck me!"

David wasn't any less disgusted, but he'd noticed something else as the crawfish had pushed its way out. Reaching a gloved finger forward, he peeled open the body's distended lips. There was a tooth missing, with enough trauma visible around its socket to suggest it had been ripped out at its root.

After closing up the shop, Andi had accepted Ro's offer of a ride home but hadn't wanted him walking her to the door. One parent finding out about their situation was enough for the night. She'd slipped in and headed straight to her room, on a mission.

Now, stale coffee left over from the morning in hand, she settled in at her IBM 5150. As the machine spun up, she plugged the dedicated phone line her paycheck from Home Video World bankrolled into a direct-connect port in back, and soon, she was logged into Usenet, a sprawling message board system typically reserved for educators, researchers, and professionals. Thanks to a connection, her father, Devon, had gotten Andi access, and she'd proven her worth within the community, frequently providing solutions to hardware and engineering quandaries. She was proud of the reputation she had built up, which made what she was thinking of doing all the more fraught.

She and Ro had found no more leads in the old trades at Home Video World. But someone out there had to know something about *Polybius*. Or Sinneslöchen. She hoped that if her post avoided paranoia about connecting the game to the strange behaviors she'd been witnessing, she wouldn't draw any flack. She created a new thread in the rec.* and comp.* newsgroups and began typing.

From: AndiDVT

Is anyone familiar with the arcade game Polybius or the company Sinneslöchen? The game is all anyone wants to play where I work. It was bought at auction, and I can't find any information on it. I don't know games, but friends who do say it looks and plays like something years ahead of everything else on the market. I do know hardware and coding and can confirm it's unique. I'm including some of its source code below. The language isn't one I recognize. Any info?

Andi's fingers hovered over the keys, hesitating. Deep down she knew her nerves had nothing to do with her reputation on

Usenet. Nothing in her message hinted at what she suspected was going on. It was about her committing to a theory. If she didn't think *Polybius* was harmful, why care? Why ask? The message, the act of sending it, represented the belief something was wrong. *Her* belief.

Fuck it, she finally decided. *Maybe I'm wrong*. A few keystrokes later, and the message was sent.

A new week didn't bring a break in the weather. The rain was starting to cause problems around town. Roads were washing out, roofs were leaking, electrical and phone services were showing signs of struggle. And it had made it difficult for David and Charlie to search the banks of Peck Creek for any additional evidence connected to the sweltering body Charlie had fished out of the water.

Upon arriving at the office early Monday morning, David had Evie find and dust off the emergency phone tree. Containing the names and numbers of volunteers, it was typically updated every year then filed away until the next, with no occasion to put it to use. Now, David had to assemble a search party to comb the area where the body had been found.

He'd already tried calling in help from neighboring towns and even the state police, but the rain was impacting everyone. Someone had been scheduled, again, to arrive that morning to pick up Robby Sapp Jr. and now Kelly Braun—the young woman who'd broken into Home Video World the day before—but their transfer to the county jail had been scuttled due to the weather.

There had been a moment the night before, after arriving home and swapping his soaked sheriff's uniform for something drier and more comfortable, where David felt like locking the doors to his house and being done with whatever the hell was happening. Carl Delano's horses. The fight at Bar Harbor. The break-in at Home Video World. The dead body—murdered and, thanks to the tooth, almost certainly connected to the chase that nearly cost him his own life the other night. Bob Colson's missing trainee. David had seen things like this in LA, sudden bursts of violence across communities. But that was in a city of two and a half million, during summer months when long stretches of sweltering days tended to push people over the edge.

He began pinning notes to a corkboard, outlining potential connections. The body found in the creek *might* have been dumped the same night the horses were killed, but *unlike* the horses, it hadn't been mutilated. Its wounds looked more like the work of brute force, done by hand and not an implement like the billhook. Bob Colson's supposedly missing person was another story. Until they were able to identify the Peck Creek body, David couldn't rule out that it might belong to Michael Newton, the family friend Bob had hired and who'd disappeared several days back.

As Andi searched for Ro in West Bay's cafeteria, she realized how strange things had become. Not just around Tasker Bay at large but in her own small corner of it. She'd gone from a loner who was set to skip town, drama free, to someone with *friends*. With something brewing between her and Ro that she liked, but still didn't fully understand.

Spotting her, Ro and Laurel waved her over. "I was telling Laurel about the body," Ro said.

"Did your dad say anything?" Andi asked, taking a seat.

"No. I haven't even seen him since he left the shop."

For a moment, the three picked at their food in silence. In fact, it was quieter than usual in general. As she took stock, Andi noticed fewer kids sitting together. Those who were weren't saying much.

"It's weird in here," Laurel finally said. Andi nodded, heartened hearing that someone else could sense it too. "I saw, like, six people get into fights at that party you bailed on," she continued. "Have you had anything happen?" she asked Andi. "To you?"

Andi shook her head, not following.

"We both had these dreams, or whatever," Laurel said, gesturing at Ro.

Andi glanced at him. "What she's talking about?"

Ro turned to Andi. "I don't think it's anything. It was a nightmare. About my dad. I didn't want you thinking I'm—I don't know."

Crazy, Andi thought. Exactly how she felt last night, staring for five minutes at the message she finally posted to Usenet. "I get it. But if we all really feel like things are . . . *weird*, maybe we should start telling each other whenever something weird happens."

Ro was about to agree with her when a lunch tray clattering to the floor interrupted. A fight was breaking out between Mark and Cliff, the linebackers who'd been kicked out of Home Video World after nearly beating Andi up the week prior.

As a crowd of students ringed them in, Cliff snatched a tray off a table and swung so hard it cracked in two against the side of Mark's face. Still gripping half the tray, he slashed its jagged melamine edges at the momentarily dazed Mark, who sprang forward, knocking it away then wrapping his hands around Cliff's throat, squeezing.

Desperate to break Mark's hold, Cliff swatted at a metal napkin dispenser, gripping and sailing it against Mark's face, ripping a series of deep gashes that somehow failed to faze him. Mark squeezed harder in response, blood streaming down his face and onto Cliff's, who gasped for air. The enthusiasm that bubbled as the fight started evaporated as the brutality escalated.

Realizing Mark might kill Cliff, Ro moved to intervene but was jostled aside by a posse of football players pushing through, trailed by a shell-shocked teacher. It took every one of them to pry Mark off and hold him at bay as an oxygen-deprived Cliff was helped up and hurried off by a handful of other students.

Charlie took the call about the fight. After confirming Mark was calm and under observation, he looked in on Cliff, who was lying in the school nurse's office, his face swollen, neck bruised, breathing raspy. If the boy knew why his friend had attacked him, he wasn't letting on.

But Charlie wasn't thinking about Cliff's lack of answers. What stuck out were the marks around his neck. Whether they'd match the ones around the neck of the Peck Creek body. But a violent outburst, resulting in someone nearly being strangled to death, felt like too big a coincidence to ignore. He made plans to radio David as soon as he had Mark in holding back at the station.

Instead of heading straight to work after school like every other day, Andi rode home to see if anyone on the rec.* or comp.* Usenet boards had responded to her message.

For days now, she'd been struggling over whether to believe there was a link between *Polybius* and the strange behavior around town. After standing feet away from two of her classmates as they tried to murder each other, she was done struggling. The horses, the body from the creek, she couldn't reconcile. But the fugues people were experiencing, the violence at the shop and at school, the break-in, the brawl that Robby Sapp Jr. had started after he'd played the game on and off for hours the night before—all of them tied back to *Polybius*.

At home, logged onto Usenet, she scrolled through the replies to her message in rec.* first. One mentioned Sinneslöchen. The poster had a roommate who had applied for a job there. As far as they knew, the company specialized in optics—that was their roommate's area of expertise—and wasn't involved in making games. The roommate never heard back about the job, and the poster recalled hearing that the company had been acquired. They weren't sure by whom.

Responses to at comp.* were no more illuminating. Most dismissed the code she'd posted, suggesting errors with the dump and offering advice on how to fine-tune her reverse universal programmer.

Loath to admit she wasn't infallible, Andi still jotted notes. If she had to, she'd try again. But coming to the final reply, she froze.

FROM: 1077NE

Join my group: 1077.*. There is a message for you.

"What the fuck?" Andi asked, under her breath. It felt unreal. Like she was embracing the fantasy that she was embroiled in some sort of mystery.

Still, it couldn't hurt to look.

Andi had the message up in a few moments. What she read chilled her blood.

FROM: 1077NE

Where did you/your shop acquire this cabinet? It's a prototype and ought to be pulled from your floor immediately. Don't share this any further than you have, delete your posts, and destroy your dump of the code. Do it today.

CHAPTER 11

TO DAVID'S FRUSTRATION, THOUGH NOT SURPRISE, THEY'D MADE NO PROGRESS scouring the area surrounding Peck Creek. Daylight was waning, and he'd pushed his volunteers as far as he could in the cold, wind, and rain. They'd dragged the creek around the area where the body had been discovered in search of a wallet, keys, anything that could help identify it. And they'd combed the woods for a square mile, radiating out from where the body had been snagged by debris the night before. All for nothing. At this point there wasn't anything else to do but pack up, dry off, and hope for something revelatory from Clarence.

As they made their way out of the woods and back toward their cars, David overheard one volunteer, Paul Nantz, jawing at the others. Paul was a self-proclaimed survivalist who hunted wild game for families in the area, disappearing into the woods for days on end. Other than guns and gear, Paul didn't want much. He liked living rough. And he liked to talk.

"I'm going to start going out on recces at night. Any of you want to come, let me know. Unless we find out this was an accident," Paul said, throwing a pointed glance David's way, "somebody needs to do something." David had rejected Paul's application to become a deputy multiple times over the years—he seemed to want the power that came with the badge a little *too* much—and Paul was relishing the opportunity to call him out.

David didn't take the bait. But as he loaded bags of soaking-wet gear into his cruiser, he could hear other volunteers approaching Paul, offering to help. Tasker Bay didn't need a band of wannabe vigilantes roaming the streets, but David had bigger problems to solve.

Among the crowd at Ford's Diner, through the halls of West Bay High, over beers at Bar Harbor, in passing at Greene's Market, on the docks, or on the streets, people were talking about the shadow that had been cast over Tasker Bay.

Not an *actual* shadow. For that you'd need sun, which hadn't been seen since the storm had arrived last week. It was more of a sense, a feeling that people they'd known for years—family, spouses, children, themselves—were suddenly different. Prone to raise their voices, cry, lose track of time or their sense of direction, swing wildly in between moods. Friends and neighbors swapped unsettling stories at the end of their driveways or in line at the post office, no one able to point toward anything to help explain the changes they were seeing or experiencing firsthand.

"She hasn't been out of the house in days."

"My son isn't sleeping."

"I keep catching my daughter staring at me."

"I've been having nightmares, every night, the second I close my eyes."

"He hasn't shown up for work since last week."

"Someone found me sleepwalking. I *don't* sleepwalk."

"I feel like I'm being watched."

Runs had started on essential goods. For a town that was used to hunkering down in the face of inclement weather this wasn't unusual, but the things people had started buying up were. The local hardware store was running out of two-by-fours and plywood, locks, and lengths of chain. Knives, guns, and ammo were all disappearing from behind the counter. At Greene's, Paulson's, and the local pharmacy, food and first aid supplies were dwindling.

And people continued crowding Rachel's office with complaints about paranoia, anxiety, unease. Symptoms were a divergent swirl of insomnia, restlessness, full-blown panic attacks, and, in a few cases, catatonia. After seeing dozens of these mystery ailments, Rachel had started looking for patterns, but so far, she'd found none. She was growing worried for the family, friends who were bringing these people in. They looked tired, confused, frightened. In their own way they were going through this too.

As she checked the chart for her next patient—*Cliff Young, trauma to throat*—the phone on her desk flashed. For every patient she'd seen, she'd taken twice as many calls. As much as it was starting to pain her, she still picked up. "This is Dr. Winston."

"Rachel? It's Sheriff Kemp. David. Have you seen a patient by the name of Cliff Young today? He would have had pretty severe bruising on his neck, maybe a concussion."

"Seriously?" Rachel glanced down the hall toward the waiting room. "He's here right now. Why? What's going on?"

"We found a body in Peck Creek last night. It looks like it was strangled. I'm thinking about a connection between the person who attacked Cliff."

"I can't share information from an exam." Rachel was surprised he'd ask. Didn't like that he had.

"Maybe I can see notes on the injury to his neck—just the injury, nothing else—so we can compare them to the coroner's report on that body. Mental notes if you want. Anything. I wouldn't ask if . . . I'm sorry I have to, but I need your help."

Shit. It wasn't like Rachel could really know, but David *seemed* like an honest cop. As she let the receiver drift from her ear, a thought occurred that could make things slightly more ethical for them both. "What if I sat in on the coroner's exam? If something sticks out, I could tell you."

After she'd told Ro about how she'd imagined gutting Christine Abernathy, Laurel felt like she'd been steadily descending. Everything seemed to be pulling away from her. Senses, feelings were atrophying. Taste fading, sounds growing distant and indecipherable. Family and friends had become foreign to her, saying and doing things she found nonsensical or shocking. The world around her had grown alien and frightening.

In her room, on the floor with the lights off, she stared at the ceiling and waited for whatever had gripped her to finish squeezing the life from her. She just wanted to close her eyes and sleep.

Sleep. Sleep. The word began to stretch out inside her head, and suddenly she was struggling to stay awake. *Sleep.* She could feel it coming. Knew that if she could just rest, she could get her head right. *Sleep . . .*

But something started tugging, pulling her back from the brink. At first she wanted to cry, to scream out *I just want to fucking sleep!* But then she heard it. A question, feeling. *An idea.* Something was beckoning. Laurel had no clue what, but she could feel it giving her life again.

Sitting up, she could see something standing in the far corner of her room. Tall and wide, at once human but also not. Its eyes—no, something else, sharp and angular—glinted from the dark. She recognized it. She'd been running from it in the game, in her dreams.

The figment.

But here, inside her room—in her world—it didn't strike fear. It suggested purpose. *Chase*, its presence intoned. *Don't be chased.*

She found herself reenergized, on her feet and back to work at her parents' store that afternoon, but the desire to *understand* gnawed constantly. A distant idea kept calling out. It was something she *knew* she had to do, which meant she *had* to know what it was, only she didn't.

What am I supposed to know?

How am I supposed to know it?

Whenever she could, she'd close her eyes, concentrating, listening for that same voice in the hope it would clarify her task. Why had she seen the figment? Was the knowledge she was seeking with it, hidden somewhere inside the game?

After clocking out from her shift at Greene's, Laurel walked the two blocks to Home Video World, intent on playing *Polybius* until she found an answer.

As she approached, she could see a crowd ringing the cabinet. She started for the door then stopped abruptly—having moved to a different vantage, she suddenly had a clear view of *Polybius*'s screen. Eyes locking onto it, she stood in the rain, absorbing wave after wave of light that, to her eyes, was radiating from the game, through the crowd, and onto the street around her.

While the crowd played, Mal circled. He'd avoided the shop for as long as he felt he could, so that morning he forced himself out of the house in order to open. He'd stewed over his missing hours long enough. It was time to do *something*. Sitting at home, trying over and over to recall whether he'd gone anywhere near the Delanos' stables just wasn't helping.

Sometimes he'd see *things*. Flashes. Abstract bursts of violent motion. *Maybe I'm going crazy*, he thought. After years of quaaludes and bennies and LSD and he'd forgotten what all else, maybe he'd finally, fully rewired his thought process into something he could no longer interpret.

Every now and then, in brief moments, he'd feel a rush of blood. A good feeling, as if his fog had lifted, but it failed to last. And it was in *those* moments, the aftermath of his strange, fleeting highs, that Mal was at his lowest. It showed him that his tough-guy kingpin self-image was bullshit. He couldn't even live with the *thought* of having done something awful, forget whether he'd actually done it.

He was *scared*. It was pathetic.

Forced to confront the fact that the hold he imagined having over

Tasker Bay was an illusion, Mal contemplated what it would take to move on and start over. Sooner or later the sheriff's office would have *something* on him. With the way he'd been acting, there was a good chance he'd let something incriminating slip all by himself.

But to leave, he'd need cash. Selling the shop wasn't an option. Who knows how long it would take, and the bank still owned most of it. If he was serious about finding a way out, he knew he'd have to come up with something better than the few thousand in loose change sitting in back.

If Mal had been a believer in fate, seeing Ed Sanko wander through the door that afternoon would've qualified. Ed owned the Tasker Bay Bottle Shoppe down the block and had likely been on his way home when the crowd had drawn him in. If Ed still banked on the same day as Mal, he'd have cash on hand—a lot. And unless Ed had decided to modernize, that money would be hidden behind a false panel beneath the register, not stored in a safe.

It had been a year ago that Ed had drunkenly mentioned the false panel at Bar Harbor one night. That detail had stuck with Mal, as if he'd been planning something in the back of his mind since.

Maybe he had.

After half-assing his portion of the closing routine, Mal had taken up a spot in front of *Polybius* without a word, leaving a frustrated Andi to finish up. At least Ro had arrived in time to help.

Despite trying to avoid the game, Ro had been drawn in by watching Mal, stepping up to the controls after he'd left. Mal had turned away from the screen abruptly, as if something was silently calling, disappearing out the front door without a word or even so much as a glance at Ro. Not that Ro would've noticed.

Returning to find Ro locked in and unresponsive, Andi was forced to pull the plug. She stepped away, giving him room to come back on his own, which he did after a few lost moments. The shop floor was quiet. *Polybius* was dark.

"Come in back," Andi said, not waiting for Ro to follow.

A knot was forming in her stomach. Ro wasn't going to take her seriously. He hadn't seemed to consider that his symptoms—the panic attack he'd experienced—could be connected to the game. She second-guessed saying something, but if it turned out she was right and said nothing, then he might go on playing, potentially harming himself further. As could a lot of other people.

"I posted a message about the game on a bulletin board service," she said. "I asked if anyone had heard of it, or Sinneslöchen. There was this . . . message someone left for me, in private. They said the game was a prototype, and we needed to take it off the floor. The way they wrote it was . . . I don't know. Like there'd be trouble if we didn't do what they said."

Ro cocked an eyebrow. "Did they say you were in trouble?"

"No," Andi admitted. "But it felt like a threat. Or a warning."

"Can you find out who sent the message? See if you need to take it seriously? Maybe somebody's messing with you," Ro offered, trying his best to sound reassuring.

Andi shook her head. "It's anonymous. Unless you know the other person. You can ask, but if they don't want you to know, you won't."

"Okay." Ro shrugged. "So, what do you want to do—what they said? Pull the game?"

"When I got here, there were forty . . . two people waiting to play. I watched nineteen more come in and line up before you got here. There's *nothing* I could say that would convince Mal to take it off the floor. It's printing money."

"Then Mal's the one who gets in trouble for having it, right?" Ro was starting to lose the thread Andi was attempting to weave. "It's his shop. I don't see how it could come back on you as long as you at least tell him what you heard."

"It's not about that." Andi drew a deep breath, dropping her head in her hands for a brief moment. "What if the reason they wrote that message—wrote it the way they did—is because the game's not safe to play."

Ro started to protest, but Andi cut back in. "Think about everything that's been happening. When it *started* happening. People fighting. Freaking out. Everyone who's come to see my mom with anxiety or insomnia in the last week. She said that some of them just started screaming in the exam room. Or they go blank, like they can't hear her. That fight at Bar Harbor? I heard someone almost got stabbed. The break-in here. *You* out there, just now. Laurel, Mal. People come in here, they play, and—and what if it's not random? I mean, why would it be, all of a sudden? So, what if it's the game?"

Ro didn't know what to say without saying something he probably shouldn't. He didn't believe her—didn't think he did, at least. "I mean, if that's true, and there's some reason behind . . . whatever's gotten into people, then you could say it's the weather. It changed about a week ago, and people have been acting weird since."

Andi shrugged. *Sure.* "But you can't prove that."

"Can you prove *this*? And if everyone who plays or watches

people play or whatever is getting sick, then how are *you* okay? You played. You've been watching people play all week. You've probably seen it more than anybody." Ro didn't want to sound exasperated but increasingly couldn't help it.

"I know," Andi finally said, unhappy having perhaps the biggest hole in her theory pointed out. "And I know what that sounds like—"

"So doesn't that disprove it?"

"I don't know." Andi shook her head a little. "Maybe I'm going crazy."

"So it *did* get you," Ro said with a small smile. Andi rolled her eyes, uninterested in joking around. "Come on. You know you're not crazy. Look, I agree. Something *is* going on, but I think it's . . . something in the air. Not literally. Something's getting people wound up. Other people notice, and that gets them wound up. Like an echo."

"Okay, but an echo has to start somewhere. Where did it start? What started it?"

"Those horses," Ro said, more suggestion than definitive statement. "People hear about something like that, and they worry whoever did it might still be around."

Ro wasn't being unreasonable, but Andi still wasn't buying it. She was ready to die on this hill. "Okay. And what started *that*?"

"Are you serious?" Ro was tired of feeling interrogated. "Somebody acting crazy. People can be crazy. I don't know."

"Nothing happens in this town for forever, and suddenly somebody snaps and juliennes a barn full of horses. *That* can happen?" Andi shot back.

"Maybe, yeah."

"And everybody else starts freaking out and fighting and dumping bodies in the river? You believe that? It's happening to you, too, Ro. You really think it's because someone killed some horses?"

Ro's hand shot up in frustration. "I don't know!"

Andi rose, storming off toward the front of the shop. She felt like an idiot for bringing it up, embarrassed at sounding crazy and for failing to convince Ro. *What am I even trying to do? Who do I think I'm helping?* Maybe it was *her* problem. She'd started making changes in her life, and look what happened. She'd gone right down a rabbit hole, the first one she saw. It *was* crazy.

Ro knew he'd been pushing Andi, but he just wanted to understand. He hadn't meant to upset her. As he followed her onto the shop floor, watching her walk toward the door, he found himself slowing, stopping.

There was Andi, leaving. Walking away.

The same crushing sense of absolute solitude he'd felt the other night, when he'd convinced himself that his dad was gone, crept forward from the back of his mind. The world around him was turning into one big sensory deprivation tank. Total blackout. Suddenly unable to support his own weight, Ro crashed to the floor and started convulsing.

Spinning at the sound, Andi froze for a moment, watching in shock as Ro thrashed. Then she rushed in, dodging and grabbing an arm as it swung past her head. Feeling hands on him, Ro fought back. Realizing she couldn't subdue him on her own, Andi knew she was too late—*he* was gripping her now, squeezing tighter as the tremors worsened.

"Ro, stop!" She screamed at him to let go, pleading for him to calm down, hoping he'd somehow hear.

As one of his hands accidentally found her face, a kind of recognition came over him. His convulsions lessened, body calming moment to moment as the tension that was coiling his muscles began to dissipate. Finally, withdrawing his hand, he motioned around his eyes and ears, shaking his head. "I can't hear, see," he managed, unsteady. "Is that—Andi?"

Still wary, she touched him on the shoulder, watching as relief flooded over him. Telling herself this wasn't Ro, that *something* was doing this to him, she took his hand, placing it on her face then putting her own on top. The connection seemed to work. Ro stayed still, the fury that had grabbed hold of him continuing to drain away.

Andi found herself staring at him, absorbed by the strange sensation of looking at someone who couldn't look back. She'd been stung when he hadn't believed her, but he'd heard her out. Hadn't derided her. Tried to find ways to rationalize what was going on. And she'd let her own insecurities get the better of her. She wanted Ro to believe her but didn't need him to. She had her theory, and if she had to prove it on her own, she would.

She was so lost in thought, she failed to realize he was finally looking back up at her. "Should we have a staring contest?" Ro asked as he moved to sit.

"You're okay?" she asked. He nodded, clearly still groggy. "You need to talk to my mom about this. Tomorrow."

Ro went to speak but paused a moment, chewing over what he was about to say. "Both times this happened, I'd played the game. I'm not ready to jump into all this headfirst or whatever, but I don't see what's wrong with talking about it some more. If you want."

Andi leaned in, softly kissing Ro's lips before feeling something in her arm pinch, then pulling away to inspect where he'd been squeezing her moments earlier.

Ro looked horrified. "That was me? I did that?"

"Not on purpose. But that's why you need to see a doctor. If it happens again, someone *could* get hurt. Including you." Andi climbed to her feet. "I don't think I've ever mopped this floor. You don't want to be down there. Come on," she said, extending a hand to help Ro up.

As they headed into the back, Andi realized a vague unease had come over her. Ro was behind her; she couldn't see him. Didn't know whether he was still himself or something else. She glanced back and caught his eyes. He was fine. But for how long?

Mal wasn't sure what had brought him back around to the waking world. At some point, he'd stepped away from *Polybius* and walked out of Home Video World, climbed into his truck, and pulled away. Instead of heading home, he drove here, there, circling a few times to confirm when Andi finally killed the lights, locked the doors, and left for the night.

Just after eleven he pulled up to the back of the shop and slipped out into the rain. Moving along a narrow alley that ran behind the block, he kept his head down and stayed in the shadows.

As he approached the rear of the Bottle Shoppe, he pulled the .38 from beneath his jacket and swung it against a window set into the rear entrance. The storm provided cover, masking the noise as glass shattered. He reached through, unlocked the door, and slipped inside.

Closing the door behind him, he waited, listening on the offhand chance anyone else was there. But the commotion hadn't drawn any interlopers out of the shop's darkened corridors, so he proceeded deeper in. Passing an oversized rechargeable flashlight clipped to the wall, he nicked it and, keeping the beam low, swept the floor as he wound his way through a stockroom cluttered with liquor boxes and dusty promotional signs.

On the shop floor he passed a row of refrigerated cases, compressors and fluorescents humming. At the counter he wasted no time, shifting everything stored below it out of the way, finally revealing the temporary panel Ed had drunkenly bragged about. It was just as he'd described it, save for one vexing detail—*a lock*. For a moment Mal just stared, feeling stupid that he hadn't expected it.

But it didn't matter. A lock wasn't stopping him.

Spotting a screwdriver nearby, he snatched it up, jammed it into a seam running along one side of the panel, and pried. The construction itself wasn't state-of-the-art, and he could hear the frame starting to splinter after just a few moments. Bearing down, Mal tore the panel loose from one of its hinges.

As the panel gave way, he lost his balance, tumbling backward into a wire rack of sparkling wine. Bottles crashed, glass cracking and shattering, contents fizzing out over everything, including him. Undeterred, Mal scrambled back over to the counter, jamming his hands inside the panel and working with animal intensity to tear it all the way clear.

Had he not been making so much noise, he might have heard the rear entrance creaking open and the crunch of footfalls over shattered glass. But it wasn't until Ed Sanko emerged from in back, clutching a weathered Winchester Model 1892 that had belonged to his father and normally rested in a dusty corner of the shop's storage room, that he realized he was no longer alone.

"What in the hell are you doing here, Mal?" Ed stared down at a man he'd considered a friend, crouched on the floor of his shop, seemingly on the verge of stealing around six thousand in cash.

Mal stared blankly at Ed, setting the money down, then raising one hand as if to say, *You've got this wrong*. At the same time and under the cover of darkness, his other hand dipped to the .38 he'd tucked behind his back earlier that night.

"Mal, *what* are you doing? Stand up." Ed's hand tightened on the rifle's stock, but before he could level it, a shot rang out, bottles on the rack behind Ed exploding as a bullet passed through his chest. Two more shots quickly followed. The Winchester clattered from Ed's hands to the floor, and a moment later, Ed followed it down. Pupils dilating as life waned, he stared at Mal and tried to speak but could only sputter blood. He'd come back for his wallet. As his mind flooded with scattered memories and thoughts, he realized he was never leaving this place again.

It took the ringing in Mal's ears subsiding to snap him back into the moment. As realization dawned, reaction followed. Doubling up a brown paper bag, he stuffed cash inside by the fistful. Clambering to his feet, he hurried for the stockroom door. But glancing back and seeing Ed's body—the mess he'd made of the counter and left on the floor—his mind began to race. Someone was going to find this, and he'd be fucked. Even if he left town right then, sooner or later he'd be fucked.

Caroming back through the shop, Mal snatched up the screw-driver he'd used to pry open the hidden panel along with the flashlight and made for the wall behind Ed's body. He needed to find the rounds from the .38.

Sweeping bottles off shelves, he found a splintered ring of plaster and dug in the screwdriver, probing, popping out a dented slug coated in a patina of whitish-brown dust that clung to Ed's blood. *One down.*

Working his way down the wall, he found another round crumpled against the shelving unit's metal frame. *That makes two.*

But whatever confidence he'd gained in recovering two-thirds of the evidence without much trouble vanished just as quickly—the third slug was nowhere to be found, leading Mal to a horrible revelation.

It was still inside Ed.

Triangulating where the missing round had entered Ed's chest, near the center of his left lung, Mal knelt down and turned his body over. There was swelling, but no exit wound. He rose to his feet and made his way back to the counter, rooting where he'd found the screwdriver until he came upon a pair of needle-nose pliers.

Hovering over Ed's body, Mal stared ahead for a long, awful moment as he worked up the nerve to go through with what he was planning. As if ripping off a bandage, he suddenly jabbed the tip of the pliers into the wound, striking something hard almost immediately. Hands beginning to sweat, he struggled to maintain his grip on the red, rubber-coated handles as he seized then twisted the slug out of Ed's chest. What was in reality about thirty seconds' worth of work felt like an eternity to Mal, who—after the round was freed and tucked into his pocket along with the other two—staggered to his feet and began to heave.

Able to collect himself, he searched the aisles for grain alcohol.

Bottle after bottle, he doused the shop in it, gradually making his way back toward the door leading to the stockroom. He tossed a match and was momentarily transfixed by the wall of flame that rose before him, the heat already searing. As he moved into the stockroom, he happened to glance down, realizing he was no longer carrying the paper bag containing the money. He'd left it somewhere near the counter when he'd gone back to recover the slugs.

"*Fuck!*" The fire was already in Mal's path, but he had no choice. Shielding his face, he barreled through, searching for the bag as the blaze quickened. Finally spotting it, he angled for it as a massive wisp of flame shot up, setting it alight. Ignoring the sizzle of his own flesh, he grabbed the bag then snuffed it out as he stumbled back toward the stockroom door.

Cold night air coupled with what was now a driving rain soothed Mal as he sprinted back down the alley, a swirl of smoke and steam rolling off him. Upon reaching his truck, he climbed in, then tore off, catching sight of thick black smoke spiraling into the night sky in his rearview mirror.

CHAPTER 12

DAVID STEPPED CAUTIOUSLY THROUGH THE CRAGGY, BLACKENED REMAINS OF the Tasker Bay Bottle Shoppe. Despite the rain, which persisted even now, the fire that had sparked sometime late the night before had been difficult to stop, with volunteers fighting the blaze until just before dawn. The Bottle Shoppe and the businesses butted up against it on either side—a small department store and a bookshop—all housed a mix of accelerants and tinder that helped the fire flare back up every time it seemed under control. In the end, all three took substantial damage, but only the Bottle Shoppe was gutted.

David's deputy Jeff had found the body. Assumed to be Ed Sanko, it was so badly burned there was no way to identify it onsite. Clarence Meeks carted it away shortly after David arrived.

There was no easy way to tell what had sparked the blaze since there wasn't much of the store left. The answer, David suspected, would lie with Ed. If he'd gotten drunk and passed out with a cigarette in his mouth, it'd be no less tragic, but at least it wouldn't add to the concerns weighing down his office. If Clarence returned *another* verdict on cause of death . . . David didn't want to think about that just yet.

Foul play or not, the fire served to darken the shadow that had been cast over Tasker Bay since the incident at the Delano farm. Tragedies were mounting. What effect would today have, David wondered? Would people automatically assume the worst, that someone was coming for *them* next, since the worst had seemingly become the norm?

While he hadn't admitted it to himself yet, deep down some part of him knew that the situation had already spiraled out of his control. Like a wave that kept crashing over him, there was no respite, no chance to get back on his feet before it pummeled him again. David hoped, between Clarence and Rachel, he'd find out something that could help him push back.

Paul Nantz had shown up to help deal with the fire, and he'd kept quiet while doing it. But after it was out, David watched him sling a rifle over his shoulder and start down the sidewalk with a couple of other locals in tow, an armed neighborhood watch on patrol. The longer it took to offer people a rationale, David knew, the more irrational they'd become.

Leaving Jeff to oversee the volunteers still mopping up around the remains of the Bottle Shoppe, David started the short drive to Clarence's mortuary. Before being called to the fire, he'd spent the better part of the night mulling over whether Mark Casey really had it in him to take a life. Everyone Charlie had spoken to when he'd picked up Mark from West Bay High had said it hadn't seemed like he was going to stop his assault on Cliff Young; he'd had to *be* stopped. Maybe he *had* done it before, then dumped the body in Peck Creek. David knew full well what people were capable of when, for whatever reason, that primal side took hold. But pulling up in front of Meeks's Mortuary, he tried to clear these kinds of thoughts from his head. There was still a chance this wasn't murder.

"It's definitely murder," Clarence said as he tapped the end of a pencil against the marks crisscrossing the Peck Creek body's sallow neck.

"We have a pattern of horizontal circumscription across the neck. Pinpoint hemorrhages in the surrounding skin and conjunctiva of the eyes. What's left of them. Incised curvilinear abrasions here and here, where whoever did the deed dug in their nails."

"So that's it—cause of death? He was strangled?" David asked, trying to cut through the haze.

Clarence nodded. "There's other blunt-force trauma on the body, but I can't say with any certainty that's not the result of him getting hit by whatever else came down the creek while he was in it. I can tell you he was dead before he ever hit the water. There's no sign his lungs collapsed, and the laryngeal sphincter's still open."

David shot Clarence a look—*English?*

"When you go underwater, your airways close reflexively. That's the laryngeal—"

"Sphincter, yeah." David nodded.

"You didn't know there was one in your throat," Clarence said, smirking. The human body was endlessly fascinating to Clarence, and he got a kick out of shining a light on its stranger byways.

He moved to the victim's feet, waving David over. "As far as an ID goes, this is your golden ticket. Your man had an extra left toe.

Next to the pinkie. Polydactyl. It's actually not that uncommon, but it ought to be enough to set a John Doe apart."

A knock at the exam room's door drew their attention. Rachel stepped halfway inside with a timid wave. "Dr. Winston. David said you'd be joining. Please." As Clarence gestured her over, he noted trepidation in her step. "He won't bite," Clarence said as he tapped the body on its shoulder with his pen. He proceeded to watch it for a moment, pretending he didn't trust his own advice before shooting Rachel a sly, reassuring smile.

"Sorry," Rachel offered. "I haven't been around too many of these since med school. Never really got used to it."

"Well, if you're doing your job right, you shouldn't be. I've got a date with our new arrival. If you need something, you come and let me know." Clarence shuffled off to begin his examination of what were assumed to be the remains of Ed Sanko in an adjoining room, leaving David and Rachel alone with the body.

"Someone was killed in that fire?" Rachel asked as she approached the exam table.

David nodded, then gestured at the Peck Creek body. "You're sure you're okay with this?"

"I'm here, so let's not overthink it," Rachel said, forcing a smile. She moved closer, craning her neck for a better look at the marks encircling the victim's throat.

David stepped back, making sure to give her space and time to evaluate without feeling any pressure. If a link was going to be made to Mark Casey, it needed to be as concrete as possible before he could be questioned. News that a well-known, well-liked minor with important parents was being looked at for a murder would spin Tasker Bay completely off its already wobbly axis.

Rachel made her way around to the other side of the table, continuing to scrutinize the body. She dug in her purse and pulled out a Polaroid photograph, tilting it to match the angle at which the body lay. After a long moment, she looked up at David. "What's going to happen to him?" she finally asked.

"Who?"

"The other boy," Rachel said. "The one who attacked Cliff Young."

David looked away, around for a moment, considering how best to answer the question. "It depends. If a connection can be reasonably drawn between Cliff's injuries and this body, we'll question him." David realized Rachel had begun feeling the weight of what he'd asked her to do. "That doesn't mean we're arresting him or putting him in jail. No one's jumping to conclusions. That's part of my job, to make sure we don't."

"It's just . . . this isn't what I do," Rachel said, uneasy at the prospect of potentially controlling Mark Casey's fate. "I think you need to look for yourself."

She handed David the Polaroid she'd taken of Cliff's neck, allowing him to compare it to the marks on the body. The similarities were unmistakable—the spacing, the width of the bruising. He looked to Rachel and understood why she didn't want to be the one who said it.

"Okay," David finally said, resigned to what would come next. "I'll walk you out."

The two made their way from the exam room and into a lobby ringed by caskets, part of the business side of Clarence's operation. "You've been here awhile, right?" Rachel asked.

David nodded.

"Have you ever seen anything like this before?"

"In my experience, people here tend to live at the same speed. They don't suddenly put their foot on the gas. And if someone does, it's some*one*. Not the whole town, all at once," David said as he opened the front door, the two of them stepping outside. "If you look at this place now and three, four years ago, there are a lot more people than there used to be. With a lot more money. That's the biggest change. By far."

"So us transplants are ruining your utopian way of life?" It wasn't a serious question, and Rachel's tone made that clear, but she knew this *was* how a lot of locals felt. Some had told her as much to her face. She wondered about David's point of view.

"You know, every utopian society failed," he pointed out. "Or we'd all be living in one."

They lingered in front of the mortuary for a quiet moment, neither excited at the prospect of heading back out into the rain. "You should've seen the looks I got when I showed up with a Black wife and mixed-race kid. *In the seventies*. Jesus." David shook his head, bits of unpleasant memories drifting back. "After a while it didn't matter anymore. Or as much. But that took time, and my family was one variable. Now there are . . . I don't even know how many. People are losing jobs, working for someone they don't know, don't necessarily trust. Losing their homes." He noticed Rachel shifting a little as he spoke. "It has nothing to do with you. Or most of the folks moving here. But there *are* people who know because of how isolated we've been there's room to take advantage. And they press it, as much as they can."

Rachel nodded a little. It wasn't a comfortable conversation.

David glanced up at the metal canopy overhead, rain pinging ceaselessly off it. "This weather can't be helping. Just grim."

The suggestion—offhanded patter, not meant to be taken seriously—drew Rachel's focus to a torrent of rainwater rushing along the curb, past an overflowing storm drain. *Could there be some sort of environmental explanation?* It was too big an idea to easily take hold of. It'd have to wait until she was alone, when she could sit with it and think it through.

After David thanked her and she climbed inside her car, she had an epiphany. She knew exactly who to call for help with her theory. She also had a problem—her car wouldn't start. Glancing over, she saw David still sitting in his cruiser, jawing on the radio.

By the time he'd circled with every surrounding county, Jeff was staring at an inch of faxes and teletypes, all for recent and unsolved reports of missing persons. He'd already heard from David that they'd be questioning Mark Casey about the Peck Creek body, so it was imperative they come armed with as much information as possible—the identity of the victim being key.

He was tired. Everyone who'd weighed in had told him that being a new parent would be exhausting, and while he'd taken these overtures seriously, he'd decided they'd all undersold it. Whatever state of being existed beyond exhaustion, that was him. As he glanced down at the photo of his wife Meghan and baby daughter Emily at the hospital, taken a few hours after her birth six weeks ago, he wished he was home. He knew Meghan felt like even more of a zombie than he did. He wanted to be there to help her. And to take a very long nap after.

He'd barely made a dent in the files when David called in with news—the victim had an extra toe. Digging through Michael Newton's medical records, which came via a connection of Bob Colson's, he confirmed that Michael had an extra toe on his left foot, same as the victim. There wasn't enough of the face left to make a positive ID, but they had a unique physical feature, a body that fit Newton's weight and height, and a timeline that worked.

As Jeff went to radio David and Charlie, Carl Delano's booming voice nearly made him jump out of his seat.

"Where's David?"

"Jesus Christ, Carl. Trying to give me a damn heart attack?" Jeff asked as he swiveled around to face his unexpected visitor. Prominent on Carl's hip was a ten-inch bowie knife, tucked into its sheath but no less imposing for it. Jeff approached the reception desk, where Carl was waiting. "Going hunting?" Jeff asked, nerves poking through.

"I want to talk to the sheriff."

Jeff nodded. "I hear you. He's out right now, but I'd be happy to have a talk with you. Why don't you come in, sit down? Coffee's on if you want a cup."

"You know who killed my horses?"

"I—no. We don't know yet," Jeff said, annoyed at himself for stumbling. He'd let Carl rattle him.

"Then why would I want to talk with you?" Carl asked, eyes cold.

As Jeff went to follow up, Carl drew the bowie knife and slammed it down on the desk separating the two of them. Jeff's hand dipped to his sidearm; he didn't draw, but he was ready. "I need you to put that away, Carl," Jeff said, tone firm. He waited, hoping a moment or two to cool down would help. But Carl didn't budge. "I'm giving you a chance I probably shouldn't. Put that knife away and go home. I'll tell the sheriff to call you when he's back. That's the best I can do."

Slowly Carl withdrew the knife. "You all know as well as I do it's those goddamned people after our land, trying to drive us off it. That's my dad's house. You know when *his* dad came out here? The goddamned gold rush. My family's been here over a hundred years, and *we aren't leaving.*"

As they stepped into the waiting room at Rachel's office, Andi and Ro found themselves sitting with a dozen others, several of whom they recognized from Home Video World, all of whom they'd seen playing *Polybius.* None looked sick, but they didn't look well, either. They seemed distant, tense, minds occupied to the point they might as well have all been on separate planets. No one spoke. Most didn't even move, staring off at nothing or down at the floor.

Ro's leg bounced with quiet fury, the by-product of that unique sense of vulnerability that only a visit to the doctor's office can provide. What was wrong with him? What would happen when he found out? Did he want to know? He'd spent too many hours in too many waiting rooms with his mother, where the news her doctors delivered was never good. He hated these places.

"Andi?" Looking up, the two of them saw Rachel *and* David walking into the office.

"What's . . . going on?" Andi asked, worried to see her mom being escorted by the sheriff.

"The car wouldn't start. David gave me a ride," Rachel said.

"And came in for some coffee," David added, hoisting a weathered, gunmetal thermos. "What are you two doing here?"

Andi and Ro found themselves in an exam room with *both* their parents, explaining what had happened to Ro. Rachel looked him over and ran through a few cursory questions about his well-being. Nothing revealed itself.

"You seem fine," she offered, trying her best to sound reassuring. "But I still think you ought to see a neurologist. I have someone I can refer you to in San Jose."

"When were you going to tell me?" David asked, incredulity loud and clear.

"I haven't seen you. And it's not like it's easy to explain," Ro shot back. "I didn't think you needed anything else to worry about."

"Maybe you want to talk in private," Rachel suggested. "Andi, we can wait outside."

But Andi didn't move. Believing they'd withheld a key piece of information, that Ro's symptoms coincided with his playing *Polybius*, she decided it was time to speak her mind. "We might know what caused it," she blurted out, drawing everyone's attention all at once.

"What?" Rachel asked, more confused than curious.

Andi glanced at Ro, who was unsure about saying *anything*. But he nodded, a little, then tipped his head toward their parents. *You tell it.*

"There's a game. It came into the shop last week. You saw it the other night," Andi said, gesturing at David. "It was the only thing anyone was playing."

Slowly David nodded. He remembered how a display on the shop floor had grabbed his attention. How it had been a struggle to turn away.

"We've been watching everyone who comes through and plays since it showed up." Andi knew this was the part where she'd lose them, but she'd started this. She had to finish it. "It's affecting people. Doing something to them. Everyone who plays, they're . . . spaced out, or angry, or scared. Violent."

"Mark played it, Dad. Cliff, too," Ro added.

Andi nodded. "We saw them beat the crap out of some guy in front of the game last week. On Thursday. Mark came after me for trying to stop them."

"And the break-in?" Ro asked. "Did she say anything to you, the girl who broke the window? Why she did it?"

"Just that she wanted inside," David said, slowly working his way through the story as they told it.

"We know you arrested Robby Sapp. We watched him play it for hours. Dad, have you *ever* seen Robby hurt anybody?" Ro asked.

David had to shake his head no.

Andi kept on. "People have nightmares or—or visions."

"Laurel's having them. So am I," Ro admitted.

"You played it?" David asked, before turning to Andi. "Both of you?"

Andi nodded. "Yeah, but I—" She raised her hands, knowing how it would sound. "I haven't had problems. Not like Ro or Laurel. Or . . . anyone else."

"How can—" Rachel started, before realizing she didn't know what question she even wanted to ask. "Okay. First. People *can* have photosensitivities. Flashing lights can trigger seizures, but you need an underlying condition to be affected, and that condition's rare."

"We're not talking about seizures," Andi cut in.

"Exactly," Rachel replied. "What you're talking about . . . there's *no* scenario in which something that dangerous makes it out into the public." She glanced at David, looking for some reinforcement. "Right?"

"Call the manufacturer," David suggested, wheels still turning. He wasn't ready to accept *or* dismiss anything just yet.

"We don't know who made it," Andi said. "It's not in any of the trades. Or Ro's books. There are no logos. When Mal bought it, it didn't even have a marquee."

For a long moment, the room fell quiet. Again, Rachel looked to David, trying to figure out whether or not she had an ally in putting this theory to bed. "Why are *you* okay?" she finally asked Andi.

"I don't know," Andi admitted.

"Then don't you think—"

Andi cut her mother off, losing her temper. "If we knew every single answer, we wouldn't be in here, would we?"

"That's enough, Andi," Rachel admonished.

"No! You're not seeing it. *We're* seeing it. Ro's *living* it. There is something wrong in this town, and it started when that game showed up!"

David raised a hand, asking for calm. He looked to Andi. "When did Mal put it on the floor?"

"Last Wednesday," Andi said, trying to keep her voice in check.

"Everything that's been going on started *after* it showed up," Ro said. "We're not saying something like Carl Delano's horses or the body from the creek have anything to do with it, but it's a pretty big coincidence."

"We're not saying they don't, either," Andi added.

David finally looked to Rachel and shrugged. "We've been pulling our hair out looking for something that ties all of this together."

"I have too," Rachel said. "It could be environmental. And I'm going to make some calls. But you don't think—"

David shook his head, certain, turning back to the kids. "I *don't* think it's a video game. But I understand why you do. From what you said, it sounds like it's a custom thing. What do you know about it?"

"It's advanced," Andi said. "Years ahead of anything else. We think the screen was made by a company called Sinneslöchen. We got a message from somebody on Usenet who said it was a prototype and that we needed to take it off the floor."

David's brow furrowed. "Usenet?"

"It's a bulletin board. On a computer. You type questions here, someone from somewhere else can answer it."

"Sounds like the easiest thing to do is to ask Mal to take it off the floor," David offered.

"He won't. It's too much money." Andi was certain.

Ro looked to his father. "Could you ask?"

David was quick to shut this notion down. "Anecdotal evidence and the lack of a paper trail on wherever this thing came from don't make for cause."

"We're not going to stop trying to figure this out," Andi said before glancing at Ro—it wasn't just her choice to make. "I'm not," she said, trying to gauge his level of commitment. Ro nodded.

Rachel and David glanced at each other. Both knew that when their kids made up their minds, they were impossible to change.

"Find out where it's from. Who made it. That's the easiest way to get answers," David said. He didn't expect those answers would illuminate anything to do with Tasker Bay's sudden crime spree, but he could admit that the game had a certain kind of pull he'd never experienced before. It couldn't hurt. "Just don't be pushy, and don't do anything you know you shouldn't. You aren't police. Or private investigators. You're kids. So just . . . act accordingly."

David spent the drive over to the Casey house putting what Ro and Andi had told him out of his mind, while walking through the uncomfortable conversation he was about to have. Given the severity of the crime, he was certain the family would involve a lawyer before he could get too deep into questioning Mark. He might simply be turned away at the door. But with the body identified, he felt a sense of momentum. Anything he could glean from Mark would be better than nothing, which is what he had at present.

Mark's parents, Mary and Roger, were better off than a lot of Tasker Bay's longtime residents but by no means wealthy. Roger ran a boat repair shop by the dock, and after years of managing the Tasker Bay Savings and Loan, Mary had found work as an office manager for Bob Colson at his real estate development firm, Bayview Holdings. This had afforded them a new, larger than average home, nicer cars, and, for Mary Casey, one of two seats on the town council *not* filled by newcomers.

As he approached the front door, David could hear voices inside. *Christ,* he thought, *they have company.*

Ringing the bell, he took a step back. Roger opened the door. He had a frame like his son's, buried under the strata of middle age, and his face tightened when he saw David.

"Afternoon, Roger. Would you mind stepping out for a moment?"

"Is there a problem, Sheriff?"

"That's actually why I was thinking you and I might—" David tripped over his own words as he caught sight of Cliff Young passing by behind Roger. "Sorry." He tried to continue but needed to understand what he'd walked into first. "Sorry. Again. *Was that Cliff Young?*"

Roger nodded, exhaling sharply. "I suppose *that's* why you're here. Cliff and his parents came by a little while ago and said Cliff wanted to bury the hatchet. The boys are fine. You're not going to hear anything else about what happened."

"That's, uh, good. Good to hear," David said, nodding. "I still think it'd be better if we talked out here."

Growing annoyed, Roger stepped out.

"I suppose you heard about the body we pulled out of Peck Creek?" David asked. Roger nodded but didn't have anything to add. "The autopsy was conducted this morning, and we have strong reason to believe it was strangled before someone dumped it in the creek. I'm not saying there's anything to this, but the marks on that body's neck are damn near identical to the marks on Cliff's. That your boy left."

Roger stared in disbelief. "What are you saying?"

"I'd like to know where Mark was a week ago Thursday. And if it's all right with you, I'd like to talk with him about it myself."

"Wait. You think—what? That my son did *what*?"

"I'm asking where he was, I'm explaining why I want to know, and right now that's it."

"Right now." Eyes burning, Roger flung open the door and turned, barking, "Mark!"

"Hey, Sheriff," Mark offered as he approached. "How's Ro?"

"The sheriff needs to ask you something," Roger interjected, brusque.

"Ro's fine, Mark. I'll tell him you asked. Can you tell me where you were last Thursday night?" David asked.

"I was with Cliff," Mark said. "We were at the arcade for a while. His house after. Then I came home."

"About what time was that?"

"When I got back? A little after midnight." Mark shot a glance at his dad. "It's supposed to be eleven thirty."

"Your dad said Cliff's here?" David asked.

Nodding, Mark turned and called inside. "Yo, Cliff!"

"For fuck's sake," Roger spat as he pushed past David, walking to the far end of the porch. He needed to put some distance between them, his patience rapidly depleting.

"Hey, Sheriff Kemp," Cliff said as he approached.

His neck was still badly bruised, voice hoarse. *Why the hell are you here after what he did?* David thought. "Cliff, I was wondering if you'd tell me what you were doing last Thursday night?"

"Last Thursday, uh . . ." Cliff started but trailed off, glancing at Mark. Mark went to speak, but David half raised a hand, needing to hear from Cliff without any influence. "We were at the arcade.

Me and Mark. Then we went to my place and watched . . . I don't know. Nothing really, just flipped around."

"Wrestling," Mark said.

Cliff nodded. "Yeah, for a little while."

"Did you boys see anyone else you knew that night?"

"Yeah. Ro. Laurel. A lot of people," Cliff said. "We kind of got into it with somebody over cutting in line for a game, and Ro broke it up."

It wasn't too far off from the version of events Andi and Ro had told David earlier that morning, but it wasn't the same, either. Cliff seemed to be omitting details—namely, that they tried beating up a girl—that would've painted them as more aggressive. Less reasonable.

"What games do you two usually play while you're there?" The question was odd, not the kind you'd expect a cop to ask, and for a moment it threw both boys. David hadn't planned on asking, but Ro and Andi were on his mind. And again, it couldn't hurt.

"I think you've heard enough," Roger said, stomping back across the porch.

"Roger. I just—"

"Said enough too." Roger turned to the boys. "Inside. Now."

As Mark and Cliff retreated, Roger leaned into David's face. "I don't give a shit about the gun, the badge. Any of it. If you *ever* come here again asking questions about my boy and a *dead body*, I'll put your ass in a goddamned wheelchair."

CHAPTER 13

DECIDING IT WAS BEST TO DIVIDE AND CONQUER, ANDI LOGGED BACK ONTO USENET to see if she'd received any other replies, while Ro studied a sign-in sheet Andi had swiped on their way out of Rachel's office. She figured Ro would be better at putting faces with names, and she was right, as he quickly ID'd dozens of people who'd been part of the crowd obsessing over *Polybius*.

Andi had taken David's words to heart—if they wanted answers, whoever created the game would probably have them. Maybe she was talking to them now, over Usenet, and just didn't know it. *How could 1077NE know any of this? Why did they seem so alarmed, so adamant about getting rid of the game?* Earlier that night, she'd composed a follow-up, posting it in the private chat 1077NE had created.

FROM: AndiDVT

The cabinet was bought at auction in San Jose. There are no markings to indicate who made it or where, and there are no copyright notices on it or the attract screen. I want to learn more about it. What else can you tell me? And can you offer proof to explain how you know all of this? Could we speak on the phone?

A new message was waiting for her.

FROM: 1077NE

I'm sorry but I can't give you my number. Based on your original thread describing the display I assume you opened up the cabinet. You can find my initials etched into the aquadag coating on the CRT, beneath the gasket that covers the flyback transformer (top center on the back). "NE."

I am/was the founder of Sinneslöchen. The display was designed and custom-built by a small team that I lead and was the reason Sinneslöchen was created. It was not a game company, and I did not program the game; it was an optics research and development firm.

Sinneslöchen was acquired and to be clear, the company and the game are not in any way mine. But I know the people who acquired Sinneslöchen would not want Polybius playable on your floor. And I know they would take action to make sure it was removed if they found out. I want to be as blunt as possible about this: the game is not safe to play. Some of the patterns displayed by the screen can trigger seizures. This opens players up to harm and your shop to liability. I understand that you're curious, and my last reply was vague. I hope I've given you enough information for you to trust me. I can't give any more. Please. Remove it.

As she clicked the lock on the door of her practice, Rachel didn't bother retreating to her office to unwind, slumping down on a waiting room couch instead. She was exhausted. The crush of patients with vague ailments and the intense way they reacted to *everything* around them was taking a toll. The best she'd been able to do was to prescribe Valium for a few of them. But the pharmacy was already out, and good luck getting more during what had turned into monsoon season.

She still had one more job to do, before she could cut the lights and head home. Andi and Ro's theory had thrown her for a loop. Crazy as it was, it wasn't so different from the working theory she'd been developing since leaving the mortuary that morning, that something in Tasker Bay's environment was to blame for the strange turn the town had taken.

She picked up the phone at reception, then dialed the office of a med school friend who worked as an infectious disease specialist at the Centers for Disease Control's office in Sacramento.

She noticed the box of Halloween decorations tucked under the reception desk. There hadn't been time to put them up, and October was almost over. *Maybe this will all turn out to be the world's worst prank,* she thought, as the phone rang and rang.

It was after hours, and the call was eventually routed to an answering service. "Molly, hi, it's Rachel. Winston. I know this is really out of the blue, but I'm hoping you can give me some perspective. I've had over a hundred people come through my office in the last week. They're all outwardly healthy, but they're exhibiting these extreme emotional swings with, I'd say, half of them experiencing some kind of accompanying physical outburst. Screaming fits, aggression, sensitivity to light or touch or sound. I'm wondering if there isn't something I should look for in terms of the environment or the food supply that could cause something like this. I can get better data and a breakdown of the symptoms to you, but I'd really appreciate any thoughts you have. I'm just trying to understand what's going on."

While she knew she shouldn't have been, Andi was still surprised at the sixty-plus crowd mobbing *Polybius* when she arrived for work that Friday after school. There was a home football game that night at West Bay, which usually meant the shop was empty. But things had changed.

Right away she found Mal's stoner friend and off-the-books part-time employee Patrick struggling to clear a jam from the register. He looked beyond harried. Sensing people had been waiting awhile, Andi motioned him out of the way so she could take a look. Patrick gladly stepped aside.

As a child, Patrick had overheard an aunt describe him to his mother as having a cloud over him. To look at him made you feel a little sorry, or sad. The fact that his mother hadn't pushed back had stuck, and had colored his perception of himself from then on. Capable of more introspection and deeper thought than he was ever given credit for, Patrick understood that this damaged self-image informed his and Mal's relationship. It was why he let Mal walk all over him. It was also why he'd topped out, at age thirty-four, as a part-time handyman who moonlighted at an arcade. The artificial limits his lack of self-confidence imposed upon him had, over the years, calcified into something more real. He knew he'd never try for anything greater in life, because he'd convinced himself it'd be a waste of his and others' time if he did.

It took Andi all of thirty seconds to clear the jam by pulling off the drawer face then forcing a stray bill weight back into place. Sometimes she wondered how Patrick made a living doing *anything*. Stowing the tool kit, she left him to fend for himself so she could find Mal and lay into him for being such a shitty boss and bad friend.

As she stepped into the back, she found him seated in the middle of the room in such a way that he still had a view of the shop floor. He wore a heavy coat and gloves and had the windows open, keeping the back room noticeably colder than the rest of the shop.

"Patrick looks like he's about to have an aneurysm. What are you doing?" Andi asked.

Mal wouldn't even acknowledge her.

She looked him over, trying to figure out whether he was just being an asshole, or if something was genuinely wrong. "Mal?"

As she started toward him, he sprang upright, chair clattering over behind him. Andi froze. Her eyes darted over him, looking for the .38—thankfully, she didn't see it. Raising a hand, she took a step back. "I was just making sure you were okay."

Mal continued ignoring her as he bent down to right the chair, gritting his teeth when he gripped it as if in pain. The whole time his eyes barely broke from their view of the shop floor, where *Polybius*'s glowing screen was visible.

"What's up with the windows? And the coat? Are you sick?" Andi asked, glancing around.

Mal seemed to think about it for a moment before finally looking at Andi and nodding slightly.

"Maybe you should go home," she said.

Mal didn't respond.

Giving up, Andi crisscrossed the room, shutting the windows before heading back onto the floor.

Once Andi was gone, Mal slowly flexed his gloves, wincing as the burned skin they concealed pulsed with pain.

Having wandered away unannounced from her shift at her parents' store, Laurel again found herself drawn to Home Video World, staring through its plateglass facade at *Polybius*. Unlike the crowd inside swarming the cabinet, she had no desire to play or even be near the game. It was enough to observe it from afar, to allow the light that seemed to pulse ever brighter from the display to wash over her.

"Laurel? Hey. *Laurel.*"

It took Andi calling to her repeatedly to pull her out of her trance.

Andi rolled a trash can to the corner, then walked over, taking in the sight of Laurel. She was soaked to the bone, as if she'd been there all night.

As she glanced around, looking for context or a clue as to why she was there, Andi caught a glimpse of *Polybius* through the window. Laurel's eyes were locked on it, just like Mal's. "What are you doing out here?" Andi finally asked.

"What are you doing out here?" Laurel parroted, staring dead-eyed at Andi long enough to raise the hair on the back of her neck.

As Andi took a step back, Laurel scoffed, then started to laugh. Andi forced a smile and waited for Laurel to stop, watching the same dreamy veil descend as she grew quiet.

Andi waited a moment longer, making sure Laurel was done. "Seriously, what are you doing? You're soaked. Do you want to come in?"

"No." *Isn't that obvious?* Laurel wondered.

"Were you . . . ?" Andi turned toward *Polybius*, Laurel's eyes following. After a moment Andi looked back, watching as she stared at the screen, standing impossibly still. Stepping around to block her view, she wondered if Laurel's senses would return if she couldn't see the screen.

Andi found it hard to stand face-to-face, the focus in Laurel's eyes so intense it was unnerving. But she finally started to move, parts of her body coming loose in waves.

Satisfied she was "there" enough for a conversation, Andi asked, "Why were you looking at that game?"

"I have to chase it," Laurel said, forming her thought along the way, "to understand."

Not following, Andi pressed in a different direction. "How do you . . . feel when you see it?"

"It gets clearer," Laurel replied, voice flat.

"What does?" Andi asked. "What do you *see* when you look at it?"

Laurel shook her head. "You can't see it. You have to understand. I can't let it chase me anymore. I have to chase it."

She was talking in circles, and Andi was growing frustrated. "Laurel, you're not—"

Laurel shuddered—she could feel it again. Clarity. Sudden, like a bolt of lightning. With a breathless "sorry" she left, climbing into her mother's car and driving off. Whatever Andi was saying as she called after, it wasn't important.

Winding through roads being swallowed by standing water, Laurel finally turned into the parking lot for Paulson's, the chain poised to put her parents' store out of business.

Situated as a convenient last stop for Silicon Valley commuters on their way into Tasker Bay, in less than a year it had siphoned off nearly two-thirds of the revenue that Greene's used to bring in. For a long moment Laurel stared at its sprawling facade. Just looking at it pissed her off.

For half an hour, she aimlessly wandered every aisle end to end before finding herself in front of a set of double doors marked EMPLOYEES ONLY. She stared, gradually aware that there was no one around to stop her from walking through them. Which is what she proceeded to do.

Ro arrived at Home Video World an hour after Andi had run into Laurel. The two of them held down the counter, waiting out the crowd so they could reopen the cabinet and check for the initials NE. She made a point to position Ro's seat to keep *Polybius* out of his eyeline.

Andi told Ro about her strange encounter with Laurel, unable to shake how disconnected from reality she'd seemed. "She talked about it like a puzzle. Like it was *there*, but she couldn't *see* it. Then she just took off."

Ro was listening, but he was also fiddling with a metal spike near the register where Andi impaled carbon receipts from video rentals. An idea hit him suddenly. "Where'd Mal buy it—the game?"

Andi's eyes widened—she hadn't thought of that. "I don't remember the name, but there should be an invoice." Ducking down, she rifled through the mess beneath the counter—what she was looking for wasn't there. Andi thought for a moment, finally glancing over her shoulder at Mal, still camped out in back of the shop.

"I think I know where it is," she finally said. Her tone suggested that Ro wouldn't like the answer.

Forty-five minutes later Ro was parked in the shadows around the block from Mal's bungalow, debating whether it was too late to back out of what he knew was a shit plan.

Andi hadn't pressured him. But she *had* made it clear that, if they were going to get ahold of the accordion folder into which Mal stuffed all his receipts—including, she hoped, the invoice from the day *Polybius* was delivered to Home Video World—now was their best shot. Mal wasn't just going to hand it over. He'd snapped at her for going near it before, leading her to believe he must have kept notes in there on his back-alley customers. If the folder wasn't under the counter or on his desk where it normally lived, he'd have taken it home.

She couldn't leave her shift, and someone needed to keep an eye on Mal, so it was going to be up to Ro. And Ro *would* be walking in, not kicking down the door or breaking a window—Andi knew where Mal kept a spare key. She'd heard Patrick mention it a while back and, knowing just how lazy Mal was, doubted that he ever bothered refreshing its hiding spot.

Still believing this was a mistake, Ro climbed down from his Land Cruiser and started toward Mal's. He found the key where Andi said it would be—hidden in a busted window frame around back—and let himself inside.

Ro's eyes watered and nostrils burned as he adjusted to the smell. The state of the interior matched the acrid odor. Everything was everywhere, as if a localized earthquake had hit and spilled Mal's life across the floor. An unsettling realization quickly dawned on him—*how could anyone ever find anything in this dump?*

Unwilling to let his nerves get the better of him now that he was inside, Ro began rooting around the house for the folder. He started with the obvious spots—dining room table, bookcases, cabinets—without success, growing more anxious with every failed attempt. Making his way deeper into the house, Ro found more endless clutter, with no sign of the folder.

Ending up in the kitchen, he checked cupboards, drawers, and corners but found nothing. On the verge of giving up, he spotted a detached garage through one of the kitchen windows.

Catching sight of Mal leaving the shop, Andi tried stepping in front of him.

"Hey. Mal. Mal? I was thinking, if you let me take *Polybius* off the floor for a few days, I could clone it. It's doing so well, having another one makes a lot of sense. I've probably got everything I need in back to do it." She knew she didn't sound like herself, too eager and placating, but she had to slow him down.

But Mal barely even acknowledged her as he wandered past the counter and out the front door. His grim expression suggested his mind was occupied, thoughts someplace dark. If he caught Ro rummaging around his house, there was no telling what he'd do.

Following him outside, Andi tried to slow him down once more. "Hey, are you leaving? We don't close for another hour and a half. I'm tired of running this place on my own. I'm going to quit, Mal. I'm sick of this shit. Are you listening? Hey!"

Her outburst rated a hollow look back over his shoulder, but Mal still didn't take the bait and just kept on toward his truck.

With no idea where Mal was going, Andi raced back in, grabbed the phone, and started calling his house, but the line just kept ringing. She didn't know Mal had ripped the line out of the wall in a random, rage-fueled fit the night before.

And neither did Ro, who wasn't near the phone anymore, anyway. The rain blew in sheets as he locked the back door, replaced the spare key, then hustled to the garage. Finding a side door left unlocked, he ducked into the darkened space.

With his bearings thrown by the lack of light, he banged straight into a workbench strewn with tools that clanged to the concrete floor about as loudly as anything could. Finally spotting a pull chain, Ro yanked it and breathed a sigh of relief. The garage was somehow messier than the house. There was no way anyone would notice what was or wasn't on that workbench, let alone scattered across the floor.

The faint overhead light didn't help much, but it was better than nothing. He searched, checking a wall's worth of rusted metal cabinets but finding only repurposed glass jars filled with random fasteners and tools that looked like they hadn't been touched in years.

Resigned to failure, he started to leave just as the yellow glow of headlights pierced the seams of the garage door—someone was pulling into the driveway. Panic seized Ro as he realized it was most likely Mal. *Why didn't Andi call like we planned?* As the car creaked to a stop, Ro reached up, cut the light, then stumbled over to and quietly closed the side door. He had no idea if he'd been seen and no idea of where in the darkened maze he could actually hide. As he waited for his eyes to adjust to the lack of light, he could hear the engine cut off. Spotting a few faint points of light along the back wall, he moved toward them, the outline of a blacked-out window slowly taking shape as he inched closer.

Thinking he'd seen the interior light flicker off inside the garage, Mal was unnerved. He needed painkillers, and not the crap they sold at the supermarket. All he wanted to do was duck inside, swallow a handful of pills, then head back to the shop to play *Polybius*.

It had become the only respite from the anxiety he felt building inside him. But he had secrets to keep and couldn't afford anyone snooping around, so his meds—and the game—would have to wait.

He made his way inside the garage and pulled the chain, finding the space empty. Had he been a step quicker, he would've caught the window on the back wall being quietly lowered shut from outside.

Crouching beneath the window in the rain, Ro heard the door shut then crept along the side of the garage, peering out to see Mal cross the backyard and head inside through the back door.

Staying low, Ro moved onto the driveway. The sound of the back door swinging open forced him down and into cover next to the passenger-side door on Mal's truck. He listened as garbage can lids rattled. *At least he's taking out the trash,* Ro thought, trying not to panic.

As the back door snapped shut once more, Ro peered over the edge of the passenger window toward the house. He had a chance to slip back down the block toward his car, but something inside the truck caught his eye: a tattered accordion folder.

Ro tried the passenger door—locked. So close to what he'd come for, he couldn't walk away. Steeling his nerves, he darted around the truck. In full view of a bay window jutting out from the side of the home, he grasped the driver-side handle. Locked too. *Fuck.*

Quickly ducking back around into cover on the passenger side, Ro pulled off his jacket and balled it around his fist. The rain was crashing down—maybe Mal wouldn't hear him breaking the truck's window. While his mind assessed and reassessed the risk, his hand sailed and shattered the glass. He reached inside and popped the lock, opened the door, grabbed the folder, and took off down the drive.

The noise drew Mal back outside. Seeing the truck's dim interior lights glowing, he hurried over to find the passenger window broken and the door ajar. Hustling to the end of his driveway he scanned the street up and down, but all he saw was rain and darkness.

Ro headed back toward town, his heart still pounding in his chest. He kept checking his rearview mirror, expecting to see Mal's headlights racing after him. He caught a break as he ran into a long stream of traffic leaving West Bay High. Blending into the crowd gave him peace of mind, but something else was off. Ro checked his watch—it was way too early for the football game to be over. As he passed the school, he could see a trio of red-and-blue rack lights flashing near the field.

CHAPTER 14

HALF AN HOUR EARLIER, DAVID WAS STROLLING AROUND THE FENCED-IN PERIMETER of West Bay High's modest football field while a smaller-than-average crowd cheered on their hometown Titans. He'd spent a lot of nights in the rain like this over the years, but it had been easier when Ro was on the field. Now it was just another beat. He told himself the weather had deterred the crowd, but in the back of his mind he wondered whether it had to do with the ongoing torrent of bad news. Whether people no longer felt safe around one another.

The incessant rain had transformed the field into a morass, and frustrations on both sides had been building since kickoff. The visiting San Rafael Bulldogs had played the Titans to a standstill, with a series of late hits and skirmishes after the whistle enflaming tension on the field and in the stands.

West Bay had returned after halftime possessed by a kind of grim determination, willing to push the Bulldogs' buttons and goad them into mistakes and frustration if they couldn't outplay them. Clipping, horse collaring, chop blocking. Penalties were mounting on both sides, keeping the game in a kind of limbo where neither side was advancing, but both were building up nasty heads of steam. Cliff Young single-handedly broke through three offensive linemen to level the Bulldogs' quarterback and force a fumble that he managed to scoop up before finally being dragged down at the twenty-yard line in Bulldog territory. As West Bay's offense jogged onto the field, in position to make a move, energy began coursing through the crowd.

The Titans' quarterback sailed the ball, the wide receiver managing to snag it and plant a foot before stumbling out of bounds. One of the Bulldogs' outside linebackers, having watched his side roughhoused into a turnover, executed a brutal late hit and sent the Titans' player skidding across the rain-slicked grass and into a fence ringing the infield.

Incensed, West Bay fans were screaming bloody murder at the referees, who hurried toward the scene. But they were a step slower than Mark Casey. Rushing in, he gripped the Bulldogs' outside linebacker by his face mask, yanked him into the air, and hurled him a solid five feet across the field. It was such an incredibly brutal display of raw, angry power that for a moment no one knew how to respond.

But then players on both teams charged, clashing with whoever they could lay hands on. Mark slammed, swung, tossed bodies around the crowd, fighting his way to the center of the action as if his life depended on it. He grabbed a random Bulldog player and threw him to the ground, ripping his shoulder out of its socket, then kneeling and breaking his arm at the elbow.

At the same time fans were pouring down from the stands, massing at the fence that ringed the field. Most wanted to break up the scrum—protect their children—but a few were looking to join the fight. The fence quickly gave way, several people falling with it, trampled underfoot as the crowd surged forward.

David scrambled toward the brawl, desperate to break it up before it escalated further. He could see players who'd been knocked down trying to crawl clear, taking spikes to the back, air pressed from their lungs. "All units, to the field at West Bay, *now*!" he barked into his radio.

Sprinting past West Bay's dazed-looking principal, David grabbed and shook him awake. "Get on the PA and tell these people to get the hell out of here!" Charging ahead, he joined a line of coaches, referees, and level-headed locals trying in vain to pull the warring factions apart.

As the principal's shaky voice crackled over the PA system, ordering everyone off the field, lights and sirens began drawing near. None of it mattered. Bodies were still colliding, crashing to the ground. David tripped over someone from the stands, laid out and unconscious with bloody gashes from players' cleats crisscrossing their face, then struggled back to his feet. Pulling his revolver, he fired two shots into the air, sending enough people running from the field that it looked like he could re-establish control.

Mal's number just kept ringing. Eventually Andi gave up trying to warn Ro, stewing behind the counter while she waited for him to return as planned. Once she'd cleared out the crowd and locked the doors, she wedged herself back inside *Polybius*'s service door and confirmed—using a flashlight and small mirror stuck to the end of a pencil with a piece of chewing gum—that NE's initials *were* scrawled on the edge of the display as promised.

Relief flooded her when she heard Ro knocking at the front door, and the two headed for her house after, to dig through the contents of the accordion folder. Upon arrival they found a note from Rachel—she'd been called to an emergency at West Bay's football field and didn't know when she'd be back. Knowing they had the place to themselves, Andi and Ro settled on the floor in the living room and dumped the contents of the folder. Hundreds of individual papers, years of receipts, notes, and God knows what else stared back at them, filed without rhyme or reason.

"Ugh. Hang on," Andi said, disappearing into the kitchen for a few moments before re-emerging with a six-pack.

"You sure your mom's not going to miss those?"

"They've been in the back of the fridge since we moved in," she said as she tossed him a beer. "Take a pile and start looking. The delivery date was October twentieth."

Both dug in. The work was tedious, looking for a date stamp that was never in the same place twice and sometimes wasn't there at all. Once they'd filtered out everything that wasn't a receipt, Andi started looking for purchases out of San Jose, while Ro searched for anything dated within the past month. They'd been picking through for an hour and a half and finished off the very stale six-pack when Ro struck gold. He handed Andi a pink sheet of carbon paper and watched as she looked it over.

"This has to be the one. Gordon-Smith Antiquities. Sparrow and Myrtle in Palo Alto." Hopping up, she grabbed the phone and dialed, holding up the receiver so Ro could listen too. A prerecorded message began to play. "You've reached Gordon-Smith Antiquities.

We host auctions every Tuesday, Thursday, and Saturday, beginning at ten thirty a.m. Please call back during our normal hours of operation to—"

The message cut out as Andi hung up. "Mal's bought cabs from them before. I know where it is. We'll drive down. Tomorrow."

They weren't close, but closer. They'd pulled something off, together, and the electricity of the moment grabbed hold. Andi leaned forward and kissed Ro, the two of them sinking to the floor. As paper crinkled underneath, Ro suddenly felt uneasy and pulled away. "Wait, wait. I saw the inside of Mal's place. I don't think we want to be on top of these."

Breathless and flustered at the interruption, Andi stood, then helped Ro to his feet—only to push him down onto the couch. As she climbed on top of him, Ro flashed a hand at her. "We should probably wash our—" But she kissed him before he could finish the thought, and a moment later it was forgotten.

David had just laid down on the shabby couch in his office when the phone rang. He shot up and stumbled his way over to answer. Slivers of daylight crept past the blinds covering the sole window, suggesting it was sometime early Saturday morning. He heard Clarence Meeks on the other end of the line.

"I heard about the brawl. Everybody okay?" Clarence asked, voice leavened with concern.

"We wound up airlifting seven over to Petaluma that Rachel couldn't treat. Medivac barely got here through the storm. There were a lot of broken bones. I know one was still unconscious when they took him—a kid, from San Rafael. It was bad. I don't . . ." *Know where to start*, David was going to say, but exhaustion got the better of him, and his words just drifted away. He was starting to wonder if he'd ever get a full night's sleep again.

"Jesus. Well, I hate to be the bearer of bad news, but Ed Sanko's death *wasn't* an accident. I found trauma in three regions consistent with gunshot wounds. I wasn't able to recover any of the slugs, but they were smaller caliber. Two were through-and-throughs; the third I think was removed."

Still processing the fact that he had *another* murder on his hands, David took a moment to realize what Clarence was saying. "Wait. You said *removed*?"

"Dug out of the chest cavity," Clarence said. "I didn't pinpoint the wounds until I was almost done with the autopsy. I'm going back over everything this morning to make sure I didn't miss anything else."

"I'll get back over to the Bottle Shoppe to see what's left. Between the fire and the rain, it's going to be tough finding anything. Especially a bullet. Just keep me posted." David hung up and went to pull on his department button-up but found himself staring at his sheriff's star. He wasn't afraid of introspection, but this wasn't that. It was doubt, straight up, about the job he'd done the last couple of weeks. He'd lost control, and more and more people were paying the price. Carl Delano, Michael Newton, Ed Sanko. Things just kept ramping up, and David couldn't see a way to regain control. But he couldn't stop searching for one either. He finished dressing and grabbed his coat, ready to head back out into a storm that showed no sign of letting up.

But before he could, the phone rang again—Ro was on the line. "Dad?"

David brightened a little, hearing his son's voice. "Hey. You good?"

"Yeah. Andi and I are going to drive down to Palo Alto. We found the auction house that sold Mal the game. And an address for the company that made the display."

David thought for a moment, trying to choose his words carefully. "Ro, I'm not sure—"

He didn't get to use them—Ro was quick to interrupt. "I'm not asking whether I can go. I just wanted you to know where I'd be."

"Well," David said, knowing his son wasn't going to be talked out of it. "Just . . . be careful."

"We will. Once we get out of Tasker Bay, the roads won't be as bad."

"That's not—obviously, drive safe. Especially with someone else in the car. But I meant when you're talking to these people. Don't lead them. Don't say more than you need to. Ask a question and let them talk. Don't interrupt, don't say anything until they stop. And whatever you two know or *think* you know, keep the idea that the game's . . . dangerous to yourself. People are always reluctant to talk. And you're kids. If they think you're crazy, forget it."

A few hours later, Andi and Ro were inside Gordon-Smith's lobby, a trendy space trimmed in white and chrome. Andi and Ro were younger than the other buyers but a few of the faces didn't look much older, and Andi's minimalist style fit right in.

While she lingered at the front desk, looking for someone to speak with about the invoice, Ro waded through a mix of office managers, start-up CEOs, and hobbyists who'd come in search of a deal. Photos of the items up for auction, tacked to boards and placed on easels, ringed the space. As Ro looked them over, he passed one display that was smaller and set back from the rest. Sitting on a table alongside a bouquet of flowers, it held a newspaper clipping, an obituary for a woman named Mila Novik. Twenty-three years old at the time of her death, she looked pretty and youthful in the photo featured.

Ro was about to walk over and join Andi when something in the corner of the memorial for Mila caught his eye. Someone had tacked *another* article behind the one on display, with the headline POLICE INVESTIGATE PALO ALTO MURDER-SUICIDE. The subheadline read LOCAL BUSINESS OWNER, THOMAS MAZZY, MURDERS FOUR BEFORE KILLING HIMSELF.

Mazzy. The name was familiar, but Ro couldn't place it. He scanned the article and obituary again, but none of the details clicked. Spotting Andi searching for him in the crowd, he waved her over. "What happened?" he asked.

"I said we were having problems with the cabinet and wanted to find out about the manufacturer so we could try and have it serviced," Andi told him. "They just kept saying they didn't warranty anything. All they'd give me was the name, Sinneslöchen. Which obviously doesn't help."

Ro glanced around, resigned to the fact that they were leaving empty-handed. "Let's try Sinneslöchen's old address, I guess."

"What is that?" Andi asked, nodding at the obituary.

"Memorial. She worked here," Ro said, indicating the obituary before flipping it over to reveal the story on Mazzy's arrest. "Somebody killed her."

Andi leaned in for a closer look. "God, that's awful. Look at her. She looks so young."

"Do you remember hearing about this?" Ro tapped the article on the murder. "On the news, or in the *Trader* or something? I feel like I know that name."

"No. I don't think I . . ." Andi trailed off at seeing the name Mazzy. She dug in her bag and pulled out the *Polybius* invoice, scanning the faint details on the carbon until she found it—*Mazzy Asset Management*, scribbled under a line item labeled "Procurement."

Stuffing the paper in Ro's hand, she leaned in to read the clipping, zeroing in on part of the copy that read *owner of a Palo Alto salvage company, Mazzy Asset Management.*

Andi pulled the article loose from the easel and stuffed it into her pocket. "Let's go," she said as she started for the door, Ro on her heels.

They hustled through the rain and climbed into Ro's Land Cruiser. Andi scanned the text. "It says he killed everybody he worked with, went to her house—that woman—took her hostage, killed her, then killed himself. No note, no reason." Andi set the article on the dash, unsettled by the contents.

Ro picked it up. "Is there a date? When did it happen?" For a moment, he searched. "October fifth."

"After the cabinet sold," Andi added.

Setting the article down, Ro let his gaze drift, suddenly unable to look at Andi. "You think he played it?" he finally asked.

She did but didn't want to say it, because if she was right, the implications for Ro—for others in Tasker Bay—were beyond grim. "We need to find out more."

Ro fished a map off the dashboard, homed in on their location, then walked his fingers to a spot nearby. "There's a library a couple of miles from here. I'll drop you off. See what else you can find out about Mazzy. I'll try his old office. And Sinneslöchen's. Divide and conquer."

Mal dragged a chair from his kitchen into the living room and positioned it next to a window so he could watch the street without being seen.

Eating and sleeping had become secondary concerns to an increasingly pathological paranoia, which saw him staring out the window for hours on end, convinced someone was coming for him. Or waiting for him to try to skip town, at which point he'd be pinched for *something*. That "something" would inevitably become something else, and then something else, until every sordid act in Mal's past up to now would come roaring back to haunt him.

So he sat, waiting for an uncertain point in time in which he'd somehow know it was safe enough to take everything he'd skimmed from Home Video World, plus what he'd stolen from the Bottle Shoppe, and head out of town with no looking back. Only he didn't know when that would be, or how he would even know. All he had was a belief that the voice inside his head, that had been driving him to acts of greater and greater criminality, would eventually light the way.

Pain from the burns covering his hands started pulsing. As he shuffled into the bathroom, he carefully removed the dressing from both hands, intending to rewrap them. Swallowing another mouthful of painkillers, he locked eyes with himself in the mirror and experienced a brief moment of clarity. It had been days since the fire. A week since he'd been questioned about the horses. Yet here he was, afraid and puttering around his house. He'd even sawed the stock and much of the barrel off his father's weathered Ruger Model 44, making it easier to conceal in the event he had to make a run for it. But despite everything he'd done, and the paranoia infecting his every waking thought, so far nothing had come back on him.

Nothing.

Before he could determine the meaning of this revelation, the sound of a knock at his front door froze him. He stood there, listening, hoping he was imagining things.

He wasn't—another knock, louder and more urgent.

He made his way toward the door. Assuming this was someone from the sheriff's office, he faced a choice—allow them to get the drop in the event they'd come to arrest him, or take control and cut them down first. Lifting the Ruger off the floor, he inched closer to the door and waited.

More knocking. Mal raised the rifle in response, training it on the door. The knocking suddenly stopped, replaced by a voice. "Mal. You there? It's Patrick. What the hell's going on, man?"

Hearing his friend's voice instead of David's, Charlie's, or Jeff's did nothing to calm Mal's nerves. His finger, resting on the trigger, began tightening.

"Come on, man. I see your car. I just want to make sure you're okay." Milling on the front porch, Patrick waited for a reply. "You know the shop's not open, right? There's a bunch of people outside waiting to get in. Somebody's gonna break another window. I tried calling to tell you, but it just kept ringing."

The lock clicked and the door opened a few inches, a chain still in place. Mal peered out through the crack. "Andi didn't show?"

Patrick returned to his spot in front of the door. "Guess not, no. You, uh, want to open the door?"

Mal stepped partially into view. "What'd it look like at the shop?"

"A bunch of people standing around, waiting in their cars and shit. It seemed like they were kind of pissed." Mal still hadn't undone the chain, clearly uneasy. "Hey, for real, are you okay?" As Patrick sidestepped to get a better look at Mal, his eyes shot wide open. Not only was Mal still holding the gun, he'd forgotten to re-bandage his hands. "Mal, why are you holding a gun— Holy shit, what happened to your hands?"

A cold sweat rushed over Mal's body, and his eyes darted down. Raw, blistered skin could be seen between bloodstained strips of loosely wrapped gauze. He knew it had already taken him too long to reply as his eyes drifted back up to meet Patrick's bewildered gaze, but the words just weren't there.

"Looks fucked-up," Patrick blurted out in a kind of involuntary verbal spasm. "How did you—" He stopped as Mal shut the door in his face. After a moment the chain rattled off, and the door swung all the way open, Mal stepping aside to allow Patrick to enter.

Patrick knew how Mal lived and had been to his place dozens of times over the years, but the level of chaos that greeted him this time was surprising. The way Mal was acting, the horrific state of his home, the gun—it was obvious something bad had happened.

Mal nodded toward the couch, then disappeared into the kitchen. Patrick sat and surveyed the room, eyes landing on the sawed-off Ruger, propped by the front door. He shifted uneasily at the sight of it, mind flashing back to the time Mal had badgered him into going hunting. Patrick drank himself into a blackout the night before to avoid it.

He heard the refrigerator open, Mal rattling around inside a drawer, and two caps popping off. A moment later he emerged—in gloves—with two bottles of beer, placing one in front of Patrick.

Retreating to the chair he'd been using to keep watch, Mal downed half his drink in one gulp. "You hear about the fire?" he asked, keeping his eyes trained out the window.

Patrick shook his head in sympathy. "Yeah. Poor old Ed."

"I was at the shop when it started. I saw Ed was there, so I tried running in. Burned my hands on the door. Whole place caught like a minute later," Mal said, still staring out the window.

"Fuck, man. Good on you for trying, at least." Patrick raised then tipped his bottle. *Cheers to you.* Mal didn't notice. "Are you doing all right? Your hands? Any—anything else?" They didn't have this sort of relationship, and Patrick wasn't sure how to suddenly navigate it, but something was so obviously off that he had to try.

Mal shrugged, then shifted a little so he could look Patrick in the face. "Fucking sheriff. He came at me about the horses. Carl Delano's horses?" he asked, continuing off Patrick's nod. "Just making me nervous. And you see what's going on. All this crazy shit all at once. I don't want them around here. Anyone."

Mal cocked an eye at Patrick, who nodded—*made sense.* It didn't, but Patrick didn't think pushing Mal about anything right now was a very good idea.

"I don't know what Andi's deal is," Mal huffed. "Said something about quitting the other night. Somebody should go get the doors open. You mind?"

"Oh. Yeah. For sure." Patrick chugged what was left of his beer, puzzling over where to leave his empty given that everything was covered by a pile of something else, and the trash can was spilling onto the floor. Finally, he nestled it upright between two cushions on the couch before walking to the door and grabbing the keys to the shop. He didn't want to be the one to open but didn't know what else to do. "Feel better, man."

Mal watched as Patrick climbed into his rusted-out Chevy and cranked the engine—again—until the piece of shit finally fired on and pulled away.

His mind flashed back to the moment before Patrick had knocked on his door. He'd broken a chain of thoughts that Mal had been clicking together, but the visit had actually reinforced what he had been starting to realize moments earlier in front of the bathroom mirror—that he can get away with this.

All of it.

CHAPTER 15

IN AN ISOLATED CORNER OF A SMALL PUBLIC LIBRARY, ANDI DROPPED A STACK OF newspapers from the last few weeks on a desk and set to work. She was looking for anything on Mila Novik and Mazzy Asset Management, something that could give her and Ro another thread to follow.

As she flipped through page after page, cheap ink staining the tips of her fingers, she found herself thinking about Ro. About whether he could become the next Thom Mazzy.

She cycled through the same questions, over and over, looking for some piece, an idea that could provide an answer. *Does everyone who plays the game wind up going crazy and killing at random? What about me? Should I be afraid of Ro? Should he be afraid of me?*

It didn't take long to find a series of in-depth reports on the killings. Police had first been alerted to the murders at Mazzy Asset Management's office by the owner of a neighboring business who'd found it strange when the Mazzy staff hadn't moved their cars the day the streets were regularly swept. Thinking he'd be saving everyone from a ticket, he instead found the front door unlocked and three of the company's four employees dead inside. They'd been beaten so savagely, per an onlooker's account, all three were carried out in pieces.

Thom Mazzy wasn't among the dead. That sent police to his home, then, after finding its interior destroyed but empty, on a hunt across the city. Mila had been reported missing by a coworker the day before her and Thom's bodies were discovered in an abandoned building. She'd been slowly tortured, subjected to extensive "ritualistic cutting," and left chained to a wall for all four days she was held captive. Portions of her tongue, fingers, and toes had all been removed and, at least at the time the story was reported, hadn't been found. Next to the room where Mila's body had been discovered, police found Thom Mazzy in a heap with his wrists slashed.

The awful details caromed around Andi's head. The terror Mila must've felt when she realized what was going to happen to her, the pain she must have suffered. The other victims' families, living with the knowledge their loved ones were *butchered*. People who'd known Thom described him as someone with a chip on his shoulder, a little bitter about ending up—as he was known to put it—"a garbageman." But that was it, they all said. There was no *real* venom inside him, nothing that could have possibly foreshadowed what happened.

Thom had, it came out, repeatedly asked Mila out and been turned down over the years. Reporters speculated that he'd grown obsessed.

But what finally triggered him? Andi wondered.

Roughing out a timeline with help from the date on Mal's delivery receipt, Andi figured that Mazzy Asset Management must have found and delivered *Polybius* to Gordon-Smith Antiquities just a few days before Thom snapped. Had he played? Could it cause that kind of extreme psychotic break, that fast?

The articles were starting to blend together, reiterating the same information plus or minus small details, illuminating nothing new. Feeling lost, Andi pushed herself away from the table and stared at the mess in front of her. Lots of pieces, no discernable whole.

She picked up another paper, finding yet another recounting of the crime. It was longer—part of a Sunday edition—and as she scanned the text, she saw a detail the other accounts hadn't touched on: a break-in at Gordon-Smith in the days preceding Mila's disappearance. The perpetrator, a man named Nicolas Engle—*initials NE*, Andi realized—was a San Jose resident and freelance engineer. He'd been apprehended by a security guard after breaking down Gordon-Smith's rear door. He was subsequently questioned in Mila's disappearance but cleared of any suspicion after her and Mazzy's bodies were found. According to sources with the Santa Clara Sheriff's Department, Engle had broken in to destroy an item—*an unspecified arcade game*—he'd claimed was dangerous. He'd come off like a tinfoil-hat loony.

To the reporter, it was just another strange detail in a story full of them. But if this was the person Andi had been in touch with over Usenet, 1077NE, then it made sense. This was why he'd been so adamant about shutting the cabinet down. He knew what it could make people do.

At the reference desk, Andi traded her stack of newspapers for a copy of the white pages, finding three San Jose residents listed under the name N. Engle.

After a long night spent setting broken bones and stitching lacerations at West Bay High's football field, Rachel was back to work first thing on Saturday, starting with a house call. She piloted her car, back on the road with a new battery she'd installed herself, down a narrow, waterlogged road toward the Purcell home. She knew the family: mother Elise, daughter Samantha, son William. And she'd heard the worry in Elise's voice when she'd phoned.

Both children were exhibiting symptoms that sounded like the other cases Rachel had been seeing, but Elise hadn't been able to get them out of the house and over to her office. Ten-year-old William had abruptly turned sensitive to light, while sixteen-year-old Sam wouldn't stop moving—pacing back and forth over the home's ancient floorboards at all hours, tapping her fingers and hands in a series of inscrutable, repeating patterns. According to Elise, Sam's fingertips had been worn raw by the repetitive motion, leaving traces of blood all over. Neither child was eating, sleeping. At this point, Elise wasn't either.

Being a single mother, Elise sometimes struggled to give her children the attention they deserved. She had to keep the lights on and, even with Sam finding after-school work at Greene's Market, still caught whatever extra shifts she could at the docks to try to make ends meet. She'd grown up in Tasker Bay, working with her fisherman father every summer to save up for a college education that never came to pass. Instead, Sam was born, and Elise's path in life was reset. So it was that, on many nights, the kids were left to fend for themselves. Thank God for that arcade, Elise often thought. At least there they couldn't get in much trouble.

Rachel was quietly alarmed by the state of things when she arrived at the Purcell home. Because of William's sudden sensitivity, Elise had not only drawn every shade but blacked out the windows with heavy wool blankets. She was keeping most of the light fixtures turned off too. Clearly distraught over the kids, Elise's nerves were compounded by the two days of work she'd missed as a result of their sudden, strange behavior.

Sam could be heard slowly stalking back and forth in the upstairs hallway, floorboards creaking in a staccato pattern over and over. The sound, coupled with the darkness cloaking everything, put Rachel on edge the moment she walked into the home.

Elise's thoughts poured out upon seeing her. "I don't know what I'm supposed to do. I can't leave them here like this. And I haven't used a sitter in years—Sam always does it. I don't even know who to call, and I— What if something happened when I was gone?"

"Can I see them?" Rachel asked. Elise nodded, casting an eye toward the stairs. Rachel realized too late that she wasn't coming with her.

As she ascended the darkened staircase, Rachel followed the wall with her hand to keep from stumbling. Despite trying to check her nerves, she could feel her skin growing cold, hairs on the back of her neck rising. This place, which days ago had been an ordinary home with an ordinary family, frightened her. As she reached the landing, she caught a glimpse of Sam stepping into a room at the far end of the hall, door closing behind her. Every instinct told her to turn around, but Rachel steeled herself. *These are children who need your help.* She stepped forward and knocked gently on a door adorned with a wooden sign featuring William's name.

If a few shafts of light made it past the makeshift barricades Elise had erected downstairs, she'd allowed no such margin for error on the upper floor. William's room may as well have been a tomb. Even then, with almost no light penetrating the dark space, the boy still sat in a corner with a sheet over top of him. Unsettled at the sight—he would've looked more at home on the street for Halloween—Rachel paused in the doorway.

"William? It's Dr. Winston. Your mom asked me to see how you're doing." Rachel waited for a response, but none came.

The makeshift shroud billowed with each breath. William raised his hands, vigorously rubbing his eyes through the sheet. Rachel could hear the fabric grating on his skin.

"I'm going to need some light to do that, okay?" She stepped into the darkened room. "I'm going to open these curtains a little and have you lift up the sheet."

Rachel carefully crossed the room and moved the blanket that was blacking out the window, parting the curtains just enough to faintly illuminate the space. The sheet covering William vibrated faster, his breathing accelerating as dim light filled the space. Realizing the boy needed a moment to adjust, Rachel took a seat on the floor opposite. "We can take our time, okay? Can you tell me what's been going on? How's your head feeling?"

"It hurts." William's already small voice, muted by the fabric, was barely audible.

"When did it start?" Rachel asked. No answer. "Does the light make it hurt worse? And being in the dark makes it better?"

She waited a moment, watching as William's breathing intensified even further. "William? Are you okay?"

"It's not a headache," he finally replied.

"Oh. Because your mom—"

"She doesn't know," William cut in, tone curt.

The sound of a door creaking open drew Rachel's attention toward the hall. Expecting to catch sight of Sam walking past, she instead heard the door close. Then open again. Then close. Rhythmically, every few seconds, over and over.

"It makes me see things I don't want to," he added, voice small and worried again.

Rachel turned back toward him, unsettled by his response. "What makes you see things?"

The boy could barely manage a response, nearly breaking into tears as he spoke over the sound of the door continuing to open, shut, open, shut. "I just want it to stop. I don't want to see it."

"What's 'it,' William? What are you seeing?" As Rachel asked the question, she gently lifted the sheet over his head. The skin around his eyes was puffy, raw from being obsessively rubbed. She stifled a gasp.

"Goddamn it, Samantha!" Elise's voice shrieked from downstairs. Rachel could hear her as she bounded up the stairs, saw the fear, agitation on her face as she stormed past William's room toward Sam's.

"I'll be right back, okay?" Rachel said as she rose from the floor. William immediately pulled the sheet back over his head and resumed rubbing his eyes.

Down the hall, Sam continued opening and closing, opening

and closing the door to her room. Grabbing the doorknob, Elise yanked it out of Sam's hand and slammed the door shut in her face. She'd reached her limit.

Rachel, now standing just down the hall, watched as Elise backed away, beginning to quietly sob. But before Rachel could even try to speak with her, Sam began ramming the door from inside with the full weight of her body. Again and again, backing up each time for a running start.

"Elise, I think maybe you should—" But before Rachel could finish her thought, Elise sprang forward and threw the door open, bouncing Sam hard off the other side and onto the floor.

Careening into her daughter's room, Elise began screaming as Sam staggered to her feet. "I want you to stop this. Now! Stop it stop it *stop it*!"

Sam shoved her mother back, Elise feebly grabbing at her to no avail, suddenly desperate for things not to escalate any further than they already had. Shoving with all her weight, Sam sent Elise out of her room and into the wall, the back of her head hitting so hard it cracked the plaster.

Quickly moving aside and allowing an unworried-looking Sam to glide past, Rachel hurried to Elise, who had slumped to the floor. The wall was ringed in blood where the back of her head had impacted.

"I'm fine," Elise said, the distant look in her eyes suggesting otherwise.

Rachel put a hand on her shoulder, reassuring but firm. "No, you're not. You might be concussed. I need to—"

"I said I'm fine!" Elise snapped as she shoved Rachel back and staggered to her feet.

From down the hall, shockingly loud in light of the fact that he could barely muster an audible response before, William shouted, "Stop drawing that!"

Both women turned toward the commotion. Not seeing Sam, Rachel assumed she'd gone into William's room and hurried back to head off another potential altercation. But she wasn't there, only William, who'd inched closer to the doorway to see what the fuss was about. "William, who are you talking to?" Rachel asked, following his eyes—just visible between the folds of the sheet still wrapped around him—toward the staircase.

"Stop drawing that. Stop drawing. I don't want to see that. Stop. Stop it!" he shouted.

The fear *and* fury in his disembodied voice shook Rachel to the point she backed out of his room. Hearing the stairs creak, she turned and followed the sound until she found Sam on the steps, descending one at a time, tracing a kind of runic shape along the wall with her bloodied fingertips over and over.

"Sam, what are you doing?" Rachel asked, voice shaky. It felt to Rachel like everything had suddenly, violently started falling apart.

No answer came as Sam reached the bottom of the staircase and disappeared into the house below. Rachel felt Elise push past her, racing downstairs after Sam, who was walking outside.

Rachel followed her. "Elise, can you—"

"Get out of my house," Elise snapped, not bothering to turn around.

"Y-you called me," Rachel stammered. "I came here to help you. And this is—"

"You're not. You're not helping. You're passing judgment on me. Telling me how to deal with my kids. *My* kids."

Rachel's mind raced. *What the fuck is going on?* "I'm not. Elise, honestly. But I think that—"

Elise whipped back toward Rachel. "Get out!" she screamed, before continuing after Sam. "Samantha, get back inside. Goddamn it, listen to me!"

Shell-shocked, Rachel didn't know what to do. Turning, glancing back at the door to William's room, she thought about returning to the boy to continue her examination. But everything about the situation felt off. Threatening. And Elise had sounded *very* certain.

Self-preservation outflanking duty, Rachel made a line for the door. It was a dangerous environment, and by the time she'd made it back to her car, she'd decided to report it to the sheriff's office. She could see Sam wandering along the edge of their property near the woods, finger whipping through the air in an inscrutable pattern, over and over. Elise stood on the porch, hand on her head, watching with no idea of what to do about any of it.

As she drove away from the home, Rachel glanced up in time to see the curtains being pulled shut inside William's room.

Having failed to learn anything at the former site of Sinneslöchen's office—the building was in the process of a remodel, and the handful of contractors working overtime knew nothing about the previous tenants—Ro was pulling up in front of Mazzy Asset Management's offices to try again.

His eyes were immediately drawn to the graffiti sprayed over its facade. "Murderer," "rapist," "freak," had been rendered in bloodred block letters. Windows were smashed and boarded over. A handful of bouquets, all rotting or dead, littered the entrance. It had a kind of final, almost apocalyptic quality to it. Whatever it had been, for a long time it would only be thought of as a place where innocent lives were ended.

Snatching up a Polaroid camera he'd grabbed off his dresser before they'd left town, thinking it seemed like the kind of thing that people conducting an investigation ought to have, Ro stepped out. After trying the front door and finding it locked, he followed a narrow alley between Mazzy's offices and a neighboring business and hopped a fence into a parking lot with access to a staff entrance. The knob was loose, and with a little force, Ro managed to nudge the door open, then stepped inside.

The police seemed to have removed anything of potential evidentiary value—files, invoices, receipts, personal effects. Ro walked carefully around splotches of dried blood that covered the carpet, stepping over a series of smaller, taped-off outlines that must not have been for bodies but . . . *parts.*

Increasingly overwhelmed by the oppressive atmosphere—stale air, dim light, bad vibes—he passed through the other rooms, all devoid of anything that might have given a window into Thomas Mazzy's state of mind. It was already looking like another dead end.

While there weren't placards on the doors, the last he came to lead into a larger personal office, the only one like it, which he assumed had once belonged to Thom. As with the rest, it had been emptied out. A desk, chair, phone, and empty filing cabinets were all that remained.

But scribbled on the walls, in what he assumed was blood, was a series of abstract shapes. Out of context, they could've been mistaken for something occult—runes or glyphs—but Ro recognized them as symbols seen on the cavern walls in *Polybius*. They covered the room floor to ceiling.

He wondered what the police had done to try to discern their meaning, surely failing to realize they were on full display in an arcade a couple of hours to the north. Thom Mazzy had clearly seen, almost certainly played, *Polybius*. And when he'd snapped, it had been on his mind. Perhaps, somehow, *in* his mind.

Ro began taking pictures with the Polaroid, documenting as many of the bloody symbols as possible. It was the clearest link yet between the game and someone suffering a mental break, and he wanted to be sure he had it down on record before—like Sinneslöchen's offices—Mazzy Asset Management's dark past was plastered over.

As the camera's shutter snapped and photos whirred from the exit slot, flash whining as it recharged, Ro could've sworn he saw something moving. One of the symbols that Thom had scrawled over the walls, a circle with curved lines radiating out and reaching upward, shuddered.

Lowering the camera, he watched, waiting to make sure his eyes had been playing tricks. The symbol didn't move. But on his periphery, another—a series of right angles cobbled together in such a way they looked like a primitive sketch of an insect—seemed to twitch.

As Ro's eyes whipped toward the phantom motion, a cold sweat started forming across his back, neck, chest. *I shouldn't be in here.*

Backing away, he stepped out into the hall. Breathing deep, trying to get ahold of himself, he started back toward the main office then froze. Shafts of dim, gray light filtering past the plywood sheets that covered shattered windows glanced off something standing in the distance. It towered, its head forced into a bow by the ceiling.

Ro recognized it immediately. *The figment.*

He could see its chest rising, falling, its bulk pushing briefly into the light before receding back into shadow. Deep, raspy breaths clawed their way out. *How is it breathing. How is it here?* Instinctively taking a step back, Ro froze as the figment took a thudding step forward.

Ro didn't know what to do, where to go, how *not* to provoke it any further. From the corner of his eye, he saw the Polaroid still dangling from his shoulder and slowly began leveling it. His index finder inched toward the shutter button. He wanted evidence of the figment, assuming he could survive its sudden appearance.

As his finger plunged the button—the flash fired, the shutter snapped—he spun back into Thom's office, slamming the door and throwing himself against it. He could hear the figment charging toward him, fast, heavy steps barreling down the hall. Ro squeezed his eyes shut, certain he was dead.

But the footsteps ceased, and the hoarse, heavy breathing that he'd heard moments earlier was gone. Slowly he peeled himself off the door, turning to face it. Reaching for the knob, he drew a deep breath, then opened the door.

On the other side, nothing. Cautiously stepping out into the hallway, Ro darted his eyes everywhere. Had he not been moving so slowly, he might have missed the photo he'd tried taking of the figment. It rested on the floor where it had fallen after he'd bolted into Thom's office.

Stooping to pick it up, afraid of what it might reveal, Ro saw nothing—just a blurry shot taken by an unsteady hand.

CHAPTER 16

BY THE TIME EVIE HEARD FROM RACHEL ABOUT A POTENTIALLY VIOLENT SITUATION at the Purcell home, she'd taken eighteen calls in less than an hour. There had been reports of vandalism—windows on businesses, homes, cars, and boats broken; property trampled or destroyed. People were witnessing random acts of violence; some had been attacked by friends, neighbors, strangers. Inexplicable behaviors were causing alarm and paranoia. People loitered in the street, wandering as if in a stupor, exhibiting strange tics and even stranger patterns of movement. The sense of panic that had been slowly building for the past week was finally boiling over.

Then there was the storm. Power and phone service were hit or miss, roads impassable. Evie reminded caller after caller about the access road, that it remained open if they *had* to leave. Remote and, after years of budgetary neglect, in serious disrepair, it wasn't exactly safe. But it was still a way out.

The transfer to take Robby Sapp Jr. and Kelly Braun to a county facility still hadn't shown. Rob Sr. had been coming by the station regularly to visit his son, bringing him home-cooked food and changes of clothes, and Evie could tell he was growing impatient with the stalemate. Robby Jr.'s nerves seemed to come and go. He'd sleep, at random, for hours—wake and profess remorse for attacking Elliot and John Kerr at Bar Harbor—then slip into what seemed like a kind of trance, staring at nothing, eyes hardening as if lost in horrible thought.

Realizing no one was coming for Kelly, Evie had tried taking pity, providing her with necessities and trying to chat, but where Robby Jr. had moments of lucidity, Kelly seemed further gone. The only time Evie had seen her brighten was when she'd heard a song on the radio—"Crimson and Clover," something she'd said her mother used to play around the house. But once the song had ended, she'd drifted away again.

Andi met Ro as he pulled up in front of the library, hurrying to his car through the rain. "We have to find someone named Nicolas Engle," she said as she climbed inside. "*NE*. He knows about the game. He broke into the auction house to try and destroy it."

She fished out the article that featured details on Engle's arrest and unfolded it on the dash for Ro to see. While he scanned the text, she found a page she'd torn from the phone book with the three entries for N. Engle.

Finished with one, Ro took the other. "We can find them," he finally said, tucking the pages into a notebook. "Take a look at these." He passed a stack of Polaroids to Andi. "They were on the walls at Thom Mazzy's office. Those symbols are from the game. They're on the walls inside the cave. Mazzy must have played it."

"Is that blood?" Andi asked as she flipped through.

Ro nodded. "I think so."

As she came to the out of focus image of the hallway—Ro's failed attempt to photograph the figment—he plucked it from the stack, looking it over once more. "Thought I . . . saw something. From the game. I tried to . . ." He shook his head a little, knowing it didn't make sense.

Inside a bustling chrome diner trimmed in neon, Andi and Ro found seats at the counter. They ordered breakfast for dinner—eggs, toast, coffee, which Ro still coudn't stomach—then searched for something to discuss within earshot of the other customers that didn't involve brain-scrambling video games or spree killing. It was a struggle. That was all their lives were suddenly about.

Clearing a space, Andi spread a map out between them. "We should figure out where the Engles live," she said.

"You don't want to call?" Ro asked.

"I'd rather have someone tell me I'm crazy to my face, I guess," Andi said, charting a course around the city, address to address. "I'll be right back."

Stepping away to find a restroom, Andi left Ro at the counter. As he repositioned the map in front of himself he nudged Andi's notebook aside, and the Polaroids he'd taken spilled out onto the counter. Before he could sweep them up, he found his eyes locking onto them, lights and sounds around him beginning to dim until everything—save for the bloody symbols in the photos—was cloaked in shadow.

As their server set their food down in front of Ro, she noticed he seemed rigid, eyes fixed downward. "You okay, hon?" she asked, craning her neck for a look at Ro's face before glancing down at the photos. The vague unease she felt ticked higher at the sight of the gruesome images, and she found herself reaching for one to better understand what she was seeing.

Sliding the top picture toward herself, the server froze as Ro's hand latched tightly onto hers. "Let go. Hey!" she snapped. Beyond his hand, Ro hadn't moved, wasn't looking at her. "I said let go of me!"

"Ro?" Overhearing the commotion on her way back to her seat, Andi hurried forward. "Ro, let go of her!"

Other staff closed in, trying to pry Ro off their coworker.

"No!" Andi called as she fought her way through, afraid of what could happen if they triggered Ro any further. "Don't touch him! He—he's sick. It'll pass. Let me—stop—please!"

As a burly cook grasped Ro's arm to pry it loose, Ro ripped free, letting go of the server then snatching a cup and sailing it across the counter. Barely ducking clear, staff scattered as the cup smashed into a stack of plates, ceramic shards exploding everywhere.

"Ro!" Andi screamed, spinning him around, squaring his face with hers. "Stop!" Alight with angry energy, he seemed like he might strike her next, but she held firm, never breaking eye contact, silently pleading with him to come back.

Slowly his look began to soften.

Hearing the server on the phone with the police, Andi quickly gathered their things and pulled Ro toward the door. She quietly snatched up a steak knife that had been left on a table and tucked it away, frightened by Ro's outburst and unwilling to let herself be caught off guard. To become the next Mila Novik.

Andi fished the keys from his pocket, helped him into the passenger seat, then climbed behind the wheel and tore away.

The drive to the first N. Engle took them across town, through the center of San Jose and past Mineta Airport, into the neighborhood of Rosemary Gardens. While Andi drove, Ro said little, keeping his eyes trained out the window. He watched rain streak here and there across the glass, catching colorful flashes of light from offices, shops, homes. It felt peaceful, helping him find his center after what had happened in the diner.

They stopped outside a 7-Eleven so Andi could use a pay phone to call her father, Devon. She'd charted a path between the three Engles that would end with them in range of his place—her old home. She'd hoped they would've had more to bring him but still wanted his insight on the game's construction and code. She assumed they could crash there too, seeing as neither wanted to drive back at night and in the rain, but she couldn't reach him. The number had been disconnected. It was odd but had to be a mistake.

Their first stop brought them to *Noreen* Engle, pushing eighty and none too happy to find a couple of kids banging on her front door. She had no kin by the name of Nicolas and no connection to the tech industry. Her father, husband, and now her son ran a dry-cleaning business, Andi and Ro discovered, moments before having the front door slammed in their faces.

It took another half hour to reach the second address. It led them to an apartment in a building with six units, one of which *had* been rented by a Noah Engle. Per the landlord, he'd moved out two months ago and had worked construction while staying there.

They drove on in silence, each thinking through what they'd do if they couldn't find the man they were looking for. By the time they reached their final stop, a large Stick-style home nestled on a quiet, tree-lined street in Almaden Valley, neither was champing at the bit to knock. The last rays of gray twilight disappeared as Andi rapped an iron knocker against the front door. She waited a few moments then tried again, this time loudly and by hand. As she reached out to knock once more, both froze as a light fixture overhead burned to life.

"What do you want?" a voice called out from inside, tinged with what sounded like Scandinavian roots.

"We're looking for Nicolas Engle," Andi replied. "We want to talk to him about a game we think he worked on. *Polybius*. I think you—he's been communicating with us about it. Over Usenet. I'm AndiDVT. You're 1077NE, right?"

For a long moment, nothing. Quietly tipping open a mailbox that was mounted near the door, Ro fished out a letter and indicated the addressee's name to Andi—Nicolas Engle.

"I'm not interested," the voice finally replied. "Leave, or I'm calling the police." With that the light cut out, and footsteps could be heard receding into the house.

Andi knocked again, but there was no response. As a light on a neighbor's front porch clicked on she backed off, and the two retreated to Ro's Land Cruiser. For a moment they stood together, staring up at the house.

"It's him," Andi finally said.

Ro nodded. "What do you want to do?"

"The paper said he pled guilty to breaking into the auction house. If he leaves, he'd be in more trouble, right? We'll come back tomorrow," Andi said, somewhere between desperate and resolved.

It was past ten as they pulled up in front of Devon's home. It was a bland piece of newer construction, in a subdivision full of the same. Ro seemed to remember a *Twilight Zone* episode where a couple found themselves trapped in a similarly styled neighborhood that was so visually indistinct, they couldn't find their way out. He thought about mentioning it to Andi but knew this was where she *wanted* to be. So he bit his tongue as they walked toward the entrance.

Producing a spare key from her pocket, Andi went to unlock the front door, only to find it wouldn't fit. She tried again, tried other keys on the ring she carried in case she'd been mistaken. None worked.

As she rang the bell, someone shuffled inside, padding up to the door. Whoever was there, for a moment they said nothing. Andi was about to speak when the dead bolt twisted, and the door opened halfway.

Devon stepped outside. "Andi?"

"Hey, Dad." She hugged him, a gesture he returned a step too late and a touch too unenthusiastically for her not to notice. While Devon clocked Ro, his presence didn't seem to be the issue as he pulled away from his daughter and took a step back into the house, leaving the two of them outside on the threshold.

"Dad, this is Ro." She moved over, trying to bring him into the conversation. "Ro, this is my dad, Devon."

"Nice to meet you," Ro said with a nod. A handshake would've meant approaching Devon, which seemed like a bad idea. His energy felt all wrong for someone getting to see his daughter out of the blue.

Devon nodded back absentmindedly, attention still on Andi. In his late thirties, with curly brown hair that had grown a touch too long for him to keep under control and several days' worth of stubble covering his face, Devon looked tired and unprepared for company. "What, uh, what are you doing here?"

"We're in town for a project," Andi said. "There's some code I can't make sense of. I was hoping you could take a look. And that we could stay the night." The vague uneasiness on Devon's face seemed to harden with her requests. Andi wasn't sure what was wrong. "I tried calling, but the phone was disconnected. You know that, right?"

"Come in," Devon said as he disappeared inside, not bothering to wait for them.

Andi went to follow him, but Ro tapped her arm, voice hushed. "Are you sure this is okay? He seems . . . I don't know. Like he doesn't want us here."

"It's fine. He's an engineer. They're all weird. Besides, we need his help." But Devon had seemed more *off* than usual to Andi, too.

As they moved into the house, one reason for Devon's odd behavior became apparent. Most of the lights were out, leaving much of the space shrouded in darkness. There was no furniture, save for a card table shoved into a corner of the dining room, a few folding chairs leaning against it. A handful of shabby moving boxes stuffed with papers and random electronic components sat stacked haphazardly. Stains covered the carpets, in a few spots leaching up the baseboards onto the walls. Sections of drywall showed signs of distress, as if they'd been hit—repeatedly—by something with serious heft behind it.

Her mind fluctuating between confusion and concern, Andi took in the scene as she followed Devon into the kitchen. Things there were no better. Trash bags—all full—dotted the landscape. Paper plates, cups, napkins had been crumpled up around their half-finished contents and left at random. The room's sour odor hit Andi and Ro as they entered, both trying not to reflexively flinch.

"I wish you'd called," Devon said, suddenly aware of the wasteland in which he'd been living.

"I told you, I tried—the line was shut off," Andi said. "And you changed the lock?"

"Oh. Yeah. I had some . . . a disagreement with some people. I wasn't thinking I'd have to tell you like this, but I'm, uh, leaving. Moving. There's an opportunity down in Austin."

"Moving? Wait, you said Austin. *Texas?*" Andi couldn't hide her bewilderment.

"Yeah, it's really—there's a lot of money down there right now. A lot of tech people are getting sick of the Valley and going to Austin. It's a different energy," Devon said, trying hard to sell Andi on the idea. "I really think it's the right move. I've got an idea. I just need to find some funding down there to help settle things up here, then I can really get started. And look, once I get down there and get on my feet, you can—"

Andi cut him off. "What happened?"

Devon shook his head, not following.

Andi gestured at the mess. "Are you in trouble?"

Ro hung back, wishing he'd opted to wait out front. Or in the car. Or back in Tasker Bay. Glancing down, he saw a stack of mail, most of it with overdue notices stamped in imposing letters, along with a summons to court. New locks, paranoia over opening the front door, slipping out of town without telling his family, court papers—it didn't take being a cop's son to figure out something more was going on, although he doubted they'd ever know the full picture.

"What? No," Devon said, feigning shock but failing to sell it. "I took some funding and had some problems with my prototype. I just need to get out from under it. The bank is, um, taking the house. I was hoping I could sell it and use that money to . . ." He trailed off, barely able to look at Andi as he spoke. "I just need to get down to Austin. It's going to go better down there. Lot of opportunity."

Andi's mind flooded with dozens of questions, but she could only think to ask one. "When are you leaving?"

"Soon. I had to sell a few things. Obviously. Consignment. I'm supposed to get paid tomorrow, and then I need to go. I can't really be here any longer. I've gotta be out of the house. So, yeah. Probably tomorrow. So, you know, you can't—it's not a good idea for you to stay. And I don't think—I don't have the headspace to help you. Not right now. I'm sorry, A."

A. Devon's nickname for Andi's nickname. Why her parents had chosen Andrea when neither of them wanted to call her that occasionally baffled Andi. But right now it was everything else her father was saying that was throwing her off.

Devon hung his head after he'd finished, staring blankly at his shoes, aware of just how badly he'd fucked up. Finally lifting his gaze a little, batting too-long hair from in front of his eyes, he tried to look at Andi but couldn't, finding a spot just beyond her to focus on instead. "I wanted to get there and get settled before I told you and your mom. Like a surprise, you know?"

"Mom doesn't know?" Andi asked, certain she already knew the answer.

"No. And it'd help me if you didn't tell her. Let me do it once I'm settled."

"Once you're settled," Andi repeated, voice hollow. Looking around, she could feel her dream dying. Devon had understood her, pushed her to push herself when she was younger, given her something to work toward. But in this moment she was realizing something she'd known for a while but hadn't been able to admit. That he wasn't a person to idolize. That it wasn't worth trying to live up to an image. What was real was what mattered, and Devon's reality was finally in full view.

She searched for something to say, but the words weren't there. More than anything, she wanted to apologize to her mom. She couldn't recall ever comparing her unfavorably to Devon out loud, but she'd certainly thought it. And there was *no* comparison. The frustration was finally too much for her to bear. She felt heavy, sad. *And pissed the fuck off.* Turning and walking past Ro, Andi disappeared down a hallway and into the house.

Not knowing what else to do, Ro followed. Tripping over a laundry bag lumped against a wall, he managed to catch and steady himself on a door frame and found Andi, sitting inside. Jagged slivers of light cutting through haphazardly blacked-out windows fell around her at random.

"Hey. Are you . . . okay?" Ro asked, stepping inside.

"This was my room. There was a bed there. Computer, desk over there. I had clothes, books. *My things*—things I bought, for myself. I always figured they'd be here when I . . ." *Moved back.* She couldn't bring herself to say it, trailing off and quietly seething for a long moment. "And he just *sold* them. And I don't care about the stuff, I really don't. I care that he *didn't.* That he just did what he wanted. Like he's always done. He did this shit to my mom all the time." It hurt, saying that out loud. "He's sick. And she would tell him he needed help, to talk to somebody. But he wouldn't listen."

"I'm not going to act like I understand, because my parents . . . it's not the same. But I know what it feels like when somebody isn't there. And I know this was your plan, coming back here. You still can. Andi, you're . . . great. You are easily the most capable person I've ever met and you're *my* age. You're only going to get better. You can do whatever you want. And you shouldn't let him or anybody make you think different."

Andi took in Ro's words for a moment before sighing and flopping back on the empty floor. "That was a pretty good speech."

"Well, that's what I aim for. Pretty good," Ro smirked. "Maybe we should go. It looked like there was a motel up the road."

Glancing at Ro, Andi felt a kind of deep, peaceful happiness come over her that shouldn't have been possible, given the circumstance. She nodded a little. *Okay, let's go.*

Devon, slapping tape on boxes then sliding them across the empty floor toward the front door, stopped his work and stood as Andi, trailed by Ro, walked back into the kitchen. But she didn't engage, instead making a line for the refrigerator. Taking a case of Miller High Life from inside and shoving it into Ro's arms, she turned toward her father.

"You were an asshole to Mom. You're a liar. And this"—she flung her hands around the room—"is fucking pathetic. You need *help*, Dad. You need medicine. A doctor. Mom told you, and you . . ." It was overwhelming. Too much, all at once. "Don't call. If Mom wants to talk, we'll find you."

Andi felt like she floated down the hall as she left the house, her actions not her own. Out front, she took a can from the case of beer resting in Ro's arms, shaking it a solid ten seconds before sailing it against what had been her bedroom window. It exploded on impact, shattering glass and spraying the Champagne of Beers inside and out. Ro tugged her shoulder, desperate to get in the car before a neighbor or Devon could scribble down his license plate.

Rachel had been surprised to find David at her door. After hearing about her experience at the Purcell home from Evie, he'd come to take her account. And, while he wouldn't say it, he'd wanted to check up on her. Circumstance had forced them together, but they were both realizing they liked having the other around, especially in the middle of a dark, confusing moment.

The phone rang before he made it through the front door. "David?" Rachel called as she answered. "It's Andi and Ro."

Andi's voice echoed over the line. "Ro, your dad's there."

"Where are you?" David asked.

"Still in San Jose," Ro replied.

"*Where?*" Rachel asked, more pointedly.

"A motel," Andi said. "*It's fine. We're fine.*"

Rachel glanced at David. He didn't like the idea any more than she did, but they couldn't do anything about it from here.

"We found out about someone else who played the game. This guy Thomas Mazzy. He killed four people after," Andi said, "then himself. Ro has pictures of these symbols from the game that Mazzy drew on the walls of his office in—in blood."

"Yeah," David said. "Story was in the news a few weeks ago."

"We found the guy I've been talking to over Usenet, too," Andi added.

David looked impressed, which worried Rachel. "Hold on," she cut in, cupping a hand over the microphone. "You believe this? About the game?"

"I don't know," David said, head shaking. "Parts of it line up. It's not hurting anyone to ask. Honestly, they're probably safer there than they are here, but if you say no, then it's no. I'm okay with that, too."

"But you believe it?" Rachel asked, searching.

"I believe in them." David shrugged.

From the lumpy king bed in their room's center, Andi watched Ro finish reversing the bathroom doorknob, allowing her to lock him inside for the night. It wasn't foolproof but, without knowing what might trigger him, it seemed safer for them both.

Andi didn't feel right helping. She didn't want to be the one to lock Ro away, even if it was just for one night in the shitty bathroom of the shitty Crescent Motel. It all felt wrong. She also felt safer for it, which just made her feel worse.

Satisfied with his work, Ro flopped down on the bed next to her. "Done," he announced. "Just let me be comfortable for like, five minutes first."

Andi smiled as much as she could, grabbing them both a beer from the case they'd stolen from Devon's. Their eyes settled on the room's black-and-white TV, which in between bursts of static was tuned to a movie called *A Cold Night's Death*. As they watched a pair of scientists bicker over the cause of strange events in their isolated research station, they stayed quiet, both nervous for what the night could bring.

Finally, Ro tilted his head toward hers. "We should probably get some sleep." He rose and took a pillow and a thin blanket from the room's closet.

Andi sat, watching him as he stopped just outside the bathroom. "Maybe keep the car keys with you," he said. "If something happens, go to the police."

Andi looked at him a moment, face ashen, before walking over and hugging him. She didn't want to let go. Exhaling, suddenly wishing he hadn't volunteered to wall himself off like a B-movie werewolf, Ro pulled away and stepped into his temporary cell. Andi offered a weak smile as she closed him inside then clicked the lock. Feeling the light weight of the door, she realized if Ro wanted out, it wouldn't take much effort.

While he layered towels in the bathtub, anything to make it marginally more comfortable, she surveyed the room. Pocketing his keys, she took the blanket and pillow from the bed and settled down on the other side of the door, comforted by the fact that she was closer to Ro *and* that she'd be better able to hear with more time to run, if something happened. Taking the knife she'd lifted at the diner from her jacket, she wiped it clean and set it nearby as she shut off the lights, laid down, and stared at the ceiling. It was going to be a long night.

The bitterness in the Greene household was overwhelming. Laurel couldn't take it anymore. Her parents were barely speaking and only shouted when they did. Each blamed the other for mistakes they believed were going to cost them a business that had been in her dad Michael's family for generations. The Greenes had been some of Tasker Bay's first residents, establishing a general store a full decade before the town even made it onto a map.

To escape, Laurel had begun stretching out her reconnaissance trips to Paulson's, often wandering the aisles until close. She made acquaintances with a few employees who'd started to recognize her. All seemed nice enough. And she watched customers come and go, wondering who they were, which side of town they'd come from. Were they happy ? Alone? In love? That none of this fazed her spoke to the frightening totality of a plan she'd started piecing together after wandering unnoticed into an employees-only area of the store the other day.

She'd grabbed a smock from a hamper, pulled it on, and moved anonymously through the rooms and halls, capturing as detailed a mental picture as she could.

She wasn't sure *why* she'd wanted to. It had simply felt like the right thing to do. It was fifteen minutes before another employee spotted her and tried making small talk, asking if she was a new hire. Demurring, she quickly slipped back out and retreated to her car, where she sketched a skeletal layout of the store from memory.

In the days that followed, she'd found herself following Christine Abernathy. Laurel started leaving the store at the same time as Christine, tailing her before she arrived home and disappeared behind an imposing wrought-iron gate.

Compelled by the same dark, relentless energy that was driving her to do something she felt would fix the problems her parents could not, Laurel wanted to learn more about Christine. Her routines, her family. She began finding time to tail her every day, skipping class then school altogether so she could split time between profiling her two targets—Paulson's and its owner. She watched Christine drive her children to a private school forty-five minutes outside of town; strut in and out of meetings with members of the bullshit town council; direct dejected-looking locals to toil on and around the family's yacht, one of several massive ships that now dotted the town's small harbor and never seemed to go anywhere.

One thing Christine did not do, Laurel quickly noted, was spend much time on the family business. It drove her insane, certain people being rich enough that they could "work" by working others. Her parents did this too, to an extent, but not without spending ten-plus hours a day on store business—working the registers, bagging groceries, corralling carts, keeping books.

Having seen the dark endgame of capitalism convincingly portrayed in one too many of the high-minded sci-fi lit novels she'd devoured since finding her mom's old copy of Ursula Le Guin's *The Dispossessed*, Laurel believed firmly that *no one* needed that much money. Christine's life had revealed itself to be one of empty convenience and luxury, an existence simply to exist. It was pointless and should end, Laurel decided, along with her empire.

Escaping the tumult at home and focusing on the mission at hand had made her world clearly, blissfully simple. She resolved to take charge of the tailspin her family had been forced into, to not just stem but reverse it.

Now, in the dark, seated in her car outside a hardware store, she studied her map of Paulson's. It had become a habit for her to reference it, refine it, committing details to memory so she'd be able to move through the store as quickly as possible when the time arrived. Satisfied with her review and the results of her shopping trip, she finally pulled away into the rain.

On the floorboards behind her, rattling as she drove, sat five identical lengths of heavy-duty chain, padlocks to match, and as many empty gas cans as she could haul.

CHAPTER 17

HALLOWEEN. ON TOP OF EVERYTHING ELSE, IT WAS HALLOWEEN. FOR THE CITIzens of Tasker Bay who weren't interested in dressing up and seeking candy alongside local youngsters or getting loaded on cheap beer with the teens and twentysomethings, it was approached annually with a mild sense of dread. Trash on the streets, toilet paper in the trees, the occasional battered mailbox. All tricks, no treats.

The notion of hundreds of people prowling the streets in masks and costumes that could render them anonymous, potentially leading to more chaos, was fodder for what remained of the local rumor mill. There was talk of a curfew, calling in a consulting detective from San Jose, or even the National Guard. No one was sure what to believe.

More and more of Tasker Bay's residents had begun sequestering themselves, concerned about the instability that lurked outside their front doors *and* the flooding that had rendered their swath of the northern California coast largely isolated. Speculation festered, steadily poisoning peoples' views of their town *and* one another. Couples sat at home, nervous about how strange their neighbors had started acting, while next door, their neighbors were having the exact same conversation.

"I'll see him standing on the porch just staring at us from across the street for hours. It's creepy. I don't like going outside anymore because I know he's going to be there."

Parents walked on eggshells around their children, who'd become prone to snap in loud, sometimes violent spasms.

"She wakes up screaming every night three, four times. No one knows what's wrong with her."

"He turned around and shoved me. You should've seen his face. He was *so* angry."

People leveled accusations over the phone about who might have done what, why, and what was coming next.

"Somebody said they've been finding dead animals in the trash all over town. Cats, dogs. It's sick. And I'll bet whoever's doing it killed those horses."

"They think whoever shot Ed Sanko killed that kid they found in Peck Creek. I mean, that's a serial killer, right?"

After the riot at the football game, the sheriff's office and town council had canceled all public events until further notice. Rumors swirled that a lockdown was next.

But people were still queueing up to play *Polybius*, then roaming the streets after. And a handful of others, led by Paul Nantz, had started patrolling the streets as "citizen lawmen." Too zealous for a spot on the sheriff's duty roster, but in his element now that Tasker Bay's social structure was breaking down, Paul expanded his posse as people found an outlet for their anxiety, a means to feel powerful in a place they believed had been stripping them of power and purpose—not just now, but for the last several years.

More than one of Paul's ad hoc police force talked about seizing the moment to "take back our town."

There was an unavoidable divide between the posse and the hordes drawn to *Polybius*, who couldn't be reasoned with or intimidated into staying away. When Paul spotted and confronted Mal about closing his shop until things cooled off, Mal laughed. Paul had no real authority. When Paul flashed a gun, Mal did the same. But the standoff was over before it started, both of them backing down with a fresh grudge.

Mal couldn't see it, or didn't care, but Home Video World *was* the epicenter of the crisis. People had started leaving their cars in the street out front, sometimes with the keys inside. Anyone who felt like it could go joyriding, bailing out when the mood struck, leaving a series of abandoned and sometimes wrecked vehicles littering the area. They brawled with one another and battered whatever struck their fancy, steadily dragging themselves and the town around them over the edge.

Carl Delano had given up on getting any help from the sheriff's office. He'd begun to surveil Bob Colson's company, Bayview Holdings, which sat on the fringe of Tasker Bay's downtown. On the day news broke that a Bayview employee named Michael Newton had been killed, Carl had been sitting in his truck when a distraught Bob Colson had stepped from the office and started down the block on foot. Carl had decided to follow, and it hadn't taken long for Bob to sense someone behind him.

"What do you want?" Bob snapped as he turned to face Carl.

Carl said nothing—he simply stared, interested to see what kind of reaction he could goad from the man. "I've seen you. Outside. Out front. The sheriff knows."

As Bob started to walk away, Carl called after him. "Did you kill that boy in the creek like you killed my horses? What'd he do? What'd he have that you wanted?" Spinning around, fist balled, Bob seemed primed to take a swing. Still, Carl just stood there.

Suddenly aware he was poised to hit Carl, Bob took a breath and a step back. He wouldn't let himself be pulled into Carl's shit. *And fuck him for trying.* "You know what I think? *You* killed those animals. You're going broke fighting a case you can't win, and you need the insurance payout. I think you're a sick piece of shit. That's what I think."

Carl's face twitched, the momentary power he'd felt over Bob gone and replaced with deep, indignant rage.

"Maybe *you* had something to do with what happened to Michael. Keep stalking me and we'll see what the sheriff thinks," Bob spat. "*Fuck. You.*"

Carl lurched forward, grabbed Bob by the collar, and shoved him into a lamppost. Bob staggered back, fearing he wasn't done, but Carl just stood there staring daggers. It felt good, seeing the fear in Bob's eyes after years of being slowly bled to death in court. Here, in the street, things felt fair.

That encounter had stoked a fire in Carl that was already building. Now, days later, that fire was still burning. Carl had no endgame in mind, but everything clicked when he'd noticed his truck was low on oil. Retrieving a quart and funnel from a shed at the end of his driveway, he'd also instinctively picked up a box of twenty-gauge shotgun shells. They'd sat next to him in the truck all day outside

Bayview's office, his attention drifting to them at random. The next day, he'd brought his gun. Loaded it the day after. With each small step, his trajectory felt more and more inevitable.

Now, on October 31, 1982, a gloomy Sunday morning, Carl was back outside Bayview Holdings' office. And he was finally ready. Even though it was the weekend, he knew at least some of Bayview's employees, including Bob, would be in the office. They seemed to work around the clock, intent on razing and rebuilding Tasker Bay as quickly as possible.

Had he not sat there so long squabbling with some part of himself that was unwilling to do what the rest of his body and his mind wanted done, Carl could've caught them before they left. Instead, he watched as four employees filed out the door and into a car parked directly in front of the office. While he recognized all four faces, he only knew two by name—Whitney Hines and Greg Streiber, both transplants who'd moved from San Jose expressly for the purpose of strip-mining the town. Both had come to his home on two separate occasions to harass him over his land.

As the car pulled away, Carl found himself cranking over his own engine and following. It didn't take long for him to realize he knew the route—they were heading in the direction of his home.

While the Bayview car kept on its course, an unease settled over him. When he saw the vehicle approach his driveway and flash its brake lights, his whole being tensed. He rolled to a stop a hundred or so yards back and watched the car continue ahead, slowly, until the driver pulled over onto the shoulder next to the wire fence that Carl had helped his father install years ago. On the other side sat the land that he farmed.

It was the weather, Carl realized, or lack of it—they'd caught a break in the rain and were here to evaluate the land. They believed they'd won, that he was going to fold after what they'd done to those animals, to his business. After he'd laid hands on Bob. As his foot moved off the brake and toward the gas, the sense of inevitability he'd felt upon leaving his home that morning came roaring back. *I shouldn't have waited so damn long.*

Flooring it, he white-knuckled the wheel. The Bayview employees heard the engine moments before Carl veered off the road toward them. The truck mowed down Streiber and one of the other employees, ripping off both passenger-side doors in a shower of sparks and shrapnel as it tore past, skidding to a stop up ahead.

The suddenness of it—the violent flash of sound and motion—caused Whitney and the other employee to momentarily freeze. Then, as if coming to from a nightmare, she started screaming.

But as Carl forced open his truck's battered door, he didn't hear her terror. He heard his justice. With a rhythmic clack of his shotgun's forestock, he drew a bead on the other employee, firing off a blast of buckshot that penetrated just above the man's left knee and up the side of his body. Staggered, on the verge of collapse, the man caught sight of Carl taking aim and began to limp away, toward the fence.

Where does he think he can hide? Carl wondered. He decided to finish him off, leaving the panicked Whitney screaming by the roadside. *She isn't going anywhere.*

Approaching and leveling the shotgun at the helpless man's face, Carl heard an engine fire on. Behind the wheel, eyes wild, Whitney threw the car into drive and nearly spun out as she whipped it back onto the road, racing toward town. Carl fired at her, shattering a taillight but failing to stop her. He'd just have to catch up.

Glancing back, he realized the man was now trying to hoist himself over the wire fence. Carl chambered a round and pulled the trigger, leaving his lifeless body slumped over the fence's rusty barbs, as if floating in midair.

Carl returned to his truck, pulled it around, and quickly gained speed as he raced after Whitney. He was driving too fast to see the front door on his home as it flew open, his wife, Julie, stepping out to see what the commotion was about. As she saw Carl's truck speed away, then turned and saw the carnage he'd left in his wake, she had to brace herself on the door before staggering back inside toward the phone.

Catching sight of Carl's truck fast approaching in the rearview mirror, Whitney felt her panic go full-bore. Bayview's company car, a fully loaded Audi 5000, had more than enough horsepower to easily outstrip the relatively ancient pickup giving chase. But as she floored it, she could feel herself losing control, tires skidding over wet pavement.

Backing off the gas, she gave Carl a window, and he slammed his front end against the Audi's rear, pushing it toward a waterlogged shoulder that would surely swamp it. Whitney spun the wheel and regained just enough control to hammer her foot against the accelerator one more time. Screaming at Carl, the car, everything, she tore forward, tires spinning against then finally gripping the rain-slicked asphalt.

Realizing she was heading toward town, Carl whipped down

a back road that would shave off a quarter mile and allow him to meet her head-on. Racing ahead, he caught a glimpse of the Audi as it rounded a corner that led toward Main Street.

Keeping her foot on the gas, Whitney did everything in her power to stay focused. She just had to make it someplace where there were people. The sheriff's office was at the far end of town, but her own was close by.

After screeching to a stop in front of Bayview's office, half of the car bucking up and over the curb, a panicked Whitney scrambled through the hole where a passenger-side door had been and made for the front entrance. Stumbling, trying to find her footing, she could hear Carl's engine roaring toward her.

In that moment, it was as if time dilated. Whitney watched as Carl's truck swerved, bouncing over the curb and up onto the sidewalk. It smashed through a series of planters arranged in front of neighboring businesses, sending dirt, sparks, debris flying in a spectacle of violent motion. The truck then slammed her and half of its own length through Bayview's facade. A crag of stonework snagged the transaxle, jerking the truck to a sudden halt as Whitney's body flew through the plateglass front then into the lobby with such force, it shattered a panel of drywall on impact.

The two others left in the office, Bob Colson and Mary Casey, scrambled from in back at the horrible sound. The bright front office, walls lined with pictures of the properties they'd sold, was destroyed. They found Whitney's broken frame crumpled on the floor and the smoldering remains of Carl's truck lodged halfway inside the building. Momentarily overwhelmed, Bob suddenly snapped to.

"Phone the sheriff right now," he said, voice shaky, as he approached the truck.

As the wheels and engine spun down, Bob peered inside the cab. There didn't appear to be a driver. Moving in for a closer look he saw Carl's body on the floorboard, tilting the barrel of a shotgun toward his face.

Before she was even through talking to a frenzied Julie Delano, Evie was already radioing David, Charlie, and Jeff simultaneously. It was David who was best positioned to respond. Knowing that Carl and whoever he was pursuing were headed in the direction of downtown, he fired on his lights and siren and angled toward Main Street.

Racing through an intersection and skidding onto Main, he could see the tail end of Carl's truck sticking out of a hole smashed into the front of the Bayview Holdings building. By the time Evie radioed again with word from Mary Casey that there'd been an accident, David was already screeching to a stop out front.

If he'd stumbled back half a second later, Bob's face would have been lifted off and splattered across the ceiling. As he clambered to his feet and stumbled through the wreckage, pawing at Mary to follow him into the back, Bob glanced over his shoulder in time to see Carl staggering from the truck. Covered in blood and detritus from the crash, he fired the shotgun wildly, blasting a chunk off the reception desk but missing Bob and Mary as they ducked around a corner.

Battered and struggling to breathe from what were no doubt multiple broken ribs, Carl had come this far, and Bob—the head of the snake—was feet away. He wouldn't stop until this was over.

Spotting them as they dashed down a corridor toward a back door, Carl fired. A second volley cut Mary's legs out from under her. She spun face-first into the floor, neck snapping on impact. The forestock locked in place as Carl tried chambering another round; the gun was empty, so he pulled the massive bowie knife he'd taken to carrying the last couple of weeks from its sheath.

Bob ducked inside an office and raced to close the door but was a step too slow as Carl jammed the knife through the opening. Slicing downward with brute force, he cleaved off two of Bob's fingers and hacked into a third.

Recoiling in pain and succumbing to shock, Bob cowered as Carl smashed his way inside and grabbed his collar, jamming the bloodied knife against his cheek.

"Carl, d-don't," Bob started, but before he could sputter another word, a voice boomed out from the void.

"Let him go and drop the knife!" From just outside the door frame, David trained his revolver. "Now, Carl!"

Carl didn't turn to look at David, keeping his eyes on Bob as he spoke. "I can't, David. No one else is going to do anything about it."

"You know that's not true. Something's going on around here. What happened at your farm is part of it. Bob didn't—*none* of these people hurt your animals, Carl. You *can't* do this. You *won't*. I know you. This isn't you. Think about Julie."

"I am."

David could see Carl's hand tightening around the handle, muscles starting to twitch, and knew he had no choice. Firing a single shot, he struck Carl square in the temple, the force of impact spinning him into the wall then onto the floor.

CHAPTER 18

KNOCKING ON THE BATHROOM DOOR ROUSED RO. AFTER TOSSING, TURNING, AND repeatedly banging his head on the side of the tub all night, he'd finally fallen asleep around five a.m. Light had started filtering through the frosted windows an hour or so after, waking him up for good with a cramped body and tired mind.

Another knock. "Ro? Hey. Are you up?" came Andi's anxious voice from outside.

He labored to his feet and shuffled over. Trying the knob, he suddenly remembered relocating the lock. "Yeah, you can—yeah." The lock clicked, the door opened, and Andi—eyes a little wide—nodded past him toward the bathroom. Unable to wait for Ro's faculties to catch up, she pulled him out of the way, then closed the door behind her.

Stumbling over her makeshift bed, Ro accidentally kicked her bag aside, revealing the knife. For a long moment he stared, a sickening realization taking hold. *She's afraid of me.* Not wanting her to feel like she had to explain herself when he already understood, he covered the knife back up then lay down on the bed, trying to put it out of his mind. A few moments later she re-emerged and took a seat next to him.

"I need to stay here for, like, five minutes," Ro said, stretching out. For all its lumps and busted springs, the mattress still felt cloudlike after his night in the tub.

"Did you sleep?" Andi asked.

"Not really. The shower was dripping all night. Right on my feet."

"Thank you for doing that. Staying in there," she said as she lay down next to him, taking his hand and resting her head against his shoulder. "Did anything happen?"

"I don't think so. But I don't know. It's like a . . . hole in my memory. I go blank."

"You don't remember anything? At all?"

Ro shifted, the conversation branching in a direction he wasn't ready for first thing in the morning. "Sometimes." He glanced at Andi, hoping that was enough to put her off. But her eyes were on him, intent and searching for more. "Sometimes I see things after. Like that woman in the diner, the waitress. I can see the look on her face. When I grabbed her." He shook his head, wrestling anew with the fear he'd put into a stranger over nothing.

As Ro spoke, Andi studied him. The episodes he'd experienced were the only way to tell that he had played. If she didn't know any better, she'd assume he was fine. Normal. Only she knew he wasn't.

In another hour they were back in front of Engle's home, nerves high. Both stared at his front door from inside the Land Cruiser, reluctant to find out whether he'd talk—if he was even still there.

"What if he doesn't answer?" Andi finally asked.

"We could try and break in. I guess," Ro replied as he scanned the rest of the street for any watchful eyes. "I broke into Mazzy's office yesterday without really thinking about it. And Mal's house. It's actually a lot easier to do than you'd think. I'm not saying we should, but—"

"I think that's him." Andi pointed out the window at a lanky blond man in his thirties, hair and beard as unkempt as the stained sweats he wore under a tightly wrapped, thin robe. He shuffled from the door to with a bag of trash toward a can left at the corner.

"Nicolas Engle?" Andi called out as she approached. Glancing up at hearing his name, Engle took a step back, instinctively defensive. "I'm Andi Winston. This is Roman Kemp. We were here last night. You've been talking to us about *Polybius*. I found your initials on the back of the screen. Where you said they'd be. We need to know more about the game."

Engle shook his head a little—not in response, but disbelief. The suspicion he'd felt after leaving the project—that he'd never be able to escape it—had been borne out. "I was wondering if you'd come back," he finally said.

Ro stepped up next to Andi. "I played. Both of us have. A lot of other people in our town too."

Engle's face tightened, but he didn't respond. He also didn't move, so Andi continued to press. "You broke into Gordon-Smith to try and destroy the cabinet, didn't you? Do you know about Thom Mazzy? What he did, after he saw the game?" Engle nodded, terse. "There's a whole town of Thom Mazzys north of here. Nobody understands what's happening, but it's bad, and we think it's going to get worse unless we do something about it."

Engle nodded. "It will. You didn't listen to me before, and I can understand why. But I'm telling you, you have to take it offline. Destroy it. Every piece. It was the only prototype ever built, but if you leave anything behind, somebody could . . . It'll never end if you don't end it."

"And that'll stop what's happening? If we destroy it?" Andi asked, hopeful.

Engle hesitated, wishing he could spare them the truth. "Nothing can stop what's started. You can only keep it from spreading."

Andi and Ro stared, aghast, as Engle's eyes darted away again. His expression, which hadn't shifted during the exchange, began softening at its fringes. He turned, starting back toward his house. It had been easier to ignore them when they'd just been strings of characters on a computer screen. Disembodied voices on the other side of his front door. But here, face-to-face, Engle knew someone owed them an explanation. And no one else was able to give it.

"You can come in," he said, without looking back.

Andi and Ro followed him inside. The home was beautiful, stately and immaculately maintained despite Engle's hermit-like appearance. The large dining room had been converted into a workshop, complete with shelving and benches in place of a table. Vast amounts of raw materials—copper wire, transistors and diodes, breadboards and blank printed circuits—were carefully organized in bins, each with impossibly neat handwritten labels. As they traced Engle's steps through the home, Andi stole a glance at a project he had underway—a visor of some kind, left resting on top of a mannequin's head. It was bulky, thick umbilicals jacked in here and there with struts attached like a surgical halo, to distribute its weight for the wearer.

Engle led them into an attached solarium teeming with plants, too carefully curated to be considered overgrown but jungle-esque all the same. Rain plinked, then rolled down the curved glass walls in crooked streams. Taking a seat in a wrought-iron chair, he nodded for Andi and Ro to do the same on the opposite side of a table covered in books and papers.

No one was sure where to start. It was Andi who finally broke the silence, cutting to the quick. "We know your name, but—who *are* you?"

"Nobody." Engle had to smile a little, though the sadness hanging over him still shone through. "I'm an engineer who had an idea that was too effective. Too malleable for its own good. The hardware—screen, delivery system—those were my contributions. But I never meant for it to become what it did."

"Delivery system. For what?" Ro asked, leaning in.

Engle exhaled, sinking back into his seat as he started to speak. "The first thing you should know is I won't have all the answers. I'll tell you what I can, but when it comes to what the game's doing, you can't take any of what I say as gospel."

"Whatever you can tell us, we want to hear," Andi reassured him.

"My company, Sinneslöchen, developed a screen that could analyze its environment. Thousands of image sensors woven into the glass would relay data to a CPU, and the display would adjust. We were building something that . . ." Engle's thoughts drifted for a moment, his eyes lost in the sea of plant life surrounding them. It seemed to bring him a measure of peace.

Andi looked at Ro, growing impatient. She went to prod Engle, but Ro, remembering what his father had told him about letting people tell their stories, tilted his hand a little. *Wait.*

His focus returning, Engle kept on. "I'm not going to tell you it would've helped people. But it would've made TV screens, computer monitors, things people spend their money on work better. I felt good about that. We needed funding before we could move into production."

Stopping, Engle glanced around the room, as if there were other people involved in the conversation they couldn't see. "Have you heard of ARPA?" he asked.

Andi had to think for a moment before it clicked. "Like Arpanet?" She glanced at Ro, correctly suspecting he was lost. "It was Usenet before Usenet."

Engle nodded. "Except now it's DARPA. *Defense* Advanced Research Projects Agency. They come up with technology the government might want to use and help develop it. Sometimes they do that in-house; sometimes they contract. After we'd demoed our display at a trade show, they agreed to fund Sinneslöchen. They wanted access to our research and prototypes. They saw something in what we were doing. I didn't know enough to ask what that something was."

Engle stood, nerves buzzing. He paced as he spoke, picking up a spray bottle and misting a few plants. "When I finally understood what they wanted to use it for, I told DARPA I'd pay them back and keep my research. But I couldn't stop it. And they didn't want me around anymore."

"Stop *what*?" Ro asked.

"They wanted to use the screen for a game. *Polybius*. The code came from someone else I never met. It was supposed to drive the screen to 'read' a player's psychological makeup based on how they responded to the game. Tracking how their eyes dilated, body temperature changed. How their musculature tensed, or relaxed. Then the game would adjust, to trigger a response. It could make you angry. Or paranoid. Scared. It could calculate what you'd buried, secrets you kept. Fears, anxieties. Then it would raise them to the surface. Things you might not know about yourself, or that you'd buried, deep. The game could find them. They called it psychological warfare, psyops. Fighting without weapons."

Nervous energy spent for the moment, Engle sunk back into his seat. "The government wanted a way to covertly destabilize communities, creating a pretext for intervention. Drop the game into a city, people play and start acting out. Everyone around them who *didn't* play starts acting out too, because suddenly they're paranoid over how their neighbor or their kid or whoever's acting. And there's no way to tell who's played and who hasn't. No physical effects. That was intentional, to create confusion. Chaos. *How do I know if you're still you?*"

Clocking Andi's and Ro's expressions, Engle could tell they were struggling to process. They *needed* to understand how dangerous, how insidious *Polybius* was if they were going to do what he hadn't been able to. "A state of emergency gets declared, then martial law, and finally the government steps in to suppress the threat and seize control. The way I heard it put was, if you were a moral person, the game made you frightened. If you were immoral, it made you aggressive. Of course, people don't come that way," Engle said, bitter amusement in his tone. "No one's perfectly moral or immoral. Good or bad. There are shades in everyone. And I think that's why it was so dangerous, because people are already unpredictable on their best day."

"What's it doing in *our* town? Who could honestly give a shit about Tasker Bay?" Andi threw out, exasperation getting the better of her.

Engle shook his head, wishing the answers weren't so messy. It was toxic knowledge he was bestowing—dark truths about the world that would leach into Andi and Ro, permanently reformatting their points of view. "Did you know the US has lost nuclear submarines, nuclear missiles that were never recovered? This government is great at making messes and terrible at cleaning them up. By the time I had a sense of what they were doing, the prototype was finished, and there had even been a beta test. In some . . . installation somewhere. The effects were horrible."

Engle seemed to drift off again, lost for a moment in a dark memory. "I ran into someone who'd worked on the game, and they said it'd been scrapped. The cabinet and . . . everything else had just been left in the warehouse where we'd been working. I started looking into what really happened to it. That's how I got arrested. I tracked it to that auction house. I tried getting to it before it sold. Obviously, I failed."

A phone began to ring in the other room and Engle rose to his feet. As he started to step away, he gestured around the solarium, into the house. "To really know, you're going to have to ask them. They're listening. They don't trust me anymore."

Ro stood up, eyes drifting around the room as Engle wandered off. *Is someone actually listening?* What Engle was saying sounded insane; only they knew it wasn't. He was probably telling the truth about this, too, then.

Something on the table centered in front of their seats caught Ro's eye, pulling him out of his thoughts. Sticking out from under the edge of the day's paper was the textured grip of a handgun.

Before Ro could slide the paper back, Engle reappeared in the solarium's entryway. He clutched a manila folder in his hand, but his attention went to the gun. "It isn't for you. If that's what you were thinking," he said matter-of-factly as he retook his seat and gestured for Ro to do the same. But Ro wouldn't budge. Andi tried taking his hand, pulling him away, but he stayed rooted to the spot.

"You played it?" Ro asked, the implication clear—*no one who played should be trusted with a gun*. Ro didn't like guns, but thanks to his dad he still knew how to handle them. He slipped the snubbed-nose Astra .44 out from under the paper, depressed the release, then pushed the cylinder away from the frame. A single round was inside. He shook the bullet loose and set both it and the weapon back onto the table in plain view. "Did you play?"

Engle nodded. "There's a . . . flaw in its design. It can't affect people who have certain impairments to their vision."

Andi stiffened. "Wait. What do you mean?"

Her tone and the sudden shift in body language were enough for Engle to realize what she was really trying to say. He tapped underneath his right eye. "Glass," he said. "You too?"

Andi nodded. *Close enough.*

Wary of the answer, Ro still asked, "What about everybody else?"

Shaking his head, Engle lowered his gaze. "I know that they were searching for a way to reverse the changes the game made to a player's mind. As far as I know, the project was shuttered before they found it." Engle watched his words wash over Ro and Andi, overcome with shame. "You can still destroy it."

"What if it—if you hadn't played it that much? If you're not . . . all the way *gone*?" Ro asked, desperation seeping in.

Engle shook his head. "It's like a poison. The more of it you take the faster it works, but once there's even a little inside you, there's no stopping it."

For a moment, Andi and Ro just sat, absorbing Engle's blunt decree. "Why don't you come with us," Andi finally asked, "back to Tasker Bay? You could help."

Engle shook his head, certain. "That's what I'm doing now." He passed the folder he'd brought back with him over to Andi. Opening it, she found dozens of papers covered in very official-looking markings, denoting them as "top secret" and "eyes only."

"That's everything I could get copies of," Engle said. "It might help if you decide to go to the press. I never felt capable, but you two seem braver. Just be careful if you do. The people who made the game made a mistake. They'll do whatever it takes to keep that a secret."

After watching Andi and Ro pull away, Engle disappeared back inside, locking the door behind him. He trudged through the home, gathering what he'd left in the solarium—stacks of newspapers as well as the handgun and solitary bullet—then dumped it all onto the bench occupying the center of his dining-room-turned-workshop.

Turning on a bank of IBM 5150s that lined one wall, matrixed together to help drive the visor that rested nearby, Engle booted the device. As fans hummed and drives churned, he glanced around, taking everything in—the world he'd made for himself, things he'd created from his own mind's eye, hoping for but never truly finding solace within any of it.

He carefully removed the visor from its stand and fitted it onto his head, adjusting the struts until the device was stable. Dozens of small screens that lined the inside of the device flickered to life, displaying an immersive, panoramic image of a pastoral field—the kind he'd grown up playing in and around as a child in the Swedish countryside.

Since reading about NASA's Jet Propulsion Laboratory conducting experiments in a new field called virtual reality, Engle had been obsessed with crafting his own device, something that could give him passage out of this world into another. He wanted to get away from what he'd done. Away from *Polybius*. As light from the display danced across his face, he seemed to finally relax.

He picked up and loaded the gun, cocked the hammer, leveled it against his temple, and pulled the trigger. As sparks showered, Engle slumped. Damaged but not destroyed, the visor flickered off and on, mutant colors rebounding off the lifeless face beneath it.

Roughly two thousand miles away in an anonymous, intentionally shabby-looking field office hidden in an industrial park in Fort Wayne, Indiana, junior Signals Intelligence Analyst Rebecca Liddy—tasked with monitoring a handful of feeds from US citizens under federal surveillance—yanked off her headphones and jerked back from her desk.

The feed from Nicolas Engle's home had been a source of consternation since it had been assigned to her two weeks ago. Nothing happened. *Ever.* She'd become so used to it, she would routinely monitor other sources simultaneously, confident she wouldn't miss anything.

When Engle had visitors the night before, then invited them inside earlier that morning, spilling what sounded like government secrets, she rushed to record the feed and take notes. With the volume on her headphones cranked up to clearly hear what was being said, she hadn't been ready for the concussive gunshot.

SIGINT agent Liddy grabbed a line that automatically dialed her on-duty superior, then ran down what had happened. Included were the names of Engle's guests and the location of the "outbreak" driven by the game: a town to the north of San Jose, Tasker Bay.

It had been half an hour since Andi and Ro had moved. A flash flood had washed out their route so, when the line of fifty-odd cars in front of them started making K-turns and heading back toward the city, they had no choice but to follow. With a map that didn't offer enough detail to navigate around the closure, they decided to pull into a gas station to pick up another.

Neither had said much since leaving Engle's. He'd given them more than they'd hoped for, just not a reason for hope. As they'd pulled away, Andi—who'd taken Ro's keys, wary of him suffering an episode while driving—reminded him that she still had the game's code and that members of the project team had been working on a cure. There *had* to be an answer other than "live with it," and they would find it, together. Ro had nodded but said nothing back.

Now, as he searched for a map in the narrow aisles of a convenience store attached to a gas station, Ro found himself sinking to the floor next to a walk-in cooler plastered with faded stickers for ice cream bars and candy. He sat, staring ahead, lost in dark thoughts about what his lack of a future held. He kept thinking back to the gun on Engle's table, the single bullet in the cylinder.

That was one way out.

Andi tried reaching her mom and then the sheriff's office on a pay phone in front of the store—hoping to convince someone to destroy the game now and find out why later—but phone service in Tasker Bay was out on account of the storm. Resigned that they'd have to get home as quickly as possible to tell their story in person, she headed back inside to find Ro.

Other than a bored-looking cashier, spinning from one station's coverage of the storm to the next on a transistor radio, it looked empty inside. "Ro?" Andi called out, anxiety building as she walked the aisles. Finally spotting him sitting on the floor as she rounded a corner, she assumed he was slipping into an episode and rushed over, grabbing him by the shoulders. She was surprised when he looked up. "What are you doing down here?"

"Checking out the floor. Pretty gross."

Andi slumped down opposite him, against a rack crammed with bags of chips. "Are you okay?"

Ro waved his hand around his head—*scrambled.* "None of this is okay."

"We're going to figure something out. We found out about Mazzy. We tracked down Engle. There's a folder in your car full of proof that we were right about the game. We can do this, too." Andi eyed Ro, seeing whether her words had had any effect. She couldn't tell. Feeling self-conscious, she hugged her knees. "Sorry. I don't give pep talks. You're supposed to be the optimist."

"They're bullshit. I used to hate when they'd do it before a game.

We're on one team, they're on another, let's just play." Ro's eyes finally met hers. "But yours was pretty good."

"Yeah, well, that's what I aim for," Andi said, parroting Ro's words to her back at Devon's. "Come on," she said, rising to her feet and offering him a hand up.

New map in hand, Andi and Ro were soon back on the road, following a course through higher elevations and around the flooding. Still riding shotgun and now navigating, Ro figured as best as he could that this new route would add at least two hours to their trip. But it was still better than being stuck in San Jose, without a way to warn their parents.

Despite what Andi had said, Ro doubted there was any way out of what he'd stumbled into. He was scared about what would happen, angry it was happening at all. Assuming they could destroy the game, what were they supposed to do after? Just sit around and wait for everyone, including him, to go crazy? Even if there was some sort of cure, he doubted it could be found in time.

Whether she saw or sensed that he was spiraling, Andi reaching over and taking his hand felt like a lifeline. He didn't want to let go, afraid he might slip over the edge if he did. Bad as things were, they could be worse. He was the only person going through this with someone who understood. Who still believed whatever darkness inside him the game had revealed, he was still good, and worth holding on to.

As the car climbed a hill, he glanced out the window. Even under the circumstances and shrouded by rain and fog, it was beautiful. Rolling green hills, broken by jags of gray serpentine rock, dotted the landscape before disappearing into the storm's haze.

As the road began to twist, Andi slipped her hand from his to take the wheel. Watching the scenery whip by, Ro experienced a darkly amusing moment of self-realization—he'd been preparing to disappear for a while now. He'd hoped the vague process of self-discovery he'd undertaken, leaving his old life behind in search of something new and more fulfilling, would've led to a better place than *this*. But as much as anything else anymore, it actually made sense. And perhaps made it easier. Having withdrawn from everyone, he wouldn't be missed now—or at least they'd miss him less. There was nothing left for him to do but wait for the world to go dark.

Which, strangely, it suddenly was.

"You better slow down," he said, glancing skyward.

"What?" Andi asked, reflexively easing her foot off the gas but failing to share his cause for alarm.

"The storm," Ro said, shocked she couldn't see it darkening everything around them. "You don't *see* it?" Then it hit him. He reached up and yanked on his seat belt's shoulder strap to lock it and pin himself in place, then clutched his arms and began breathing deeply, in and out, over and over. It wasn't the world going dark; *it was him*, his mind falling prey to the game's unpredictable thrall.

Realizing what was happening, Andi began to slow the car, but there was no shoulder, nothing but hillside to the left or right. "Hang on. You're okay. Ro? *You're going to be okay.*"

As his breathing accelerated, Andi reached over to lay a hand on him, to try to calm him, but he was already gone. His body bucked so violently at her touch that he broke his belt's retractor and began flailing in his seat, smacking Andi away and distracting her long enough that she lost control of the car.

As they skidded off the road and started careening down a hillside, the Land Cruiser clipped an outcropping of rock and flipped, landing on its roof. It skidded another hundred feet before slamming against a tree, coming to a dead stop. Rain sizzled as it pelted the still-hot undercarriage.

CHAPTER 19

RAGE. IT WAS THE ONLY WORD CLIFF YOUNG COULD PUT ON THE FEELING THAT HAD overtaken him that night. They'd been having fun, playing games. Well, just the one. *Polybius*. But still.

From the moment he and Mark Casey had tussled with the scrawny stranger at Home Video World—it was several days later when Cliff learned the man's name was Michael Newton—the aggression that had always simmered inside him had come to a boil.

When they'd spotted Newton leaving Bar Harbor later that night, they saw a chance to finish what they'd started. They'd tried to confront him on the street and, when Newton ran, gave chase. Mark had launched himself through the air, tackling Newton, and together the two had dragged him down an alley where they had taken turns beating him.

No stranger to violence on the field, Cliff had still never let loose on another person like that before. The smaller man's face had crumpled beneath his fists. He'd watched with perverse exhilaration as Mark—with a pair of rusty pliers from a tool kit kept in the trunk of his car—worked one of Newton's teeth out of his mouth at its root. If they hadn't been spotted by the sheriff, they would've taken turns pulling the rest, one by one.

Instead, the two wound up driving Newton deep into the woods, past a well that sat near Peck Creek. They'd battered him until they lost interest, dumping him into the creek and driving off.

Unlike Mark, who'd gone back to his old life and old self as if nothing had happened, Cliff felt like he never left those woods. He couldn't sleep, couldn't focus in school or at practice, had retreated deep into his own thoughts and steadily grown distant. While no one was going to accuse him of being overly introspective—a word he probably couldn't have defined if asked—he wanted badly to understand *why*. What had happened—what it had meant—who he'd become as a result.

As he made his way through the woods, the sights, the soundscape—the rush of the creek, the hum of the pumps connected to the nearby well—drew his mind back into that moment. Why was he compelled to relive it, to trigger a specific horrible memory over and over when it was the kind that any sane person would try to bury, or rush to confess?

Was his obsession with that night a sign? To truly understand what had happened, did he need to relive it?

Phone service in Tasker Bay had gone from bad to worse. David had dropped off a radio with Rachel the night before, tuned to the police band. The storm was poised to kill phone service all across town, most likely for days.

The strange turns people's mental health had taken. Andi's stranger theory as to why. Everything had seemingly landed on *her* doorstep. The lone bright spot in all of it was turning out to be David. She had started to wonder, when it was all over, whether there might be something between them worth exploring. It was a hopeful thought, the kind she needed, but it would have to wait. To her surprise, the phone was ringing.

When Rachel heard the tone in Molly Jiang's voice, she suddenly had a very bad feeling. Molly was her contact at the CDC. The two had met as med students at UCSF Fresno, rooming together for most of their rotations and growing close in a crucible of long hours and self-doubt. They'd kept in touch even as their career paths diverged, with Rachel going into private practice and Molly nimbly climbing the ladder in a regional office of the CDC.

"They had someone come and install it," Molly said about the fax machine that hummed day and night in her spare room. The line hissed and crackled as she spoke. "I never used it. Ever. But I then heard your message and this came in and I—" Molly exhaled, clearly uneasy at what she'd been dragged into. "I'm just going to read it, okay?"

Rachel listened as Molly recited the fax she'd received word for word, the connection threatening to give at any moment.

> All information contained in this memorandum must be considered Eyes Only. Tasker Bay, a village and census-designated place located in Sonoma County, California, is experiencing a mass outbreak of an unclassified neurological disorder. Any agency personnel contacted by civil servants or private citizens from Tasker Bay seeking assistance should

refuse, inform the caller that a government task force is mobilizing a response, and immediately report all details from the call utilizing the phone tree found on the attached contact sheet.

The outbreak is believed to be the result of exposure to a genus of bacteria, clostridium, found for as of yet undetermined reasons in Tasker Bay's primary water supply. Clostridium is understood to inhibit the release of serotonin, which can result in unprovoked and unpredictable aggression. The strain of clostridium in Tasker Bay significantly amplifies those effects. Anyone living within the village's twelve-mile radius must be considered a threat to themselves and others.

Ongoing inclement weather has created a temporary cordon around the village, which until further notice is a designated hot zone. Do not attempt to offer any assistance. Only the task force is authorized to respond.

Rachel just sat there, phone to her ear, silent. While the big picture tracked—people had turned aggressive for no apparent reason—details did not. "Who's . . . testing our water?" she asked, more puzzling out loud than she was expecting Molly to answer. "I mean, why were they even looking at Tasker Bay?"

"I, uh, I don't know." Molly hadn't expected pushback. Rachel was sounding paranoid.

"And if they're testing our water and making determinations, that takes time. This has been going on for two weeks. Have they known that long?" Rachel asked.

"I just thought you should know. If you're that worried, you could test the water yourself, I guess," Molly replied.

Earlier that morning, before Carl Delano's rampage, David had been up and on the radio, asking the National Guard for assistance. As a result of the storm, their services were in demand across the northern part of the state, but David *was* hoping his description of other events around town might set off alarm bells. From where he sat, Tasker Bay was on the verge of full-blown violent upheaval, but nothing he said broke through.

With the Guard promising they'd continue to liaise, David was left wondering what else he could do to try to keep things from escalating further. He had no idea the same message about Tasker Bay that the CDC had received had been making its way to *other* state and federal agencies too, chilling any reception to his request for help.

Deciding a stay-at-home order would at least keep people from triggering one another in public, he'd started drafting one that morning before being called away. Now, after the tragedy at Bayview Holdings, he wanted nothing more than to go home himself, draw the blinds, and be left alone.

For the first time in his career as a law enforcement officer, he'd been forced to kill someone. He'd done so to prevent an innocent man's death, and while the fact that he'd saved a life mattered, he could only see the pain frozen on Carl Delano's face as he lay on the floor, bleeding out.

He needed space to rest, reflect. Take a fucking breath. Only there was none. The number and intensity of the events around Tasker Bay seemed to hit a new clip daily, each surpassing the last. So, instead of taking a moment to recognize the trauma he'd experienced, he'd returned to the scene at the Delano farm to help Clarence Meeks with the Bayview employees' bodies and to speak with Julie Delano.

The woman had seemed numb to David, absorbing then burying his words somewhere deep inside. When he'd said his piece and she'd offered the faintest acknowledgment, he was all too relieved to go.

He'd taken on the responsibility of contacting the next of kin for Carl's victims too, which included Mary's husband, Roger Casey. The acrimony Roger had felt toward him, for suggesting his son Mark could've had something to do with the Peck Creek murder, came roaring back as David delivered the solemn news about Mary. Roger screamed, shoved David down the steps and off his porch before storming back inside and slamming the door so hard, a pane of glass embedded in it cracked. David had said nothing, just letting him vent, remembering what it felt like as he'd watched his own wife pass. He'd wanted to find someone and beat the life out of them, so he could give it to her.

Of course, things didn't work that way. But sometimes that didn't matter.

Andi came to, uncertain how long she'd been out. Everything was upside down. Bracing herself, she unbuckled her belt and thumped out of her seat onto the Land Cruiser's headliner. She'd been shaken up, pushed and pulled hard against her restraints, but nothing looked or felt broken, and she didn't see enough blood to worry.

Ro was slower to come around, any harm the crash might have inflicted blending with the lingering, disorienting effects of the spell he'd just been under.

"Ro? Can you hear me? We have to get out. Come on." Moving in, Andi helped to buttress him. "Can you undo your belt?"

Reaching over, Ro fumbled with the release for a moment until it clicked. With help from Andi, he lowered himself out of his seat.

They collected the papers from Engle, then climbed out through the shattered passenger-side window.

It took effort to scale the rain-slicked hillside. Finally reaching the top, Ro looked back at what was left of his car. Starting in eighth grade, he'd worked every summer and during his limited off-season windows to save up for it. His dad taught him how to change its oil; together they'd replaced the brake pads and spark plugs. During spring and summer, he'd spend the weekend mornings washing, waxing, detailing. Now, he wasn't even sure he could point out its location on a map.

It was also, incredibly, the least of their concerns. They'd plotted a specific path on small roads through hilly areas to try to avoid more flash flooding. It had worked, but they were now in the relative middle of nowhere and faced a pair of unappealing choices: backtrack in the rain for several miles toward a housing development they'd passed, or forge ahead on foot and try to hitch a ride.

Consulting their map to try to gauge how far they'd have to walk before reaching some sign of civilization, Ro spotted something more promising. Roughly six miles in the direction of home was a bus stop, on the edge of a small town. If they followed a straight line across the countryside instead of sticking to the road, those six miles could become two. So they set off. There was no way of knowing the bus schedule, but they were moving in the right direction. Once they reached the stop, they could follow the road and look for anyone willing to take them farther north, bus or otherwise.

Neither said much as they struggled through the terrain, still disoriented and aching. The weather made everything more difficult, both of them wiping out as they tried ascending a moderate hill only to stumble down the opposite side.

"What's your favorite movie?" Ro asked as they huffed along, breaking what had become a too-tense silence.

"Hm?" Andi's mind was elsewhere.

"Movie. Your favorite. I don't think we ever talked about it."

"I don't . . . know." Initially put off by Ro's obvious attempt at small talk, Andi found herself drawn into finding the right answer. "*The Wizard of Oz*. I think?"

"Oh, that's a good one. My mom took me to see that when I was like, five? When the flying monkeys showed up, I freaked out. She had to take me into the lobby so I could calm down."

Andi glanced at Ro, the frustration, anger at the situation she'd been feeling dissipating for the moment. He was good like that, finding ways to cut the tension. He listened, shared. She thought back to the effort she'd put into avoiding this kind of connection, seeing now she'd done so because of the toxic example set by her parents. But she hadn't wanted to face the hurt that seemed inextricably tied to caring for someone besides yourself either. Through Ro, she'd come to realize those risks could be worth it.

"I was going to say *Tron*, but *Wizard of Oz* is a classic. Guess I should go with a classic."

"*Tron* was cool," Andi offered as they navigated their way up a slope.

"Yeah," Ro said. "I guess—did you ever see *Point Blank*? Lee Marvin? My dad took me to see it when we were in San Francisco a few years ago. I'm pretty sure his character's dead, but he's going after these people who tried to rip him off. He's like a ghost. But with a gun. He was this *force*, you know? Nothing was going to stop him."

Andi could hear the marvel in Ro's voice and wondered if he was recalling a story that, favorite or not, gave him a dark sense of hope for his future. As the two talked, they crested the slope they'd been climbing—at the bottom of the next hillside sat the bus stop, denoted by a lonely roadside sign and bench. They were almost there. Making their way down, a noise grew in the distance, drawing closer—a bus, half a mile from the stop and heading their way.

"Come on," Ro said, taking Andi's hand and picking up the pace. As they cleared the hillside, splashing across an overgrown field toward the stop, the bus roared ahead. It was outpacing them—they were going to miss it. Snagged by a divot, Ro went down hard. Andi skidded, intending to go back and help him up, but he waved her on. "Go!"

Racing ahead, Andi could only watch as the bus passed the empty stop and continued on. She screamed, waving her arms, chasing after until her legs could no longer propel her forward.

But someone, driver or passenger, must have seen her. Before the bus was set to round a bend and disappear from sight, it lurched to a stop, brake lights burning red. Glancing over her shoulder, breathless, Andi saw Ro limping after. She hurried to him, tucking under his shoulder for support, the two of them hobbling to meet their ride.

As the door hissed opened and they climbed on board—wet, muddy, bruised—the driver looked them up and down for a long moment, alarmed. "Jesus. You two okay?"

Andi and Ro glanced at one another, then nodded. Neither saw a point in slowing things down with details. "We need to go north. Tasker Bay," Andi said, still huffing and puffing.

The driver shook his head. "This route gets you close, but that whole area's flooded. Nobody's going in or out."

"Drop us as close as you can," Andi said as they limped up the steps. Pooling their cash for the fare, they stuffed it into the driver's hand, then found seats nearby. As the bus pulled away, Andi took out the folder Engle had given them, resting her head on Ro's shoulder as she started paging through the documents.

It had taken Rachel half an hour to reach the path leading to the town's well, near Peck Creek. What was normally a ten-minute drive had extended on account of two washed-out roads. A sample from her own tap would've been easier, but she wanted data as close to the source as possible and uncorrupted.

As she made her way into the woods, she noted another car

parked nearby that hadn't been visible from the road. A week or so ago the thought wouldn't have crossed her mind, but with everything she'd seen and heard, it gave her pause. Turning around, she grabbed the police radio David had given her. Just in case.

She reached Peck Creek and followed it to the location of the well from which most of the town's drinking water was drawn. As she walked, she continued parsing her conversation with Molly. Supposing there *was* something wrong with the water—which, she had to remind herself, had been her initial suspicion too—it made sense for the government to try to quietly investigate before making any sort of announcement. But when Molly had read the memo over the phone, one line in particular stood out.

The strain of clostridium in Tasker Bay significantly amplifies those effects.

If whoever was responsible for the memo understood that this was a unique variant of a dangerous bacterium, why wasn't more information given? It felt intentionally obtuse, and it was sticking in Rachel's craw. In an emergency, sharing as much common knowledge about the problem as possible was the best way forward. If something truly significant was impacting the citizens of Tasker Bay, shouldn't they be warned? Protected?

Rachel wasn't naive. She'd come of age in the era of My Lai and Watergate. Government scandals and malfeasance had become a disappointingly accepted part of American life. But she still found it hard to believe that lives would be put at risk to cover up something like a bacterial outbreak.

She wasn't sure, but as she approached a pumping station attached to the well, she took heart in the fact she'd soon know more for herself. Examining the small pumping station, which drew on a natural aquifer beneath it, Rachel found and muscled open a rusty valve that allowed her to quickly capture samples. She'd have been done, if a voice hadn't called out from behind her.

"Dr. Winston?"

Rachel's heart jumped. She spun, dropping one of her samples, the vial shattering as it hit the ground. Standing twenty-some feet away was Cliff Young, who looked as surprised to see her as she was to see him.

"It's, uh, Cliff. Young."

Still shaken, Rachel nodded. "Yeah, I remember. Wh-what are you doing out here?"

"I don't know," Cliff said after a too-long pause, sounding genuinely confused.

Rachel scoffed a little, uncertain how to take him. "Well," she said, trying to mask her nerves, "I'm on my way home. You have a jacket? Umbrella? It's cold out here. And wet. Obviously." Her attempt at small talk seemed to bounce right off him. Cliff's face betrayed nothing, a blank slate onto which Rachel found herself projecting a growing sense of threat.

Finished securing the surviving samples, she went to close the bag and saw the police radio inside. Discreetely taking it, she offered a tight smile as she started away. "Take care of yourself, okay?"

With a little distance between herself and Cliff, Rachel considered radioing Evie but wasn't sure what to say. He'd acted strange but hadn't done anything other than startle her. Then she saw it—movement, on her periphery. She pulled the radio to speak, but it was already too late as Cliff cut across the woods at full speed, face red and eyes burning with rage. He lunged, grabbing her arm and spinning her to the ground.

Stunned, Rachel could only watch as Cliff snatched a heavy stone then knelt beside her. Coming around as he raised the rock into the air, preparing to strike, she swung the police radio and slammed it against the side of his head. Cliff reeled back, but with her lifeline now in pieces, Rachel's only choice was to get back on her feet and run.

Backtracking, she sprinted deeper into the woods. It felt counterintuitive, but she couldn't outrace him to her car, and the ground cover was thicker farther in, offering a chance to hide. Cliff was already back on his feet, and she could hear his hulking stride quickly gaining ground.

As she passed a wide, towering box elder, she circled around it then skidded to a stop, waiting for Cliff to race past. Snatching up a jagged branch, she froze, back to the tree.

Realizing he'd lost her, Cliff slowed, scanning the terrain. Stalking back toward the tree—toward Rachel—he had no time to even raise a hand in defense as she spun out of hiding, swinging the branch at his face with such force it snapped in half—one part in her hands, the other embedded deep inside Cliff's right eye. He screamed, flailing, gripping then yanking it free.

For a moment Rachel just stared in horror, shocked she'd managed to hit him, maim him for life with one swing. Some deep instinct told her to help him, that he was just a kid—then he swiped at her, clawing her face and screaming furiously.

The pain snapped her awake, propelling her forward. There were hollows closer to the creek, places where she could disappear. If she could draw him back in that direction, she'd give herself more space to turn around toward her car. She'd wounded him badly, and the longer she kept him moving, the more likely he'd wear down.

Rachel spotted an outcropping of soil that clung to the roots of a black oak, climbed down, and ducked underneath into its hollowed-out root structure, eyes darting back and forth as she watched for Cliff. At the same time, she searched for something she could use as a weapon, finding a rock with enough heft that it could do some damage.

She spotted him as he angled his way down an embankment a dozen yards away, toward the overflowing creek. He'd lost his coordination with his eye, whipping his head back and forth, struggling to find an angle on his surroundings as blood flowed down his face.

As he approached, Rachel inched back to try to stay out of sight but realized the roots were blocking her. She grabbed and smeared a handful of dirt over her face, instinctively trying anything to blend in. But as Cliff drew nearer, she panicked at the thought of being cornered and ran.

He gave chase, gaining on her before lunging and snaring her ankle. They splashed into the fringe of the swollen creek. Rachel kicked, striking Cliff in the face multiple times until, overwhelming him with fresh pain, he let go.

Both staggered to their feet. As Cliff charged, Rachel swung the rock she still carried but missed, stumbling and falling back into the water. Rising up, she saw him circling toward her, and she scooped up a handful of sediment from the creek bed and flung it into his face. Recoiling, Cliff slipped on a mossy log and fell, hard, head thumping on a rock beneath the surface.

Rachel clambered past and didn't stop until she'd made it back up the bank. Turning back, she looked for Cliff, but he hadn't made it out. He was already twenty yards down the creek, struggling feebly against the current as it pulled and buffeted him back and forth. Eventually he slipped under and, for a long moment, stayed there. When Rachel finally saw him again, he was floating face down, drifting away.

CHAPTER 20

THE LATE OCTOBER SUN SEEMED TO SET EARLIER THAN IT SHOULD'VE THANKS to the storm. Through static-filled bursts relayed over his car's radio, Patrick could overhear a DJ talking about it in historical terms—there hadn't been this much rain in northern California in close to fifty years.

It had been dark for days on end, wearing on everyone in deep ways they weren't able to articulate. As he drove through downtown, Patrick realized the massacre at Bayview Holdings that morning had actually brought people back out onto the streets after many had spent the past few days in hiding.

The people he saw looked angry, frightened, confused. The storm had trapped them just as something inexplicable seemed to have gripped the town, drawing out the worst in everyone. They weren't getting answers to their problems and had no way out, creating a combustible mix of personalities pushed to the edge.

It felt to Patrick like an echo chamber. If you weren't angry, you were scared. If you were scared, you felt no choice but to get angry, so you could be ready to defend yourself. *Around and around.* As he left the crowds behind, driving across town, he had a horrible sense they'd all be at one another's throats before the night was through.

Eventually he found himself in front of Mal's door, knocking and waiting. Mal's truck was gone, and normally Patrick would've just assumed he wasn't home, but with the way Mal had been acting, he couldn't be sure. He tried again, this time calling Mal's name—nothing, still.

Several years ago, Mal had shown him where he kept a spare key, so Patrick could check in on the place while he was out of town for a funeral. Since then, they'd arrived at an understanding where, if Mal needed something and couldn't get home, Patrick could drop in and grab it for him. He could also pick up a dime bag from the stash Mal kept hidden behind the bathroom mirror, so long as he left enough cash to cover it. Mal didn't do "friend" discounts.

This is what had brought Patrick out of hiding. It had all gotten to be too much around Tasker Bay, and he needed something to take the edge off while he hunkered down to ride out the storm. Finding the spare key, he knocked one more time before making his way inside and out of the rain.

Maneuvering through the mess and into the bathroom, Patrick jimmied the mirror loose. The stash looked off. Mal had consolidated everything into one corner with no apparent rhyme or reason. He may have been a slob when it came to most areas in life, but Mal had always been meticulous about his product. The "shelf," just a board wedged in place between the two-by-fours that framed the house, seemed loose as well. Maybe it had broken, Patrick reasoned; just from him moving the mirror, it seemed to wobble. Suddenly afraid he might accidentally knock thousands of dollars' worth of contraband off the shelf and in between the walls of Mal's home, he moved everything out onto the sink, then decided he'd try to secure the shelf a little better. That, he figured, Mal wouldn't mind.

But as he removed it, he saw the brown paper bag. Generic, the kind you'd get from any shop, it had one obvious quirk—black singe marks that darkened one side. Pulling a lighter from his pocket and striking it, Patrick lowered it into the narrow space behind the bathroom wall. Telling himself he'd take a quick look to satiate his curiosity then put it back, grab some weed, and go, he fished the bag out. Thousands in cash sat inside. Patrick had never seen so much of it at once.

As much as he found himself enjoying the sensation of flipping through bill after bill, this was none of his business. As he went to stuff the money back into the bag, he noticed something tucked into one of the wads that had been rubber-banded together—a slip of paper. It was an impromptu ledger of some kind, numbers scribbled in handwriting that Patrick knew wasn't Mal's. It was written on an otherwise blank receipt with the Bottle Shoppe's name printed along the top.

What the fuck is this?

He started counting the money. The prospect of Mal walking in—what he'd think, what he'd do—loomed, but something deeper was compelling him. The numbers aligned with the ledger. Mal had hidden nearly six thousand in cash, in amounts that corresponded with an accounting not in his handwriting and scribbled on a blank receipt from a shop that had just burned down under mysterious circumstances. Mal had been there that night, burned his hands trying to save poor Ed Sanko.

Or . . . ?

A block away from his house, Mal rolled to a stop when he saw Patrick sprint out the front door. He moved with urgency, not to keep out of the rain but with some larger purpose. Mal watched him swivel around as if checking for something, someone.

What was he doing inside that made him so paranoid somebody else would see?

As Patrick sped past, Mal crept back onto the road and followed him in the direction of downtown.

Mal's head swam with conspiratorial thoughts as both vehicles made their way onto Main Street. Patrick's willingness to turn up whenever a hand was needed, at home or at the shop. His loyalty when it came to keeping quiet about all of Mal's illegal side grinds. What had it meant? Where had it led?

What the fuck was he doing?

While the drive he felt to leave town hadn't waned, Mal *had* decided he needed to button a few things up first. He'd stopped by Home Video World earlier that day, taking whatever cash was on hand—including several hefty bags of coins—before throwing open the doors and walking away. Assuming the chaos in the streets continued, the store would almost certainly wind up looted, trashed, maybe—hopefully—burned. It was better, he'd decided, if he had no hand in any of that. The loss of the store would provide cover, in the event people began asking questions about his disappearance. David had *already* been too interested in him, after what had happened at the Delanos' stables.

He'd convinced himself the only option was to run, but as he followed Patrick through downtown, he was gripped by a vague notion that whatever was going on here wasn't through with him yet. He was still wrestling with the question of who he was, whether the hardened criminal he imagined dwelling inside him all these years had been an illusion.

Slowing, he watched Patrick pull to a stop across the street from the sheriff's office, step from his car, then hurry toward the entrance. Clutched tight in his hand was the bag containing the money that Mal had stolen—*killed for*—from the Bottle Shoppe.

He had to get it back. Wasn't leaving without it. From nowhere a voice hissed inside his head, jolting him awake. *If you are what you say you are, walk in there and take it. Then burn this whole place to the ground on your way out.*

Rachel sat in her car along the roadside for what felt like an eternity. She could see Cliff Young's truck parked up ahead and kept thinking, *Who's going to pick it up?* It was the least of anyone's problems, but it was the one directly in front of her, and she needed something to focus on to keep from falling all the way apart.

She already felt frozen in place. An adrenaline-fueled sprint had taken her back to her car from the creek, and now she could feel herself coming down, liable to crash then and there. She just wanted to close her eyes and wake up somewhere, sometime different from now.

But she found her hand fishing keys from her pocket and firing the ignition, and through the storm she navigated back to her practice. *I should find David,* she thought, but muscle memory took over. She'd planned on returning to work, so that's what she was doing.

She pulled up and hurried inside, grateful beyond words no one was waiting for her out front. Knowing she had to report what had happened, she decided she'd better test the sample she'd nearly lost her life obtaining first, while it was still stable.

She was still processing the fact that she'd killed someone. *A kid.* She'd done it in self-defense, but that was cold comfort as she keyed inside her office. She locked the door then retreated to a small room in back that served as a combination supply closet and low-end lab.

Clostridium wouldn't be visible on a stock microscope like the one Rachel kept on-site, but then, hers was no longer stock. A few Christmases ago Devon had, in an unusually selfless and thoughtful act, taken hers and modified it with Andi's help, incorporating computer controls for more precise adjustments and swappable lenses that increased its magnification tenfold. The device's accuracy and convenience were enough to make Rachel overlook the fact that seeing it always reminded her of what he was capable of, and how seldom he rose to those levels.

As she prepped a series of slides from the water sample she'd taken, her hands proved too shaky. She lost two slides and, in a stubborn effort to show her nerves who was boss, dropped a third to the floor, where it shattered along with the others. Her sample was dwindling, and she sure as hell wasn't going back out there.

Drawing a deep breath, she managed to steady her hand and was soon studying the samples through the custom eyepiece Devon and Andi had machined in their garage. Slide after slide told the same disturbing story—one that, on any other day, would've been welcome news. Tasker Bay's water was pristine.

As best Andi and Ro could figure, the bus had dropped them roughly four miles from the center of town. Night had already fallen by the time they disembarked, with nothing but a long, dark, waterlogged hike ahead. Before the driver had pulled away to finish his route, he'd taken sympathy and tossed them a flashlight he kept under his seat. As they made their way, navigating increasingly deep, invisible pools filled by fast-moving currents, it was a literal lifesaver.

The ride down had given them time to examine the documents from Engle. Taken together, they painted an incomplete but still startling picture of a project irresponsible in conception, execution, and eventual abandonment.

One of the most shocking documents detailed a list of possible-use scenarios for the game, including "American ghettos," with neighborhoods in San Francisco, Los Angeles, Chicago, and New York explicitly mentioned as possible targets.

A weapon paid for by us, to be used against us.

By installing cabinets in strategic locations, the government theorized it could covertly instigate riots, then send in police and military authorized to use lethal force to pacify them. Minority populations would be driven off or worse, paving the way for redevelopment and gentrification. The implications were as frightening in scope as they were staggering in scale. That the project was ultimately abandoned offered cold comfort. The cabinet really was akin to the loose nuclear weapons Engle had offered in analogy. Forgotten, but no less potent an agent of destruction.

Huddled in their seats, chatting in low voices, Andi and Ro had taken what was on the page and extrapolated to the point each felt like they could see an apocalypse on the horizon, a world where every image you saw had the potential to rewire your brain. But now, as they trudged over ground that gave way with every step and threatened more than once to swallow them up or sweep them away, those thoughts had been back-burnered. They just needed to stay on their feet, destroy the cabinet, find David and Rachel, then look for a way out of town. The world would have to be warned later.

Off Engle's insistence that *someone* was listening and a fatalistic strategy for containing people affected by the game found in one of the white papers, it was clear that someone was coming to clean up the mess that was Tasker Bay. And they would cover it up, no matter the cost.

After an hour on foot they saw the outlines of several large, darkened homes, part of Aurora, a Bayview-backed subdivision. At the first multistory sprawl they came to, they made the mistake of letting their flashlight's beam cross one of the windows. Before they could even knock to ask for help, the door opened and the barrel of a hunting rifle swung out, firing over Ro's head. Lighting out, they dodged another shot before coming to a line of cars that gave them some cover.

The line kept going. As they followed it, they heard noise—music, voices—booming from a massive new home, the site of a riotous Halloween party. The power was out here, too, but fires burned and a few pickups with high-intensity rack lights flooded the area. People in costumes darted in and out of the beams, scuffling, staring off at nothing. The house was trashed, most of the furniture on the lawn or piled into a roaring bonfire.

"Think they have a phone?" Ro asked.

Shattering a second-story window, a heavy lamp flew out and landed in front of them.

"You want to go in there?" From her tone, Andi clearly didn't. "The keys have to be in those trucks, right?"

Ro took Andi's arm and pushed through the crowd toward a distant pickup, the easiest to steal without being noticed. But he caught sight of Laurel and Mark arguing near the edge of a bonfire, where a group of kids far too young to be there were piling on furniture, clothing, towels, anything from inside the house they could find.

"Hang on." As Ro started toward them, he could hear Mark raging at Laurel.

"Shut the fuck up! I said I'm going—"

"I'm not." Laurel's voice was flat, unemotional and unbothered.

"Get in the fucking car, Laurel!" He grabbed her, yanking her through the fire's edge toward him.

Clamping a hand on Mark's shoulder, Ro spun him around and pushed him away from Laurel, sending him onto his ass and skidding across what was left of the lawn.

Laurel strode toward him and raked a hand across his face, slicing skin. Mark screamed and clawed after her, but Ro slammed a foot on his chest before he could raise himself off the ground and kept it there. Mark spat at him, finally working his way out from under but staying down.

Seeing Laurel walking toward her car, Andi tagged Ro's shoulder—*Time to go*—and the two of them hurried to an F-150 with blazing halogens parked near the edge of the commotion.

At the door, Ro paused, glancing back toward Mark. He was up, huffing away into the dark, no longer a threat to Laurel.

"Ro? What's she doing?" Ro followed Andi's voice to Laurel, who was heading back toward the party, lugging a plastic gas can. She tossed it into the center of the fire, turning back and walking away after. The gas quickly caught, and the bonfire exploded in a massive fireball, spraying liquid flame across everything and everyone in a radius that reached the side of the house. The crowd erupted in panic and celebration as the fire spread.

The lights in the sheriff's office had started stuttering as soon as Patrick stepped inside. The first time the space dipped to black he'd spun, expecting to see Mal behind him, hand on the switch. He knew he was about to cross a line that would end a decade-long friendship. His only one, really. It was the right thing to do, but it made him uneasy. In more ways than one.

Now, sitting across from Charlie in the office's small bullpen, watching as he scribbled details into a notebook, Patrick tapped a nervous thumb on the desk. This was taking too long. He was ready to be done and locked down inside his small bungalow on the fringes of town.

Around them, Evie busied herself gathering flashlights, candles, and radios that still held a charge as the lights continued to flicker and dim. "I'm going to start the generator," she called, disappearing in back.

"I understand what it took for you to come in," Charlie said, finally looking up from the report, "and I appreciate it. Until we're able to talk to Mal, I advise that you don't."

"When he finds that money's gone, he's going to ask me about it. I don't think anyone else knows about the spare key. Or where he was keeping the money," Patrick said. "He's not . . . himself all of a sudden, you know? And if he really did something like this, I don't know what he'd do if he knew I was here talking to you all."

Charlie understood. Patrick was right, Mal probably *would* come looking for answers, and he was the most obvious person to give them. "You're welcome to stay here until we pick him up. You can go home, but I don't advise it. If you do, just don't—"

Patrick never heard the rest of Charlie's advice, as a slug from Mal's sawed-off Ruger Model 44 carbine slammed into the back of his skull. The force of impact jerked Patrick to the floor.

Standing in the doorway to the bullpen, Mal trained the still-smoking gun on Charlie, who snapped to and dove clear as Mal began firing. He crawled between desks, desperately searching for cover as the room exploded around him.

At the sound of gunfire, Evie abandoned the generator, leaving the office to stutter in and out of darkness. Peering out as Mal stalked toward Charlie, she ducked back out of sight, quietly fumbling through her keys as she padded toward the office's small evidence locker. She clicked open the lock and seized the shotgun Carl Delano had used that morning during his assault on the Bayview Holdings office, along with a handful of shells found in his pocket.

Moving carefully through the back hallway, she passed the holding cells where Robby Jr. and Kelly had both been roused from their malaise and stood near the bars listening, waiting to see what would happen next.

Mal let go of the Ruger as it clicked empty, a strap slung across his chest dropping it to his side, and pulled a revolver from behind his back. Springing out of cover, Charlie fired but Mal didn't budge, didn't flinch, blasting back. Three rounds pierced Charlie's chest, sending him to the floor.

Evie watched Charlie's fingers twitch, grasping at something invisible until they slowed and finally stopped. Rage, instinct, something pushed her out from cover, and she fired on Mal, buckshot shredding the bullpen and pockmarking his shoulder. As the shotgun clicked empty, Mal stalked toward her, snatching up Charlie's revolver and firing the remaining rounds. Evie spun, stumbling against the holding cell doors as she sprinted away, the shotgun and her keys dropping to the floor. But she didn't slow down or look back, crashing through an emergency exit and out into the night.

Mal didn't bother to follow, reloading the Ruger with a steady focus. Hearing Evie's keys jingle as Robby Jr. reached through the bars of his cell, he paused. The two locked eyes as the cell door clanked opened. Tossing the keys into Kelly's cell, Robby Jr. disappeared through the emergency exit, unconcerned with the bloodshed that had just unfolded a few feet away.

As the equally disassociated Kelly let herself out of her cell, Mal walked past and into the evidence lockup, gathering a handgun, shotgun, and loose rounds for both, all confiscated over the past few days from the would-be vigilantes and self-appointed "town security officers" being goaded on by Paul Nantz. But his eyes kept being drawn back to a long, curved blade resting on one of the shelves and wrapped in a protective plastic bag.

A billhook . . .

Mal could suddenly see himself, standing in dull moonlight in front of the Delanos' stables . . . letting himself in . . . staring at the horses lumbering in their stalls, eyes covered by fly masks . . . finding the billhook hanging alongside a rusted set of farrier's tools . . .

It was me. But the realization didn't hit the way he might have expected. Some part of him had known, and in the haze of the last weeks had been looking for the right moment to remember. He didn't recoil or chastise himself. It was a part of him, a part of who and what he was finally becoming.

He reveled in knowing.

With the billhook tucked into his belt, he stepped back into the hall, where Kelly was clutching the shotgun Evie had dropped as she fled the office. For a moment the two stared—Mal across at Kelly, Kelly down at the gun.

Reaching back into the lockup, he grabbed a half-empty box of shells and tossed it over to her. A deep, concussive boom sounded from outside, distant but unmistakable—an explosion, powerful enough to rattle the office and everything in it.

Bemused, Mal headed out into the rain while Kelly reached down and gathered the ammo.

It was almost closing time when Laurel pulled into the Paulson's lot. A drive that should've taken twenty minutes had lasted over an hour thanks to a growing number of washed-out roads, and she was quietly relieved to find that the store was still open. Its lights were still on too, on account of a massive generator humming out back.

Her aim was simple: make people too scared to ever set foot inside a Paulson's market again. Her plan, though, was another story. She had to lock the building down. Haul in then distribute a dozen cannisters of gas. Set fire to enough of the store that it wouldn't stop burning until it ran out of fuel. All of that, without being stopped.

Hauling a canvas bag that looked like it weighed more than her from the back of her station wagon, she made her way around the building's exterior, sealing each exit shut with thick-gauge chain and a heavy-duty padlock before coming full circle to the front entrance.

Having pulled into a spot along the lot's edge moments earlier, Mark Casey watched Laurel as she pushed a shopping cart back to her car and filled it with cannister after cannister of what he assumed was gas. Loaded down, she left the cart sitting just outside the front entrance, then walked in.

If his head had been clearer, his mind right, Mark might have wondered *why*. But his focus was on Laurel, not what she was doing. Having followed her all the way here from the party, he was set on making her regret rejecting him, and not just tonight.

Laurel whisked past the handful of customers still shopping, making a line for aisle three, where charcoal, lighter fluid, liter bottles of propane, and paper products were stocked side by side. *Poor planning,* she thought. She grabbed bottles of lighter fluid and emptied them over everything in the aisle. About to strike a match, she spun at the sound of a clerk's voice.

"Hey, what did—what are you doing?"

Laurel had seen him before as she'd wandered the aisles, formulating her plan. He was around her age, maybe a year or two older, and had seemed nice when he'd asked before if she needed help.

Oh well.

As he approached, she turned one of the bottles on him, spraying him with accelerant, then striking a match and tossing it. He caught like dried brush, spinning into the shelves. The rest of the aisle ignited in seconds, streaks of fire chasing wild sprays of lighter fluid, paper bursting into flame. Laurel had chosen well.

It took the staff and remaining customers a moment to realize what was happening, which gave Laurel a window to wheel in the shopping cart filled with gas cannisters she'd left outside. After chaining the front entrance shut then setting it ablaze, she pushed the cart with everything she had through the store.

No one's getting out of here alive. Me included.

Mark, who'd made his way in before Laurel had sealed the store, caught sight of her as she sped around a corner, iridescent trail of gas shimmering in her wake as cannisters glugged onto the floor. He went to follow, but Laurel ignited the fuel, sending a river of fast-moving flame zigzagging through the aisles. The fire chased him, leaping off the floor through a cloud of fumes, leaching onto the soles of his shoes. Mark swatted, trying to put them out, setting fire to his hands instead. Viscous, burning strings of melted rubber began sizzling down past skin and muscle to nerve and bone—he couldn't stop it, couldn't pull it off without completely tearing all the skin from his hands.

Laurel finished dumping fuel then stepped back, smiling, watching the fear escalate as the crowd found one exit after the other locked. Her gaze fixed on Christine Abernathy as she searched for a way out, steadily thickening smoke slowing her frantic pace.

Suddenly Laurel was seized from behind, and Mark slammed her into a shelf filled with pots and pans. She found her bearings as he charged again, snatching up a baking dish and cracking it against the side of his head.

With the blaze crawling over everything, it was getting harder to see. Drawing Mark into the thick of it, weaving around a half dozen bodies violently choking from smoke inhalation, Laurel thought she'd lost him, only to have Mark spring at her and cinch his hands around her throat. But before he could finish her off, she was on him instead, jabbing her thumbs into his eyes with animalistic force. Flailing, Mark sent her skidding across the floor then dove after. As they wrestled, rolled, the shelving around them began to collapse. Grabbing a boiling-hot metal can—adrenaline blunting the pain as it cooked her skin—Laurel swung it, shattering Mark's nose and knocking him senseless.

She scrambled clear moments before another shelf folded over, flaming contents spilling onto Mark and igniting his clothes. Engulfed in seconds, he collapsed, spasmed, then went limp.

Breathless from battle, Laurel was gulping too much smoke to stay upright. But as she wilted to her knees, a voice echoed.

"Come on! Get up, come on!"

Through the smoke and haze Laurel caught sight of an outline, a figure rushing toward her. Collapsing to the floor, she never knew it was Christine who'd come back for her or that neither of them would make it out of the store alive. Flames sucked into the generator's air intake sparked a massive explosion that ripped through and razed the store in a wild, violent flourish.

CHAPTER 21

FROM ITS INCEPTION, THE ARCHITECTS OF PROJECT LETHBRIDGE—ENCOMPASSING the conception, design, and fabrication of *Polybius*—recognized that its effects had the potential to rapidly spiral from bad to much, much worse. Act too late and "reasonable force" would no longer be enough to control an affected area. More drastic action would be required.

In Tasker Bay, the window for reasonable force had long ago closed.

A platoon of soldiers with the Seventh Infantry Division, stationed at Joint Base Lewis-McChord roughly eight hundred miles to the north, was being mobilized in response to intel picked up via surveillance feeds in Nicolas Engle's home. Given the same cover story as other federal agencies—that Tasker Bay's citizens were suffering en masse from an irreversible bacterial infection, driving an escalating outbreak of violent, homicidal behavior—the soldiers were warned that engagement with US citizens would be inevitable.

But it wouldn't be on them to clear out the entire town by

hand. Four Hughes 500P helicopters, modified to run silent a decade earlier for clandestine work in Vietnam, would fumigate Tasker Bay with sarin gas sprayed overhead from pressurized tanks. A nerve agent so toxic that just a fraction of an ounce on the skin is considered lethal, it had been requisitioned from the Deseret Chemical Depot just outside Salt Lake City, Utah, and was en route to a private airfield twenty miles to the east of Tasker Bay. Thirty minutes after the choppers completed their run, giving the sarin time to dissipate, soldiers from the Seventh Infantry Division in NBC suits—designed to protect against nuclear, biological, and chemical exposure—would sweep through and mop up any survivors.

It was a draconian response, but there were no other viable options in the eyes of the limited pool of high-level decision-makers aware of the situation. There was no known method to reverse *Polybius*'s effects. This made so-called real exposures—those who'd played the game—a permanent threat to themselves and others, and the need to cover up the game's existence *and* accidental release paramount. There was no other choice. Tasker Bay would be wiped off the map, and a combination of spin and deflection would have to run at full tilt for years after to avoid the truth *ever* coming out.

While a Caribou cargo plane rushed tanks of sarin westward, soldiers were being moved south in the belly of a massive Lockheed C-5 Galaxy. The operation, code-named Centralia in recognition of a ghost town created by an industrial accident in Pennsylvania circa 1962, was set to commence at 2330 on Sunday, October 31, 1982.

A horror show.

It sounded too trite to do it justice, but it was the only turn of phrase that came to mind as Andi and Ro navigated the remains of Tasker Bay's downtown.

Trash, clothing, furniture, fixtures had been flung onto Main Street—some through shop windows, some of it set on fire—creating a slalom around which Andi had to navigate.

Costumed faces could be seen dipping in and out of the shadows in violent motion, fighting or fleeing, laying waste to whatever they happened upon at random. Streetlights were busted or flickering, as power continued to fluctuate. Most of the light came from fires uncontained and spreading. The sound of sporadic gunfire echoed, its sources unseen.

A group of kids in Halloween costumes lit fireworks and chucked them through shattered windows, while a young woman covered in blood attempted to break down a shop door, someone throwing their weight against the other side and screaming for help that wouldn't come soon enough.

As they passed Home Video World, Andi slowed. Cabinets were on the sidewalk and street, in pieces. Ribbons of glossy black videotape covered everything, ripped from their reels and whipped about by the wind.

Someone had fired on a generator that Mal kept in back. Not even the rolling blackouts could bring *Polybius* offline. A crowd at least eighty-strong was gathered, disciple-like, around the game. Its members surged at random, scuffles breaking out that would radiate from person to person like ripples in water.

Ro noticed eyes drifting toward the rumble of the F-150, drawn to the prospect of something new to destroy. Seeing the mob starting to encroach, Andi hammered the gas and tore down the street, hands slapping at the bed as people tried in vain to climb on, then spilled hard across the street as they failed.

Out of nowhere the rear window exploded, catching a stray bullet from somewhere in the dark. Andi and Ro ducked, swerving onto the sidewalk and narrowly missing a lamppost before veering wildly back onto Main Street.

Rising up out of cover just in time to see a figure in the middle of the road, Andi hit the brakes. She and Ro stared wide-eyed at Robby Sapp Jr. crossing the street in front of them, dragging two lifeless bodies behind him. Large shark hooks pierced their chests, attached to rusty lengths of chain slung over Robby Jr.'s hulking shoulders. Wide streaks of blood trailed behind them.

Andi kept on, the chaos dying down as they moved toward the edge of downtown where the sheriff's office sat. Andi pulled the truck to a stop out front, and she and Ro piled out and rushed inside, freezing at the sight of Charlie and Patrick sprawled over the bullpen floor.

"Holy shit." The words fell from Ro's mouth as he slowed. He'd known Charlie for years, remembered when his dad had hired him. Like that, he was gone. "Do you think Robby—"

"I don't know," Andi said. She felt a sudden, unexpected pang of sadness looking down on Patrick. He was a mess but thoughtful, kind in his way. And who out there would miss him? He deserved better.

The office had been trashed, but Ro managed to find a radio. "You know how to work that?" Andi asked, eyes on the entrance. She didn't like being there, near the bodies. And how long did they have until somebody else decided to wander through?

"We're trying to reach Sheriff David Kemp," Ro said into the handset. "If you're on this channel, please respond."

"Ro?" David's voice crackled. "Where are you?"

"Your office. Dad, you need to— Charlie's dead. And this—this other—"

"Patrick," Andi said, still keeping her eyes trained ahead, watching for movement in the dark.

"Patrick," Ro parroted. "A friend of Mal's—someone shot them, both of them."

"Are you sure he—"

"Dad, he's . . . I don't know how many times Charlie was shot, and Patrick's head is, it's— They're *gone*."

Andi suddenly spun, as if she'd heard something. The bullpen was empty; beyond it sat a dark corridor leading to the holding cells.

"What?" Ro asked, alarmed.

"I . . . I don't know. I thought I—" Andi froze.

"*What?*" Ro's voice was desperate. He still didn't see anything.

"Ro?" David asked over the radio, panic rising. "Are you still there?"

"*Listen.*" Andi reached over and lowered the volume on the crackling handset.

Ro finally heard, and it sent a chill straight down his spine. Somewhere in the dark, from the sound of it back near the holding cells, someone was *whistling*. Soft, melodic. He recognized the song. "Crimson and Clover."

"I want to go" was all Andi said as she turned and started toward the door. Ro followed, arranging over the radio for them to meet his dad at Andi's house.

Outside of downtown, things were no better. Andi and Ro passed a roaring house fire and two recently crashed cars before coming upon a line of trick-or-treaters that pelted the F-150 with rocks. The last child's costume—a traditional bedsheet ghost—had been made into something deeply unsettling with wet, bloody circles for eyes that they kept rubbing. Andi kept the pedal down, pulling the vehicle into her driveway a little after nine. She raced to the front door but couldn't open it—it was barricaded.

"Mom?" Andi waited. No response. She called out again, desperate. "*Mom?*"

"Keep your voice down," Rachel hissed at them from inside. "Hang on."

After clearing the dining room chair she'd tucked under the doorknob, she pulled Andi in, wrapping her in a tight hug while waving Ro forward.

Before they were even inside, David's cruiser roared to a stop in front of the house.

Rachel and David sat in silence, paging through the documents Engle had stolen. The story that Andi and Ro told—Engle's work in optics being co-opted to further a destructive government psyop that wound up canceled, forgotten, then sold off to an unwitting Mal—still sounded crazy. But it was no longer unbelievable.

For his part, David had followed the drip-drip-drip of stories exposing government-backed corruption, atrocities, and incompetence in Vietnam since coming home from the war. Whatever faith he'd had in higher institutions doing the right thing, the smart thing, had atrophied in the years since.

If she'd missed Molly's call, hadn't been able to test the water, or if those tests had revealed something, *anything* out of the ordinary, Rachel would've balked. Instead she and David found themselves listening to an incredible story detailing Andi's immunity to the game's effects and her and Ro's accident on a backroad north of San Jose, before reading and rereading a series of alarming summaries from an incomplete memorandum in Engle's file titled "Report on Pacification of Areas Exposed to Project Lethbridge."

> INTRODUCTION (see LT-102A.3 for full project background): In areas where Project Lethbridge (PL) achieves 10% real and 5% adjacent saturations within a target population, widespread social disruptions leading to violence should occur within six days of those benchmarks. As real and adjacent exposure to PL continues, these behaviors will escalate exponentially, resulting in a trigger point where total lethal action may be required in order to regain control over affected population centers. Between days eight and ten is the ideal point at which to pacify, allowing for a rise in violence that clearly justifies an armed response, without tipping into a trigger event. See pp. 4–27 of this report for full introductory thoughts.
>
> PACIFICATION: Areas of effect will be evaluated beforehand, to develop case-by-case cover stories for actions taken. Generally speaking, a combination of detainment

and lethal action will be required. Target numbers for each tranche will be provided, developed from population data. Special emphasis should be placed on protecting and cultivating adjacent saturations, who, due to lack of direct exposure, will present as reasonable and can be coached into providing statements that align with a given cover story. Real saturations should be considered for long-term detainment or lethal action only. See pp. 30–121 of this report for full pacification protocols.

TRIGGER POINT: If action is not taken before day eleven, projections suggest the standard pacification force (as defined in LT-103A.9) will no longer be able to provide an adequate response. Unless a more robust military response offers strategic value, total lethal action will likely be required. This is undesirable and should, in an overall ideal application of PL, not be utilized. See pp. 124–198 of this report for full trigger point protocols.

"They're going to try and cover it up," Ro finally said. "Engle said they wouldn't want any evidence to get out."

"We should leave. But we have to destroy the game first," Andi added. "That's the only way to stop it from spreading any further."

"There's the access road, through the hills to the east," David said. "That truck out front could get us there. But I passed the store on the way here. It was packed. It's too big a risk."

"Engle said it draws out . . . destructive parts of your personality. The more they play, the worse they'll get." Andi tapped the memo as she went on. "Even the people who don't play—'adjacents' or whatever—turn violent. We can't let them or the government or whoever destroy the game before we get to it. We have to take it offline, but we have to keep the boards intact if I'm going to figure out a way to undo what it's done." She glanced at Ro as she spoke, trying to send a message to their parents. *His life depends on it.*

"We'll split up. We'll take care of it, then meet you somewhere after," Ro said.

David looked at Ro—battered, bruised, sick with something no doctor could diagnose. He should've felt pity, but the resolve Ro was showing humbled him. It was an odd time for Ro to find the determination he'd lost over the past few years, but David could see it in his eyes. *He'd* thought about walking away more times than he could count over the last two weeks but hadn't. For better or worse, here was Ro, following in his footsteps. "All right," he finally said. "You three take the truck and leave now. I can take care of the game."

"I'm *coming*," Andi cut in, offended anyone would think otherwise.

"Me too," Ro said.

Rachel nodded. "We need to stick together."

There was no fight to be had. David turned to Rachel. "We're going to need flashlights, first aid, anything you keep around for emergencies. You have a gun?" Rachel shook her head. "I've got a shotgun in the car," he said. "You know how to shoot?"

Andi was surprised to see her mother nod yes. "Self-defense classes," Rachel clarified. "With a pistol. Not a shotgun."

"Same basic principle," David replied as they both climbed to their feet.

Grabbing Andi, Rachel headed off into the house to gather what they could to help get them through the night.

Making her way to her room, Andi started gathering everything she'd acquired about *Polybius*—the code she'd dumped, notes she'd taken. As she emptied textbooks from her backpack then started cramming her research inside, it hit her that they might never come back here. How could they? She lost one home the night before, and now she was about to lose the other.

Passing by, Rachel caught her daughter staring off and quietly stepped into her room. "Andi? Are you okay?"

Without looking back, she shrugged a little, then shook her head.

Rachel nodded. She wasn't either. "We'd better keep going."

"I saw Dad," Andi said, finally turning but still unwilling to face her mom.

"I thought you might. You didn't say on the phone, so I wasn't sure."

"Yeah. He, uh . . ." She decided it wasn't the time to tell her that Devon was moving, but there was still something she felt she needed to say before they threw themselves to the wolves. "Mom, I—" About to break, she cut herself off for a moment to try to settle, eyes ducking away. Her voice shrank as she spoke. "I'm really sorry."

"For what?" Clearly, something had happened with Devon, but Rachel still had no idea where this was coming from. It worried her.

"Everything?" Andi didn't know, or couldn't prioritize. "You're the one who—" Again, she felt her throat catch. *Who's here. Who tries. Fights. Survives.* Any would've sufficed, only she kept tripping over her words.

But Rachel understood. She saw on Andi's face the desire to

open up and bridge, even just a little, the divide that had grown between them. "I know. Okay? Your dad is . . . his own person. We have to be our own too. And, Andi, you don't need to apologize for *anything*. I mean, look at us. You figured all of this out, on your own. You're trying to save lives. That says . . . everything. I'm proud of you. And I love you."

Glancing up, a small smile breaking through, Andi finally met her mom's gaze.

Downstairs, Ro watched his father as he inventoried everything he had on him and in his cruiser. Service revolver, speed loaders for the same, a shotgun and a box of shells, road flares, extra radios. "How are we supposed to clear everybody out of the shop?" he asked. "Even if you had enough ammo—"

"We're not shooting our way in. Or out," David interrupted. "Guns are a last resort. There's a weapons locker at the office with riot gear. Nonlethal. Hopefully nobody's found a way in yet. We'll have to—"

Before David could finish his thought, the radio clipped to his belt squawked—a staticky, panicked-sounding voice on the other end. He ducked into another room, responding in an anguished, hushed voice Ro couldn't clearly overhear. Whatever it was, it was bad. He made his way across the room, listening as his father signed off then solemnly tucked his radio away.

"Dad? What is it?"

David turned toward his son as he stepped into the room. "Jeff. He— I sent him home. They've got the baby, and . . . I don't see a point in trying to control this anymore. People just need to do what's best for them." He paused for a moment, the horror of what he'd just heard still roiling within. "Someone burned down

Paulson's. Fifteen, maybe sixteen people were trapped inside. Rain might put it out, but there's no one else to—there's nothing left we can do. The focus has to be on the four of us getting out of here, with whatever you two need from that game to set this right."

CHAPTER 22

RIGHT OR LEFT?" RACHEL ASKED AS THEY PULLED UP TO A DARKENED INTERSECTION. She'd taken the wheel so David could keep watch—and a gun trained, just in case. While both routes led to their destination, neither promised safe passage. Through the storm's haze a faint orange glow could be seen encircling downtown—fire, a lot of it, with more than enough fuel to keep burning despite the steady rainfall.

Rachel started to turn right but cut left instead, uncertain. David raised his gun, slowly sweeping for signs of trouble. Thick woods bracketed one side of the road, a run of darkened houses the other. If anyone was hiding, he doubted he'd be able to see them until it was too late. "Can you go any faster?" he asked, as Rachel crawled them forward.

"I can't keep it steady," she said, casting an eye out the driver-side window. "I can't even see the road. There's half a foot of water out there."

In back, Ro caught Andi staring over her shoulder, focused on something in the dark. "What is it?" he asked, trying to figure out what she saw that he couldn't.

"I don't know. I thought I saw—shit!" Figures were sloshing through the water, six, dark Halloween costumes all, advancing from behind. "Mom, drive!"

Rachel glanced at the sideview mirror to see what was going on moments before a chain whipped from the dark and shattered it. Screaming, instinct taking over, she jammed her foot on the gas. The truck fishtailed, spinning jets of water into the air that splattered the converging pack but didn't slow them down.

As chains, rocks, clubs began battering the exterior, David took aim. But their attackers were Ro's age, younger, and he hesitated.

No longer under Rachel's control, the truck angled away from the road and into a ditch. She jerked the wheel and worked the clutch, but was unable to regain traction—they were stuck.

"That house, there." David indicated a dark, two-story home. The closest to them, it was still at least a hundred yards away. "Go!" As he climbed out, he dodged a baseball bat that zipped toward him out of the dark. It put a dent in the truck's side instead, the force of impact reverberating through the bat and into the attacker's hands, a boy of no more than fifteen who was left momentarily stunned. David took advantage, cracking his revolver against the boy's face and shoving him back, then firing into the air. Undeterred, the others kept swarming, clambering into the bed, battering the windows and body as Andi and Ro rushed out, carrying with them whatever they could grab.

Splashing away from the truck, they made for the house, but gunshots split them apart just a few yards into their sprint. Identifying the shooter—another teenager, a girl, perched on top of the hood—David fired back, trying to send her into cover. She didn't care, firing wildly until her gun clicked empty.

At the same time another member of the pack, fishing out a rifle left in the truck's back seat, began firing at random.

With bullets chewing up everything around them, Ro and Andi were forced away from David and Rachel.

David panicked as he saw them disappearing into the dark but knew that stopping meant kill or be killed. He and Rachel continued sprinting toward the house at the end of the street. Kicking open the front door then barreling inside, David realized he knew where they were. As they slammed the door shut, the rhythmic *ca-clack* of a shotgun shell being chambered stopped both in their tracks.

Stepping out of the dark, Bob Colson swept his gun back and forth between them, finger tensed on the trigger. "David? What the hell are you doing in my house?"

After leaving the sheriff's office, Mal started toward his car but kept walking instead. The voice in his head demanded action, so he set off, uncertain where, intent on sowing chaos.

Whatever self-doubt he'd earlier felt vanished in the wake of killing Patrick and Charlie. He was just as dangerous as he'd imagined, and it was time to find out what else he was capable of. The anger, resentment he felt toward a world that hadn't offered him more, what he felt he deserved, had become manifest in violence. His true self was emerging, and the destruction of his old self—along with the systems that governed him, everyone, everything else—was necessary.

Eyes panning up and down the street as fires burned, shots

echoed, and screams followed, he could feel the smack of the billhook against his thigh and found his mind drifting back to the night he'd slaughtered Carl Delano's horses. A line could be drawn, he believed, from that moment to the mounting dread that followed. It had poisoned Tasker Bay, leading to this day's bloodshed.

He'd done this. All of it. And it was sublime.

Footsteps approaching snapped him awake. Gripping the billhook, spinning, Mal slashed and cleaved open a young man who'd been charging toward him. He fell away, eyes wide, no idea what had just happened, only the sense that the world was steadily growing darker around him.

Tucking the blade away without bothering to wipe it clean, allowing the blood to smear over his clothes, Mal walked toward the young man. Approaching, he pulled the Ruger and fired before bothering to look any closer.

But the young man hadn't been gunning for him—he'd been running, having robbed the Tasker Bay Savings and Loan. A pair of canvas sacks, the bank's name stenciled in black ink onto their fronts, sat a few feet from the body. Mal scooped them up and looked inside—cash, a lot of it. After unceremoniously dumping the contents into a pack slung over his back and tossing the empty bags onto the body, he started away.

But he hadn't made it ten feet when someone in the shadows behind him opened fire. Mal blindly fired back, and a round from his Ruger nearly entered Paul Nantz's skull, bouncing off the side of a building and whizzing past. As the Ruger clicked empty, Mal grabbed a pistol from behind his hip, emptying it over his shoulder as he cut down an alley.

The house Andi and Ro had ducked into seemed empty. They stayed low, flashlights off as voices began drawing near—*the pack*. They moved deeper into the home, taking up a defensive position inside the kitchen. At least from there they could see who was coming.

In the only bag either of them had managed to grab as they fled, Ro found a loaded revolver. He didn't want it but didn't want to put that burden on Andi, either. As he went to draw the weapon, she nudged him, indicating a mudroom with a door that appeared to lead into the backyard—a way out.

As the pack smashed its way through the front, Andi and Ro ducked out back, but their relief was short-lived. A figure in the distance, clearly armed, was running toward them. Slipping into the shadows nearby, they listened as the pack laid waste to the home within, watching as the figure approached without. Andi's hand found Ro's arm, tightening its grip as the figure passed by, missing them even as its face fell into focus—*Mal*, loaded down with enough weapons to start a war.

"What's he doing here?" Andi whispered.

Ro responded with a raised hand—*wait*—then directed her eye toward a cluster of flashlights whipping back and forth in the distance, coming toward them from the same direction. Mal was being followed.

Ro started digging in the bag, unable to find what he was looking for. "You have a radio?" he asked Andi, voice hushed. She shook her head *no*. As the cluster of flashlights approached, Ro nodded in the direction David and Rachel had fled. "Let's just go. We can find—"

Chaos suddenly erupted inside. Mal and the pack were shouting, scuffling, an explosion of gunfire shattering windows. The distant flashlights froze in response, one after another dipping from sight. From the dark, the sound of clasps rattling, bolts cranking open and shut, shells being chambered drew Andi and Ro's already-fractured attention. A moment later they were scrambling for cover as a fusillade slammed into the house, round after round tearing up everything.

From the dark Paul Nantz's voice called out, "In the bushes!"

Spotted *and* misidentified as a threat, Andi grabbed Ro's hand and pulled him back through the mudroom into the house, where they nearly stumbled over the lifeless body of a young pack member, his throat slashed.

"Front door," Ro whispered, revolver shaking in his hand. "Don't stop, no matter what."

Andi nodded and they started to move. A saloon door lead them from the kitchen to the dining room, where Mal, barricaded behind a massive table flipped on its side, was reloading his arsenal. "What the hell are you two doing here?" he spat.

Before Andi or Ro could answer, the back door was kicked open and a handgun jammed inside. Firing blind, Paul emptied an entire clip into the kitchen.

As Mal spun and fired back, Andi and Ro scrambled from the dining room but found themselves pinned down as the rest of the posse entered through the front door and spread through the home, surrounding Mal and inadvertently cornering the two of them in the process. With nowhere to go, they fled deeper inside, climbing a flight of stairs to a second story as Mal and the posse traded fire.

Buckshot splintered the railing as the two rounded a corner into the upstairs hall, some of it digging into Ro's calf. Grabbing him as he stumbled, Andi pulled him through the first doorway she saw, into a child's bedroom. Quietly closing the door, she shoved a dresser in front of it as a makeshift barricade. As she stepped back, an errant shot from below tore through the floor and into the dresser, exploding the drawers and frame.

That shot, reflexively fired by a posse member in the throes of death after Mal's Ruger had punched a quarter-sized hole in his neck, meant it was now three against one. Crashing into the living room, Mal was followed by the posse's youngest member, Paul's nephew Barry. No more than sixteen, the boy was so caught up in the moment that he failed to check his periphery. Mal swung the Ruger from out of the dark, flattening the boy's face and staggering him long enough to plant a pair of rounds in his chest.

A shot from Barry's stricken father clipped Mal's ear, spinning him out and into the open. Mal fired back until the Ruger clicked empty, failing to land a hit before pulling a shotgun off his shoulder and discharging both barrels, sending the man to the floor to bleed out feet away from his dying son.

Having retreated to circle around the house outside, Paul crashed through the front door ready to fight—but Mal was gone. Clicking on his flashlight, seeing his family dead on the floor, he paused in horror before spotting a blood trail leading up the stairs.

Upstairs, Mal tried the first door—on the other side, Andi and Ro watched, gun trained, as the knob jangled and the already splintered barricade shuddered. But after a moment, Mal moved on.

They listened as he tried another door. Finding it blocked too, this time he forced his way in. Screams followed—*there was someone else inside.*

"He's going to kill them," Ro said over the commotion. Andi knew he was right and pulled him back onto his feet. Somehow, they had to help. As they worked to move the dresser, they spun at the sound of the closet door opening. It was a pass-through from the other bedroom. At gunpoint, the home's owners and their young daughter hurried through, Mal trailing behind. Still gripping the revolver, Ro snapped his aim onto Mal, and for a moment everyone froze.

"Mal. What the hell are you *doing*?" Andi hissed.

As Mal shifted the gun onto Andi a tremor shot through her, but she stood firm. His finger began tensing on the trigger.

"Mal," Ro snapped, gripped by survival instincts, ready to shoot if it meant protecting Andi. "Don't."

Footsteps in the hall broke the stalemate. Mal shifted his aim from Andi to the door as the knob began to move. He emptied his gun into it, then dropped it and pulled another off his shoulder as he raced back through the closet and into the other room.

An explosion of shots from the hallway followed as Andi, Ro, and the family hit the floor in a desperate bid for cover. After a few horrible moments the house fell silent, save for the rain plinking overhead.

Andi and Ro looked at each other, making sure they were both in one piece, then slowly made their way into the pass-through. Laid out on the floor in the other bedroom was Mal, bullet in his side. Slumped against a blood-splattered wall in the hallway was Paul Nantz, shot through too many times to count.

The rattle of Mal shakily trying to sit up caused Andi to spin on her heels. He was pawing at the Ruger resting across his chest.

"Mal, don't," Ro shouted, as his grip tightened on the gun he still carried.

"For once in your life, don't be an asshole," Andi implored. Mal wouldn't listen, finger wrapping around the Ruger's trigger. "Goddamn it, Mal!" she shouted as he started twisting the barrel toward them. "Stop!"

He wasn't going to.

Andi grabbed Ro's hand—the same one holding the gun—and pressed her finger down on top of his, firing and hitting Mal dead center. "Fuck you!" she screamed as he slammed back against the floor.

This time, he didn't try to get back up.

CHAPTER 23

BOB WOULDN'T LEAVE. MAYBE, DAVID TOLD HIMSELF, IT WAS THE RIGHT CHOICE, he and his wife Carol would be safer holed up, drawing less attention while waiting for help to arrive. Only he wasn't sure any was coming.

According to the papers Andi and Ro had shared, the government had orders to eliminate anyone even tangentially exposed to the game. In other words, *all of them.*

David had been uncertain what to say, how far down the rabbit hole he ought to go, to convince Bob to make for the access road. There were no guarantees it'd be passable or even reachable, given the chaos in the streets. But the alternative, waiting an indeterminate amount of time in a home that was big enough it would inevitably become a target, felt like a mistake.

By the time Ro called, using a radio lifted off Paul Nantz's body, David knew they were leaving there alone.

It didn't sit right with David. He still had a duty to the people of Tasker Bay. He gave Bob a spare radio he'd taken from his cruiser, telling him, "If we make it to the access road, I'll call. You ought to follow. And if you see anybody, hear from anybody who seems like they're okay, stick together. You're going to be safer in a group."

David and Rachel hurried down the block, spotting Andi and Ro waiting in the shadows. Ro's bloodied leg and the haunted look on Andi's face left no doubt that they'd been through something.

"You good?" David asked, angling his flashlight for a better look at his son's injury.

"They followed us," Ro said, ignoring the question as he glanced back at the house. "Paul Nantz showed up, and it . . ." Trailing off, he could only shake his head—*they're all gone.*

As she looked Andi over, Rachel keyed to the pack slung over her shoulder. "Whose is that?"

"Mal's," she replied in a flat voice, still processing what happened.

David's head jerked toward the house, hackles up. "He's in there?"

"He isn't coming out," Andi said.

One look at the F-150 and it was clear the pack had trashed it beyond repair. They set off on foot through a dense run of firs butted up against the rear of the home, heading toward town.

Rachel had quickly cleaned and bandaged Ro's leg before they'd started off, but it hurt more with every step. He tried hard not to let it slow him down. The chain of flashlights moved slowly, conditions and terrain combining to hobble them. A series of towering firelights in the distance—the low skyline of downtown, much of it ablaze—guided them in. So did the noise, a growing rumble of shouting voices and random destruction that put them further on edge as they approached.

Forming a tight cluster, they passed through the outer edges of downtown. At the other end, a full eight blocks away, sat Home Video World. But they had to make a stop at the sheriff's office before running that gauntlet, to retrieve the riot gear hopefully still stashed in the weapons locker.

They found the office ransacked, worse than when Andi and Ro had passed through earlier that night. Every window had been smashed, furniture overturned and ripped apart. Anything that wasn't nailed down was either gone or crammed some place it didn't belong.

Stepping into the bullpen, David swept his flashlight. Eventually, the beam hit Charlie's body. Ro had warned him, but he still wasn't prepared to see his friend sprawled on the floor.

Not wanting to look at Charlie or Patrick again, Ro and Andi kept up the pace. As she followed him through the bullpen and into the hallway that led to the holding cells and the office's small weapons locker, the beam of Ro's light glanced on something, and he froze.

Bumping into him, Andi had to step back. "Ro, what—"

But she didn't need to finish asking to see what had stopped him in his tracks. The walls were covered in symbols, painted in blood, like the ones inside Thom Mazzy's office. From the increasingly frantic way Ro was moving his light, Andi knew he was starting to panic. She pulled him back into the bullpen, where Rachel and David rushed to meet them.

"What happened?" David asked, taking hold of Ro, who just shook his head. He clocked Andi, who looked just as scared and lost. "Just wait near the front; we'll get what we need," he said, trying hard to sound reassuring.

As he watched them go, Ro knew he had to try to focus his mind elsewhere. He scanned the space, looking for anything that might be useful. He could no longer see the others but could still hear them as they moved through the back of the office, gathering the riot gear. But as he continued to sweep his light, he became gradually aware that it had grown completely silent.

"Andi?" No response. "Dad?" Nothing, still.

Glancing down, Ro realized his flashlight beam was starting to dim. The world around him was fading away, the same thing that happened to him on the road, in the diner, in his living room.

No, he told himself.

This is not reality.

This is not happening.

No.

"No!"

"Ro?" Andi's hand on his shoulder felt like a bolt of lightning. Ro spun away from her, nearly tripping on an upturned chair. David and Rachel were soon there too. "We heard you shouting. Is everything—are you okay?"

The look on Ro's face said he wasn't, but he nodded. He could feel their eyes on him, inspecting. Judging. *They don't trust me*, he thought. *They're afraid of me.*

He remained on the periphery as David hefted a pair of canvas bags he'd retrieved from the weapons locker onto the reception desk, then pulled a silver cannister roughly the size of a soda can from inside.

"Tear gas," David said. "Pull the pin and chuck it. You'll have a few seconds before it pops." Next came gas masks. One each, plus a handful of extras. As each slung one around their necks, David tucked the remainder away. In the other bag were batons, flares, a pair of revolvers, another shotgun, and boxes of ammo.

"When we get to the shop, Rachel and I take the front. Ro, you and Andi go to the back. We toss six cannisters each to cover as much of the shop as we can, then wait for the crowd to clear out before we go in."

They were set. But David found himself hesitating, something else on his mind. He debated for a moment, then told the others, "Wait here."

"Dad, what are you—"

"I can't leave Charlie like that. I won't be long. Be ready to move," David said as he disappeared down the hall, back into the bullpen. His guard remained up as he approached Charlie's body, then knelt beside it. David didn't know what to say. For a moment he just hovered over him, searching his thoughts.

Balled up in a far corner, unseeable in the dark, Kelly Braun had her eyes fixed on the stray beam of David's flashlight. After Mal had left, she'd wandered the station, giving it some color by drawing the symbols she saw every time she closed her eyes on the walls. She'd watched crowds come and go, including the boy and girl—*Ro and Andi*—who'd been through there earlier that night.

And now it was him, the man who'd first evicted her, then arrested her and held her in a tiny cell for days on end. Humiliated her, over and over. *Him*. Right in front of her. Hands tightening around the shotgun she'd scavenged off the floor earlier that night, she rose to her feet. Unheard, unseen on David's periphery, she stepped silently toward him.

Hand shaking, David unpinned the star from Charlie's uniform, intent on using it to somehow honor him once they'd put distance between themselves and Tasker Bay. The gravity of the moment had his full attention, leaving him unaware as Kelly drew within just a few feet. She stopped, looming, head slowly cocking to the side as she quietly studied him. Finally, she raised the shotgun, aiming down the sight to the dead center of his skull.

Star in hand, eyes closed in silent prayer, David snapped awake to the sound of gunfire. As he drew his weapon and spun, he saw the shotgun fall from Kelly's hand and her body collapse. Across the room, gun still trained with smoke rising from its barrel, stood Ro.

"She was going to kill you" was all Ro said, eyes distant. Nodding a little, David pocketed Charlie's star, stood, then stepped around Kelly, intending to help Ro lower the gun. But as he tried to push down on his son's arm, Ro went rigid, the gun still trained dead ahead toward where Kelly had been standing.

Ro wasn't looking at his father anymore. In his place was the figment, shrouded in a kind of fluid darkness. Black lines crawled across its body in blocky ripples, suggesting it had stepped out of the game and into our world. It towered in front of Ro, waiting for him to move so it could catch and consume him. *Ro was sure of it.*

Seeing his fingers tensing on the trigger, Andi shouted, "Stop! Just—step back." David looked to her, confused. "Let him come out of it."

David pulled his arm away but didn't move. "Ro?" he pleaded, hoping to snap him out of his trance. Instead, Ro swung the gun toward David, the barrel inches from his face. Trying to step back, David tripped and Ro fired, the round slamming into the wall as David hit the floor. Shooting back onto his feet, David moved to force Ro's arm upward, only to find him going limp. Catching him, he took the gun, then lowered Ro into a chair nearby.

Andi stepped in, kneeling and taking Ro's face in her hands. Over the next few moments, the tension in his body began to melt away, and the world around him came into focus, Andi at its center. He reached up and put his hand on her face, Andi clasping hers on top. Watching, David and Rachel shared an uncertain glance, struck by everything—but especially the intensity of the bond their children appeared to share.

Mal's eyes slowly opened. There seemed to be a film, a layer of some kind over them, the world gauzy and indistinct. He knew he'd been shot, although he wasn't sure how many times or how much damage had been done. As he tried raising himself up off the floor of whoever the hell's house he was in, he felt a sudden surge of pain from the hole Paul Nantz had blasted in his side. *Asshole.*

A struggle ensued, Mal climbing to his feet as his body, the room, everything pulsated around him. The Ruger, which had absorbed the shot Andi had fired, was bent and worthless. As he tossed it aside, he could feel something burning around his ribs. The force of impact had surely broken them. How many he didn't know, or particularly care.

Patting himself down, he took comfort that the billhook was

still tucked in his belt, but he quickly realized that his guns and pack—*his money*—were gone. Before he could process what had happened any further, the beam from a flashlight whipped past a nearby window. Mal hobbled toward it, waiting until it was gone to look out. He watched as four lights bobbed away into the woods, studying the silhouettes of those carrying them in the faint moonlight, able to make out Andi among them.

Slung over her shoulder was his pack.

Gaining confidence with each step, he started downstairs to see what weapons he could salvage. He'd have to catch up to them, to take back what was his.

The shop was just two blocks away, and tensions were silently rising within the group. They were about to conduct a raid, something that even a few hours ago would've sounded like a joke without a punchline.

Still hobbled by his leg, Ro had at least recovered from his episode and was able to move on his own. He'd taken up a position at the group's rear again, glancing periodically over his shoulder at the odd sound—*things* seemed to move in the dark, but none had designs on them. For now.

He was still struggling to process what had happened back at the sheriff's office. Some part of him was lashing out because of the game. Something deep, which he'd managed to repress or avoid all these years, had been clawing its way up, reaching out through him and into the world. He couldn't control or understand it. He could only reflect on moments he remembered.

He'd been trying to piece together a theory, going over his previous episodes, but nothing quite fit. Arriving home late, he thought his father might be in trouble, and he had an episode. When Andi walked away from him at the shop, he had another. Another, when he thought about dying on the drive home from San Jose. And another here, when *again* he thought he might lose his father to Kelly's shotgun.

But if that was it—if he was being driven by a fear of death, of losing people he loved—then what about the diner? There'd been no threat. Or the times Andi had pulled him away from the game, and he suddenly felt hot, angry, like he wanted to lash out?

Was it simpler than all that? he wondered. Was there just anger and violence inside him that was waiting for an opening, a mental green light so it could explode out and cause harm? If so, if that kind of darkness was truly innate, how much was bubbling beneath the surface for the rest of Tasker Bay?

From time to time, Rachel clocked Ro, concerned over both his state of mind and his injury. A warped ring of blood had been steadily darkening the bandage she'd applied to his leg. She stepped closer to David, voice low. "Ro won't make it all the way to the access road on that leg. We're going to need another car."

David glanced back and saw his son hobbling, face peaked and straining. While a random car sat here and there, their clearances were all lower than the F-150 and their engines nowhere near as powerful. "If Charlie's cruiser's still at the station, it might work. It's a V-8. Otherwise, we're going to need another truck," David replied.

A burst of gunfire from behind sent them running. As they scampered toward the shops lining Main Street, looking for cover, the shots zeroed in tighter. Rounds glanced off the pavement and walls, cleaving debris that fanned out in fiery streaks.

"David!" came a sudden call from across the street—they were near the mortuary, where Clarence Meeks was waving them in. "Come on," he shouted as he opened fire on the anonymous gunman with a hunting rifle, buying the group time to dart over and duck inside.

Once they were through the door, Clarence slammed and locked it, then rolled a cart with a casket strapped to it in front. A quick look suggested the mortuary was relatively safe. The door was barricaded, steel shutters covered the window, and a generator kept a handful of lights on even as the grid continued to stutter.

"Everybody all right?" Clarence asked as he looked them over, not waiting for an answer before retreating to a heavy-duty fire door leading to the exam room in back. Ushering them forward and through, he double bolted it behind them. "Hope you don't mind being stuck back here with the stiffs. What the hell's going on out there?"

"An infection," Rachel said, deciding that the round of twenty questions sure to follow after they blamed the chaos on a video game wasn't worth their time. "I have a contact at the CDC who told me they're quarantining the town."

"Quarantine? What kind of infection?" Clarence asked. "I haven't seen signs of anything in any of the bodies coming in the last few days."

"Clarence? What was—oh my God, David!" The voice, out of nowhere from farther in back, registered immediately—Evie. She stepped out of hiding and rushed over, hugging them all, including Andi, who she didn't actually know.

"You mean we can't leave?" she asked, turning to Rachel.

"We're going to the access road, to see if we can get out," David said.

"People are getting killed out there." Clarence shook his head, tone grave and seemingly rooted in firsthand experience. "And if there's a quarantine, don't you think we ought to stay put? It's safe here."

"It's the government," Andi said. "They did something that made people sick. And they don't want anyone to know. We don't think it's safe to be here when they show up."

Clarence looked to David, who nodded—*it's true*. "We have to make one stop," David said. "And honestly, we could use some more help to do it."

Evie looked past them, toward the steel fire door, locked down tight. "I—I'm sorry, but if somebody's coming to stop all of"—she waved a hand at the door—"then we're not a part of that. I think we should wait."

"I have remains here," Clarence said, wishing that weren't true. "Half the block's burning. Sooner or later, someone's going to try and set this place on fire. If I let that happen, I'm—I can't."

David pulled his last surplus radio from his bag and presented it to Evie. "Bob Colson's on channel ten. Let him know where you are in case either of you have to move."

Suddenly, something loud thumped from the show floor. David and Clarence shared a worried glance. Moments later, what sounded like an axe thunked against the fire door.

Clarence ran toward the door and attempted to push a cabinet in front—the others raced to help as the axe continued cleaving into the door's other side. With the cabinet in place, they all stepped back.

"You can't go back out there," Evie reasoned, eyes pleading for the group to stay together.

Andi turned to Clarence. "Is there another way out of here?" He nodded toward an emergency exit, ALARM WILL SOUND stenciled across it in red block letters.

David took a step forward, looking it over. "That's fine," he said. "We can use it."

Mal kept pounding on the door with an axe he'd pulled off a wall, bent on getting at Andi however he could. Recovering the cash she stole had become secondary to exacting vengeance on her for shooting him. That, and everything else. Mal knew he'd been intimidated by her. Afraid of her, even. Ever since he met her. *A fucking teenage girl.*

It was pathetic. But cutting her head off would solve that problem, and the opportunity had neatly presented itself. Mal felt invincible, like there was a light shining down. Nothing divine, just a sense that he possessed something no one else in town did—a willingness, perhaps even an eagerness, to kill. After years of holding himself up as a local villain, he'd become something worse. Which, he was certain, was better. He'd settle his scores here, move on, then burn down the next town he came to for good measure. He was chaos embodied.

The sudden loud clanging of a fire alarm snapped him out of

his narcissistic reverie. He burst back onto the street, looking for a way around the building in order to find the fire exit he assumed had triggered the alarm. If the mortuary followed the same layout as his and every other building on Main, the fire exit would lead into an alley that ran in back, which is where he raced.

Careful to make as little noise as possible while still moving fast, Clarence and David slid the cabinet from in front of the fire door. David then moved into the hall—empty. He waved, and Andi, Ro, and Rachel followed him out.

The quartet moved through the ruined show floor and onto the street. The streetlamps flickered, then cut out and stayed off. Other than firelight, Tasker Bay was dark. But up ahead they could see the crowd milling around Home Video World, light still spilling out from inside.

As they neared an alley that ran alongside the shop, the group split, Andi and Ro around back, David and Rachel out front. As David handed Rachel a cannister of tear gas, his radio chirped—Ro and Andi were in position and ready.

"Go," David whispered into the microphone. The four strapped on masks, pulled the pins from their cannisters, and lobbed them toward the shop. Some sailed inside, others clattered across the sidewalk in front, noxious vapor hissing out and sending the crowd into a confused panic. People rushed out, pushing, shoving, tripping over one another to get clear of the gas and catch their breath, but it just kept coming, a dozen cannisters soon covering the area in a dense, suffocating fog.

Waiting a moment for the stampede to thin out, David and Rachel pushed past a few flailing stragglers and made their way inside.

At the same time, Andi and Ro were moving in through the back. Andi buried a hatchet in the generator that had been keeping the power on, killing the lights and cabinets. As she and Ro made their way onto the floor, they headed straight for *Polybius*. Spotting David and Rachel, Ro waved them over.

Off Andi's nod—*this is the one*—David pulled a hammer from his bag and drew back but thought twice, handing it to Andi. Over and over she swung, finally cracking the dense screen as she smashed toward the boards concealed inside the cabinet.

David and Rachel fanned out, keeping watch. The gas was already thinning. "Let's hurry it up," David called.

"We need the boards," Andi said breathlessly between swings.

Ro dropped his bag and rifled through it for a pry bar, looking to speed things along. As he found it, he heard something other than the steady crack of the hammer that Andi continued to wield against the cabinet—a deep, heavy wheezing. Squeezing his eyes shut, trying to block out the sound, he couldn't. It was still there.

Ro started off, determined to find what he was hearing. To prove to himself that it wasn't the figment. But the vapor still hanging in the air scattered his flashlight's beam—he couldn't see a thing. Then the power stuttered back on, long enough for him to see a face reddened by the gas screaming toward him. Mal tackled him, slamming him hard against the shop floor. As his head cracked, Ro's world went dark.

Everyone spun at the sound, catching sight of Mal hauling Ro through the fog before the power cut out again.

"Roman!" David shouted, charging after. Unable to get a clear line on Mal in the dark, he started striking and tossing flares, but this quickly added to the haze, making it harder to see.

As plumes of glowing smoke filled the room, Mal gripped Ro's skull and bounced it hard against the floor before clawing off his gas mask and pulling it over his own face. Casting Ro off, he stayed low, spotting and evading Rachel before zeroing in on Andi. Pulling the billhook, he scurried toward her then rose, grabbing and slamming her against *Polybius*, ripping off her mask and planting the knife's bloodied curvature at her throat. In one move, he could rip it wide open.

David and Rachel approached, weapons trained. Mal pulled Andi back a few steps from the cabinet to give himself cover. As the blade pressed against and broke the skin of her neck, Andi tensed, and David trained his gun on the quarter of Mal's head he could see. It was an impossible shot, made worse by Andi physically struggling to breathe thanks to the tear gas still lingering in the air, but he was going to have to take it.

Then the power stuttered back on.

As the fluorescents flickered overhead then burned on, light shone through and was rerouted by the jagged remains of *Polybius*'s screen. Beams cast everywhere, including onto Mal's face and eyes. Blinded, he stumbled back, pulling away from Andi. Slices of light tore at his skin and set fire to his clothes.

Watching Mal stumble then crash to the floor, Andi snatched up a massive shard she'd cleaved from the screen and launched herself forward, slamming it into his chest. She could feel her palms burning as she let go, falling backward as light flowed through the shard, exploding in a prismatic array. The heat it generated cooked Mal from the inside out, shafts of impossibly bright light blackening then lancing his skin. He quaked with pain until his nerves surrendered, and he was left only to smolder.

Andi stumbled for a bank of switches, killed the lights, and kicked away the flares, dampening the screen's assault. She looked around. "Where's Ro?"

They fanned out, panic rising, which is why David's eyes were elsewhere when a broken chunk of an *Asteroids* cabinet sailed from the dark and clipped the back of his head, sending him to the floor.

Racing toward the sound, Rachel stopped short just as the makeshift weapon cut across the haze inches in front of her face. Grabbing and pulling her back, Andi shone her light, catching sight of a figure twitching in the darkness—Ro, caught in a deep trancelike state and swinging his bludgeon erratically.

"Ro," Andi shouted, hoping to break through. But blinded by the gas—eyes sealed, ringed by massive red pocks—he could only follow sounds and keyed to her voice. Realizing she'd made a mistake, that this was far beyond any episode Ro had experienced before, she stumbled back, snagging her foot on Mal's body and crashing to the floor.

As Ro stalked toward her—jagged piece of splintered wood in constant violent motion—Andi emerged from beneath the haze with Mal's billhook. "Roman, stop!"

His head whipped toward her, and he lurched, slamming into a cabinet. "Stop! It's me. Ro, it's Andi. Mal's gone! We're safe—*please*!"

From the dark Rachel rushed forward, slamming into him. Failing to bring him down, she still threw him off balance long enough for Andi to join the fray and knock the jagged shiv from

Ro's hands. Fighting him to the floor, Andi hovered over him, struggling to focus his eyes onto hers, hoping to bring him back from the brink once more.

It felt like being dragged over rough terrain, thumping up, down. But it was cramped and confined. Eventually, Ro was aware that his feet were pressing against a car door, and he was laid across its back seat. Looking up, he could see the outline of a face, staring out the window—Andi's.

We're on the access road.

As he tried to move, to reach and brace himself to sit up, he realized that his hands were cuffed. Then he remembered. What he could, anyway. Flashes of motion inside Home Video World, struggling with someone, light shining in his face, his eyes. Floating. No, being carried. The rumble of an engine.

"Is everyone okay?" he finally asked, throat dry, voice hoarse.

David, behind the wheel, glanced in the rearview mirror. "Ro? You good?"

Beside him, Rachel turned in her seat. "How are you feeling?"

As the rest of the cruiser's interior started coming into focus, Ro noticed a bandage wrapped around his father's head. "What happened? Did I . . . ?"

"What do you remember?" Andi asked, adjusting her position so she could clearly see his face.

"I don't know. Why am I . . . ?" *Handcuffed,* he meant to ask, but the crush of sudden awareness was making it difficult to navigate his thoughts.

"Can't worry about it now. Here," David said, passing a key back to Andi, who unlocked Ro's cuffs. As they dropped to the cruiser's floor, she helped him sit up.

Ro's gaze drifted toward the window. Catching his reflection in the glass, he realized the skin around his eyes was red. His memory suddenly jolted, he could see Mal looming over him, ripping the gas mask from his face. As quickly as it emerged, the thought retreated. Turning back, taking in the scene inside the cruiser, he thought that their mood should have been lifted. They'd made it out. "What about the game?" he asked, looking to Andi.

"Gone. I took the boards. Some of the screen. Maybe I can . . . I don't know," she said, sounding distant.

"What *happened*?" Ro asked her, his voice hushed.

She looked away, unable to explain. But realizing what saying nothing actually said, she turned back. "It's over. We'll talk about it once we get out of here. We're close."

Andi reached across, taking his hand with a small smile. But as her fingers glanced skin worn raw from the handcuffs, Ro sensed that something between them had changed.

As he worked to keep them on the decaying access road, David split his mind between the task at hand, his son, and the people they'd left behind. Evie, Clarence, even Bob were all stranded in the middle of a riot. His sense of duty to them weighed more heavily with every mile he put between himself and Tasker Bay. Even if those same people—one of them, anyway—were set on abandoning *him*, it felt wrong for him to abandon *them*.

At the same time, the holes in Ro's memory were beginning to fill themselves in. The fight with Mal was clear, to a point at least. After, things came in waves, incomplete and all the more harrowing for it. He could remember the sensation of striking someone—his father, he assumed. Chasing after a voice—Andi's, he was certain. Being hit, dragged. Blurry flashes of Andi and Rachel over top of him, a blade in someone's hand as they fought.

I was just like the rest of them.

Ro was a threat. And he knew all too well that there was no way back.

As the cruiser crested a hill, David slowed at an unexpected sight in the distance—lights, a lot of them, where there shouldn't have been any. Clustered together, some moved in a way that suggested a temporary installation still under construction. Killing the cruiser's headlights and pulling over, David knew in his gut that something was wrong.

"Must be the National Guard. Right?" Rachel asked, eyes flitting between the lights and David, who stared ahead, spooked by the sight for reasons she couldn't discern.

About to reply, he suddenly stopped, raising a hand—*wait*. The others did, long enough without any noticeable change that Rachel finally, quietly asked, "What is it?"

David pointed to groupings of multicolored lights slowly rising, as if on auxiliary poles, only they kept going up, until they were several hundred feet in the air. The lights began moving forward, approaching fast.

"Down!" David suddenly shouted.

As Andi, Ro, and Rachel all huddled in their seats, four remarkably quiet helicopters flew overhead. Felt more than heard, they cut a line straight toward town.

Before they had time to react, light suddenly crept over the cruiser's rearview mirror—another car, approaching behind them. A pickup with a bed full of people looking for a way out of town, it rambled past, picking up speed at the sight of the lights up ahead. *Salvation*, the driver must have thought. But as the vehicle neared the cluster of lights, an explosion of automatic gunfire caused the truck to skid, swerve, and finally roll to a stop, left to smolder in the middle of the road.

For a horrible moment, no one in the cruiser spoke. They just stared, processing what they'd seen, the realization of what it meant for them dawning.

"The white paper," Andi finally said, referring to the grim primer Engle had given them, on how the military would deal with a populace affected by *Polybius*. "They're not letting anyone out of here alive." The evidence was there in her lap—and being cleared from the road in the distance.

"The three of you are going to walk. Wide, at least half a mile around the blockade," David said. "Go south and you'll hit Route 101 in about two miles. Find a ride. There's . . . I don't know the name, a motel. It's the only one if you're heading that direction, before you hit Novato. You won't miss it. We'll meet there."

"Wait, what about you?" Ro asked, confused.

"I'm going back for Clarence and Evie. Bob. Whoever else they pulled in. I can't just leave them there."

"You just saw what happened to that truck—" Andi started, David cutting her off.

"That's why I'm going. I'll find them, and we'll follow you. I'll be a couple of hours behind. That's all." Doubts obvious, David moved quickly to try to reassure everyone, including himself. "Just stay out of sight, get to the motel, and I'll meet you there."

Ro's mind raced as his father spoke, but he stayed silent. He saw another way.

"Why can't we just walk up there with our hands up? Or drive? I mean, it's a police car. They'll just . . ." Rachel started. Desperate and searching, she couldn't finish her thought. She knew it wouldn't work.

"It's still my job to protect these people. And no one else is coming to help. We have to do this, now. Come on."

Outside the car, Ro strapped the parts from *Polybius* to Andi's back while David and Rachel gathered anything else that might help—flashlights, flares.

As David started saying his goodbyes to the others, Ro stepped away, retrieved the keys from the trunk's lock, and moved toward the driver's seat. Reaching inside, he picked up David's service revolver but kept it at his side.

"Dad?" he finally called. As the others turned toward him, Ro could feel his composure starting to break. With everything he had, he willed himself steady. "You're not going back. I am."

David didn't follow. "What? No. Ro, you're—"

"Sick. Like them." He nodded toward town. "After tonight—the last few days—I'm getting worse. I'm going to get Evie, Mr. Meeks, whoever else, and—"

"You're not," David said, voice firm. As he took a step forward, Ro cocked but still didn't show the revolver. David froze at the sound, turning to Andi. "Talk to him. Please."

Andi felt paralyzed. They'd made it. And suddenly everything was falling apart. "Ro, we have the code. And the hardware. We can figure *something* out. *I know* we can figure something out."

"You will. I don't think there's anything you can't do," he said, admiration shining through the horrible moment. "But it's too late for me."

"Ro—" Andi tried to start, but he was quick to cut her off.

"You can figure it out. What happened here, to us. All of it. You have to get out," Ro said as his gaze shifted onto his father, "and I can't help you. One way or the other, my leg, or . . ." *Me trying to kill somebody again*, he thought. "I'll just slow you down."

Andi went to respond, but engines started rumbling on in the distance, trucks ready to move out toward town. As headlights fired to life and formed up, Ro started climbing into the driver's seat.

"Ro!" David shouted, starting toward him. Ro raised the gun, but David, still on the other side of the cruiser, didn't stop. Suddenly aiming away from his father and into the air, Ro pulled the trigger. As the muzzle flash lit up the dark and the report echoed, everyone but Ro froze.

"Dad. I'm good," Ro said before nodding at the distant cordon, suddenly buzzing with activity. "You better go." He offered Andi a last, sad smile as he fired on the engine, whipped the car around, and raced back toward town. He kept his eyes fixed ahead, afraid that if he looked back, he'd lose his nerve. Instead he watched as, in the distance, the helicopters swept back and forth over Tasker Bay.

After spotting a handful of bloodless bodies along the roadside, Ro fished a gas mask off the cruiser's floor and pulled it on. *Something was wrong.*

As he drove, he saw more, frozen in horrible, crooked contortions brought on by some invisible agent. They looked as if they were just trying to find a way out of town. *Polybius* hadn't done *this.*

He had no way of knowing, but long before he reached Main Street, most of Tasker Bay's citizenry was dead. The amount of sarin sprayed on the town made it impossible to avoid, no matter how many locks were on a door or pieces of furniture shoved in front of it. It flowed past rotten seals around windows, down chimneys, through soffits. It choked the life from everyone it touched, failing to discriminate between those who'd been victims of *Polybius* and those who hadn't.

No sooner had Ro made his way to and inside the mortuary with a pair of masks for Clarence and Evie, hopeful they'd avoided whatever was killing off everyone else, than he heard the sound of automatic gunfire.

Rushing back to the entrance and peering out, he saw a military convoy at the far end of Main Street, soldiers in gas masks and white suits with M-16s fanning out and firing at anything that still moved.

He slipped back into the mortuary, made his way to the fire door, and knocked, calling out for Evie and Clarence. No response came. Debating what to do, whether he should run or hide, Ro could feel the exposed skin on his hands and neck starting to burn.

EPILOGUE

IT HAD BEEN A LITTLE OVER A DAY. ANDI, RACHEL, AND DAVID HAD BEEN WAITING for Ro at the Road King Motel, just outside Novato, when news started to break about an "industrial accident" involving Tasker Bay's water supply. Massive casualties, numbering in the high hundreds, were being reported. The area had been completely cordoned off, deemed unsafe for anyone beyond a team of specialists sent in by the government to assess the situation.

There were, apparently, no survivors.

At the end of the fourth day, Andi and Rachel spoke together with David, having decided it was time to figure out what came next.

Rachel had a brother in Denver. She suggested they could stay with him for the time being and leave word for Ro at the front desk to come and join them. But David refused, unwilling to hear further arguments about abandoning his son. The last image he had of Ro—in the middle of the road, gun raised, intent on sacrificing himself to save them and to preserve the truth—haunted him.

Andi had found the money Mal stole, tucked away in the pack

she and Ro had taken after they shot him. Against David's repeated objections, she divided it among them. If the government was serious about erasing evidence of what had happened in Tasker Bay—and based on the news, it seemed like they were—then they needed to stay off the radar for a while. The cash would help and wouldn't be missed. Still reluctant, David knew Andi was right.

Rachel gave him multiple sets of information that he *and* Ro, she was quick to add, could use to find her and Andi after they were reunited. Names, phone numbers, addresses for family and friends, a trusted network she and Andi planned to move between. Someone would know where to find them.

Andi watched, curious, as her mother and David embraced, lingering in each other's arms long enough that it started to suggest some deeper meaning. Deeper feelings. Finally saying their good-byes, Andi and Rachel boarded a bus headed for Denver, leaving David to wait for Ro.

Two months on, the discovery of dangerous concentrations of toxins in the soil of a small municipality in Missouri resulted in the sudden creation of *another* overnight ghost town and a juicier, more current story for reporters to follow. Tasker Bay had officially become old news.

The government spent untold sums covering up what had really happened. That included tracking down Andi and Rachel. The pair quickly learned two truths: that they escaped made them dangerous, and what they knew made them bulletproof.

After their names eventually re-entered the system in Denver, they were targeted by military intelligence personnel who "wanted to talk." Rachel made it clear: anything that felt off to her would result in a public reckoning over what really happened in Tasker Bay, including hard evidence of the government's role in creating *Polybius* being leaked to the press. A tenuous deal was struck—they'd be left alone, *alive*, in exchange for keeping that knowledge to themselves. This threat extended to Rachel's unwitting brother, sister-in-law, and two young nieces. They had no choice but to comply.

While they never saw David again, Andi once took a call from him. He was working as a security guard at a casino in Las Vegas. He'd never found nor heard from Ro. Disappointed that he'd missed Rachel, he promised to call again but never did. More than once, Andi and her mother talked about flying down and casino-hopping until they found him, but the plan always ended up seeming like a violation. He'd made his choice; they chose to respect it.

A long period of careful, quiet planning went into their eventual disappearance, the two of them feeling their way through a process that came without guardrails or guarantees. New names and backgrounds took them cross-country where, in October of 1985, they settled into a remote home just outside Bucks County, Pennsylvania.

While Rachel would never again practice medicine, she found work as an office assistant at a hospital in nearby Philadelphia, quickly rising through the ranks to run her own department.

As she'd planned all along, Andi eschewed college in favor of work, quietly amassing a series of patents for peripheral technologies that earned her the right to do what she wanted with her time.

In the years that followed, she searched obsessively for cracks in the facade the government had built to cover up the events in

Tasker Bay. While she'd sometimes find new kernels of information, bits of evidence that had been forgotten or carelessly misfiled, a full picture of what had happened eluded her.

Both she and Rachel looked fruitlessly for survivors, keeping tabs on their extended families, people the government paid handsomely for their suffering *and* silence, to no avail.

She also dug for mentions of *Polybius* itself, but its existence remained a void, a black hole from which nothing escaped.

When she wasn't researching the events surrounding *Polybius*'s appearance in Tasker Bay, she pored over a printout of its code, looking for . . . she didn't know what. It at least provided her with some focus, for which she was grateful. Whenever she *wasn't* focused on something, she saw ghosts, among them Ro's. A day seldom passed when she didn't think of him. What he gave up when he drove into the dark that night. What might've been.

For a time, she blamed herself for his death, steering clear from others out of fear she'd end up hurting them, too. If she'd just kept ignoring him and stuck with her plan to avoid making connections in Tasker Bay, maybe he wouldn't have been drawn into what happened. Would've gotten out and gone on to live his life. But deep down she knew, and gradually accepted, that once *Polybius* had arrived in town, *all* their fates were sealed.

Even with those qualms laid to rest, she struggled to build any kind of life away from home. Living under an assumed name made her doubly cautious in how she interacted with others, how close she'd let them get. But despite those hang-ups and the heartache inherent in relationships of all walks, she slowly forged new bonds.

The gradual evolution of online communication made it easier for her to meet and feel people out before transitioning things to a real-world setting. She made friends, dated from time to time, achieving a level of comfort with the past that allowed her to appreciate the present and contemplate the future.

That, she decided, was the lesson to carry from her and Ro's brief time together—life wasn't meant to be lived alone.

The rest of her time was spent studying *Polybius*, looking for an explanation about how it worked. Within that, she believed, would be a means to stop it. With the salvage they'd taken from Home Video World, she rebuilt the cabinet, keeping it locked in a secure room to avoid accidental exposure, no different from the way high-level biosafety labs dealt with dangerous pathogens. It was her duty to keep it contained within those air-gapped walls where it was secret, safe . . .

. . . except, of course, for the portion of its source code she'd published on Usenet all those years ago.

She couldn't have known the implications of what she'd done. It had been a necessary evil that led her and Ro to Engle, to the truth. It had saved her life. And the likelihood that the code was still out there was infinitesimally low.

But if it *was*, or if a copy lurked in some dusty government archive, waiting for someone to unwittingly stumble onto it like Thom Mazzy did all those years ago, she had to be ready.

Late at night, she'd retreat to the safe room and open the game's files, picking through block by block in search of some magic elixir she may have missed. A key to unraveling how the game had unraveled Tasker Bay.

In those moments, Andi failed to see that *Polybius* had its hooks in her as much as it ever had anyone else. It had come to dictate the course of her life, that flashing attract screen always calling her back for one more round, one more attempt to crack the byzantine logic behind its design. *Somewhere*, it whispered, *answers lie.* And like the crowds that used to ring the cabinet on the scuffed linoleum at Home Video World, she'd been lured in by its dark magic, its promise of a release from malignant thoughts and feelings that coiled deep inside. As it had with everyone else who'd played, *Polybius* had grabbed ahold of a darkness hidden inside her. And it would never let go.

ACKNOWLEDGMENTS

Polybius wouldn't exist without the contributions of many individuals whose insights and enthusiasm helped bring the book to life. Chris Cook at Skyway Entertainment read draft after draft and encouraged me to see things through when I wasn't sure what I was writing or where it might go. Parker Davis, Liz Parker, and Emma Kapson at Verve Talent & Literary Agency saw the potential in my manuscript and expertly positioned it to succeed. Ed Schlesinger graciously brought *Polybius* into Gallery Books, where Kimberly Laws's deft, challenging editorial notes helped to evolve it in ways I could not have foreseen. And my wife and children lived with, supported, and loved me during a long, unpredictable creative process; without them, none of this would have been possible.

ABOUT THE AUTHOR

COLLIN ARMSTRONG has worked in the entertainment industry for over a decade developing, writing, and producing material for outlets including 20th Century Fox TV, ABC Family, Bleecker Street, Viaplay, Discovery, and the LA Times Studios. *Polybius* is his first novel. He lives in Los Angeles with his wife and children.